THE
Great
WITCH
of
BRITTANY

By Louisa Morgan

A Secret History of Witches

The Witch's Kind

The Age of Witches

The Great Witch of Brittany

THE
Great
WITCH
of
BRITTANY

LOUISA MORGAN

REDHOOK

Redhook Books/Orbit
Hachette Book Group
1290 Avenue of the Americas
New York, NY 10104
hachettebookgroup.com

First Edition: February 2022
Simultaneously published in Great Britain by Orbit

Redhook is an imprint of Orbit, a division of Hachette Book Group.
The Redhook name and logo are trademarks of Hachette Book Group, Inc.

The publisher is not responsible for websites (or their content) that are not owned by the publisher.

The Hachette Speakers Bureau provides a wide range of authors for speaking events. To find out more, go to www.hachettespeakersbureau.com or call (866) 376-6591.

Library of Congress Cataloging-in-Publication Data
Names: Morgan, Louisa, 1952– author.
Title: The great witch of Brittany / Louisa Morgan.
Description: First edition. | New York, NY : Redhook, 2022.
Identifiers: LCCN 2021029334 | ISBN 9780316628747 (hardcover) |
    ISBN 9780316628778 (ebook) | ISBN 9780316628754
Classification: LCC PS3563.A6732 G74 2022 | DDC 813/.54—dc23
LC record available at https://lccn.loc.gov/2021029334

ISBNs: 9780316628747 (hardcover), 9780316628778 (ebook)

Printed in the United States of America

LSC-C

Printing 1, 2021

This novel is dedicated to the wonderfully engaged readers who asked for Ursule's story. I hope each of you enjoys getting to know her as much as I did.

THE
Great
WITCH
of
BRITTANY

The
BOOK OF AGNES AND URSULE

1

1762, outside Carnac-Ville

Thirteen-year-old Ursule Orchière knelt in the shadow of the red caravan to watch her mother lie to people.

Agnes was very good at her job. Her dark eyes flashed convincingly, and she spoke with just the right amount of hesitation, of warning, and of promise.

Ursule's responsibility, one she had shouldered since she was six, was to collect the payment after the readings her mother gave. The pretense was that Agnes, the fortune-teller, gave no thought to money. The truth was quite different, and Ursule had learned early that not a penny should escape her.

The customers would arrive on foot, or in a pony cart that rumbled along the rutted road from Carnac-Ville. They wound through the field of menhirs where the clan camped, gazing wide-eyed at the circle of scarlet and blue and yellow caravans. They shrank away from the narrow-eyed, bare-chested men, gaped at the women in their gaudy scarves, and sometimes smiled at the half-dressed children running about among the stones.

Ursule met these seekers in the center of the circle, beside the remnants of that morning's cooking fire, and guided them to the red caravan where Agnes sat, shaded by a striped canopy, the Orchière crystal before her on a small table.

Often the customers glanced over their shoulders to see if anyone had followed them.

Ursule offered no reassurance. It was better if they were anxious. There was energy in their nervousness, in their fear of someone knowing they had come to have their fortunes told. Frightened customers never held back when it was time to pay.

Ursule added to her mother's drama whenever she could. She had always been plain, but her eyes were large and black and thick-lashed, and she used them to good effect, producing a flashing glance that implied danger. Sometimes she spoke in rapid Romani, and the seekers thought she was speaking in tongues. At other times, kneeling at her mother's side, she let her eyes roll back as if she were in a trance. Often she moaned, underscoring something interesting in her mother's patter.

It was an act, and Ursule was good at it, but it was the crystal that convinced the customers. It was an ancient stone, a chunk of crystal dug out of a riverbank by the *grand-mère* of Agnes's *grand-mère*. The top was smoky quartz, rubbed and polished until it was nearly spherical. Its base was uncut granite, the same rugged shape as when it emerged from the mud.

A generation had passed with none of the Orchières seeing so much as a spark in it. Agnes and her sisters swore that their grandmother could bring the crystal to life just by touching it. They widened their eyes and lowered their voices when they told the tale, claiming the crystal bloomed with light under her hands.

Ursule doubted the truth of this, and with good reason. The Orchières were notorious spinners of stories, even for their own family members. She suspected that her mother's *grand-mère* had simply been more adept than Agnes at fooling everyone.

Her mother had devised a way to make the crystal appear to glimmer as she moved her hands across its cloudy face. It required a strategically placed lamp at her feet, a twitch of her foot to move her skirt aside, a practiced motion of her hands to hide the reflection in the crystal and then, at an opportune moment, to reveal it.

Agnes excelled at reading her customers, if not at scrying in the crystal. She gave them a flood of rosy predictions, marring the optimistic future with just enough bad news to make it all seem real. The seekers handed over their money, for the most part, without demur. If they didn't, they learned how fast Ursule could run and how loudly she could shout.

Today a townswoman had come with a friend, the two of them clinging together for courage. They were dressed in traditional Brittany fashion: dark fabrics, with white scarves over their bodices and lacy aprons. They rolled their eyes this way and that, sniffing at the odors of cooked hare and boiled beans that hung over the encampment, eyeing the bright, ragged dresses of the Romani. They lifted their skirts to avoid the dirt of the camp, and shrank away if any of the grimy children came too near.

After Ursule seated the customer on a stool opposite her mother, Agnes told the woman's fortune, at great length. When the two women turned to leave, she called out to the other one. "Wait, *madame!* I have a message for you, too!"

Ursule lifted her scarf across her face to hide her smile. There would be two fees today. She was ready to add her persuasive touch to the process, but it turned out there was no need. The second woman turned back and took the stool opposite Agnes, eager to hear what her own future held. She listened openmouthed as Agnes predicted a sudden stroke of good luck that would bring money into her house. Agnes followed with a warning about being careless with the money, because someone was watching her, someone not afraid to steal. The woman nodded and cast a meaningful glance at her friend, as if she knew just who that would be.

Ursule collected the double fee and watched the two satisfied customers hurry off toward the village, arm in arm, giggling together over the success of their reading.

Her uncle Arnaud appeared at her elbow, holding out his broad dirty hand for the coins. She dropped them into his palm, and he scowled. "Where's the rest?"

Ursule blinked. "Uncle Arnaud, what do you mean? That's the payment."

"This isn't enough," he growled. "What did you do with it?"

"Me? I did nothing!"

"They cheated you, then."

She hung her head to hide the gleam of her eyes. "If they did, I didn't know it, Uncle. Perhaps I counted wrong."

"You, count wrong?"

It was a preposterous claim for her to make, of course. Everyone in the clan, no matter how odd they thought Ursule to be, acknowledged her talent for numbers. They called her clever when they wanted to flatter her, or when they needed her to translate from their patois to French or Breton. When they were angry, they said she didn't know how to keep her place, that she should stop showing off, that she should leave business matters to the men. For those reasons and more, Ursule hugged to herself the greatest secret of her young life. Even her mother didn't know.

She could read.

The Orchière clan, like the other Romani who traveled the roads of Europe, was illiterate. It was part of their identity. Their tradition. Reading, in their way of thinking, was unnecessary. Uncle Arnaud said it was better to learn from your ancestors than from foolish words some stranger had written. Books were for churchmen or landowners, collections of words used to oppress the peasantry, and the Romani with them.

The Romani left drawings of bears or boar on trees or standing stones to mark their passing. They sang or recited their family histories. They counted on their fingers, or made slash marks in the dirt to tot up what was owed to them or what they owed. To be a reader, Ursule had always understood, was to be a rebel. To offend the traditional ways. To risk being isolated even more than she already was.

Ursule had been just three years old when she realized that the letters on shop signs or in advertising posters spoke words to her, as if the writers of those letters were whispering their meaning in her ear. Her cousins mocked her because she didn't talk until she was five years old, but that turned out to be a blessing. By the time she began, she realized the letters that told her so much meant nothing to her mother or her aunts or uncles. She couldn't recall ever learning to read. It was simply there, the way her uncle Omas had always been able to play the harp, and Aunt Genève always knew how long to roast a hare. It was her gift, but she knew better than to reveal it.

Her clan already viewed her as a misfit, first because she had been silent for so long, and then because, when she did begin to talk, she spoke like a miniature adult. She refused to learn to sew or cook, and preferred to be alone rather than gossip with the other girls. The boys mocked her, trying to make her cry, but she refused. She was small, but her fists were hard and quick.

She was eight when she discovered there was a book in the Orchière camp. It was a single, real book, and it was in her very own caravan.

She had gone to fetch the scrying stone before a reading. When Ursule knelt down to pull it out from beneath her mother's bed, a random beam of sunlight exposed an object unfamiliar to her, a rectangular shape wrapped in burlap and tied with a strap. She believed she knew every bit and bob of their meager possessions. Surprise and curiosity drove her errand from her mind as she pulled the thing out into the light, untied the strap, and peeled back the burlap.

It was the first real book she had ever held in her hands, heavy and old and smelling of dust and ink. Ursule lifted the top cover and saw the first parchment page, the top written in French in a trembling script, with three illustrations of herbs decorating the bottom. She gingerly riffled the pages. There were dozens of them. She could hardly breathe with excitement over the treasures it must hold.

"Ursule! What are you doing?"

Ursule gave a start that made her drop the book with a thud. A little cloud of ancient dust swirled from it, tickling her nose with the promise of secrets within. "Daj, I—"

Agnes fell to her knees beside her and began hurriedly rewrapping the big book. "Never touch this!" she said. "Never ever. Promise me!"

"Why?" Ursule plucked at the burlap, but Agnes slapped her hand away. *"Daj!"* she cried. "You never told me we have a *book!"*

"And you can never tell anyone else, Ursule. It's dangerous."

With decisive motions, Agnes rewrapped the burlap and tightened the strap that held it all together. She bent to shove it as far under her cot as it would go.

"But, Daj, what is it? Where did it come from? Why do you hide it?"

Agnes settled back on her haunches, her skirts pooling about her feet. "Bring the stone, Ursule," she said tightly. "I have readings to do."

"Tell me!" Ursule demanded. She took the scrying stone into her lap and covered it with her arms. "I'm not moving until you do."

Agnes's hand rose again, but when Ursule didn't budge, she made a wry face and lowered it. "I will tell you, daughter, but only if you promise never to tell anyone."

"I promise," Ursule said. "But tell me!"

"It's called a grimoire," Agnes said. "It belonged to my *grand-mère*, and her *grand-mère* before that, and even more *grands-mères* before her."

"Why is it called a grimoire? What does that mean?"

"I don't know. My *maman* couldn't read it. She kept it hidden, and we have to do that, too."

"Why?"

"Witch hunters," Agnes said, spitting out the words as if they burned her mouth. "A grimoire is a book for witches. A book of witchcraft. If they see you looking at it, they might think you're a witch."

"I'd like to be a witch," Ursule said.

"You'd like to be burned alive?" her mother hissed. "That's what they do if they catch witches. They burn them, and stand around laughing while they scream!"

The fear in her mother's voice, even more than the ghastly images, made Ursule shudder. She never said it again. She never told anyone there was a book in her caravan. And she never looked into the grimoire—unless she was certain her mother would not find out.

Her uncle Arnaud said now, "Turn out your pockets, Ursule. Quickly!"

She did, tugging out the frayed fabric of her pockets to show they were empty. One had a huge hole in it, and she spread it open with her fingers so her uncle could see.

He glared at her for a long moment. "If you are stealing from us," he began.

Ursule promptly broke into a convincing bout of tears, and Arnaud, grunting, shoved her away from him. She stumbled back, sobbing.

"Stop that!" Arnaud snapped. When she only cried more loudly, he swore and said, "The sooner Agnes finds you a husband, the better! You need to settle down!"

"I don't even have my monthlies yet, Uncle!" Ursule wailed.

"Well—well—hurry up with them, then!" He gave her another push, and she ran, stuffing her pockets back into her skirt.

Her mother was waiting, holding open the flimsy door of their caravan. She glared at her brother as Ursule jumped past her, up the step and inside. Agnes looped the rope lock behind her.

The lock was symbolic. Arnaud could break in easily if he wanted to, but long ago Agnes had sworn if he ever bothered her or her daughter in their own wagon she would put a curse on him. He never set foot in her caravan after that. Women had very little power, but they were known to cast terrible curses.

Ursule plunged her hand through the hole in her skirt pocket so she could fish the extra coins out of the *posoti* sewn into her drawers. She held the money out on her palm, all pretense of tears gone. "Double, Maman."

Agnes snatched up the coins and jangled them in her fist. "Well done, daughter! Well done."

"I need a new dress. This one barely reaches my calves, and the others laugh at me."

"I know they do. I'm sorry." Agnes turned to the old cracked jar she kept hidden behind a curtain and poured the coins into it. "Arnaud is right about one thing, though. You're going to need a husband soon."

"I don't want one."

"What does that have to do with it?"

"I'm only thirteen!"

"I was thirteen when I was wed to your father."

"And what a mistake that was," Ursule said. "Married to an old man. Widowed before I was born. Dirt poor your whole life."

"Well," her mother said with a shrug. "We're all dirt poor. And widowed is not so bad. I make my own choices."

"I'm going to make mine, too, and marrying some lout of a blacksmith or a basketmaker is not one of them."

"Ursule," Agnes said, shaking her head but smiling at the same time. "You speak like a woman of eighty."

"Born old," Ursule said. "You've said that often enough."

"Yes. You had no childhood."

"It would be over now, in any case."

"I am sorry for that, little one."

Ursule shrugged. "It doesn't matter."

Her mother blew out a breath and began taking off the beads and scarves she wore for telling fortunes. "You'll have a new dress. We'll buy fabric when we get to Belz."

"Are we leaving Carnac-Ville already?"

"Your uncles say we must. The witch burners are about again."

All Romani knew better than to risk confronting the witch burners. The bloodlust swept through the countryside at regular intervals, like a bout of the Black Death spreading from village to village. The witch burners craved the screams of accused witches, the smell of burning flesh, the manic screeches of those who came to watch. There had been no witches among the clans for generations, but that made no difference. They were the perfect targets. They were darker. Wore different clothes. Were grindingly poor. They were *gitans*, gypsies, believed to be thieves and liars, rumored to carry disease.

People said the gypsies cast curses, causing illnesses and accidents. It didn't matter whether it was or was not true. When the blood fever seized the land, truth made no difference.

Ursule had asked her uncle Omas once why the clans didn't band together for strength and protection. "Not our way, little one," he said, shrugging, tugging at his long black braid. "We're rovers. Travelers. We move when we want to, stop when we wish."

"Why not settle someplace, all the clans? We could protect ourselves! All of you men carry *churis*—why not use them?"

He stuck his pipe between his teeth and squinted at her through the smoke. "Not our way," he repeated. "Too many of them, not enough of us."

She stared at him, waiting. Omas was her mother's younger brother, the one of her clansmen who would take the time to explain things to her, answer her questions without too much impatience. He took the pipe from his mouth to give her a rueful smile. "Hard to go against tradition, little Ursule. We Romani are slow to change. Impossible to organize."

Afraid to try, Ursule thought. *Now, if I were the head of the clan*...But there had never been a female clan head that she knew of. She supposed the men would never allow it.

On the night Agnes earned her double fee, the clan clustered around the cooking fire as the autumn dusk closed in. The little ones were quiet, ready for sleep. The adults, Agnes and her brothers and their wives, spoke in low, grim voices. Ursule, as always, sat alone.

It always seemed to Ursule that the sea, just across the lane from the field of stones, sang louder in the darkness. The waves beat drumlike against the stone sea stacks, and the tide made its own music, humming up onto the beach, withdrawing with a hiss like an indrawn breath. She loved the way the scent of salt intensified at night as the daytime odors faded away.

Belz was also on the sea, or at least on an estuary leading to the sea, but she would miss the menhirs scattered around this field like ancient sentinels, watching unperturbed as years and people passed by. Often she pressed her palms to their rough surfaces, feeling the vibration of age through her skin. The menhirs held their places for years, centuries, even millennia, no matter what human tumult swirled around them. That seemed infinitely wise to Ursule.

Arnaud's harsh voice distracted her from her thoughts. "It's the archbishop," he said, tossing a bone into the fire. "He's gathering his witch hunters again."

"The bastard wants to be a cardinal," Omas said. "Thinks burning a few witches will get Rome's attention."

"And it will," Arnaud said.

An ember popped, sending up a fountain of sparks like red stars to wink out in the darkness. Everyone sighed. It was an omen.

Arnaud scowled across the fire at Agnes. "It's too bad we don't actually have a witch in our clan, since they're going to accuse us of it anyway."

"The gift is gone, Arnaud," Agnes said, her lips set in a sour line. "The line has died out."

"And whose fault is that?" he snarled back at her. "None of you can produce daughters?" It was an old argument. Ursule had heard it a dozen times, but it saddened her. There were no more witches. But what could any of them do about it?

"It's no one's fault." Her aunt Marina rarely spoke aloud and almost never contradicted one of the men. Everyone turned to look at her in surprise, and she averted her face, shying away from their intense regard.

Ursule said, "Aunt Marina is right. Don't stare at her that way."

"Mind your betters, girl," Arnaud snapped.

"How are you better, Uncle Arnaud?" she snapped back.

"As you can all see, I have a daughter," Agnes said dryly.

"Is she a witch?" Arnaud demanded.

"She's a child. If you want a witch for the clan, why not become one?"

"Would if I could. Women's work."

Ursule burst out, "Why do you leave everything to the women?" making her aunts click their tongues in disapproval and the other children laugh behind their hands.

Omas spoke mildly, as he always did. "It is a pity, isn't it? The crystal lies there as if it were dead."

"It died with Grand-mère," Agnes said. "Those were great days, when the crystal lived, but those days are no more."

"And so we run like frightened deer!" Arnaud said.

"What else do you suggest?" Agnes demanded. "Do you want to stand and fight, hundreds of them and only a dozen of us?"

One of the children began to whimper. Céline hushed him, but everyone shifted uneasily, the peace of the evening fractured. Even the horses, hobbled among the menhirs, stamped and snorted.

It was Omas, always the peacemaker, who tried to change the mood. "Let's have a story, Agnes."

Agnes blew out a breath in an obvious effort to ease her temper. "Which one, Omas?"

He looked around the circle. "What would you all like to hear?"

It was one of the other children who piped up. "Grand-mère. Tell us that one."

Ursule, along with the others kneeling or sitting cross-legged around the fire, settled down to listen. She could have recited the familiar story herself, but she loved to hear the way her mother told it, her voice rising and falling, melodic as a song. The rosy light from the dying fire gleamed on Agnes's mahogany cheekbones and sparkled in her eyes. The tale never changed, nor did the rhythm of her recitation. Even Arnaud ceased grumbling, and the clan settled in, harmony restored, to listen.

Violca had been the *grand-mère* of Agnes and Omas and Arnaud. The whole family referred to her as Grand-mère, though she was the great-grandmother of Ursule and the other children and had died before any of them were born. Her story, and some believed her ghost, lived on in the Orchière clan.

"They say," Agnes began, as all the storytellers did, "that when Violca was born, a great light streaked across the sky from west to east. It blinded the baby in one eye, and gave her the second sight in the other."

A sigh went around the circle at the tragedy and wonder of it.

"She was a sickly infant, weak and small and half blind, and since her mother had hardly any milk in her breasts, no one thought little Violca would survive. One of the uncles said they should leave her to die, but her own *grand-mère*, a true seer, swore that the crystal said she would live. She insisted that all the aunts nurse her."

Agnes paused, and lowered her voice. "Violca suckled at every aunt's breast, in addition to her mother's. She drank in their gifts, and grew into them. She became a harpist, like one of her aunts, and a teller of fortunes, like another. She was a seer, like her mother. She was a witch, like her grandmother."

She went on to describe Violca's life, dramatizing every detail. When the tale was finished, she raised her head to speak into the night wind. "And the crystal showed her when the witch burners were coming!"

Another long exhalation rippled around the circle. None of their clan had been caught by the witch hunters in a very long time, but other Romani had not been so fortunate. The witch hunters had seized an old woman from a clan near Vannes, a clan that had never had a witch among its people. They took another Romani woman from the eastern border. They didn't know if she was truly a witch or simply another poor old woman with no one to protect her. Both women were tried and convicted within hours, and burned within days. It was a tale all the Orchières knew. It was not one they wanted to hear again.

There had been a few years of peace, but now, with a new and bloodthirsty bishop, the burning times were on them again.

After Agnes finished her recitation, the clan sat in solemn silence, watching the last embers of the fire turn to ash. Arnaud said, after a time, "Remember, there will be no celebrating the Sabbats while we're in Belz. Too dangerous."

A sigh of regret swept the circle. The Orchières always observed the Sabbats and had recently held a bonfire to mark Lammas, but they knew Arnaud was right. Few of the clans celebrated the Sabbats anywhere near a town. The people of Brittany—and of France, and Italy, and the countries to the east—considered such rites heathen practices. It was one more way to attract the dangerous attention of the witch hunters.

A nightingale called from the field of stones, and Ursule glanced up. She could just see the little bird perched on one of the menhirs, its nearly colorless feathers illumined by starlight. It seemed to warble its farewell just for her, and she felt a thrill of premonition shiver through her body.

That stone, with its drab little songmaker, was calling to her, speaking to her blood and bone and spirit.

For an intense instant, she yearned to understand its message right at that moment, as the salty breeze ruffled her hair and the brilliant stars glittered over the standing stones.

But she recalled one of Grand-mère's lessons, one Agnes repeated often: *Remember the past. Live in the present. The future will come when it's time.*

The stone's message was about her future, and that was why she couldn't understand it. Her time had not yet come.

·····›››››› • ‹‹‹‹‹‹·····

The Orchières broke camp as soon as the sky brightened enough for them to harness the horses. Ursule could have hitched up their skinny mare, but Agnes never allowed it. "Let the men do it," she often said. "Whole months go by when that's the only work they do."

It was true enough, although Ursule had never heard any of the other women say it. She stood back and watched as the horses were backed into the hafts, harness adjusted, buckles buckled, and straps tied.

She and her mother had lashed most of their possessions down the night before. As the sun rose and Agnes stepped up onto the box to take the horse's reins, Ursule saw to the final task. She cushioned the old crystal with the blankets from her cot, nestling it in a basket she could tie securely to the front frame of the caravan. The frame was the sturdiest part of the wagon, with the driver's box above it and the front axle beneath. In case of a bad rut or stones in the road, the crystal would be safe.

Ursule also wrapped the old book and stowed it safely beneath her bunk before she climbed up on the box beside her mother, wrapped in a shawl against the early-morning chill. As they set out, Arnaud's wagon leading the way and Omas coming last, Ursule cast a final look at the menhirs as the Orchières rattled off toward the road and turned to the north. She would be back, she was sure of it. She wished she knew when that might be.

Agnes said, unnecessarily, "Did you put the stone in its basket? Tie it to the frame?"

"Of course, Maman."

Agnes blew out a breath as she snapped the reins against the horse's hindquarters. "I wish you would call me Daj, Ursule."

"You're happy enough to have me speak French or Breton when you want to barter."

"But with me, you can speak Romani."

"I can do both," Ursule said. "It's good practice!"

"Such an odd gift, Ursule, a knack for languages. I think Grand-mère must have her eye on you."

"There, you see? You use the French word."

Agnes laughed. "You're right about that. Violca preferred it. It became a habit."

"Your French is almost as good as mine, Maman. You even speak a bit of Breton when you need it."

Her mother shrugged. "A little. I save it for the customers. They like my accent."

"Which you pretend to have!"

"They don't need to know everything. No one needs to know everything." Agnes nudged her daughter with an elbow. "It's good to have some secrets, my Ursule. Keep some things to yourself. You never know when it might be useful, to know something no one else does."

As their caravan jolted and bumped along the winding northern road, Ursule wondered if her mother knew her own great secret. She avoided the topic, asking instead, "Do you truly think there are no more witches?"

"I can only say, daughter, that there are no Orchière witches now. As to other clans, I don't know. Not the Vilas. Nor the Franks, or the Pereiros, as far as we know. No doubt if they have witches in their midst, they keep the secret. It's a dangerous one."

"Will the Orchière line die out, then?"

Agnes shrugged. "The Goddess knows the answer to that one. It would be a great wonder if a successor to Grand-mère appeared after all."

At that, Ursule subsided, chewing on a finger as she pondered the mystery and watched the scenery pass by.

The day's journey was long and tense. The caravan stopped twice for food and water for people and horses, and a third time for the women's necessaries, which were accomplished as hastily as possible. When a cart appeared ahead of them, or a galloping horse behind, Arnaud and Omas and Thierry loosened the *churis* in their sheaths and tugged their caps low over their eyes. The women pulled their scarves across their faces and ordered the children, riding inside the wagons, to stay away from the windows.

They pressed on long past the dinner hour. The children whimpered with hunger, but Arnaud insisted they couldn't stop until they reached the camp. They rolled and clattered through the thickening dusk, peering ahead for some sign that their goal was near. The first evening star glowed in the sky before the flames of a cooking fire flickered through the gloom. Several of the adults groaned in relief. Cautiously, Arnaud called a greeting.

A response, just as wary, came from the encampment. A figure appeared, making its way through the wagons clustered around the fire pit. Firelight silhouetted the thick body of a man with one slumping shoulder and a shock of hair shining silver through the darkness.

"It's all right," Arnaud said, turning so his voice could carry to the Orchières. "It's Edouard Vila."

The adults recognized the name, though they couldn't yet see the man's face. He was the head of the Vila clan, known to be a tough old man who had brought his family through many hard times. He carried a lantern in one hand as he limped toward the newcomers. His other hand clutched the hilt of his *churi* until he came close enough to recognize the Orchières.

"Arnaud," he said, in a deep, hoarse voice. He released the knife hilt, letting the blade slide into its sheath, and he lifted his lantern higher. *"Sar san?"*

"We're all right, Edouard. And the Vilas? *Sar san?"*

The old man grunted. "All right." He waved toward the circle of wagons, where the Vilas were now standing around the fire, ready for company. "Unhitch your horses. Come and join us. We'll build up the fire."

Set free, the children clambered down from their caravans and scattered through the Vila camp. More slowly, the Orchière adults set about drawing their wagons up beside a stand of cedar trees. They replaced their horses' harnesses with hobbles and set out grain and water buckets. Ursule hid the crystal in its basket once again, with the old book underneath it.

Ursule reflected, as she carried water to fill their horse's bucket at the slow-moving brook, that the Romani were a people of secrets. Clans kept secrets from other clans and from the villages they passed through. Family members kept secrets from other family members, just as she did. It was simply the way her people were, although sometimes it made her feel lonely, knowing there was no one in the world who knew everything about Ursule Orchière.

She was glad to join the Vila encampment, to be in company with other Romani. The old people settled on rocks and stools. The younger ones squatted or sat cross-legged on blankets. Several mothers nursed babies. Others gathered their children into their laps. A harp came out, and a bombarde. As the harpist began to pluck his strings, a bird answered him out of the dark.

Ursule's aunts, Céline and Marina, worked over the fire pit, dicing turnips and carrots and tearing a leftover bit of venison into bite-sized pieces. The smell of simmering stew rose into the cool air, and the children tugged at their mothers' skirts and begged them to hurry. One of the Vila women, a crone with no more than three teeth, brought out a loaf of bread and sliced chunks of it for the smallest children to gnaw on while they waited. Ursule found a spot to settle, kneeling on a blanket, wrapping herself in her shawl against the growing cold. The brook gurgled, tumbling between its banks, and a thousand brilliant stars glittered over everything.

While the Orchières ate their belated meal, the harpist and the bombardist played the old songs. Sometimes they sang. When there were no words, they hummed, and others hummed with them. When the meal was over, and Céline and Marina and the other women were gathering the wooden bowls to clean in the brook in the morning, the men began to talk in low, tight voices.

Ursule, her stomach full and her eyelids heavy, bent her legs and wrapped her arms around them, resting her forehead on her knees. She closed her eyes, trying to focus her ears on the splashing of the brook, the chirping of the night birds, the sweet high voices of little children resisting sleep, anything but the evil news.

The men's words broke through despite her efforts. She couldn't block them out, the names, the stories, the threats.

Vannes, the home of the archbishop, which made her think of the cathedral where he preached hate. Grand-Champ, where three accused witches were burned in one day, the last left to listen to the screams of the others before facing her own agony. The thriving market of Lorient, where the Romani often did business but had now been forbidden by the bishop even to enter.

The hastily cooked meal roiled in Ursule's belly.

She was thinking of getting up to go to her bunk, where she could pull a pillow over her head to shut out the voices, when she felt a prickle on the top of her scalp. Someone was looking at her.

She lifted her head from her knees and opened her eyes.

A man sat on the other side of the fire, staring at her. When she met his gaze, one corner of his mouth quirked, making his long mustache quiver. He tucked his chin, acknowledging she had seen him.

He was heavily built, like all the Vilas. His black hair hung in tangled locks from the kerchief he wore over his forehead. He wore his *churi* prominently, the sheath on a strap across his chest. Thick eyebrows shadowed his eyes, but even at the distance she could see how small and dark they were.

Her stomach roiled again, this time with a new anxiety. She felt like a fox kit under the eye of a hungry wolf, and it made her angry.

She jumped to her feet, and seeing that the man was still watching her, she spit into the dirt before spinning away with a flounce of her skirt. His eyes followed her, burning into her shoulders as she stamped toward the relative safety of her caravan.

Her mother was already there, shedding her skirts and scarves. "Temper again, Ursule?"

"That man, that Vila. He's looking at me."

"Bound to happen. You're of that age."

"I'm too young."

"He may not know that. Born old, remember?"

"I don't like him."

"You don't know him, Ursule."

"I know I don't like him, Daj."

"Ah, now you speak Romani to your mother. Because you want something."

Ursule began undoing the tie on her skirt. "Will you protect me?"

"I would fight to the death for you," Agnes said, hard-eyed. "But I'm just a woman. You must watch your step."

There was little comfort, either in Agnes's assurance or in the warning. Ursule knew how some Romani men took brides, and if it happened to her, her uncles would never accept her back into the clan. She would be ruined. Trapped.

She wished with all her heart the Orchières had not left Carnac. As she lay down on her cot and pulled up her blankets, she muttered a curse against the witch hunters who had made it happen. *May you suffer for your cruelty as you make others suffer.* Before she fell asleep, she added another curse, this one for the insolent Vila man staring at her as if he had the right. *May the Goddess punish your arrogance.*

If only she really were a witch instead of a powerless thirteen-year-old girl! If she were a witch, her curses would be dangerous. Would be meaningful. That would be a very good thing.

D awn over the Étel estuary came in porcelain shades of rose and blue and violet. The moment the sun rose above the heath to the east, the Vila and Orchière children spilled out of their wagons, scattering among the bilberries and willows that grew along the brook. Childish voices pierced the morning with laughter and shrieks, and the Vilas' two shaggy dogs ran around them, barking. The adults called greetings to each other as they emerged from their caravans and went about the chores of feeding horses and collecting brush and wood for the fire.

Agnes, roused by the noise, peered outside the wagon at the women gathering around the cooking fire. "Looks like they're doing pottage again. Céline will want *pufe* to add to it. Lot of people to feed."

"Do you have buckwheat?"

"Enough for today."

"How about some bilberries?"

"Good idea. Hurry, because the children will be hungry."

Ursule took up the market basket and stepped outside, leaving her mother stirring buckwheat and water in a pottery bowl. The fearful shadows of the night faded in the brightness of the morning, and she lifted her face into the sunshine, sniffing the charcoal smell of the fire and the spiciness of the cedar branches dangling above the wagon.

It had been too dark when they arrived to appreciate the charm of the campsite. The little stream flashed blue through clumps of prickly sea holly and spiky glasswort. Green and yellow fields stretched to the east, where narrow streams of smoke rose from the stone cottages of Belz.

At this moment, Ursule understood why the Romani preferred to travel, to see fresh sights and breathe unfamiliar air as often as they could. It was invigorating. She wished she weren't too old to run and shout with the children.

But she was nearly a woman now. Her mother needed her help. She hooked her basket over her arm and set out at a dignified walk toward the brook.

"Ursule, wait!"

Ursule turned to see one of the Vila girls trotting toward her with her skirt flaring around her ankles and her long apron flapping. She came up panting and laughing and embraced Ursule awkwardly around the bulk of both their baskets.

"Bettina!" Ursule exclaimed. "I hardly recognize you!" Bettina's face was rounder, and she wore her hair tied up under a scarf, as the grown women did. "We were little girls when I last saw you."

"I'm a married woman now," Bettina said, proudly smoothing her apron over a round, obviously pregnant belly.

Ursule took a step back. "Bettina, you can't—you're not old enough!"

Bettina gave her a brilliant smile. "I'm fourteen! I've been married six months already."

"I—oh, my—I'm just surprised." Ursule knew she shouldn't offend Bettina, the only childhood friend she had, but the very idea of the pregnancy sparked a feeling of revulsion in her. She averted her eyes, hoping Bettina wouldn't notice.

When she had finally begun to speak, the other children had stared at her as if one of the dogs had suddenly started talking. They avoided her, and she knew they pointed and laughed behind her back. It was different with Bettina.

One of the happiest times of Ursule's young life had been a meeting of the Vila and Orchière clans, because of Bettina. She made a friend for the first time, someone to play with, to whisper with, someone who didn't care how odd she had been as a child, how different she and her mother were from the other big, noisy families.

And now her only friend had fallen into the trap that awaited all Romani girls: early marriage, too many babies, no life of her own—the very trap that yawned before Ursule herself.

Ursule fought a sinking sensation, as if the last shreds of her childhood were draining away from her. She struggled to make conversation as they walked together toward the stream. "Who is your husband?"

"His name is Mikel. He comes from the south, but his clan was small, so he became a Vila." Bettina caressed her belly again. "He paid the highest bride price any Vila girl has ever received."

"My goodness," Ursule said. She didn't believe it, of course. It was the sort of lie the Romani told each other all the time, but she made herself smile and nod as Bettina chattered about babies and families and weddings until they reached the brook.

The little stream chuckled over shining gray stones and splashed up the banks where willow roots and drowned grasses hung like the fringe of an unraveling shawl. On the level ground along the stream, bilberry shrubs grew low to the ground. Their rough green leaves hid the berries as if they meant to keep them for themselves, but the girls' deft fingers flicked through the branches, and dark blue berries began to rattle into their baskets.

"Mikel says bilberries are good for the eyes," Bettina said. "I'm going to eat a lot of these so my baby will have perfect vision." She popped several into her mouth.

Ursule doubted bilberries had any special properties aside from sweetening the fried *pufe*, but she didn't say so. Her shock over the fact of Bettina's pregnancy began to fade before her friend's obvious pleasure in everything to do with her marriage.

"Mikel is the best hunter in the clan, you know," Bettina went on. "That's why there's always meat in our pottage. Last year he brought down a wild boar all by himself!"

Ursule murmured something admiring, then said, "I think this is enough. My mother wanted me to hurry."

Together they bent to rinse their blue-stained fingers in the water before starting back toward the camp.

They were halfway there when Ursule felt the prickle on her neck that meant someone was watching her. She increased her pace, but Bettina groaned. "Ursule, I can't go so fast!"

Ursule was forced to slow her steps, and the prickle on her neck grew more intense. She didn't want to look behind her, to give him the satisfaction, but she sensed him there, as if he could cast a shadow over her. The brightness of the morning seemed to dim and the air to grow chilly. She didn't even know his name, but she didn't need to. She knew what he was.

As she and Bettina joined the women laboring to put breakfast together, Ursule took a surreptitious glance over her shoulder to confirm what her instinct was telling her.

He was squatting in the shade of a caravan painted a blue so dark it was nearly black. He stared up at her, as if daring her to spit again. She refrained. She probably shouldn't have done it the first time.

She averted her face instead and hurried toward the fire pit. Agnes had set her much-battered iron griddle across two flat stones, with a pile of hot coals beneath. Several small children clustered around her, watching hungrily as she spilled a bit of duck fat onto the griddle. It hissed invitingly.

Her mother looked up at the sound of her footsteps. "Oh, Ursule, good! You found some. Pour them into the bowl, will you, and give it a good stir."

Ursule put aside her unease about the Vila man as she smiled at the little ones, and gave each a bilberry before she spilled the rest into the bowl. She swirled them into the batter and handed the bowl to Agnes. In moments, half a dozen cakes sizzled on the griddle.

The Vila women had warmed up the pottage from the night before, and added wild onions and mustard greens from someone's stores. As the children took hot *pufe* in their grimy hands, the women scooped pottage from the enormous pot, everyone using bowls from their own wagons. Some used spoons. Most used their fingers.

The children tossed the cakes from hand to hand to cool them, then ate them in three bites. They were a scruffy lot, these Vila little ones. Two were wearing trousers that might have belonged to a dozen children before them. One wore a man's shirt but nothing underneath. Its hem dragged against the ground. Two little girls wore real skirts, but most wore remnants of this and that, the fabric colors leached out long ago.

Bettina came up to her elbow, her own bowl of pottage in her hands. "My son is going to have proper clothes," she said, indicating the children with her chin.

"How will you manage that?" Ursule couldn't help asking.

"Mikel will sell hides at the market," Bettina said, with blithe confidence. "We'll always have money."

Agnes caught Ursule's eye above Bettina's head, one skeptical eyebrow raised. Ursule bit her lip to keep from laughing.

The men gathered for their own meal, sitting on rocks and tree stumps while the women brought them bowls of pottage. Agnes scraped the last of the batter out of the bowl for a few more cakes. Ursule took the bowl from her hands.

There were other women on the path to the brook, carrying bowls and spoons to wash. Ursule started after them, but paused. The stare of her tormentor stopped her as if it were a wall she couldn't climb.

She took one small step, then another, casting around for a way to get past him. He sat on the ground with his back against the wheel of his wagon and a group of three other men around him. He was no more appealing in the bright light than he had been in firelight the night before. His skin was thick and pocked, his hair shiny with oil. Ursule was small, shorter than her mother, but this man was even shorter than she was, with the thick shoulders and wide hands all the Vila men seemed to have. His gaze made her skin crawl as if he had actually touched her.

She drew a breath, steadying herself for the ordeal of walking close to him.

The man on his left leaned forward, jostling his knee. "Dukkar! I think that nag of yours needs a shoe. You should take better care of her!"

Another man laughed. "Dukkar's nag always needs a shoe, or a bridle mended, or one good meal!"

Now Ursule knew his name, and as he turned to respond to the banter, she hurried out of the camp toward the water.

She found a spot beside the other women where she could crouch to splash water into the bowl. She rubbed it clean with a handful of sand and rinsed it, then set it aside. The clear water, sparkling in the sunshine, held her for a moment. Fish darted between the smooth stones, tiny silver arrows almost too quick to see. Ursule plunged both hands into the stream and splashed her warm cheeks and neck, sighing with pleasure.

She combed her dampened hair back with her fingers and retied her scarf, then stood, her bowl on her hip. Reluctantly, loath to leave the peace of the brook, but with chores waiting, she turned back toward the circle of wagons.

She had taken a few steps when she heard an unfamiliar sound. It rose and fell, sometimes blending with the gurgle of the water, sometimes rising above it. The notes were sweet, with an airy, hollow timbre that reminded her of the wind playing through the dolmens near Carnac. She peered through the drooping willow branches, searching for the source of the music.

She glimpsed a slice of red shirt, vivid against a backdrop of purple sea holly. It moved, disappearing behind a drooping branch, then shifting back into view. The music wound on, a slender twist of melody almost too fragile for the open air. As the Vila women walked past, their chatter drowned out the music, so Ursule left the path, pushing under the nearest willow branch and into the copse.

A few steps brought her out of the trees and into the clearing where the musician stood. He was taller than any of the Vilas, and from the look of his narrow shoulders and skinny hips, not yet done growing. His hair fell in straight lines to his shoulders, not the dense black of the Vilas, but a light brown, glimmering gold where the sun caught it. He seemed to be fully immersed in his music, his head bent over the instrument he held in his two hands.

Ursule stepped on a dried twig, and the crack of it startled him. The melody broke off, and he whirled to face her.

"I'm sorry—" Ursule began, then stopped, startled into silence.

He was young, as she had guessed, perhaps three or four years older than herself. His face was as narrow as the rest of him, with a straight, aquiline nose and clean-shaven chin, and fine eyes of amber that glowed like the turning leaves of fall. Those eyes turned in her direction, but without quite finding her face. He couldn't see her. He was blind.

Ursule clutched her bowl over her chest, where her heart gave a sudden lurch of sympathy. "I heard your music. It's beautiful."

"I don't know you," he said, and she understood he meant he didn't recognize her voice.

"I'm an Orchière," she said. "We arrived last night. I'm called Ursule."

He nodded and pushed back a long strand of hair brushing his chin. His shirt and trousers were as worn and grimy as those of any other traveler, but his hands were clean, fine-skinned and long-fingered. They moved her somehow, distinguished him from any man she had ever met, and her heart gave another bump. He held his musical instrument in a confident grip, and he stood easily, legs slightly apart, without the anxious leaning of the few sightless people she had encountered.

"You must be a Vila," she ventured, when he didn't introduce himself.

"*Non,*" he said, shortly, softly. "I only travel with them."

Ursule frowned over his accent. "You're not Romani."

"*Non.*"

"You're French?"

"I am mostly French."

That explained his narrow features, his pale complexion, his light hair. It was unheard of, in her experience, for a traveling clan to be joined by someone from the outside. "Oh! How did you come to be—" she began, but he had already turned away from her, his instrument pressed to his chest. He strode away almost as surely as if he could see his way, one hand trailing along tree branches and thistle tops.

Ursule watched him go for a little before she turned toward the camp, her bowl on her hip. She wished the boy had stayed to talk with her. Had played more of his haunting music that called to her in a mysterious way. She wished he had told her something about himself.

The Vila camp was suddenly much more interesting than it had been an hour before.

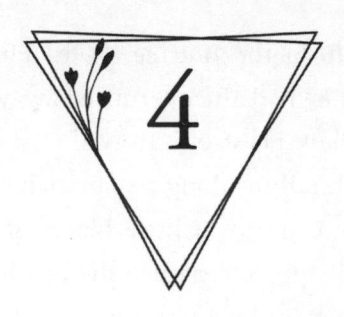

4

To call Belz a village was to exaggerate. No more than ten or twelve of the traditional stone houses scattered like spilled dice around a small green. The farmers and artisans of the commune had set out their produce on benches and tables, but there weren't many of them. The Carnac market was four times the size of this one. Though Ursule's precious coins jingled invitingly in her *posoti*, it was easy to see there would be no fabric to buy.

Still, it was almost Mabon, high harvest season, a time of good things to eat and to drink. The yeasty fragrance of fresh bread trailed from a baker's oven outside the village's single shop, and from somewhere, the scent of apples rose from a cider press. Slanting autumn sunshine splashed trees and grass and houses with golden light. It glistened on the villagers' brightly colored vests and sparkled on aprons and headdresses crusted with Breton lace.

The voices of the Belzois vendors calling their wares competed with the efforts of three Vila musicians. The French boy played alongside the harpist and bombardist, and when they took a break, he played on alone, his strange, sweet music making his listeners crowd closer to hear him. Ursule, shopping basket on her arm, paused, enchanted by the sound. Several village girls in their lace caps surrounded the musician, their faces rapt with admiration. Ursule experienced a flash of jealousy, though she understood. What young woman could not help but be enchanted by his music, his fine features, that spill of straight hair?

"Ursule, enough woolgathering." Agnes appeared at her shoulder, having finished her rounds, promoting her skills as a fortune-teller.

"Let's start back. There's no one here selling dress fabric." She put a hand under Ursule's arm to lead her away.

"Wait, Daj, wait." Ursule pulled free and gestured to the musician. "I want to listen."

"Who is that?"

"He didn't tell me his name, but he travels with the Vilas. I met him outside the camp. He's blind."

"He doesn't look blind," Agnes said, squinting through the sunshine for a better look.

"No, but he is." Ursule pushed the basket into her mother's hands. "You go back, Maman. Uncle Omas and Uncle Arnaud are ready. I'll walk back with Bettina and Mikel."

"Don't speak to these Belzois," Agnes said, slipping the basket over her own arm. "I don't like the way they look at us. I don't trust them."

"You don't trust anyone."

"No. Nor those Vilas, either." Agnes indicated a little gaggle of men congregated at one side of the green, joking, bumping each other with their shoulders and elbows. They had been drinking ale all afternoon, which was obvious from their raised voices and raucous laughter. Dukkar was one of them, his coarse voice unmistakable.

"They're just in their cups, Daj. Nothing to worry about."

"They shouldn't be drawing attention to themselves that way. I don't like the look of that musician, either. He's not Romani."

"Perhaps that's a good thing," Ursule said.

"How could it be? He's not one of us."

"So he's a misfit, like me."

"What a silly thing to say!"

"You know it's true, Daj, but never mind. Go on now. I'll see you in an hour."

Still scowling, Agnes hooked her basket over her elbow and went to find her brothers. Ursule watched her mother until she saw she had met Omas, then edged closer to the musicians' corner through a little clutch of people. The harpist and bombardist had returned, and the familiar strains of Romani songs rose into the waning afternoon. The music was disappointing now, the poorly tuned strings of the harp and the bleating of the bombarde too strident for the French boy's fragile music. A woven basket with a few *livres* in it rested on the grass before the trio. Whenever they finished a tune, the harpist gave the basket a push with his toe to draw attention to it. A cluster of Belzois children danced to the music, clapping, singing in shrill voices.

One little girl, skirt swirling as she spun, collided with Ursule's legs and almost fell. Ursule caught her, lifting her up by the hands, but before she could set her on her feet, one of the village women swept the child away from her grasp. She carried the little girl away, ignoring her wails, scowling over her shoulder at Ursule.

Ursule turned her back on the woman's sour face, but the moment had been spoiled. That little one would no doubt grow up to believe gypsies were dirty and dangerous. It was always the way.

The trio played two more songs, eliciting a few more *livres* for their basket, before they began to pack up their instruments, and the harpist scooped up their earnings. As the village girls started to reluctantly disperse, Ursule stepped forward. The French boy was just sliding his instrument into its leather case.

"*C'est moi,*" Ursule said. "The girl from the camp."

He tilted his head as he recognized her voice. "Ursule?"

"Yes." Her heart quivered with pleasure at his recalling her name, and at the delicious sensation of jealous glances on her back. It was rare for anyone to envy her for anything, and she decided she liked the feeling very much. "Wouldn't you like a cup of cider? You've played a long time."

He nodded. "I would. I'm thirsty."

"You must be." She tucked her hand under his elbow, finding his arm thin and wiry beneath her fingers. Her own muscles were thicker than his, made strong by daily labor. His arm felt like that of an aristocrat, the slender limb of someone who didn't do physical work. She said, "Come this way. There's a cider press on the other side of the green."

He walked beside her in such relaxed fashion it was as if he knew the way, guided only by the slight pressure of her fingers. They wound through the little market as the last of the vendors packed up their left-overs or called out bargain prices to clear their inventory. Ursule dug in her *posoti* for a coin to buy two cups of cider, then led the musician to a spot beyond the cider press where they could sit undisturbed in the last of the afternoon sunshine.

As they settled onto the grass, she said, "You know my name, but I don't know yours."

"Sandor," he said.

"Sandor. *Enchantée.*"

"*Enchanté.*" He still didn't smile. It occurred to Ursule she hadn't seen him smile once, not even when the Belzois children applauded the trio's jolliest tunes.

"Sandor. Is that a French name?"

He drank half his cup of cider in one long draft, leaving his smooth lips sparkling with moisture. "It's Greek, but I'm named after my Moldavian grandfather. He left me my flute."

"Is that what it is? A flute?"

"It is. A *nai* flute." He pulled it out of his shirt and slipped it out of its case with a motion as gentle as if it were an infant in swaddling clothes. As he lifted it, a gleaming knife fell out of the case into his lap. It wasn't the characteristic Romani shape, nor even the typical size of a Romani *churi*. It was longer, with an unusual diamond-shaped blade.

"I've never seen a knife like that," Ursule said.

He caught it up and tucked it back into his case. "This was my grandfather's, too. A Spanish dagger he acquired in his travels."

"It looks dangerous."

"It's no good to me if it isn't sharp. Mostly I use it to cut new thongs." He held his flute out on his long fingers. There were perhaps twenty of its polished tubes, lashed together with lengths of slim leather into a gracefully curved shape. "Some call this a pan flute."

"Oh! Also Greek."

"Ah!" Now, at last, a tiny smile lifted the corners of his mouth, and revealed a deep dimple in his left cheek. His eyes fixed on her as if he could see her with his mind. "An educated Romani girl."

She chuckled. "I'm not educated at all. I know the story of Pan, though. It's one of the myths. I've heard it a hundred times."

His smile grew, just a bit. "I am no Pan, as you see. I have only the legs of a man, and my head lacks horns."

The charm of his conversation made Ursule's pulse race. "But you make magic with your music, just as Pan did."

"Hardly Pan's magic, I'm afraid."

"I think it's exquisite."

"Merci beaucoup, mademoiselle."

"De rien, monsieur."

"I like your voice, Ursule. You speak excellent French, too," Sandor said. She was glad he couldn't see her blush. She was unused to compliments. He added, "So few of the travelers do."

"They speak enough to get by, but they will never admit to that if they can help it. I speak it when I'm helping my mother. And Breton, of course."

"Helping your mother do what?"

"She tells fortunes."

His eyebrows, as pale as his hair, lifted. "Real fortunes? Is she a seer?"

Ursule made a wry face before remembering he couldn't see her. "No, she's not really a seer. She pretends. She does it very well, though."

"Too bad." She glanced up and saw that his face had regained its normal somber expression. "I would have liked to have my fortune told."

"Would you? What would you like to know?"

He shrugged his thin shoulders. "The usual things, I suppose. Will I be successful?"

"You mean in your music?"

"Yes. I want to play with good musicians, not—" He broke off. "Oh, sorry. I didn't mean..."

"I understand. I have wondered how you came to be with these Vilas."

"They found me," he said. "I was playing on the streets, after my father—well. That's a long story. In any case, they heard me, and said I could live in their caravan if I would go with them to play."

"Do you like it? Being with the Vilas, playing in marketplaces?"

He sighed a little. "I don't mind it, but—I think some of them resent me because I can't hunt, or fish, but I still have to eat."

"I'm sorry about that."

He shrugged again. "*Eh bien.* I wouldn't mind so much if the music were better."

She watched his expressive features and thought it would be hard to keep secrets with such a face: the sensitive mouth, the dimple appearing and disappearing. Even the movements of his fingers gave away his feelings. "Tell me what else you would like to know, Sandor."

"It's the same, in a way." There was a little pause, and he swirled the liquid in his cup so that the smell of apples rose from it. "Will I ever see again? Because if I can't see, I can't travel about on my own, play where I wish—and what I wish."

His last comment made her want to throw her arms around him as if he were a child, a disappointed child like the one who had been pulled away from the dancing.

Ursule wanted to ask how he had lost his sight, but she didn't want to break the mood. It felt grand to sit here through the fading afternoon, the last shafts of sunlight warming her shoulders and glinting on Sandor's hair. He talked with her as if they were equals, and though they were in public, they were alone just the same. She had his full attention, and when she said something, he bent close to concentrate on her words, listening for their true meaning. It all made her heart soften in a way that was new to her.

She could have sat that way for a much longer time, but Sandor tipped up his cup to drain the last of the cider. "That was good. I thank you, Ursule. It's getting late, isn't it?"

"It is." She took his empty cup in her hand and reluctantly pushed herself to her feet.

Sandor stood, and his eyes looked past the cider press to scan the green in that uncanny way he had. The crowd had thinned to a dozen or so people. Almost all the vendors had packed up and left, and the woman with the cider press was wiping out the apple hopper with a cloth. Only a few Vilas, including Dukkar and his friends, still lingered.

Sandor said, "Do you see Michel or George?"

"I don't know those names."

"The Vila musicians." His voice tightened. "The harpist, the bombardist. Do you see them?"

"No. Their instruments are gone, and their basket. I think they might have—"

He stiffened. "They left without me." All traces of his smile vanished.

"Perhaps they couldn't see you, sitting over here."

"But I—how will I—"

She touched his arm. "It's all right, Sandor," she assured him. "I will guide you. Come, we'll return the cups and start back."

He averted his face, but not before she read hurt pride in the pinch of his lips and the tuck of his chin.

She slid her hand into his and gave it a gentle tug. "It doesn't matter. My mother has already left. You and I can walk back together."

Evening shadows now stretched across the green. The estuary glistened bronze and silver in the distance as the two of them started off. Thickets of brambles tumbled alongside their path, and Ursule sniffed the faint fragrance of the dog-roses that threaded through the tangle, littering the ground with the last petals of the season.

As the path darkened, Sandor seemed to become more surefooted than Ursule, anticipating twists and obstacles. She wondered if the remaining senses of all blind people sharpened in the absence of their sight, or if Sandor was unusual. He was certainly unusual in every other way. He was more slender than any of the Romani, like a long-legged heron that had blundered into a flock of geese. She was glad the other musicians had left him behind. The touch of his hand on her arm made her skin quiver.

They were halfway to the camp when a voice sounded behind them, thick with the effects of drink.

"Hey! You, little Ursule!"

Ursule's breath caught in her throat as Sandor's hand tightened on her arm. She didn't need to look back to know that it was Dukkar, his words slurred, but his voice all too familiar.

"Hey!" Dukkar shouted again. "Afraid to talk to me?" His voice was coming closer, though Ursule and Sandor hurried their steps as much as they dared in the darkness. Ursule could have run, but Sandor could not.

Dukkar made some comment to his companions, who roared with laughter.

Sandor said in a tense voice, "They're crazy when they're drunk, Ursule."

"I'm not afraid of them," she said, though anxiety knotted her stomach.

Dukkar called again, "Hey, girl! What are you doing with that boy? He can't even see your pretty face!" One of the others hooted something rude, and Dukkar shouted, "What you need, little Ursule, is a real *rom*. Lucky for you, I'm here!" More guffaws answered him.

Ursule glanced behind her, hoping there might be someone to aid her, some of the more sober Vilas, or perhaps one of the Orchières. She couldn't see anyone behind the lurching, laughing group of men. They stumbled along the path, shouting with fresh mirth when one of them tripped and fell to his knees, swearing.

The moon had not yet risen. Ursule cast about for a place she and Sandor could step off the path, get out of the way of the louts following them, but she saw nothing but the thicket of brambles crowding the path.

"I will have to face them, Sandor," Ursule said in a tense voice. "Maybe they'll go past. Leave us alone."

His voice was even grimmer than hers. "Everyone knows he has no wife, because no one will have him."

"I won't have him, either."

A sound scraped from Sandor's throat, an involuntary groan of anxiety.

Ursule didn't want to tremble, but she couldn't help herself. Every Romani girl knew the brutal truth. There were men who resorted to rape in order to acquire a wife, and a girl who was raped was spoiled. No one would have her except her rapist, and sometimes even he would not.

"My mother—" Ursule began, but didn't finish the thought. She knew her mother wouldn't hesitate to step between her daughter and Dukkar, but Agnes wasn't here. There was no one to help her but soft-handed, sweet-voiced, sightless Sandor.

From the thicket, incongruously, a nightingale sang. The beauty of it, thrilling through the soft-scented night as if all were well, made Ursule want to weep. It hardly seemed possible the dreamlike day could end like this, devolving into nightmare.

Together, she and Sandor stopped and turned to face the threat. A faint silver glow began on the eastern horizon, the moon preparing to show her face. The Vilas came on, shoving each other, chortling, cursing. Sandor stepped in front of Ursule, a slender bulwark against the danger approaching.

Dukkar stepped ahead of his companions. In the gloom he looked dark and mean, like one of the bears some of the Romani trained to dance at festivals, with the smell of the predator around him. "You! Ursule! Why are you hiding?"

"Leave her alone," Sandor said. His voice sounded steady, though his body shook.

Dukkar grunted, "Mind your own business, boy. Come, little Ursule! Come talk to me!"

"Go away," she said, her voice nowhere near as steady as Sandor's.

One of Dukkar's companions gripped his arm. "Come on, Dukkar, leave the girl alone! She's still a child."

Dukkar grunted and threw off the man's hand. "She's old enough," he snapped.

"I'm not," Ursule protested.

"You will be soon," he laughed. He stamped toward her and Sandor, weaving unsteadily, advancing just the same.

Brambles clawed at Ursule's hair as she shrank back. Sandor braced himself, his feet set wide, but though he tried to hold his ground, one negligent shove from the heavier Dukkar threw him to one side. The moon slid up the eastern sky, shedding just enough silvery light for Ursule to see Sandor stumble sideways into the brush. He gasped at the bite of the thorns as he struggled to extricate himself.

Ursule bolted forward, attempting to dash out of Dukkar's reach, but he was too quick. His hard hands caught her, pulled her to him. Her involuntary cry of terror shamed her, but she couldn't help it.

Dukkar's attack was not subtle. He kicked her feet from under her and bore her down under his weight as crudely as if he were a wild boar mounting a sow. His breath was foul with the stale smell of ale, and his body was hard and heavy. He released her arm so he could pull up her skirts. The chill of the night air shocked her bare thighs, and she gasped with the horror of it. Her chemise tore as easily as a dry leaf, leaving her exposed, without defense.

She fought him with all the strength she had, but she might as well have pounded a wall with her fists. She could barely move under his unrelenting bulk. The only weapon she had, as he pressed her into the dirt beneath the brambles, was her teeth.

She found his earlobe with her incisors and bit down hard, relentless in her own way. Something gave. He yowled in pain, and she tasted hot, salty blood. She spit out the bit of flesh she had bitten off even as he freed one hand and struck her full in the face.

He used the same hand to untie his belt, and she felt his hairy, hot belly grind against hers as he wriggled his trousers open. She screamed again, this time a howl of pure desperation. She shouted, "No!" and then, as his gross flesh searched for hers, her voice rose to a scream. "No, please, please, no!"

His roar of lust was the bellow of a rutting animal, a brutal sound

louder than the jeers and shouts of the other men. A wave of pure
helpless panic blurred Ursule's mind until she hardly knew what was
happening to her.

Then Dukkar made another sound. A different sound.

It cleared Ursule's thoughts and brought her back to herself.

She recognized the sound he had made. It was deep, guttural,
instinctive. It held pain, and shock, and recognition. It was the sound
emitted by an injured horse when its throat was cut, the sigh of release
when a chicken's neck was wrung, the groan of a hare taken by a fox.

For Ursule, it was the sound of reprieve.

Dukkar's body went limp. His head fell to one side so that only his
greasy beard lay against her cheek. His weight still held her down, but
it was the dead weight of an animal's carcass. Sobbing now, she twisted
her body, arms and legs scrabbling through the dirt until she wriggled
free of him. She struggled to pull her clothes over her nakedness. Her
face stung where he had struck her, and the taste of his blood still fouled
her mouth. She scrambled to her feet, defiantly choking back her tears.

Dukkar's companions stood in a ragged semicircle, goggling at the
scene. Two of them half-heartedly gripped Sandor's arms, though he
made no move to flee. The moon had risen, and it showed Sandor's
face terribly white, eyes stretched wide, pupils expanded so they nearly
vanquished the irises.

Ursule followed his gaze, though with reluctance, to take in the haft
of the blade buried in Dukkar's back. The shirt fabric bunched around
it, soaked in blood that was black in the moonlight. The blade was
invisible, but the distinctive handle was unmistakable. It was the knife
Sandor had shown her earlier.

"Sandor," Ursule breathed. "Did you...?"

One of Dukkar's friends answered. "He did, and he'll answer to
Edouard for it. He's killed one of our best hunters."

Ursule said, "Dukkar tried to rape me."

"Your claim," another man said.

"You all saw it!" she snapped.

"Dark. I saw nothing," someone said.

"Edouard won't like this," the first said. "Won't tolerate violence in our clan."

Sandor groaned, a sound full of misery.

Ursule summoned her ready temper and let it blaze. "Sandor saved me, and you all know it. And so I will tell Edouard Vila! I'm a fatherless girl, not yet a woman, and Dukkar had no right—"

"Your word against his," one of the men growled.

Another said, "Dukkar won't be speaking any more words, I think."

The first said, "I thought she was grown. Didn't know she was still a girl."

"I told you!" Ursule cried. Sandor groaned again, a sound of such grief that Ursule let her torn clothes fall in a ragged curtain around her and ran to take his hands.

His captors released his arms, and she said, "Sandor, it's going to be all right—"

"No, little girl, it's not," one of the other men said. "Not for your young fella. Edouard won't care what the reasons are, he's done murder. Edouard will turn him over to the sheriff."

"That's not fair!" When no one responded, Ursule rounded on them with such fury they fell back a step, away from the fire of her anger. "You all stood back and allowed him to try to rape me! Me, a thirteen-year-old girl! Someone else stopped him, and now you want to act like men? Attack the one man who did the right thing, a blind musician who can't defend himself? Cowards! Every one of you! And that's what I'll tell Edouard Vila, I promise you!"

One of the men gave a sour chuckle. "Edouard won't care what a child has to say."

Another added, "It will go hard on your friend here, little girl. You should get him away."

"Go then," she said. "All of you men, flee back to camp like the cravens you are! Leave a girl to deal with this!"

She drew Sandor to her and stood with his unresisting arm clasped in her two hands. The men cast doubtful glances at the lifeless form of Dukkar, but they seemed eager enough to take her suggestion. There were one or two murmurs, but they made them even as they backed away, farther and farther into the darkness, until they were only shady silhouettes against the darker thicket of brambles. Then they were gone, leaving Ursule and Sandor alone with the corpse.

Ursule bent over Dukkar. It would be best if she could recover the knife, to leave as little evidence as possible. Though it made her shudder, she forced herself to wrap her fingers around the haft and pull.

It only moved an inch or two, and a gout of fresh blood spilled out around it. Sandor had held nothing back when he thrust his weapon into Dukkar's back. She would not have thought the flutist to be so strong.

Dukkar, in the moment of his passing, had soiled himself. The air was already rank with the smell of blood, and the other smell made it worse. Ursule wrinkled her nose and tried one more time to pull the knife out of his body, but her hand shook so she couldn't do it.

She gave that up and tried to shift the body into the thicket. It took all her strength just to roll the corpse to its side, then roll it again so that it was partially hidden by low-hanging brambles. The boots still stuck out, so she tried to disguise them with a bit of dry branch she found at the edge of the path.

Panting, she stood back and tried to assess the scene. Someone would have to be looking, she thought, to realize there was a body half-hidden by brambles. The casual passerby would not notice. Unless, of course, they smelled it.

Tired and dry-mouthed, she gave it up. She drew Sandor away, back down the path toward the village.

He said, "Where are we going?"

"It's not me who's going," she said, her voice broken with sadness. "Those men were right, Sandor. You need to disappear. It will go badly with you if you return to the camp."

Sandor said, in the dull tone of shock, "Dukkar's dead."

"He is, and praise the Goddess for that."

"I killed him."

"He was going to rape me. To ruin me."

"I have never—"

"Sandor." Ursule thrust aside her own revulsion at what had happened, the ghastly sensation of being assaulted, of the weight of a dead man holding her down, of the taste of a dead man's blood in her mouth. She knew it would haunt her dreams, but there was no time to think of that now.

She tightened her grip on Sandor's hand. "Listen to me. You're a hero, like in the songs you sing. I am the maiden you saved, and now I must save you. That means you have to leave the camp, leave Belz."

They walked a little way in silence, his hand in hers quivering with anxiety.

"Do you know anyone in Belz? Anyone who can help you?"

"No. I come from Lorient."

"Do you have family there?"

"I do, but..."

"Sandor, they're your family. Surely they will take you in." A Romani family would never turn away one of its members—except perhaps a ruined girl.

He said, "I don't know. Perhaps."

"You'll have to go to them."

"I have no money. I haven't yet gotten my share of today's take."

"I have money." Ursule thrust an anxious hand into her skirt. She found, to her relief, that though her chemise was in shreds, her *posoti* was intact. "I have money," she repeated. Giving it to Sandor meant she would have to continue wearing her old skirt, now ripped into pieces, but he had saved her. She didn't hesitate. "It's enough to send you home. You must buy passage on a boat, something that can carry you well away from Belz. Edouard Vila can hardly follow you out into the estuary."

"Do you not think, Ursule, truly—if Edouard knew what Dukkar tried to do..."

"I think Edouard knows what Dukkar is, but he has to be seen as strong in the eyes of the clan. He will turn you over to the sheriff in a heartbeat, and they will hang you."

"Dukkar was a brute," Sandor said, his voice going high like that of a child about to cry.

"Yes." She held his arm tighter. "I am only glad you had a knife."

"I lost my knife!" Sandor said, and shuddered. Ursule shuddered, too, at the thought that Sandor's beautiful blade was still buried in Dukkar's cooling flesh. "My grandfather's—"

"You will buy another," she said, though she doubted he would find another Spanish dagger. "You will get away. Play your flute and earn money, and buy another knife."

"My father will say I have failed. Again."

But you will be alive.

E douard Vila roared around the caravans a few times in the days
following, demanding to know what had become of one of his
best hunters, but he learned very little from Dukkar's drinking companions. One suggested Dukkar had gotten into a fight, then disappeared. The others nodded agreement and, when pressed, were vague
about who he had been fighting.

They left Ursule out of the conversation, avoiding blame for their
part in the disaster. Edouard huffed and threatened, and talked of going
to the sheriff in Belz. He didn't do it, though. Ursule knew the last
thing he wanted to do was bring attention to the Romani.

No one commented on the Orchière girl's blackened eye and swollen cheek, nor did anyone ask what had become of the blind flutist.

It was all a very Romani way of dealing with a crisis. Dukkar had
been unpopular. Sandor had been an outsider. Ursule was young and
foolish, had injured herself somehow. The Vilas and the Orchières alike
were content to leave the episode a mystery.

Agnes asked her daughter over and over if she was sure she was all
right. Ursule repeated her reassurance many times, finally saying, "Daj.
Do you think I don't know what rape is? I do. Dukkar tried, but Sandor stopped him. He stuck his *churi* right between Dukkar's ribs, and
that's why he had to get away. That's why I spent all my coins for his
fare, because he saved me."

Agnes had made a poultice, and she pressed it gingerly to Ursule's
swollen cheek. "I shouldn't have left you alone in Belz. I shouldn't have
left you unprotected!"

"I wasn't unprotected. I had Sandor."

"A blind boy!" Agnes snapped the words as if she were angry, but Ursule knew her mother. It was grief that choked her voice, and shame, and fear for the future.

"It's going to be all right." Ursule pretended to be calm for her mother's sake, but inwardly, she trembled with horror over everything that had happened. It was easier to think of Sandor's knife still lodged in Dukkar's back than it was to remember the helplessness of being trapped beneath Dukkar's weight, the revolting touch of his hairy stomach, and that other—that awful hot thing he had meant to hurt her with. That he came close to hurting her with.

It was Sandor—poor sweet Sandor—who had to live with the knowledge that he had killed someone. Ursule wished she had been able to do it herself. The memory would haunt Sandor, but it would not have troubled her at all. She had been born old. She understood what mattered.

Agnes had taken one look at her ruined skirt and tossed it into the rag bin. She dug through her modest cache of things to find an old skirt of her own. She altered it to fit Ursule, muttering a curse on Dukkar's soul with each stitch.

As Ursule accepted the skirt from her mother's hands, she thought sadly that she would always associate this piece of clothing with the tragedy that had driven Sandor away.

"I should have taken the knife," she said miserably.

"The knife?"

"If someone finds the corpse, they'll find the knife. There's no other knife like it anywhere near Belz. They'll come looking for the one who owned it. The boatman will say where he took him, won't he? If it's murder? I should have taken it!"

Agnes didn't look up but busied herself putting away her needle and thimble. "Don't think about it anymore. There's nothing more you can do."

Ursule tried to take her mother's advice, but it wasn't easy. She dreamed of Dukkar's corpse moldering under the bushes, that distinctive knife emerging into the air as his flesh decomposed. Another time she dreamed of one of the wild boar tearing the remains apart, dropping the knife on the path for anyone to see.

Her other dreams were of Sandor.

In her dreams, she yearned toward him, tried to find him in a crowd, or in the woods, or in the city, a place she had never been. It was foolishness, girlish fancy. She had barely known him, after all. Just the same, as the salt wind blew over the estuary and rattled the frame of the caravan, she remembered the sunny afternoon they had spent together. She prayed, in her irreligious way, that the boatman who had accepted her coins would keep his promise to deliver Sandor safely to Lorient. It had been awful watching that boat slip away into the early-morning fog, Sandor clinging to one of the masts, his sightless eyes searching the mist for her as he lifted a hand in farewell.

She tried to picture him safe in the bosom of his family, playing his flute at festivals and weddings and birthday fetes. She worried that his fate was the opposite, that he had reached home and his father had refused to take him in.

She didn't know if it was his music or his gentle manner—or perhaps his fine features and wonderful hands—but she felt as if he were woven into her heart, as the basketmakers wove patterns in reeds and straw. Her spirit was out of balance, torn between relief and sadness, revulsion over what had happened, gratitude that it had not been worse, grief at the loss of something she had only begun to understand.

Samhain came and went, unmarked by the Vilas or the Orchières. Agnes was out all day, so Ursule remained alone in the caravan, poring over the grimoire, longing for something she couldn't name. She felt as if she were poised at the edge of one of the sea cliffs, not knowing if she would fall forward into the restless water or backward into the clutch of the damp earth.

When the news arrived that the sheriff of Belz had found Dukkar's body, that he had died from a knife wound, Ursule and Agnes stared at each other in mutual agreement that they would speak no word about it. The other Vila men, the ones who knew, also kept silent. It was yet another Romani secret.

Then, on the night of the full winter moon, Ursule's monthlies arrived. She was a woman. Her girlhood, such as it was, had reached its end. She could hardly lament what had barely existed, but she still felt a sense of loss. What, she wondered, could adulthood offer her that she would want?

·····•·≫≫≫•≫≫≫·•·····

The sky was still dark when she woke that morning with an aching, tender belly and bloody clothes. She scrambled out of her cot, picking at the sticky fabric of her nightdress. "Daj," she whispered. "Daj, it's—it's my monthlies!"

Her mother sat up in her own cot, blinking sleepily. "What?"

Ursule twisted to show the stain on her nightdress. "I've started," she said.

"Ah," Agnes said. "Yes, I see. Here, I'll fetch you a clout." She pushed her blanket aside and started to get up, but Ursule waved her back.

"No, don't bother. I know where they are."

There was little storage room in the caravan, which was why their pans and cups hung on the walls, and their clothes mostly from hooks. For things like smallclothes and chemises, scarves and handkerchiefs, they used baskets that could slide beneath the cots.

Ursule knelt beside her mother's bed and slid out the basket that held clean clouts. She had to move the basket that held the scrying crystal to reach it, putting it to one side while she rummaged for what she needed. It was when she began to slide it back into its place that the bit of blanket protecting it fell away, sliding on the film of dust that coated the floor. Ursule reached out to smooth the blanket back into place, then froze as her fingers grazed the rounded stone.

She might have missed it had the inside of the caravan not been so dim. It was no brighter than the dull glow of a dying ember, no bigger than the flicker of the morning star. She drew a startled breath and bent forward, peering through the dusky quartz, not completely sure she had actually seen anything.

"Ursule?" her mother whispered. "What is it?"

"Daj. It's the stone…I think…"

Agnes threw aside her blanket and came to lean over Ursule. The two of them stared at the tiny spot of light glimmering from the depths of the stone. When Ursule lifted her hand, it winked out.

Agnes gasped, "Touch it again! Ursule, put your hand on it!"

Gingerly, Ursule laid her palm over the cool quartz.

This time the light flared under her hand, bright as an oil lantern, gleaming between her fingers and casting thready bars of light on the roof of the caravan and their intent faces. At the same time, the ache of her monthlies flared in her belly, connecting the two.

Agnes drew back, gazing in wonder at her daughter. "You!" she breathed, and then, choked by sudden tears, fell silent, her hand over her mouth.

Ursule lifted her hand again from the stone. The light faded slowly this time, dimming little by little until it flickered out. She gripped her hands together and turned to her mother. "Me?" she whispered. "It responded to me? But why?"

"Grand-mère always said that it started for her when she was thirteen, like you—when she became a woman. We didn't believe her."

"Didn't you see the light in the stone when she touched it?"

"We thought she faked it. We all thought that!"

"Oh, Maman! Does no one in our family tell the truth to each other?"

Agnes wiped a tear from her cheek with one finger. "I wanted to be a seer," she said, her voice thick with emotion. "I wanted it with all my soul, but it never happened. No matter how I tried, how often I rubbed the crystal or spoke to it or begged it, it lay like a dead thing, dark and empty." She sniffled and gave a little self-deprecating laugh. "I decided Grand-mère's tales of the crystal were just fables. But now—now *you* will be the seer! You will tell real fortunes! I don't know how you will learn how it works, but you must figure it out somehow."

Ursule felt the call of the old book that nestled in the basket beneath the scrying stone. She thought of its handwritten recipes and spells and instructions, and experienced a rush of excitement. The book would teach her what she needed to know. Some of it she had already learned, puzzling out the old French, wondering at the quavering hands that had written in it. Had they been Romani? They must have been.

Perhaps this was the time to tell Agnes her secret.

Outside, the light was rising, the camp coming to life. Children cried, people called out as they started their day. Ursule opened her mouth to tell her this other, great thing, but Agnes spoke ahead of her.

"We'll change places," Agnes said. "You will sit behind the stone, and I will take the money. They will come from all over for our fortune-telling!"

"No, Daj." Ursule gathered up a fresh skirt, a clout, and a towel. "I will not tell fortunes. I will not take money for my gift."

"Then what good is it?" Her mother stared at her, her mouth a little open, not understanding.

Ursule shook her head. "I don't know yet. I need to think. To see what the stone wants."

"I don't think it told Grand-mère what to do."

"Daj—I have to tell you—"

"What?"

Ursule wanted to say that the stone had told her ancestresses many things. She wanted to say that it was not only Violca, but many grandmothers, leaving their wisdom for the ones who came after. She wanted to confess that she had been reading for years, to explain that printed words—in French, in Breton—had begun to speak to her when she was tiny, but that she had been afraid to tell anyone. She was different enough in this clan—small, plain, difficult. She hadn't wanted anything to set her even further apart.

She bit her lip, trying to think how to explain why she had kept this secret for so long, but a banging on the door of the caravan stopped her.

It was Bettina. "Ursule, you lazy thing! Come out now, and let's go to the brook."

She would have to tell her mother later. "Maman, I need to wash."
"Yes, you do. Go, then hurry back. I'm hoping for customers today,
out from Belz."

········ ·›››‹‹‹·›››‹‹‹· ········

Ursule had vowed she would not use the crystal for money, but in that
she was mistaken.

It was still Agnes who sat behind the table, swathed in sashes and
strings of painted beads as she predicted events for her clients. Ursule
still crouched in her accustomed place on a cushion on the ground, just
to one side of Agnes's stool. She kept her scarf pulled over her face and
added drama to her mother's proclamations with little sighs or gasps.

But the crystal, now that it was awakened, had changed. Though
Ursule was below it, looking up at what she could see above its granite
base, its inner light was clear to her, glimmering with an insistent and
unmistakable incandescence, undimmed by the false light her mother
created. Ursule's belly responded with the ache of magic.

Agnes would speak familiar words, perhaps "A tall dark man will
appear on your doorstep. He brings bad luck." Sometimes this pro-
nouncement met with no argument. At other times, in this new province
of real magic, the crystal signaled disagreement, and Ursule couldn't keep
silent. Its messages were like an itch in her mind, an irresistible compre-
hension, like the ones she had when she realized letters formed words.

This sensation blended in some way with all that had happened to
her in recent months, a mix of excitement and longing, wonder and
fear. The convictions took hold of her, and she couldn't shake them off.
She hadn't asked for them. In truth, she didn't want them, but she felt as
if the stone had taken her in hand to instruct her, as if it had a will of its
own. She sensed the grandmothers laughing as she learned things she
had never expected to learn.

She found herself speaking the truth, good or bad. It was a compulsion. She might whisper to her mother, "No, he is short, Daj. Short and
stout." Or, "He is gray, Daj. Old."

Agnes resisted at first, frowning down at Ursule on her cushion, but her customers made it clear Ursule was right.

The customer might respond, with clapped hands, "Oh! The girl is right! I know that man—it's the sheriff." Or she might exclaim, "*Mon Dieu!* My mother's brother is coming! He always needs money."

Agnes tried to hide her resentment of the change in their circumstances, of her daughter's power ascending and hers diminishing. Ursule could see this, but she let it pass. Everything that was happening was as much a surprise to her as to her mother. It was all beyond her control.

It was a relief when, little by little, her mother's vexation began to transform into respect.

Agnes's traditional predictions—sudden wealth, a relative's illness, an offer of marriage—were enhanced by inarguable details, things no one could have guessed. The sudden wealth might be the discovery of a husband's secret purse, coins kept out of the housekeeping money and hidden among his tools. The relative's illness might be explained by too much drink. The offer of marriage was a flattering one but would never result in a wedding.

The news was not always good, but it was never wrong. The flow of customers increased, drawn by Agnes's new reputation for accuracy in her fortunes. The coins piled up in dramatic fashion, and even Arnaud smiled on the two of them. Agnes declared she felt as rich as a bishop.

Ursule was uneasy, though. She didn't always understand the stone's messages, and she could only wait for it to speak to her, because she didn't know how to ask it for anything. Worse, what made her lie awake at night, worrying, was the darkness that began to develop in the crystal over the weeks of Agnes's growing success.

It began as a faint fog that clouded the inner light and caused Ursule's solar plexus to quiver in response. The fog grew thicker and darker each time she looked into it, like the winter mists that drifted over the estuary and hid the stars. Ursule's instinct told her it was trouble, though she couldn't fathom what it might be.

Her instinct was right. Trouble it was, and it arrived in the form of the mayor's wife.

Madame Robert was young, and pretty enough, despite an unfortunate wen on one side of her nose. She was accompanied by a much older woman, a wrinkled crone with hooded dark eyes. The crone kept her seamed lips folded tightly together, dismissively shaking her head when Agnes asked if she wanted her fortune told.

Madame Robert was the eager one. She settled on the stool, her arms crossed beneath her winter cape, one foot jiggling with anticipation. "I've heard such wonderful things about you, Madame Agnes!" she said, in a breathy voice. "I can't wait to see what you'll tell me. I'm expecting again, and I'm hoping you'll tell me I'm going to have a son at last! I already have three girls, and I simply can't have another one. My husband will be so angry!"

The older woman's scowl deepened, and Madame Robert's round cheeks reddened under her angry glance.

Agnes fluttered one of her scarves, casting Ursule a sidelong glance before she bent over the crystal, sliding her fingertips over its surface. "Let us see," she intoned, as she always did. "Let us see what the spirits have to say."

"Oh!" Madame Robert breathed, hugging herself tighter. "Do tell me it's a boy!"

Agnes slid a scarf over the stone and tilted the lamp at her feet to make the surface of the crystal sparkle.

Madame Robert cried, "Is that how it works? What do you see? What does it tell you?"

Agnes drew a long, slow breath through her nostrils before she let her eyelids droop and her voice drop to a confiding tone. "I see a baby—" she began.

"I certainly know that!" Madame Robert giggled, and smoothed her dress over the roundness of her belly.

Agnes glanced again at her daughter. Ursule, gazing up into the scrying stone from her seated position, raised her left hand, and tapped the palm twice with the forefinger of her right.

"Ah," Agnes said, on a long exhalation. "Oh, my goodness, *madame*. Not one baby. Two. Twins! They are——" Her glance slid swiftly to Ursule, then back. "Yes! They are boys! They are both boys. Your husband will be very happy with you."

Madame Robert sighed, sniffling back tears of relief. The crone snorted, but Agnes smiled in triumph.

Ursule noticed none of that. The crystal commanded all her attention. She forgot entirely who else was present. Who was listening.

The light she saw, which spoke to her in such an unfathomable way, glowed deep inside the shadowy quartz, unaffected by Agnes's fluttering scarf. Ursule perceived the light with her eyes, but also with the space just beneath her heart, that sensitive place that shivered with awe at knowing things she couldn't know. It was exhilarating. It was terrifying.

As her mother murmured congratulations to Madame Robert, and the older woman frowned doubtfully at the scrying stone, Ursule received another message. It seemed a very great thing to her, bigger than twins, bigger than the gender of the woman's babies, bigger than the fee she and her mother would collect for the welcome news. It startled her so she dropped the scarf that covered her face. She forgot that *some secrets should be kept*.

She breathed, without thinking, "He is not their father!"

"What?" It was the first word the crone had spoken, and it was as sharp and fierce as a knife blade.

Madame Robert paled and began to tremble. Agnes, recognizing the crisis building before her, said hastily, "Pay no attention to the girl! She is sometimes not quite——"

Her argument fell on deaf ears. The crone, hissing like an angry snake, slapped the younger woman's cheek, clawing her skin with long yellow fingernails. Madame Robert cried out in pain and threw up her arm to defend herself. Ursule, shocked into awareness of what was happening, scrambled to her feet as the old woman lunged at the younger woman a second time. Already three lines of blood seeped from Madame Robert's fair skin. Ursule seized the crone's arm before she could strike again, dragging her backward so she stumbled, then catching both her arms so she wouldn't fall.

Agnes said something, trying to salvage the situation, but there was nothing to be done. Madame Robert and the crone instantly plunged into a spitting argument in Breton that drowned out Agnes's pleas. They spoke so fast that Ursule could get only the gist, and around the camp, people turned to stare at the sudden tumult.

The scene exploded as if someone had thrown a cup of goose fat into a hot fire. Madame Robert screamed something at the crone, picked up her skirts, and fled the camp without paying. The crone jerked free of Ursule's grip and hobbled after her, shrieking imprecations. Ursule stood, rigid with guilt, her fingers pressed to her mouth. Agnes was at her shoulder, watching helplessly as the two women disappeared down the path to Belz. Their shouts carried to the camp, dwindling gradually as they moved farther away. One or two of the Vilas laughed, but others shook their heads. Such a scene could draw unwelcome attention.

Ursule couldn't think what to do or to say. She had caused all of this, her mother losing her profit, the young woman now in terrible trouble. There was no way for Ursule to put it right. No way to take back what she had said.

There was also no way to make what she had said not true.

"The old woman," she groaned. "That was her mother-in-law. Now she knows Madame Robert has been unfaithful to her son."

"I can't think why she allowed her mother-in-law to come." Agnes's voice shook with anxiety.

"I think—they talked too fast, but I think—the old lady goes everywhere with her. She suspected something was going on, I suppose, but—"

Agnes hugged herself, still gazing after the two Belzois. "You saw truly, then, Ursule?"

"I don't exactly see. I don't have the proper word for it. I just—the crystal flashes, and I *know*. It's in my mind, all at once, as clearly as if I had seen it with my eyes, or heard it with my ears. This—it surprised me so! I shouldn't have said it aloud." Ursule turned to grasp her mother's hand. "I'm so sorry, Daj. The money—"

Agnes turned abruptly toward the caravan and began stripping off her sashes and beads. "Never mind that. Keep a thought for poor little Madame Robert. Her husband is likely to throw her right out in the street."

"It will be my fault!" Ursule said, tears gathering at the back of her eyes.

"Well, there's nothing to be done about it now. Chances are her husband knew already and sent his mother to watch over her." She bent over the crystal to wrap it, saying sourly, "Husband not doing his duty, I expect, but he'll have two sons to soothe his wounded pride."

"But they won't—"

Agnes straightened, putting a finger to her lips. "Hush, Ursule. Some things are better kept secret, remember?"

"I remember." Ursule took the stone to return it to its basket. It felt as heavy and old in her arms as one of the menhirs.

Agnes sighed. "Too late, I know. Remember for the next time."

"I'll try, Maman." But as she stepped up into the caravan, Ursule's shoulders sagged under the mantle of responsibility that had fallen on them. It was a good thing she had been born old. This dark gift would be too much for a young heart to bear.

It was almost Yule, the one Sabbat the Romani felt safe celebrating, since the Belzois would be busy with their Christmas. Ursule had always loved the days of preparation: pouring candles, making wreaths to symbolize the completion of the Wheel of the Year, collecting mistletoe to be blessed for the handfastings Ostara would bring. But this year, a sense of apprehension darkened the already-gloomy winter days, and she felt no joy.

Ursule felt about the scrying stone the way she supposed Sandor must have felt about his *nai* flute when he was a beginner: enthusiastic but clumsy. She had searched the grimoire, hoping for guidance, but she found only recipes and rites and charms and spells. None of her Orchière ancestresses had left instructions for a beginner.

There was only one hint, written in an odd mix of Breton and Cornish, its sister language. With difficulty, Ursule puzzled out the words. The writer signed herself Liliane, or it might have been Lilith, and she wrote in a spidery hand that spoke of days gone by.

The stone is the gift of Mother Earth, to be treasured and respected. Let every mother's daughter remember, and take care (or it might have been *be wary*—Ursule wasn't sure). *Power is a sword with two edges. It acts in different ways according to the hand that wields it. Some who attempt to use the stone will fail, but take heart. A great practitioner* (or artist, or performer) *will arise one day, and her line will continue beyond the horizon of memory.*

Had Grand-mère been the great practitioner? Ursule had found no reference to One-eyed Violca, the great seer, in the grimoire. She couldn't tell if any of these pages were in her hand. She couldn't guess when the ability to read had disappeared. It would take only one generation to lose it, and it was only by the grace of the Goddess that words and numbers spoke to Ursule. She wished it were as easy to read the stone.

At times it lay like a dead thing, no matter how dramatic a reading Agnes was trying to give. At others it began to glow the moment the customer sat down, as if it couldn't wait to reveal a secret. If she had known more, perhaps she could have interpreted the growing shadow in the quartz as the warning it must have been.

They came on a cold night in December, with a ground mist curling around the caravans and shrouding the waters of the estuary. The Belzois, at least twenty of them, cloaked and hooded, with a priest in their midst, marched into the Vila camp. They carried lanterns that swayed with their steps and stopped just inside the circle of wagons, the fog swirling around their ankles. The dogs snarled and barked at them, but two men with staves beat them back. The lanterns cast sickly yellow light on their faces, leaving their eyes in shadow. The leader, a skinny little man in an overlarge coat, shouted for Edouard Vila.

Men and women and a few children descended from their caravans to gaze in horror at the mob. Edouard, half-dressed except for a coat hastily thrown over his shoulders, stood straddle-legged beside the smoking fire pit, bracing himself on his cane. "What do you mean, disturbing my family at his hour?" he demanded, in passable French.

"We want the witch!" the man shrilled. "Hand her over or it will go ill with you all!"

Ursule and Agnes fell back toward their own wagon, gripping each other's hands. Ursule's heart felt as if it would pound itself out through her ribs. Agnes groaned as the crone who had accompanied Madame Robert pushed her way through the crowd.

"There she is!" the old woman screeched. Another hiss of indrawn breath swept the watching Romani, huddling in shawls and coats, pushing their children behind them. The crone pointed her yellow-nailed hand at Agnes. "That's the witch, that one!"

The Romani followed the pointing finger to the spot where Agnes and Ursule clung together. Ursule felt their gazes like knife points digging into her skin. That gnarled finger was pointing directly at her mother.

Edouard said, "There's no witch here!"

"Yes, there is," the old woman cried. "It's her! Right there!" It was Agnes she meant, Agnes the fortune-teller, who hawked her services openly in the market. Ursule shuddered. She couldn't let this happen. The fault was hers alone.

Arnaud sidled gingerly forward, obviously loath to stick his neck out but driven by family loyalty. He protested weakly, his French much worse than Edouard Vila's. *"Non, non,"* he stammered. "My sister tells fortunes, that's all. Tells people what they want to hear."

The crone's voice rose above his. "She's a witch, I tell you! She scried in that stone of hers, the devil's light shining from it as if the door to hell had fallen open! She said my daughter-in-law's babies are bastards, and she was right!"

Agnes drew a horrified breath, and Ursule took a step forward. "No!" she shouted. "No, it wasn't my mother, it was—"

Abruptly, Agnes dragged Ursule back. She stumbled, stunned to silence by her mother's strength and by the sudden, rock-hard rigidity of her body as she positioned herself in front of her daughter. She seemed suddenly bigger than she really was, broader, taller. She hissed at Ursule, *"Chut, chut!"*

Ursule moaned, "But, Daj—"

Agnes said to the crone, "A guess! It was a guess. Sometimes I guess right, sometimes not. Even now, who knows what's true?"

The crone stalked forward, her black draperies flapping like the feathers of an ancient crow. She shoved back her hood, and her eyes burned like coals in her wrinkled face. Standing directly in front of Agnes, she snarled, "She *admitted* it, witch! The slut admitted it to me, and to my son!"

"I couldn't have known that, *madame*."

"You *did* know it. You looked into that stone of yours, and you knew it! Only a witch—"

Ursule tried to move, but her mother held her with an iron hand.

"I am no witch," she said, steadily, though there was a thread of panic in her voice. Ursule's heart thudded at her courage. "I tell fortunes, and I guess at things. It's what I do—"

Omas stepped between the crone and his sister. "Leave her alone," he tried to say in French, even worse than Arnaud's. "Let her be." It did no good. The mob saw his gentleness and scoffed at it.

The leader of the Belzois commanded, "Take her!" and two other men leaped to seize Agnes, one on each side. They pulled her right off her feet, making her cry out.

Ursule screamed, "No! It wasn't her!" but no one paid her any attention except Omas, who tried to put his arm around her. She shrugged it off.

Other women were screaming, too, and men shouting. The dogs spun in circles, snapping, threatening, their hackles high and stiff. Edouard Vila tried to intervene, but it was no use. A big man shoved him back with a heavy staff. Edouard's bad leg gave way, and he fell.

The priest, in a high, thin voice, intoned in Latin as the mob dragged Agnes out of the camp and along the path to the village. Ursule could just see the top of her mother's head, bobbing helplessly in their midst. The dogs barked at the heels of the interlopers until one of the Belzois kicked the fiercest of them with his thick boot. The cur fell back with a yelp, and the other dog cowered back with him.

Someone helped Edouard to his feet. The other Romani stood frozen, their calls and shouts evaporating into a stunned silence. The men slunk to the fire pit. In a few moments everyone gathered there, their misery as thick as the fog. Women began to weep. Frightened children wailed, and their mothers tried in vain to hush them.

Ursule, in her nightdress and barefoot, was the only one to run after the Belzois, calling, "Daj! No, no, let her go! Daj!"

She didn't hear Omas pounding along the path behind her. She didn't know he was there until he seized her arm, wrenching her to a halt. She tried to break free, but her uncle, normally so mild-mannered, had surprisingly strong fingers, and his grip on her arm was one of iron.

She stared up at him, openmouthed and breathless, wide-eyed with panic. "Uncle Omas," she sobbed. "They took her! They took Maman, and they'll—they'll—"

His hold didn't ease. "I know, Ursule. I know. But there's nothing you can do."

She tried again to get away from him, even forcing him to stumble a few steps, but he held on. "Ursule," he said. "It's no good if we lose you both!"

"Lose!" she cried. "We can't *lose* her!" Her voice was thin and shrill, a voice she didn't recognize. "We have to go after her," she shrieked. "We have to reason with them—beg the sheriff—"

"The sheriff was one of the mob," Omas said grimly.

"Then, then—the mayor!" Panicked sobs garbled her words. "We'll tell him it was me, not Maman. It was me said the babies weren't his, and we'll tell him I lied, I made it up. You can tell him, Uncle Omas! You can say I'm just a silly girl—"

"They wouldn't listen to us, Ursule. You know they wouldn't! You have to think—"

"No!" She gave a tremendous pull, one that made her feel as if she had dislocated her elbow, and spun to race down the dark path. A short, thickset man blocked her way with one arm stretched out.

It was Edouard Vila, leaning on his cane. He shook his head at her. "You can't do anything, little one," he said heavily. "I'm so sorry about your *daj*, but they have her now. They don't care whether it's true or not. They just want a witch to burn."

"*Burn!*" Ursule shrieked. Suddenly she couldn't draw a breath. The world rocked around her, the stars at her feet, the ground rising to bang against her head. Her hands were nerveless, incapable of pushing her up again. Everything blurred: Edouard's grim face, Omas's stricken one, the mist shivering around them. She sighed, and for one blessed moment, she knew nothing at all.

She drifted back into consciousness to find she was being carried like an infant. She blinked and drew a shaky breath.

"Shhh, now, Ursule." It was her uncle Omas, puffing with effort. "Shhh. You'll sleep in my wagon tonight. Marina will see to you."

Ursule's head spun with shock as her uncle carried her toward the camp. He was going to be no help. The burly figure of Edouard Vila limped ahead of them, and she knew he wouldn't help, either. The stars shone overhead, brilliantly white above the mists, mocking the ugliness of the world below with their icy splendor.

Ursule pretended surrender, letting herself lie limply in her uncle's arms. She didn't have to feign the unsteadiness of her feet as he set her down in the circle of anxious Romani, all of them murmuring and whispering, their faces full of shame.

Marina came forward to fetch her, but Ursule shook her head. She could not bear the idea of lying in Omas's caravan with his wife and children, expected to go to sleep as if her world had not just been shattered.

She said in a tight voice, "Thank you, Aunt Marina, but I'll be all right."

Relief flitted across Marina's hard features, but to her credit, she made an effort to persuade her, speaking to her as if she were still small. "Come now, Ursule, you don't want to be alone." She reached for Ursule's hand and gave it a half-hearted tug.

Omas said, "Now don't be stubborn, little one, come with us. That would be best."

They thought they could handle her as they would a child. They thought they could distract her, soothe her pain, settle her as if she were a troublesome toddler.

They didn't understand that she had never been a child, and now she felt as ancient as the dead.

She freed her hand from Marina's and indicated her caravan with a weary gesture. "I'm sorry. I need to be alone."

They let her go. All the Romani still clustered around the cold fire pit watched her with pitiful, frightened eyes as she climbed into her caravan. Their helplessness made Ursule angry.

She was not like them. She refused to be like them. She might be just as shocked and frightened as they were, but she was not helpless. She was shaking with anxiety, sick with fear, but she would not give in to those feelings. She had a great task ahead of her, one she hardly knew how to perform. She knew what she needed to do, and she needed to do it swiftly.

·····•ᴡᴡᴡ•ᴡᴡᴡ••·····

Ursule lit the oil lamp in the wagon, shading it so it wouldn't bring her uncle to check on her. Still in her nightdress, chest aching with misery, she went to the chest for the scrying stone. She lifted out the basket that held the crystal and reached with her elbow to push the lid closed.

She stopped, the basket in her hands, and stared into the bottom of the chest.

She knew immediately what she was looking at, though only the point of it showed from a fold of the dyed flax it was wrapped in. She also knew it couldn't possibly be here, in the caravan, hidden in the rag chest where they kept the crystal and the grimoire.

The fresh shock of it made her doubt her own senses, already reeling from the calamity of this night. She took extra care as she set down the basket. She put out a trembling finger to push the fabric to one side, as with her other hand she lifted out the knife.

The diamond-shaped blade gleamed silver in the muted lamplight, and the curved handguard was cool and hard in her palm. All traces of blood had been washed away, but she remembered what it had looked like, dark in the moonlight, flowing sluggishly from the wound.

Her stomach contracted at the remembered horror of Dukkar's disgusting flesh pressing on her body, his foul breath against her neck. For a moment she couldn't move. She had fought not to think of that again, not to relive those awful moments. She had tried to strike it all from her mind, especially that moment when her attacker had gone still. Had given up his spirit. Had succumbed to the knife left to Sandor by his grandfather.

When she had last seen the blade it was buried in Dukkar's body. How long had it been lying here, folded into one of her mother's scarves?

She stared blindly at the wall of the caravan, trying to calm her heartbeat as she struggled to absorb the discovery and to understand what it meant.

The only person beside herself and Sandor who knew about the knife was her mother. Agnes must have walked back along the path to find the spot Ursule had described, the place where Dukkar's body lay under a hedge of brambles.

Agnes hadn't told Ursule, not in all these weeks. Their habit of secrecy persisted, even now that Ursule was grown, or almost grown, even now that they had shared the awful secret of Dukkar's death and the lingering anguish of her near-rape.

Had Agnes shuddered, pulling this knife from Dukkar's flesh? Had it slid out easily from the decomposing body, or had she had to brace herself, touch his macabre remains with one hand and pull with the other? Had she cleaned the blade there on the grass, or carried it home, still crusted with blood, hidden in her skirt pocket?

It had been a brave thing to do. A kind thing to do, to protect Sandor, who had protected her daughter. Ursule needed a chance to tell her mother that.

She made herself draw a long, slow breath and lay the knife aside. She lifted the grimoire out of the chest, unwrapped it, and laid it on her cot.

She turned the pages, skipping past recipes for charms and potions, philters and spells, finally coming to the one she remembered. The hand that had written it had been a steady one, with good ink and a sharp nib. At the top of the page it read, in large clear letters, *Preparing the Altar.* The steps were listed below in simple language.

Set the scrying stone in the center of the altar.
Take an unburned candle with a trimmed wick and set it in a plate.
Make bundles of rosemary and tarragon and lavender and savory, taking care not to break the stems. Set them at the four corners of the altar.
Sprinkle salt water in a circle of protection.
Light the candle.

The instructions ended there. Ursule could only guess at what might come next.

Ursule had no altar, but there was the stool her mother used for readings. They always kept a pitcher of brackish washing water, scooped from the estuary. Herbs hung from the roof of the caravan, and unburned candles were tucked behind their few plates and bowls.

Ursule hurried her preparations. She felt the rush of hours flowing past as if she were wading against a strong current. She shrank from imagining how frightened her mother must be, how terrified she her-self would be in her place. She set her teeth, hard, to make herself focus on her tasks, do everything as perfectly as she was able, and cling to the hope she might be successful.

As she set the stone on the stool and arranged the herbs around it, she thought she detected a glimmer in the crystal, faint as the flicker of a distant star. She bent to look closer, but the tiny light had disappeared. Perhaps it had not been there at all.

She trimmed the wick of the lantern until the caravan was nearly dark before sprinkling the salt water around herself and the stool. She did it twice in case the water wasn't salty enough. She touched a spill to the low flame of the lantern, then set the flame to the candle. Once it was burning, a small, steady beacon in the darkness, she was at the end of the instructions.

She knelt beside the stool and put her two palms on the dusky quartz.

Nothing happened. It remained inert, empty, without even the dark mists that had so worried her.

"This is not the time to be silent," she whispered, and bit her lip hard to stop the sob that threatened to close her throat. "Speak to me! I need you to tell me what to do!"

Nothing.

She bent her head and concentrated with all her might, frowning so hard her forehead began to ache. "Please," she said. She had no idea who she was speaking to, but she did it anyway, out of desperation. "Please. This is much more important than Maman's readings—please, please help me."

She lifted her head to look into the stone again. There was only the wavering flame of the candle reflected in its surface. The wind whined around the wagon, and one of the dogs, unsettled now, barked into the night.

Ursule thudded the side of her fist against her knee in frustration and growing fear. What was she doing wrong?

"Stop trying."

Ursule started so violently she nearly upset her makeshift altar. Still on her knees, she whipped around, looking for who had spoken. She peered into the shadows of the wagon, though she knew it wasn't possible for anyone to have come in without her knowing. It was cold, the damp night air seeping through the cracks of the walls and the roof, but she felt a sudden warmth over her shoulders, as if her mother had returned to put an arm around her.

"What—"

She heard the voice again, clear and low, as if someone were speaking directly into her ear, though she felt no puff of breath. *"Stop trying. It will come."*

"But—"

"Be still. It will come."

There was nothing more, but the warmth remained, an inexplicable sensation that was oddly reassuring.

Ursule exhaled a long breath, releasing the tension in her chest, and at the same moment, an ache began in her belly. It was not the damp cramping sensation of her monthlies. It was not precisely pain, either, but something for which she had no perfect word. It was intense, spreading from her womb down into her thighs, up into her chest, reminding her of the way fire spread through dry kindling. Her arms tingled with it, and her toes throbbed.

Energy, she thought. Power. A power almost too great for her small body to contain.

"Magic," she murmured, and thought she heard the unseen voice give a low chuckle.

Ursule turned back to the crystal and touched it lightly with her fingers. She didn't ask again. She didn't plead, or push, or insist. She closed her eyes and listened, while the magic spread through her body and the warmth continued on her shoulders, her neck, tingling through her hair.

Suddenly she gasped and opened her eyes.

Beneath her fingers the crystal flared with light, so brightly she feared someone outside would see it. She squinted against the brilliance and moved her fingers apart.

In the very center of the crystal was a tiny, wavering image. Ursule fixed her eyes on its vague shape, her breath coming fast. *"Be still,"* the voice had said. She waited, doing her best not to think, not to worry, not to force.

In moments the bits of the image began to coalesce, tiny dark spots taking shape, points of light collecting, shifting, drawing together to show the silhouette of a building, a sort of shack, so small that the head of the man in front of it was higher than its flat roof. There was an animal of some kind, too, knee-high, hard to make out. It might have been a dog, or a sheep.

Why show her this? Ursule tried not to wonder, and in an instant, she knew.

She knew it in the same way she had known that Madame Robert's babes were not her husband's, just as she had known a marriage proposal was false or that a visitor was going to bring bad luck.

She understood that the stone was showing her where her mother was kept. She needed only to know where this shack was.

You will. Believe.

Ursule gazed into the old crystal, calm now, oddly soothed, happy to trust in the magic. The ache in her belly eased, and the fire in her chest cooled.

She whispered, "I'm coming, Daj. Be brave. I'm coming."

Hurry. Christmas.

At this Ursule's skin prickled. She understood the meaning. The witch hunters would want the trial and the execution over before Christmas, a time they pretended to believe in peace and compassion. She took a moment to stow the crystal back in its hiding place with the grimoire, then hurried to dress in two skirts and heavy stockings, her warmest blouse and a thick ancient coat they had rescued from someone's rag bag. She dropped her *posoti*, with a few coins clinking inside, into its deep pocket.

As she opened the door of the caravan and stepped out into the cold darkness, she felt small and alone, as vulnerable as when Dukkar had attacked her. On an impulse, she turned back and retrieved Sandor's knife. She slipped it into her coat pocket, tied the door of the wagon shut, and set out for Belz with only the stars to guide her.

She had just set foot on the path when she realized she wasn't alone after all. She glanced back and saw one of the dogs following her, the fiercest one, rangy and rough-coated, the one the witch hunter had kicked. It had never paid her the slightest attention before.

It was the magic. It clung to her, tingling faintly in her fingers and toes. She supposed it had attracted the dog, but for what purpose? She couldn't guess.

The night was far gone by the time Ursule and the nameless dog
reached the outskirts of the village. The mist had dissipated, and
the stars were beginning to fade in the clear black sky. Ursule was cold
and afraid, but the dog trotted close behind her, and that gave her courage. Once or twice she thought it might give up and turn back, but
whenever the distance between them grew too great, it trotted faster,
never losing sight of her.

The scattered buildings of Belz were still dark except for the bakery, where a lamp shone through a window shade. Ursule slowed her
steps, not knowing which way to turn. She scanned the houses and
outbuildings but didn't recognize the one the crystal had shown her.
She hugged herself, shivering, wondering what to do.

Believe.

"I'm trying," she groaned. "It's so hard."

At that moment the dog trotted purposefully past her, then ahead.
It paused a moment, looking over its shoulder as if to make certain she
was there, then paced on into the village.

Voices rose from inside the bakery, spurring Ursule to hurry after
the dog. Head down and tail in the air, it led her past the bakery, past
two of the stone-walled houses, then onto a well-trodden path leading
out of the village proper and into a field lying fallow in the winter chill.
Ursule stumbled to a stop when she realized she had reached her goal.

The shack was exactly as she had seen it. It stood in the center of the
field, well away from the houses of the village. In the gray light she
made out a little, slumping structure that looked as if it were meant to

store equipment, wheelbarrows perhaps, or hoes and shovels. There couldn't be enough room under its low roof for a person to stand up.

A man drowsed against the ramshackle building, his chin dropped onto his chest and arms folded against the cold, and a dog curled at his feet.

Ursule's heart gave a painful jolt when she saw the half-built pyre. It was going to be a pyramid of wood, larger pieces at the bottom, kindling bits at the top. A tall, heavy stake rose from the middle of it, and a coiled rope hung from its top. It was only a few paces from the shack. Agnes must have huddled in her prison, listening to them build the means of her torture.

Horror prickled Ursule's arms and neck. She felt as if she might be sick.

The Vila dog began to growl, intensifying the menace. Ursule clenched her jaw against a wave of fear. She was no coward, and there was no one else to do this. She was alone.

Except for the dog. It didn't look like much, with its ragged coat and thick paws, but it was all courage. Its growl became a snarl, which turned into a single throaty bark. It leaped away from her, out into the open field, tearing toward the shack with ears and tail flying.

The guard's dog shot to its feet and raced to meet the challenge. The two met halfway, crashing together in a noisy tangle of fur and teeth and furious snapping.

The guard jerked awake and ran after his dog, yelling.

Ursule ran, too, but the other way, away from the waiting pyre and the cramped shed. She dashed around the field to approach the shed from the back. The furor of the dogfight followed her, punctuated by shouts from the guard.

When Ursule reached the back of the shack, she put a hand on the blank wall and called in a low voice, "Daj! Are you there? Get ready to run!"

Agnes's voice was weak, thinner than she had ever heard it. "Ursule? Oh, *mon Dieu*, you shouldn't—"

"Chut, chut!" Ursule hissed. "Find your way to the door. Hurry!"

Agnes gave a long, wordless groan. Ursule had to trust she would do it.

She crept along the wall, staying low, blessing the Vila cur for the cover it was giving her. When she reached the door, she found it barred with a stout piece of wood.

She tried to lift the bar, but it was secured to the wall with a thick rope.

The dogfight was moving farther into the field. The guard followed, cursing, hovering around the battle with his staff poised to strike.

Ursule yanked on the bar again, willing the rope to split, the nails that held it to break free. They didn't. Agnes was silent within, but Ursule felt her mother's tension in her own body, the suspension of dread, the agonizing temptation of hope.

Believe.

She did believe. She had found her way here. The Vila dog was doing its part, with dramatic effect. She could do this. She must do this.

Almost without realizing it, Sandor's knife was in her hand, oddly shaped but with a wickedly sharp edge, sharp enough to easily slice the braided strands of a farmer's rope.

It took three slashes, executed quickly and silently. The door of the shed fell open the moment the rope separated. At first she couldn't see her mother in the dark interior. She squatted to reach inside, and her hand found Agnes's shoulder. She let it slide down her mother's arm to her hand, which was cold and clammy to her touch. She tugged, hissing for her mother to hurry.

Agnes scrambled out on her knees, and Ursule pulled her up. They didn't speak, nor did they glance toward the dogfight and the frantic man trying to stop it. They raced as fast as they were able around to the back of the shed, then off toward the cover of the woods edging the field.

The furor of the dogfight ended abruptly with a sickening sound, the awful crack of a staff against flesh and bone, followed by one miserable

yelp, then chilling silence. Seconds later the guard shouted an alarm as
he realized his prisoner was gone. He caught sight of their two figures
laboring toward the trees and thundered after them, his footsteps like
the hooves of a galloping plow horse. Ursule's heart pounded with each
thud of his boots.

Ursule and her mother ran as hard as they could across the uneven
ground, arms and legs churning. Agnes wasn't as fast as Ursule, but
Ursule stayed by her mother's side, ready to catch her if she stumbled.
Agnes's breathing was so noisy Ursule didn't notice her own hoarse
panting until they reached the woods. The cold air ached in her throat,
and her thighs burned with effort.

Agnes and Ursule dodged between the trees, not knowing which
way to turn. They heard the guard reach the wood, bellowing imprecations. In the distance, another voice called the alarm, and more
answered. It sounded like a stampede of angry men, and the sounds
they made weakened Ursule's knees. She was now in as much danger
as her mother.

She sensed it from the rage in the men's voices. There would be no
excusing her. They would be as happy to burn two witches as one.

A mound.

Ursule's stride faltered. She nearly turned to see if it was her mother
who had spoken, but caught herself and pressed on. "Where?" she tried
to cry, but her breath was too short for her to make a sound.

Where the brook curves.

Agnes's strength began to flag, each breath a moan. Ursule reached
for her hand and nearly fell as her mother clung to her, adding her own
weight to Ursule's.

It seemed the voice had come too late. They were going to be
caught. Going to be dragged back to that awful shack, tied to that
hideous stake, the pyre flaming around them. The vision of it filled
Ursule's mind, nearly blinding her.

"No!" she said, her tone so hoarse and guttural she didn't recognize
it. "No!"

At once, as if at her command, time slowed to a near stop, like the trickle of a shallow stream drying in the sun. On its sluggish tide Ursule drifted upward, leisurely, lazily, right out of her body and up above the world. The pain of her laboring lungs disappeared. The burning of her legs vanished. As if in a dream, she looked down at the two pitiful fugitives struggling through the woods. She saw the men coming after them, dark figures plunging through the trees. In the rising light, Agnes looked small and exhausted. She herself looked almost as worn out, tiny and disheveled, striving to hold her mother upright while still dragging her forward.

In front of them was a thicket of brambles, and on the other side, out of sight from the woods, was a brook. The curve of a brook.

Beyond the curve swelled a low mound, overgrown with winter-dry grasses. A tumulus, one of the old burial mounds Bretons avoided for fear of the spirits captured there.

Ursule tumbled back into her body as time resumed its forward race, a river at full spate. There was no time to lose. She croaked, "This way, Daj! Through the brambles—never mind the scratches—shove through it—"

She didn't know if Agnes heard her. Winter had robbed the thicket of most of its leaves, exposing its long, sharp thorns. The thorns were wicked, but they were nothing compared to the waiting flames of the witches' pyre. Ursule shoved into the brambles, tugging her mother after her. Their clothes and hair and skin caught, tore, hurt. Ursule felt a thorn rip through her hand, and her scalp burned as the brambles tangled in her hair. There was no time to unwind it. She yanked herself free and felt a strand of hair give. It didn't matter.

Suddenly they were through. Side by side, they splashed across the brook. The icy water stung Ursule's fresh wounds and soaked her boots. They staggered up the far bank and pressed on, hurrying around the mound in search of an entrance.

Had she not believed it was there, Ursule would never have found it. She felt it more than she saw it, and she heard the voice again in her ear, *Here! It's here!*

The entrance to the tumulus was even lower than the doorway of Agnes's prison. They had to bend double to duck beneath the aged timber that held back the weight of dirt and stones and grass. Beyond it was a cave of sorts, deep and dark, smelling of damp earth and ancient vegetation. They fell to their knees on ground that was spongy and doubtful, cluttered with decayed leaves and grass and scree.

Safe.

"We're safe, Daj," Ursule whispered.

She tried to put her arm around Agnes's shoulders, and her fingers brushed her cheek, felt the warmth of blood streaming down it. Her own hand was bleeding, and she wiped a thread of blood from her forehead as her eyes began to adjust to the darkness.

Agnes's teeth began to chatter as her body cooled. She wore nothing but the nightdress and shawl and thin slippers she had been wearing when the witch hunters came for her.

Ursule shrugged out of her heavy coat and draped it over her shoulders. *"Chut,"* Ursule breathed, as she pulled the collar up around Agnes's throat. "Not a sound."

They huddled together, arms around each other as they listened to the voices of the men searching for them. Footsteps sounded in the woods, and along the thicket of brambles, but none of the Belzois ventured to brave the thorns. A long time passed. Ursule, straining her ears, heard voices on their side of the brook, but they weren't close, and they didn't come near the mound.

Ursule bent her head to lean her forehead on Agnes's shoulder and send her gratitude out into the universe. The Vila dog. The voice of Violca. They had gone to ground like injured animals, but they would stay where they were until the witch hunters gave up. They were safe.

8

Ursule and Agnes didn't dare come out of the mound during the daylight. They breathed damp air all day, sitting or lying on rough, cold ground. When night fell, with its welcome cover of darkness, they crawled outside, wary, stiff, thirsty. They scooped brook water up in their palms to drink, and it dribbled through their fingers, wetting their clothes and intensifying the chill. They had nothing at all to eat, and nowhere they dared go, but by the third morning, Ursule knew they couldn't stay in the mound much longer.

Agnes hadn't spoken once since the terrifying run through the woods and the painful plunge through the brambles. She barely moved, and then only when Ursule pulled her outside the tumulus. Ursule could see, even in the moonlight, how sunken her cheeks had become, how hollow her eyes. She began to fear that, despite everything, her mother would not survive.

Adding to her misery was her agony over the Orchière crystal. Their other possessions didn't matter, the clothes and pots and plates left behind in the caravan, but she felt the loss of the stone, and the grimoire with its precious recipes and notes, as a physical sensation in her middle. It reminded her of the way she had felt when Sandor left, and it nagged at her, like an injury that refused to heal. Once or twice she was tempted to slip out and go back to the camp to retrieve them, but she didn't dare leave her mother alone.

The memory of the half-built pyre was hard to shake off. It gave her a quiver of nausea, that ghastly monster of wood and rope, waiting to devour its victim. Her only comfort was knowing that the pyre was going to go hungry. She imagined the witch hunters dismantling it, pulling out the big pieces so that the smaller ones scattered on the ground, flinging them about in frustration. She pictured one of them bringing down the rope, a rope meant to restrain a woman in agony, and she wondered if such a man would experience even the slightest pang of conscience. She had seen no evidence of empathy in any of the Belzois.

At twilight of the third day, Ursule coaxed her mother out of their sanctuary. The usual winter mist lay upon the ground, but a sliver of moon glistened from the clear sky. The first stars were coming to life, casting a cool ghostly light.

Ursule led her mother to the brook to drink and adjusted the old coat over her shoulders. Agnes's eyes followed her movements like those of a lost child. When Ursule took her arm to guide her away, she complied as meekly if she had no will of her own.

Three days of huddling in the mound had made Ursule's legs shaky and stiff, and Agnes stumbled as they navigated the uneven ground. Ursule drew long breaths of the chilly air, willing her muscles to thaw. After an hour or so, she felt a bit better. When she asked Agnes if she felt the same, her mother made no response.

There was nothing she could do but press on, keeping a hand under her mother's arm. She felt light-headed with hunger, and walking in the darkness did nothing to ease that. She led the way alongside the brook, keeping the water on their right and hoping the streambed didn't curve too far west. Her thoughts were thick and sluggish, unable to conceive any plan other than to get as far from Belz as possible.

She saw occasional farmhouses, and she suffered a stab of envy for the people sleeping there, warm in their beds, safe under a roof, secure in their place in life. As the night wore on, she began to feel as if she had always been walking, always holding up her mother, who tripped often and had to be caught before she fell. She barely noticed when Agnes began to lean on her. Her arm grew numb, and her back ached with the effort.

She lost track of time, but she supposed dawn was about an hour away when the two of them skirted a stand of leafless beech trees. Past their sparse branches she spied a small farmhouse, nestled in a wide turn of the brook. It wasn't far, a walk of perhaps five minutes in their weakened state. A faint light wavered in one small window, a candle, or a lamp with its wick trimmed low. A slant-roofed structure that appeared to be a cow byre leaned against one wall. There might be food in that byre: stored potatoes, perhaps apples. Ursule was so hungry she thought she would eat hay if she could find it.

She yearned toward the possibility of something, anything, they could eat, but that tiny light frightened her. Fragile though it was, it seemed to be a warning. Someone was awake. Someone would see.

Reluctantly, she tugged at her mother's arm, and they drifted to their left, away from the temptation of that byre, though her stomach contracted with longing.

They had not taken more than four or five steps when she heard a low, rattling call from the grove behind her. A night bird, she thought, beginning to wake up.

She took another step, and it came again, a long, bubbling croon. She stopped where she was. Her mother stood blinking in confusion. Ursule pressed her free hand over her belly, where an odd throbbing began between her hip bones.

That ache was familiar. She hesitated, unable to force her tired mind to recognize it.

When the bird called again, it came to her. This was the way her body had felt when her mother was telling fortunes and she was—she was kneeling beside her, watching—

The scrying stone. Magic.

With a swift intake of breath, she spun to see what bird was calling to her from the beech grove. Agnes tottered when her support disappeared, and Ursule seized her arm with a fresh grip. She took a single step back toward the grove.

The bird's cry was louder this time, a chuckle, as if it were pleased. Ursule took another step, and it hopped forward on its branch, balancing there, wings glossy in the starlight, black eyes gleaming. It was a raven, but she had never heard a raven make those intimate, almost musical sounds. The call of a bird had never caused this feeling of compulsion, of surrender. Her head swam with it, and she couldn't think what to do.

"What do you want?" she whispered.

The raven gave one sharp caw, and with a flap of its wings, it flitted to the next tree. It perched there, head on one side, eyes glistening faintly in the shadow of the trees.

"We're going back, Daj," Ursule said. "Back to that little grove. You can rest, and I—I'm going to—" She let the sentence die away, because she didn't know what she was going to do.

In the grove, she settled Agnes against one of the tree trunks. Her mother pulled up her knees and rested her head against them, the coat pulled up around her neck. Ursule straightened her shawl around her shoulders and turned toward the farmhouse.

A cow lowed from the byre, and the door to the farmhouse opened as if someone had been waiting to be called. A small, stout figure emerged, haloed by the light from within. Whoever it was wore trousers and boots, a hat pulled low, and carried a bucket in one hand.

Ursule couldn't tell if the figure was male or female, young or old. She hesitated, torn between her need and her fear. Above her head, the raven gave one low, gurgling squawk. Ursule's belly answered with a flare of pain between her hip bones. As if in a trance, she obeyed the magic and stepped out into the open.

The person saw her and slowly, warily, swiveled in her direction.

The two of them gazed at each other across the short distance while the cow lowed again. Ursule drew an uneasy breath, squared her shoulders, and walked forward. The other person set down the bucket and waited, hands on hips.

When she got close enough to smell the scent of sweat and smoke that clung to the stranger, Ursule said, in Breton, "Good morning."

"What are you doing here?" A woman, speaking French with a rough country accent.

Ursule moved forward, close enough to see that the woman was elderly, with a deeply seamed face and black, heavy-lidded eyes. Ursule answered her simply. "We need food."

"Who are you?" the woman demanded. She pushed up her hat so she could look into Ursule's face.

The raven chirped.

The woman heard, and squinted through the dimness. "Don't lie to me," she grated.

Ursule passed her hand over her throbbing belly and surrendered to the magic. To her fate, whatever it might be. She answered in a low, even voice. "No, *madame*, I will not. I'm called Ursule. Ursule Orchière."

The old woman's gray eyebrows arched. "The witch's daughter?"

Ursule's heart missed a beat. "*Madame*, I swear to you, my mother is no witch."

"Of course she is not!" the old woman snapped. "It's just what they say. Utter nonsense. Where is she?"

Wordlessly, Ursule lifted her arm to point back to the beech grove.

"Fetch her," the woman commanded, and spun back into the farmhouse without waiting to see if Ursule complied. She left the door standing open.

Ursule dashed back to the place where Agnes still sat, her head bowed to her knees. The raven watched from its perch, its eyes glittering like jet beads in the starlight. Ursule tugged at Agnes's arm. "Daj, get up. Hurry! We're going into that house."

She had to lift her mother up. As she guided her away from the safety of the trees, the raven gurgled softly. After urging Agnes over the doorstep and into the smoky interior of the house, Ursule glanced back, but the bird had disappeared.

The simple low-ceilinged room she found herself in was wonderfully warm. A thick candle burned on a plank table that had a single bench on one side. The solitary window held a small pane of thick, irregular glass. The floor was pounded dirt. A banked fire smoked gently in the fireplace, where a kettle hung on a hob and an iron pot sat in the ashes.

A small room with a bed was just visible to one side beyond a crooked entrance with no door. Everything smelled of cows and sour milk.

The old woman pulled off her hat, releasing hanks of gray hair to straggle over her shoulders. She set the bucket beside the table as she bent to poke up the fire and toss in two thick fagots. She glanced over her shoulder at Ursule and Agnes and pointed to the table. "Sit," she said. "My poor skinny cows need milking. The pottage will warm while I do it. Pump water if you need it."

In seconds she was gone, the bucket again swinging by her side. Ursule guided her mother to the end of the bench nearest the fire, which was beginning to glow. Ursule felt weak with the relief of being within doors.

Agnes sat when Ursule told her to, and removed her coat when she suggested it, but she said nothing, nor did she look about with her usual curiosity.

"It's all right, I think, Maman," Ursule said. "We're safe for now, and we'll eat."

There was no reply.

While she waited for the old woman to return from the milking, Ursule prodded the fire with a bit of iron that lay on the hearth, then went to the stone sink to pump water into a pottery cup that stood there. She helped Agnes to sip a little, and finished the rest herself. When the old woman returned with a sloshing bucket, she hurried to take it from her and lift it up to the wooden counter.

"Got away, didn't you," the woman said, squinting at her.

Ursule said, "It was a close thing. We're so grateful to you—"

The woman threw up a hand. "Never mind that. Nasty people, those Belzois. Superstitious. Probably come after me next, an odd old woman living alone. I'm called Yanna. Forgot to tell you. Here, dish up."

She handed Ursule two bowls. The pottage was only lukewarm, but Ursule couldn't wait any longer. She ladled some into a bowl for Agnes, and some for herself. She sat down next to her mother, accepted a spoon, and thought of nothing for the next few moments but getting food into her body. The pottage was salty and not a little greasy, but she didn't care. She swiftly emptied her bowl. Yanna, with a nod of approval over her appetite, set a cup of milk before her, warm and frothy from the milking. Ursule drank it down in three huge swallows.

She was relieved to see that her mother was eating, too, though more slowly, and that she drank some of the fragrant milk. Their unlikely hostess tugged a stool across the floor and sat opposite them with her own cup, assessing them with glittering black eyes.

"So," Yanna said. "You saved your *maman*, Ursule Orchière. They're saying in Belz you spirited her away on the back of a broom." She grinned, showing a set of surprisingly strong-looking teeth.

"We hid in the mound," Ursule said.

"Ha! Ha ha!" Yanna chortled, slapping her knee. "The fools could have guessed, but they're terrified of that place. Afraid of their own shadows, truth be told." She sipped at her cup, eyeing Ursule over the rim. "How did you manage getting your *maman* out of that shed?"

"There was a dogfight."

"I heard that. Lucky coincidence?"

Ursule didn't know how to answer without admitting there had been something unnatural about the dog. She said, after a moment's hesitation, "I suppose so. The guard was distracted."

"Stupid brute. Killed both dogs."

"Oh, no!" Ursule felt a stab of grief for an animal whose name she didn't even know. "Did he do that?"

"He did. One was a strange dog, but his wife was attached to the other one. Gave him an earful when he got home, and the others gave him an earful about the witch getting away." She chortled again. "Wouldn't care to be in his shoes just now."

Somehow this loss, a poor dumb beast who bore no fault, brought tears to Ursule's eyes. It seemed there was no end to the darkness of these days.

Yanna put out a hand, the knuckles twisted with age, and patted her arm. "Don't cry for a dog, little one. They don't live long anyhow."

Ursule tried to sniffle back her tears. "It's so cruel," she said.

"Cruel people, the Belzois. Why I don't want to live among them."

"But to live all alone out here..."

"Don't even like going into the town. The goodwives turn up their noses because I smell like my cows." She turned to take a long look at Agnes. "Your *maman* is in a state," she said.

"I know. She's not speaking just now."

"Way I was when my Claude died. Killed by a boar, right in front of the house. I didn't speak for days."

"*Désolée, madame!* How awful for you!"

"*Oui, oui.* Long time ago now."

"But you must be lonely. No children?"

"No. Got my cows. Silly old things, but company. I sell butter and cheese. I get by."

Ursule watched Agnes scooping up the last of her pottage. She touched her arm and said, in Romani, "Daj, you should thank her for the food. For letting us come into her house."

Agnes put down her spoon and lifted her face. She looked a little less worn, but her eyes, her beautiful dark eyes, looked as empty as if her soul had left her.

Ursule said, fearful now, "Maman?"

Yanna said, "*Chut, chut,* little one. Leave her be."

"But I don't know why she's like this."

"You do," the woman said. "Just think. They were building the pyre right where she could hear them. Think of her terror, expecting to be burned alive."

"It's horrible."

"People are horrible, my girl. Learn that early, and you'll fare better in this world."

Yanna took a long drink of warm milk and smacked her lips.

"You are so kind, *madame.* I wish I could—"

"*Chut!*" The old woman tapped her arm with a sharp fingernail. "We are sisters. Outcasts, all three of us. If we don't help one another, who will?"

They rested through the day by Yanna's fire. At midday Yanna fed them bread and cheese, with a cup of bitter ale she had made herself. Ursule thought nothing had ever tasted so good in her life. Yanna also insisted on giving Agnes a much-mended dress and an old coat that smelled of cow. She even produced a knitted scarf, brushing cobwebs from it before pressing it into Agnes's hands. "How could they take you in just your nightdress?" she muttered. "Couldn't wait for you to dress? Shameful. No Christian charity."

In silence, Agnes accepted Yanna's gifts, and Ursule helped her into them while Yanna made up a pallet of blankets near the fire. "Your mother should sleep," she said. "You should, too. I'll wake you for supper."

"I'll get Maman to lie down," Ursule said. "But I'm not tired." It wasn't true. She was exhausted, but she felt too restive and anxious to sleep. "Can't I help with your work? I'm very strong." She made a fist to show her muscles.

The old woman chuckled. "Stronger than me, no doubt, child! Are you fifteen? Sixteen?"

"Fourteen," Ursule said. "Well, almost fourteen. But born old, Maman always says."

"Ah." Yanna's laughter faded, and she paused in wrapping a wool scarf around her neck. "Now that's a pity."

"Is it?"

"*Bien sûr.* Everyone should be a child for a while."

Ursule shrugged. "It's the way I am, I suppose. Please let me help you."

"*Eh bien*, little one. Strong, and stubborn, too." Yanna's smile was gentle, but she pointed to the hook where Ursule had hung her coat, the one her mother had been wearing. "You'll want that. It's cold in the byre."

Ursule helped her mother to lie down and covered her with a faded quilt, its patterns only pale shadows of the red and blue and green they had once been. She left Agnes already asleep and followed Yanna out to where the two cows waited outside the byre. Yanna let them in and opened the stanchions for them to put their heads through.

The byre didn't feel cold to Ursule at all after the chill of outdoors. The bodies of the cows warmed it, and their homely scent melded with the fragrance of sweet hay.

Yanna patted the smaller cow. "This is St. Anne. That's St. Thérèse."

"You call them after saints?"

"*Absolument*. Since I lost my goats to the wasting disease, my two saints are all I have. They're my salvation."

Ursule smiled, and the sensation of it startled her, as if her face had forgotten how it felt. She accepted the pitchfork Yanna handed her and used it to toss forkfuls of hay into the manger, smiling again as the cows began to munch. She stood between them, one hand on each of their bony spines, her feet nestled into the straw that softened the dirt floor, and closed her eyes to breathe in the atmosphere. Though it was not so colorful, the byre felt cozy and protective, as her caravan once had. Her breathing eased. Her thoughts spun more and more slowly, and she felt more like herself than she had since the Belzois took her mother.

She thought she could rest in a place like this, in the company of gentle cows and the mice she heard rustling through the hay.

Yanna stood up, finished with St. Anne. Ursule said, "Will you show me how to do it? How to milk?"

Yanna grinned at her. "*Bien sûr*. It's easy." She moved the three-legged stool to St. Thérèse's side and placed the bucket beneath her udder. "Sit here. Now put your forehead against her flank—she expects it, don't worry. Then, just grip and strip. Gently, but firmly."

"It doesn't hurt them?"

"No, no, they like it. Imagine your hand is a calf's tongue—you should see those little rascals suckle!"

Ursule sat and leaned her head against St. Thérèse's flank. The cow's hide felt warm and smooth and alive against her skin. She took a grip on the teats, gingerly at first, then more firmly. St. Thérèse shifted a couple of times as Ursule's unpracticed fingers blundered, but soon Ursule found the rhythm, and the cow stood calmly chewing.

It was, as Yanna had said, easy, and satisfying. The milk sang into the iron bucket, the tune changing as the bucket filled, the scent of fresh milk rising from it. Ursule closed her eyes to hear the music, to smell the warm milk.

In no time, it seemed, the bucket was full. The cow's udder hung loose, ready to fill up again the next day. Ursule surrendered the bucket and the stool with regret.

Yanna said, "Come now, we'll shoo my saints out for a while, and go start supper. It's nice to have someone to share my chores. A gift."

As they turned toward the house, Ursule said reluctantly, "Yanna, you're very kind, but I don't think we should stay here."

Yanna turned to look at her, her thick gray eyebrows lifted. "Got other plans?"

"If they know you helped us . . ."

"No one comes here," Yanna said, and opened the door. "Only the farmer who brings me hay once a year."

Ursule was greatly tempted to believe they were safe. She followed Yanna into the house, where they found Agnes still sleeping. Ursule took off her boots and went to help Yanna chop vegetables for soup.

"No bread left," Yanna said. "I'll make some tomorrow."

"I can do that," Ursule said. "At least, I can make frycakes. *Pufe*, we call them."

"*Bon*. Be good to eat someone else's cooking."

Ursule roused her mother and urged her to eat some soup. When their stomachs were full, they went out to the tiny outhouse, then hurried back into the warmth of the house. They took off their outer

clothes and tucked themselves into the pallet wearing just their chemises. Ursule was so sleepy she could hardly hold up her head. The
floor was hard, but the woolen blankets were warm, and the pillows
stuffed with goose feathers felt like heaven. She lay down with a long,
grateful sigh and was sound asleep in moments.

It was still dark outside when she started up, alarmed by a loud
knocking.

She was on her feet, her shawl clutched around her shoulders, when
Yanna hurried out of the bedroom, a long gray braid draped over one
shoulder. "What is it?" Ursule hissed.

Yanna shook her head. "No idea."

Ursule's heart pounded, and her hands began to shake. "Is there
someplace we can hide?"

Yanna made a vague gesture around her simple house, and Ursule
understood her to mean there was no place to go.

The knocking came again, but now they could tell it was not at
the door. It was the uneven glass rattling as if someone was trying to
break it.

Yanna exclaimed, *"Mon Dieu!"*

Ursule, her shawl pulled tightly across her breast, tiptoed to the little
window, the floor chilling her bare toes. Beyond the glass a shadow
quivered, barely visible in a faint bar of moonlight. When it fluttered
broad wings and bent its head to peck at the glass again, she knew. "It's
the raven!" she cried. "From the grove."

"I know that bird," Yanna muttered. "But he's never done that
before."

The bird struck at the window again, sharp, commanding raps with
its thick beak.

Ursule blinked, trying to resist the trancelike feeling coming over
her, the same one that had brought her to Yanna's house. The ache in
her belly began again, flaring through her ribs and up into her chest.
She didn't want this, didn't want to understand, but—

She knew precisely what was happening. The awareness made her feel as if her brain were swelling inside her skull, crowding out her doubts, leaving no space for anything but the truth.

The raven was sounding the alarm.

Miserably, through a contracted throat, she choked, "We have to leave, Yanna. Maman and I—we have to go. Right away."

Under Yanna's astounded gaze, she bent to shake Agnes's shoulder. "Maman. Daj. Wake up. We have to leave now, before it's light."

Agnes came awake instantly, her eyes wide with alarm.

"We have to go," Ursule whispered to her. "They're coming."

Her mother gasped and started to struggle to her feet. Ursule helped her up and fetched their clothes from the wall hooks.

As they dressed, Yanna objected and begged for an explanation. Ursule had none to give. She knew what she knew. She was without her scrying stone, but she knew just the same. The conviction in her mind was as clear as any image she had seen in the crystal.

It was awful to step out of Yanna's warm little house into the icy darkness. Ursule felt as if, for a brief while, she had been thirteen, safe, comfortable, but now the air of the winter night biting in her lungs brought her back to the hard reality she had to face. She didn't want to go. She didn't want to carry the responsibility for her mother's safety, for their survival, but there was no one to bear it for her.

On an impulse, with her throat aching, Ursule hugged Yanna. "Thank you," she murmured. "Thank you for the food, for the clothes, for taking us in."

"I still don't understand," Yanna said, as she had already said a dozen times. "Stay! You could be happy here."

"We can't stay, Yanna. It's not safe for us."

"But why let a raven frighten you away?"

"It's not the raven. It's hard to explain, but—I see things sometimes." Ursule gently freed herself from Yanna's embrace. "Now I see that the witch hunters are coming. Make sure they can't tell we've been here. Fold up the pallet, hide the bowls. Protect yourself."

"But, Ursule, you couldn't—how could you know that?"

"It's the way I am." She adjusted her mother's shawl and pulled her own over her head.

Yanna stared at her, her wrinkled eyelids lifted high, her lips open in amazement. *"Mon Dieu,"* she breathed. "It was true, then. It was, wasn't it? You—Ursule, little Ursule—you're a—a witch!"

Ursule looked into Yanna's horrified eyes and couldn't bring herself to lie to her.

Yanna held her gaze, but her black eyes glistened with tears. "Don't tell me," she whispered, her voice breaking. "Don't say it, *ma chère fille.* It's better I don't know."

Ursule hugged her again, feeling the old woman's pain in her own breast. Moments later she hurried her mother off into the unforgiving night, the frozen ground hard under their feet, the biting wind tugging at their coats. As they moved away, she heard the gentle rush of the raven's wings against the wind as it followed in their wake.

The Prophetess Liliane

*T*hey say Liliane was a foundling, a babe abandoned on a seashore, meant to be washed away when the tide rose. An old Romani woman, a childless widow, snatched her from the sand just as the sea was reaching for her and carried her back to the caravan she shared with her sister's family. They complained about another mouth to feed, but when the widow folded back the blankets that held the babe, their arguments died unspoken. The widow named her Liliane for her lily-white skin and white hair. Her eyes were the palest blue the Romani had ever seen.

They say the babe had to be protected from the sun always, or her skin burned. Her hair remained white all her days, and her pale blue eyes saw almost nothing. The widow-mother guessed her birth parents had thrown her away because of these things, but they didn't matter to her. Liliane was small, sweet, and quiet, and the widow-mother took her to her heart. She wrapped her foundling child in scarves and shawls against the sun. She led her by the hand when she began to walk and taught her to speak at an early age. She hung an amulet from the child's neck with her mark painted on it so that if they were separated, someone would bring her back.

They say Liliane began to prophesy at the age of four. She would put her little hand, so white it was almost transparent, over her forehead and speak. "The fish are running in the bay." "The rain will come at dawn." "Aunt Sofi has a baby inside." She was never wrong.

As she grew older, the clan members began to turn to her and listen whenever she put her hand over her brow. She predicted a horse would break its leg, and it did. She said the town they were passing had the plague, and they avoided it, learning later that everyone in that town had suffered the Black Death. One day, with tears in her pale eyes, she said her widow-mother was going to die, and it happened that very night, in the dark of the moon.

They say she would not let them call her witch, but her fame spread just the same. Romani came from far away to consult with her. When a soldier came, the clan wanted to forbid him to speak to Liliane for fear of the witch hunters, but she insisted he be allowed to ask his question. When she foretold a massacre in an approaching battle, the soldier fled into the countryside. They say he was the only one of his regiment to survive.

Liliane made her greatest prophecy when her clan camped near a fishing village. The village was small and poor, just two dozen stone houses, a chapel, a long wooden warehouse where they dressed their day's catch. Liliane woke the clan far into the *night, proclaiming that a great flood would come in the darkness, a wave from which no one in the village would escape. In great haste, the clan moved their wagons and horses to a bluff overlooking the town. From there, in the early dawn, they watched a towering wall of water wash over the houses. People, dogs, cats, and the rickety warehouse were swept away in one great deluge. At daybreak, when the water receded, the men of the clan went down into the wreckage. No one had survived, though the ruins of the stone houses still marked the place the town had been. The men climbed back up the bluff laden with tools and bits of watersoaked furniture, even purses of money they found hidden in the walls.*

Liliane refused to lie with any man, yet in her middle years she bore a daughter. They say she conceived through magical means, on a full moon at midsummer while the clan celebrated Litha. Her daughter was neither white of skin and hair, nor was she a witch, but she was a healthy girl who bore six daughters of her own. When the youngest was born, Liliane said, "This is the one," and gave her amulet to her daughter to pass to the child when she came into her power.

On the night the prophetess died, a shower of meteors flashed through the sky to welcome her home. No one knows whether her daughter's sixth daughter inherited her power, but the prophetess had never been known to be wrong. They say that though the girl's name is forgotten, she is to be revered as an ancestress of the Romani witches.

The

BOOK OF MAGIC
LOST AND FOUND

1772

Ursule unlatched the stanchions and backed the cows out, then shooed them out into the yard. She rubbed Izzy's well-padded spine as the cow plodded past, thinking, as she so often had these past ten years, of Yanna's skinny saints. Remy's cows were bigger and better fed and gave twice as much milk as Yanna's had. Even the goats were fat, producing rich milk for the *chèvre* to be sold at the market in Keranna.

Ursule had given all the livestock names: the three cows, the two goats, and the raven that had followed her from Belz. Madeleine scoffed at that, saying it was foolish to name animals you might one day eat, but Remy's lips twitched with amusement, and Ursule thought he understood.

Just the same, he was too lazy to bother arguing with his wife, and was probably wise to save his breath in any case. Madeleine Kerjean was never without an argument, and no one but herself was allowed to win one.

Ursule had two full buckets of cows' milk for Remy's morning deliveries. She lifted the buckets and started across the yard to the low stone building where the milk would keep cool against the July heat. One of her she-goats—well, in truth, my lord's goats, since everything on the farm belonged by law to Vicomte Alleyn—bleated at the sight of her. It was Bibi, stretching to lift her curling horns above the fence of the pen, her eyes dark and shining behind her snowy forelock.

"Don't worry, Bibi," she said over her shoulder. "You're next."

For a moment, she wondered why Mimi, the other milking goat, wasn't beside Bibi as she usually was, but the raven distracted her with his rattling call. "Drom, you, too," she said. "When do I ever forget you?"

Drom was the Romani word for *road*, and the raven had earned it by tirelessly guiding Ursule and Agnes into the south, past the port village of Auray, then inland until they reached Kerjean Farm. Two laborers had just walked away from their jobs, driven off by Madeleine's waspish tongue. Remy had hired Ursule on the spot. Drom, with a satisfied croak, had flitted up into the enormous oak tree that shaded the farmhouse and perched there until she was settled. He had never left, nor had she.

That had been the end of the magic. She dreamed of it sometimes, of Violca's voice, of the light in the stone, of the exhilaration of knowing things she shouldn't know. She grieved for the loss, and she suffered waves of guilt over having failed to continue the Orchière line.

In waking hours, she forbade herself to think of it, or to stop her chores to gaze down the lane, yearning for the freedom of the road, the laughter and squabbles of the clans, the festivals when they played music and gathered to tell stories.

Her wages were paltry, but between the byre and the farmhouse was a low-roofed, two-room cottage where she and her mother lived. She had to shoulder the work of two men, and Agnes had not spoken a word in ten years, but they were safe. No one knew who they were. No one had come looking for them. If that meant there was no more magic, she had to accept it, for her mother's sake.

Agnes had gained a reputation for her needlework and took in sewing from the village housewives. Madeleine persisted in trying to ask her questions, clicking her tongue in irritation when she received no answer. That made Agnes's cheeks redden with embarrassment and infuriated Ursule, but she held her tongue. Agnes's customers didn't mind her silence, and after the first two or three years, the people of

Keranna stopped staring at the Orchières' dusky skin and black eyes. If Agnes and Ursule didn't exactly make friends among the villagers or the other farm families, they had a place, however modest, in the community.

Ursule was glad to find the buttery deserted on this morning. She wouldn't have to listen to Madeleine's complaints. She emptied the milk buckets into the waiting vat and washed them before trudging back across the yard. Bibi was waiting for her at the gate to the byre, but she had to go out into the pen and coax Mimi inside. The little goat gave hardly any milk, and Ursule's worry over her returned. She plucked at Mimi's skin and found her much too thin. She would ask Remy if he had heard of wasting sickness going through the district.

She finished milking the goats and scattered feed for the laying hens. She rattled a handful of corn into Drom's feeder, which brought him swooping down from the oak tree.

She greeted him. *"Zi buna."*

He answered, in his throaty croak, *"Zi buna."* Good day. He had picked it up in their first year together.

She caressed Drom's back, and the feel of his silky feathers brought back the dream of the night before. It was the sort of dream she tried to put out of her mind, ones of Sandor, the boy so briefly known and so long ago. They made her feel soft and vulnerable, when she needed to be tough and resilient. When she woke from such a dream, her skin tingled and her body felt tender as a babe's, as if it would melt beneath her blankets.

Even in daylight hours, memories of Sandor could catch her by surprise. A fragment of music in the air, or the drifting scent of a cider press, recalled his straight light hair, his autumn eyes, the plaintive sound of his flute. She rarely felt the touch of a man's hand, and then only inadvertently, working with stock or hefting tools, but when it happened she remembered Sandor's smooth, soft hands. Working men's hands were rough as sawn wood. As rough as her own.

It was an odd sort of nostalgia for something she had never really had. It wasn't as if they had been lovers. No one would love her now, of course. She was twenty-three, past the age anyone would pay a bride price. Lines were beginning to show in her face, and her skin had darkened even more after years of working in the sun. The muscles in her arms and thighs bulged like those of a man, though she was so small.

Sometimes, though it shamed her, she peered at herself in the pond behind the barn, wondering if there was anything left of the girl Sandor had liked. Had killed for.

But then, Sandor had never seen her. All he knew of her was her voice, the smell of her hair, the touch of her hand. These things she still possessed, had he been near enough to experience them.

Drom pecked up his last kernel of corn, and flitted to her shoulder. *"Zi buna, zi buna."*

She stroked his wing with her fingertips and breathed in his toasty scent. "Yes, Drom, you're quite right. A good day. Come, we'll give Chou Chou a little treat and check that the harness is ready. Second cutting starts tomorrow."

Drom's talons clung to her shoulder as she strode across the yard to the barn, where Remy's only horse drowsed in his stall. Chou Chou was young, and new to the plow. She fed him an extra measure of grain against his coming labors and was laying out his harness in the aisle when she heard her mistress's shrill call. Drom immediately took wing, fleeing through the open door at the far side of the barn, off to the little apple orchard that lined the brook. Ursule sighed, dropped the hames of the harness into the sawdust, and went to see what her mistress wanted.

Madeleine stood in the doorway of the buttery, her hands on her skinny hips. "Ursule!" she screeched again, as if Ursule were out in the field instead of just across the yard.

"I'm here, Madeleine," Ursule said mildly.

Madeleine scowled at Ursule's form of address. She said Ursule should address her as *madame*, a command Ursule ignored. Madeleine responded by calling Ursule *gitane*, then pretending she didn't mean for her to hear. It was a sour game they played, and a never-ending one, despite the mounting years of their association. It made Agnes give her silent laugh and Ursule roll her eyes.

"The churning!" Madeleine barked, temper flushing her flat cheeks. The skin of her face was perpetually red, as if her bouts of temper had burned it. She was only a few years older than Ursule, but her forehead was already scarred with frown lines. "We have orders for butter to be delivered."

"I know that. I'm going to do it next," Ursule said. "The wagon harness needed—"

"Where's Remy? The harness should be his job! Is he asleep under some tree again?"

"Why don't you go look, Madeleine? Unless you're going to start the churning yourself, of course. If that's the case, I can look for your husband."

"Just do it!" Madeleine spat. She flounced away from the buttery, her long apron fluttering at her heels, making clear the churning was not her job. With a sigh, Ursule returned to the stable to finish her interrupted task.

Drom reappeared, fluttering his broad wings as he settled on the gate to Chou Chou's stall. Ursule grinned up at him. "Coward."

"*Zi buna, zi buna!*"

"Lucky bird. If I had wings, I'd fly away, too."

Drom shook his wings and clacked his beak.

"No, I didn't mean it. I couldn't leave Maman. I'll just be staying right here forever, I suppose." She propped the wooden hames against the wall between the haymow and the barn aisle. "Come on, you great baby," she told the raven, patting her shoulder. "You can wait outside the buttery. She won't be there."

Drom hopped onto her shoulder for the short walk across the yard. It was a good thing, in truth, that he avoided Madeleine. She might take against him if she caught him eating the chickens' corn or riding on Chou Chou's withers, his talons clutching the hames for balance.

Madeleine had called him "that filthy crow" more than once, and Ursule didn't dare correct her. If she truly lost her temper, she might claim he was scaring the goats or causing the milkers to dry up.

Ursule didn't want to have to fight for him. Some days Drom was the only creature in the world to speak to her, and she didn't want Madeleine to decide he had to go. Madeleine Kerjean had driven two strong men away from her farm. Ursule didn't doubt she could scare off one solitary raven.

Drom perched above the buttery's low door, preening his shining feathers in the summer sun while Ursule labored over the churn. She was not sure how this task had been added to the list of her chores. The men whose places she had taken would not have been butter-makers. More likely Madeleine had told Remy that since they now had a woman to work for them, she could do the churning.

Butter had been a rarity in the caravan, something the Orchières bought at the village market only when they had extra *livres*. It had been doled out sparingly, a special treat. At Kerjean Farm, there was an abundance of it, over and above what Remy sold on his rounds. Ursule liked working the churn, watching the solids cohere around the plunger and the thick slabs of yellow fat form. When she poured off the buttermilk, she set some aside for her mother before filling a pitcher for Madeleine's kitchen.

Remy had told her the Kerjean butter was the best in the district. "Never sour," he would say, as he slipped Ursule an extra *livre*. "Always fresh, your butter, that's what they tell me."

She wondered if he had ever said that to Madeleine, or if Madeleine knew about the *livres*. She thought not.

At lunchtime, as Drom flew off to hunt, Ursule carried the carafe of fresh buttermilk to the cottage. The sun was high and hot, burnishing the waiting hay so it shimmered gold and bronze in the still air. The cottage, with its single tiny window, would be dim and cool.

Agnes met her at the door, accepting the carafe with a nod. As she divided it between two cups, Ursule kicked out of her boots and shed the work-stained apron she wore over her smock and skirts. Too thirsty to wait, she drank her share of the buttermilk, savoring the tingle of it on her tongue, then went to the sink to wash her hands and cool her hot neck.

A salad of greens and summer herbs waited on the counter beside the pump handle. "That looks so good, Maman," Ursule said. "Your kitchen garden is doing well."

Agnes touched her lips with one finger, two taps. *Thank you.*

Agnes had learned to garden gradually, beginning with easy things—a planting of lettuce, some radishes, a few carrots and turnips. The woman who had spent her life traveling had adapted more easily than Ursule to living in a house that didn't move. Her garden now boasted tomatoes and squashes, parsley and basil, and a variety of greens. Her pottage held carrots, peas, and potatoes, enriched with chunks of meat from the tag ends of whatever Remy brought from the butcher shop. Ursule and Agnes had never eaten so well as they did at Kerjean Farm. It was one improvement over life in the caravan.

Ursule settled on a stool, flexing her weary toes against the cool flagstones of the floor, while Agnes moved the pile of her sewing to the bench beside the door and laid forks and spoons on the table. The table, along with their other furniture, had come with the cottage. It was roughly made, with unpainted planks that didn't quite match and one leg that had to be supported with a chip of wood so it didn't rock. There were two stools, the short bench, which was no more level than the table, and two low cots in the slant-roofed bedroom, covered with blankets of undyed wool. Agnes had sewn a pretty curtain for the small window above the stone sink, but there was no other decoration beyond an occasional handful of wildflowers drooping in a pottery jar. The cottage was as devoid of color as the caravan had once been full of it. Even their clothes were drab, the colors of earth and sand and rust.

Ursule longed for the profusion of colorful cushions and vivid quilts. Even now, if she closed her eyes, she imagined she could breathe the homely smells of their wagon, intensified by the small space. She missed the tang of candle wax, the fragrance of drying garlic and fennel, the nose-tingling aroma of homemade soap. She pictured their cozy beds, the hanging pots, the mismatched cups and plates.

Even more, she missed the Orchière crystal. She dreaded thinking of it discarded, or worse, stolen, to be misused by someone who didn't understand. Her greatest fear—aside from her terror of exposure, and the pyre—was that the stone and the grimoire were lost forever.

She felt her mother's gaze on her and tried to smile. "Sorry. Thinking sad thoughts."

Agnes put a hand over hers, and Ursule saw the pricked fingers, the swollen knuckles and grimy nails, all caused by days spent with a needle or digging in the garden. She covered her mother's hand with her free one. "It's all right," she said, with a catch in her throat. "I miss the caravan, the clan—everything. Midsummer is just past, Litha, and once again, we didn't celebrate." She looked down at their linked hands and spoke the most painful thing. "And I do so long for the scrying stone."

Agnes abruptly pulled free and turned to the fireplace, where the pot of last night's soup had begun to bubble. Ursule blinked in surprise. Was it possible her mother blamed the crystal for what had happened to them? Of course she had never spoken of it, because she didn't speak at all. Perhaps Agnes thought that if her daughter had not seen things in the stone, spoken things better left unsaid, she might still be making up fortunes, telling women what they wanted to hear. It might be true. Ursule might have married, given her grandchildren. They might still be living in their caravan, free to travel the roads and camp in the fields of Brittany.

Ursule was about to say this when she heard Drom's claws rattle against the roof.

She glanced up, startled. In summer, they always left their door open to the fresh air. Drom had never offered to come inside, but now she saw him perch unsteadily on the top of the door and twist his neck to peer beneath the doorframe.

"Drom?"

Agnes was just setting bowls of soup on the table when he gave a loud, crooning call. Agnes started, spilling soup over the wood surface. Ursule jumped up from her stool to seize a cloth to wipe up the mess.

"Drom! Look what you did!"

The raven called again.

Agnes lifted her head to stare at him, and Ursule stopped suddenly, the cloth in her hand, gooseflesh prickling her scalp. It had been ten years since she'd heard that hypnotic sound. The memory might have eluded her had it not been for the sudden ache flaring between her hip bones. The throb of magic brought that moment back to her as intensely if it had happened yesterday. She remembered how she had felt that winter morning, cold, exhausted, starving. Desperate. Terrified for her mother's life, and for her own.

Drom had made that sound, that chilling, melodic, bone-tingling call, when he led her to Yanna. He had done it again when he guided her here, to Kerjean Farm.

He meant to lead her somewhere again. She knew it, just as she had known his intention ten years before. But where? And why?

He called again, a long, musical, commanding tone.

Ursule's belly clenched around the node of magic, that knot of knowledge. She had not felt it in a very long time, but she knew it was a knot that would not release until she obeyed this mysterious call.

She crossed the room to the peg where her coat hung, and took it down. She pulled on her boots. "Daj, I have to go."

Agnes lifted her spread hands. *What? Why?*

"I'll be back as soon as I can." Ursule shook her head. "I don't exactly know where I'm going, but I know I have to go."

The raven cocked his head, black eyes glittering with impatience.

Agnes brought her two palms together in front of her chest. *Careful.*

Ursule crossed to her and kissed her cheek. "Don't worry," she repeated. "Drom wants—he has something to show me, I suppose. You know how it is with me." She pressed a hand to her belly. "I guess I—it seems I still—"

Agnes pointed to the lunch she had waiting. Ursule hesitated, but Drom clacked his beak, once, twice, before flitting away from the door to perch on the nearest fence post.

"Maman, I have to go."

Agnes stepped back, shoulders slumping in defeat. She took up a chunk of bread from the table, smeared it thickly with butter, and thrust it into Ursule's hands.

"Thank you," Ursule said. With the bread in one hand and her coat in the other, she hurried out to the raven. She didn't look back, but she knew her mother would be making her gesture again. *Careful.*

Drom didn't wait for Ursule to reach him. He flew to the next fence post, and the next. As she drew near, he flitted on, past the farmhouse, skirting the great oak tree. He flapped his wings to fly past the buttery, then straight down the lane toward the road.

With each of his wingbeats, Ursule's belly pulsated, vibrating with long-absent magic. There was nothing she could do but follow.

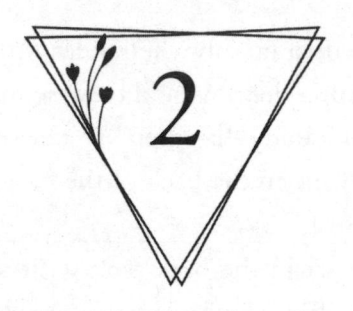

Anxiety blurred the ache of magic as Drom led Ursule farther and farther from home. As the day wore on and evening approached, she agonized over the cows begging for relief, the harness she had left unrepaired, her worry about Mimi. She kept on, blinking against the hard rays of the westering sun, because she had no choice. If she slowed her steps, the ache in her belly swelled, as if to chastise her, and Drom fluttered overhead, nervously clacking his beak.

It was clear she would not be returning this night, something she had never done, was never allowed to do. Even on festival days, she and every other dairymaid in the district had to leave the celebration to see to their cows and goats.

Madeleine would be furious and would rant about lazy *gitanes*. Agnes would be frantic. Remy would disappear into the apple orchard, where he kept his stash of brandy. Ursule prayed to the Goddess that she and her mother would not be turned out of Kerjean Farm. They had nowhere else to go.

Ursule ate the bread Agnes had given her, licking every bit of butter from her fingers. She drank from every stream they crossed, in case they didn't find another. She worried that Drom meant for her to keep walking even in darkness, but as daylight faded, the moon slid up over the horizon behind her, full and white. It cast silvery shadows from the trees and hedges and illumined the road enough for her to see where she was setting her feet.

She had forgotten the moon phase. It reminded her that Lammas was only days away, not that they would celebrate. Ursule would go to church instead.

Agnes flatly refused to go anywhere near a priest, but Ursule had decided at the beginning that it would be wise for her to attend, and it kept Madeleine from adding "heathen" to her other slights. She rode to the chapel of St. Anne in the back of the cart, with Madeleine and Remy on the bench seat.

At the chapel, she sat in the back pew with the other servants. At first the other farmworkers, the dairymaids, the cooks and the cleaners, had cast her curious glances. Not many strangers came to the village, and they tended to be suspicious, but over time, they had grown used to her. Some of them were almost as dark as she was, and their clothes were no better than hers. They nodded greetings and made space for her to sit. It was odd that she should find herself accepted in a way she never had been—not by being herself but by appearing to be like them.

She had learned to follow the Mass through imitation. She knelt, and crossed herself, and closed her eyes under the sprinkling of holy water. As everyone around her murmured Latin responses, Ursule whispered her own prayers to the Mother Goddess.

The little church had a story of its own, rather like one of those the clan had told around their cookfire. It was said that St. Anne had appeared to a plowman in a vision and told him to build her a chapel on this very spot. A statue of St. Anne stood on a pedestal at the door, a woman wearing a white veil over a drab brown robe. Ursule supposed it didn't matter that it was a crude rendering. No one, after all these years, would have any idea what St. Anne had looked like. There was another statue inside, of much better quality, of the Christian mother, the Virgin. She was robed in blue, and she gazed down from her niche with a remote expression, as if she didn't want to be there. Her white hands pressed together in prayer, and a circlet of gilt stars balanced awkwardly on her veil.

Ursule often wondered why all the priests were men, when the Catholics worshipped so many women, but she was afraid to expose her ignorance by asking.

Other things about the church also confounded her. In the chapel, the people prayed before an image of a murdered man on a cross. Was that why they were so eager to see witches tied to a stake, writhing in the flames? Perhaps it was death they worshipped, rather than the life of the natural world, like the moon lighting her path or the brooks watering the fields. Perhaps staying in one place for a lifetime, seeing the same trees, the same animals, the same people, deadened the spirit.

Lost in those thoughts, she didn't realize how far gone the night was. When a sudden cramp seized her calf, she called, "Drom, stop! I have to stop."

She sank to the leaf-carpeted ground beneath a chestnut tree, massaging the aching muscle with her fingers. The raven, with three flaps of his wings, returned to settle on a branch above her head, craning his neck to look down at her, softly clacking his beak. The moon was ahead of them now, beginning its descent. Ursule leaned against the tree trunk, curling her knees to her chest. Fatigue swept over her in a wave.

"Drom, I wish you could tell me where we're going."

Clack. Clack clack.

"No, I know you can't, but I'm so tired. I don't think I can walk anymore."

Clack.

"I have to sleep, Drom. I can't help it."

With one more gentle *clack*, Drom floated to the ground beside her. The peppery fragrance of chestnuts rose from the dried leaves as he wriggled himself into a comfortable spot. She found a few bread crumbs in the pocket of her coat and held them out on her palm. He took them, one at a time, then settled back with a rustle of his wings.

She put her forehead down on her folded arms and gave herself up to sleep.

When she woke in the pale light of dawn, dew misted her hair and the backs of her hands. She stirred, lifting her head, stretching out her stiff back. Drom stirred with her, cocking his head and blinking his bright eyes. Ursule pushed herself up and spent a moment shaking out her skirt and brushing leaves from her coat.

Drom spread his wings, hopped once, then flapped up to the branches of the next tree. He gave his strange, commanding call, and Ursule said, "Yes, I'm coming."

They were on their way again.

She plodded on in the rising heat of the morning. Her boots felt as if she had stones in them. Her head ached, and her dry eyes burned. She had missed another milking. Was there a chance Remy might have stepped in? Or were her animals aching, bawling from their pasture, looking for her in vain? She tried not to think about it, but it was no use. The habits of a decade did not break so easily. The weight of her responsibilities dragged at her heels, and her belly roiled with unease, with magic, with hunger. Only Drom, fluttering just ahead of her mile after endless mile, kept her moving.

By midmorning, she had encountered three other travelers. Two were haycarts, heading west with mounds of freshly cut timothy. The other was a pony cart with a couple on the bench seat who gave her curious glances but didn't speak. She supposed she must look terrible, having slept rough, her hair a tangle, her face dirty, her clothes stained. It didn't matter. Nothing mattered now but keeping her feet moving, answering the magic that burned in her belly.

The road led past farms fenced with miniature standing stones, like the ones at Carnac. A whitewashed church spire rose in the distance. At midday she passed a small henge, half-hidden in the summer grass, and it jolted her, as if it had called her name. She felt as if she had startled out of a dream state.

She drew a sharp breath and tasted the sea. Drom had led her into the west without her noticing. She didn't know how long they had been following the coastline. A briny tinge rode on the freshening breeze, and the horizon beyond the marshlands gleamed blue.

Drom hastened his pace, flying ahead of her faster than she could walk, then angling his wings away from the road. She watched the black gleam of him disappear into a field, settling onto something she couldn't see. She left the road and struggled to wade after him through marsh grass so tall it rose past her waist. The ground felt spongy beneath her boots, and the rough-bladed grass scratched at her elbows.

It took her a few moments to reach Drom. When she saw what he was perched upon, her breath caught in her throat, and her heart thudded. This was why he had led her here.

It lay on its side, as if it had overturned on the road and been tugged out of the way to be abandoned in a shallow ditch. It was broken beyond repair, wheels gone, empty doorway staring blindly at the sky. Its once-gay scarlet paint had faded to an unpleasant pink, and the rickety chimney was bent nearly double.

The caravan. Her caravan. Drom had heard her say that she missed it. He had guided her all this way, hours and hours of weary walking, only to find its sad remains. The sweet futility of it brought weary tears to her eyes.

"Oh, Drom," she said, her voice breaking. "It's not your fault, but... to come so far, and find this—this ruin."

He squawked, *"Zi buna. Zi buna!"* as he strutted over the wreck of the wagon, preening and cocking his head with obvious pride.

"Yes, Drom. *Zi buna.* I know you tried." With a weary sigh, she placed her hand on the cracked wall of the caravan and bent to look through the gap where the door had once hung.

There wasn't much to see. Whether the Orchières had done it themselves or scavengers had taken advantage, all their possessions had been removed. The cups and plates, Agnes's precious iron skillet, the quilts, even the curtain that had hung at the window were gone. The wooden counter lay in two pieces, stained by the weather, too splintered to be useful. Moldy blankets crumpled on the floor amid a detritus of broken pottery and bits of grass and leaves that must have blown in. Their cots had been dismantled and removed, no doubt now serving in someone else's wagon, and the baskets where they had stored chemises and scarves were overturned, empty, stained with mold. It was the final, the worst blow. There was nothing left of their lives with the clan.

In time all of this wreckage would sink into the marshy ground and disappear, just as Ursule and Agnes had disappeared. It was beyond repair. Even if she and Agnes could return to the clan, they would never live in this caravan again. No one would.

Ursule straightened and pushed herself back from the sad wreckage. There was no point in staring at it. She would have to trudge all the way back to Kerjean Farm, deal with whatever drama awaited her there, and hope she still had a job and a home. With luck, she could be back by nightfall.

She had just turned to walk back to the road when Drom gave a piercing cry, so loud and urgent that it alarmed her. She whirled, fearful he had been injured.

He obviously wasn't hurt, but he was hopping back and forth across the overturned wagon, wings bristling, hooked beak snapping angrily as he twisted his head from side to side.

At first she was relieved, and she cried, "Drom! You frightened me."

He clacked again, and hopped more and more furiously, feathers ruffling.

Ursule frowned. What did it mean? Why was Drom still—

The sudden surge of power that flared through her middle banished her headache and even her fatigue. The magic. In her disappointment, she had forgotten that element of this unlikely journey. It drove her back to the caravan's doorway, where she bent once again to look inside. At first she saw only what she had found before, the disintegrating remains of her and her mother's possessions.

She bent nearly upside down as she scanned the interior, trying to see what she might have missed.

Her eye was drawn to one of the blankets lying in a muddle on the floor. It was nondescript, a beige wool that might once have been dark brown. Its edges were frayed, and it looked as if it would disintegrate at a touch, but in the middle of it was an odd bulge that rose above the wreckage like a mountain peak above folded hills. Something lay underneath it. Something that wasn't a blanket, or a cup, or a pan. Something with bulk, disguised by the confusion around it.

Hope made Ursule's heart flutter in her throat. Her hands trembled with it, and she gave a long, noisy exhale.

She had to sit on the edge of the doorframe to swing her legs inside the toppled wagon. When she stood up, gripping the doorframe for support, her boots slipped and slid on the wreckage inside. The wall made a bad floor.

Gingerly, her fingertips braced on whatever surface she could reach to keep her balance, she slogged through the mess until she reached the mounded blanket. She crouched beside it, her breathing quick with anticipation.

She felt it first with her hand, and her heart leaped with such force she nearly fell backward. Breathing fast, she fumbled for the edge of the blanket and gradually, gingerly, peeled it back.

The basket was upside down, its contents tumbled out. The granite footing of the scrying stone peeked out from the remnants of the blanket that once covered it. With her heart in her mouth, Ursule looked past it and saw that the grimoire, still in its burlap wrapping and its strap, lay to one side, recognizable by its distinctive shape. They had been kept hidden, all this time, disguised by the wreckage. It hardly seemed possible, but everything to do with the Orchière crystal should have been impossible.

Ursule reached for it carefully, turning it right side up, letting the shredded covering fall away to expose the old, familiar, fantastical stone.

She could have wept at the touch of it, the reassuring weight in her hands, the rough surface of the granite bottom, the cool smoothness of the quartz growing out of it. She held it close to her heart for a long moment, sensing its energy through her fingers, through her breastbone. Had she not needed so desperately to get back to the farm, she might have stayed right where she was, crouching amid the ruins, peering into the scrying stone to see if it might tell her the secrets of ten long years.

She couldn't do that now. Her fears for her stock and for her mother created an undertow of emotion, pulling her home. She pulled the basket close and felt the bottom to be certain it was intact before she nestled the stone and the book back into their places. With the basket in her arms, she made her uneasy way back to the doorway. She set the basket outside, taking care that it would hold steady, before she swung herself up and out into the sunshine.

Drom was waiting for her, pacing, crooning his satisfaction. As he saw her emerge, he squawked, *"Zi buna! Zi buna!"*

"Zi buna, rascal!" He flew one wide, joyous circle above her head before dipping his wings to start back the way they had come.

Ursule climbed down from what was left of her old home. She placed one hand flat on the faded side to say farewell before she picked up the basket, threw her coat over her arm, and began the long walk back.

Ursule's heart felt as light as if she were fourteen again, instead of a weary twenty-three. She was footsore and hungry, and her arms ached under the weight of the basket, but her joy lightened these discomforts. Her solar plexus thrummed at the nearness of the scrying stone. Her eagerness to show her mother what she had found gave the illusion of shortening her return journey.

Still, it was the same distance coming back as it had been going out. By the time she drew close to home, the moon hung low in the sky behind her. She strained her ears for signs of trouble ahead but heard nothing but the whisper of the dawn breeze, pierced by the trilling of a nightjar. When she reached the farm at last, a blessed silence blanketed the fields and the barnyard. No cows bellowed in discomfort. No goats bleated. The only sign of life was a single light glimmering through the cottage window, telling Ursule her mother was waiting. Worrying.

As Drom flew away into the night to roost, Ursule tapped on the door of the cottage to warn her mother before she opened the door. A stub of candle flickered in its shallow holder near where Agnes sat at the table, sound asleep, her head on her folded arms. She woke with a hiss of indrawn breath when Ursule set the basket beside her.

"It's me, Daj. I—"

Agnes was on her feet before she could finish, gathering her into a tight embrace.

Ursule held her, patting her back, murmuring apologies. When her mother straightened and released her, she gestured to the basket.

"Look, Maman. Look what I found! Our caravan is ruined, but the crystal is safe. And look! Your *grand-mère*'s grimoire!"

Agnes reached out to touch the scrying stone, shaking her head in wonder. She turned to Ursule, her palms up. *Where? How?*

"It was a long way off," Ursule said. "Very near Carnac, I think."

Agnes crossed her hands over her breast at that, and gazed longingly at the basket. Ursule understood. "Everything else was gone, Maman. I looked. All our things, even our cots taken away. They missed the basket, though. It was hidden under an old blanket."

Agnes nodded and touched the stone again, her face softening with memory.

"I suppose Madeleine is terribly angry."

Agnes curled her hand into a claw, and shook it. *Furious.*

"But someone did the milking! Could she or Remy…"

Agnes, with a tight little smile, released the claw, and touched her forefinger to her breastbone.

"You did it? I didn't know you could milk a cow!" Ursule seized Agnes's hand and was startled by the difference between her own sturdy brown fingers, and Agnes's thin ones. Ursule felt a stab of compunction.

"How did you manage?" she said more gently.

Agnes shrugged and freed her hand so she could move to the fireplace, where a pot rested in the embers. She added fagots to the fire and stirred it up, sending the garlicky scent of warming soup into the cottage. Ursule's mouth watered. "Oh, that smells good. I'm starving."

Agnes gestured that she should sit. She brought out a plate of *pufe* and a dish of butter, and while the soup heated, Ursule ate three buckwheat cakes so fast she barely tasted them. As she chewed, she tried to picture her mother milking, hauling heavy buckets to the buttery. No doubt she would hear about all about it from Madeleine in the morning, but even dread of that could not spoil the relief that bubbled in her chest.

Her livestock was safe. She apparently had not lost her job. Her mother still had a home, and her precious crystal was in her hands again. She could survive Madeleine's temper.

She ate a big bowl of soup, watching the firelight glimmer in the smoky quartz of the crystal. When the bowl was empty, she yawned, and Agnes urged her up from the table and off to her bed. Ursule had meant to try the crystal as soon as she reached home, but she was exhausted, and it was almost morning already. Though she yearned toward it, she decided she had to put it off. At least the stone was safe. And the precious old book.

She kissed her mother's cheek before heading for her cot, stripping off her clothes as she went. She fell asleep the moment she laid her head on her pillow, so tired that even the lowing of the cows a few hours later didn't rouse her. Agnes had to shake her shoulder to wake her, and Ursule started up, blinking in surprise. She had never slept through the calls of her milkers.

Her cows were clearly unhurt by her absence, and though Mimi didn't have much milk, she seemed no worse. The chickens were content, their nests full of eggs. The byre was clean-swept, as tidy as if she had never been away. Ursule felt a surge of gratitude for Agnes's hard work.

When she carried her pails to the buttery, she found her mistress in her long canvas apron, a dozen bricks of fresh butter laid out before her on the stone counter. Madeleine disdained the labor of churning, but she insisted on being the one to shape the bricks of butter and mark them with Kerjean Farm's signature. She wielded the wooden stamp with a practiced hand, pressing the spirals of the Breton triskele into the shining yellow surfaces, smoothing and re-stamping them until they were perfect.

At the sound of Ursule's footsteps, she slapped a fold of wet linen over the brick she was working on, slid it into the pan of cold water to chill, then stood with her hands on her hips, glaring at her dairymaid. "Where have you been?"

Ursule had prepared her tale. "One of the goat kids went missing."

"It took you two days to find a goat kid?"

Ursule lifted one shoulder. "I was too far away to make it back."

"A likely story," Madeleine said. "You *gitanes*! Always wandering off!"

Ursule set her bucket on the counter with unnecessary force, so that milk splashed over the edge. She seized a cloth to mop it up, saying tightly, "You see me before you, Madeleine. I have not wandered off."

Madeleine's eyes narrowed in her bony face, and the color in her cheeks intensified. She was a difficult woman, all sharp elbows and sharp chin and sharp words. Ursule thought a passel of babes might have softened her, rounded her hard edges, but they had never come.

Madeleine said, "Did you give no thought to the milking?"

"I did, of course. I gather my mother did it for me."

"An old woman like that! Was that fair to her?"

As Ursule poured the fresh milk into the churn, she said, "Madeleine, if I had lost the kid, you would be no less furious. We lost two to the wasting sickness last year, and I'm worried about Mimi now—we could lose her, too. You're going to want this kid for the market."

"Which one was it?"

"The one with the black spot on its nose. He always wanders." Ursule felt safe in this description. Madeleine never went anywhere near the byre nor the pens if she could help it. She would have no idea what the goat kids looked like.

Remy appeared in the doorway, and Madeleine snapped her mouth shut so hard her teeth clicked.

"Ursule, you're back!" he said. "*Bon, bon*. We were worried about you."

Ursule repeated her story of the missing kid and said she would make up her lost chores.

"There's work to be done, *bien sûr*," Remy said. "But your mother did the milking! I didn't know she could do that."

"I didn't, either," Ursule said. "I supposed she's seen me do it often enough, but—"

"She didn't do a very good job. There was barely enough for our deliveries," Madeleine said. "And almost no cream."

Ursule was tying on a fresh apron for the churning. She gave the ribbons a tug and turned to look her mistress full in the face. "Did you thank her, Madeleine? For stepping in, doing something she's never done before in her life so that *you* didn't have to soil your hands?"

Madeleine drew breath to retort, but Remy clicked his tongue, somewhere finding the courage to say, "Now, now, Ursule, you must be tired. Have you eaten? Madeleine, you should get Ursule a bit of cheese, some bread."

Madeleine gave her husband a glance that could have melted the bricks of butter on their shelves, but she didn't speak. She spun away from the buttery and stamped off toward the house. Ursule bit the inside of her cheek to keep from laughing.

Remy contrived to ignore his wife's irritation. He patted his round stomach, looking around with an air of satisfaction. "Plenty of butter here. *Bon.*"

"Yes," Ursule said mildly. "There's plenty."

"The wall in the east pasture is broken. Maybe that's how the kid escaped?"

"It could be."

"We can repair it when you've finished here. Which kid ran off?"

She described it to him, and he nodded, setting his jowls trembling. "So glad you found the rascal. The Delacs want one. They lost all their goats in the winter."

"Mimi's sick, too, Remy."

"That's the little one? She does look poorly."

"If we lose one, we're likely to lose more."

"I know." Remy gave an exaggerated shrug and turned his eyes skyward. "But what can you do? It's in God's hands."

Perhaps, Ursule thought. *Or perhaps it's in the Goddess's.*

· · · · · ·꧁ ꧂· · · · · ·

Ursule hurried the churning, then hastened out to look at the broken wall. There was no sign of Remy, but that didn't surprise her. On a hot afternoon like this one, he would be enjoying his sip of brandy and subsequent nap in the woods.

The wall was built in the Breton dry-stone style. It wasn't easy to dislodge the interlocking rocks, so Ursule suspected the Delac bull had leaned on it. He was a slow-moving, dull-witted beast, usually docile, but if one of the Kerjean cows had come into heat, that could have enticed him to make an assault on the wall.

Fortunately, he had only dislodged the top two layers. Ursule set about replacing them, gathering the scattered stones, organizing them by size, then beginning with the bigger ones at the bottom, working her way up to set the smaller ones into the top.

As she handled the inert rocks, she yearned for the moment she could look into the crystal. Would it remember her? There had been no magic for her in such a long time. She had filled the void with relentless farm work, with her responsibility for her mother, but now . . .

She was impatient to use it again, to feel the magic flow through her, to feel living stone under her fingers instead of the dry, dead rocks of the fence. She wanted to hurry, to hasten the job, but she restrained herself. She didn't want to have to do the chore again the next time the Delac bull misbehaved.

Ursule was meticulous by nature, and that suited the work. She fitted the stones together with precision, searching for the perfect fit with each one. She worked right through the day, missing her lunch entirely, while the sun burned her neck and her shoulders began to ache.

Remy showed up as she was settling the final stones into place, testing its soundness with her shoulder. As if he had done the work himself, he pushed at the fence, tugged at a rock or two, and in a satisfied tone announced it whole once again. "You can get on to the evening milking," he said. "I'll finish up here."

The job was already finished, but Remy would find something to add, some jagged stones to set into the top, a bit of support at the base, something that would make him feel he had done his part. As Ursule crossed the field to the byre, she allowed herself one small, exasperated shake of the head, a gesture her master wouldn't see. There were times when she could understand Madeleine's constant state of irritation.

In the goat pen, she found Mimi listless and unsteady. Ursule stroked her head and tried to coax her to eat something, but without any luck. She tried the little goat's flat udder, but what milk there was looked gray and gave off the sour smell of infection. Ursule poured it out in the grass beyond the pen and washed the bucket before she milked Bibi.

She worried over that as she milked the cows, fed the chickens, and cleaned the byre. By the time she finished, the sun was long gone. The cooling air soothed her sunburned neck as she walked to the cottage, where her supper waited.

Ursule gazed longingly at the basket, resting now beside the fireplace, but her mother made it clear she was to eat before she did anything else, and she was too hungry to argue. She ate two bowls of thick pottage and half a loaf of fresh bread. As Agnes set a pottery bowl of fresh strawberries at her elbow, Ursule said, "Where did you put the grimoire?"

Agnes made a sharp gesture, one hand under the other. *Hidden.*

"Maman, we don't have to hide it here. No one is going to—" But her mother made the gesture again, and Ursule understood that she meant *A promise.* Agnes turned her back, refusing to talk about it further.

Ursule let it go. It didn't matter. She would find it. The cottage was small, there were no hidden cupboards, and her old promise had been that of a child. She took up a strawberry, still warm from the sun, and bit into it. It was honey-sweet, and she was reaching for another when a flash of light caught her eye.

She swiveled so quickly on her stool that she almost tipped it over. Magic stirred in her, and Agnes, at the sink, drew a noisy breath.

In a heartbeat, Ursule was on her feet. She hurried to latch the door before she lifted the basket and placed it on the table as tenderly as if it held an infant. Agnes had covered the crystal with a fresh piece of clean linen from her sewing supplies, and Ursule folded it back slowly, with reverence.

The stone must have grown tired of waiting. Light coruscated from it, stronger and brighter than Ursule remembered. It was a joyous thing, a celebratory display, an extravagant welcome.

Ursule cupped the smoky quartz between her palms. Despite the blaze of light within, it was cool against her skin. The power of it radiated into her work-hardened hands, through her labor-toughened bones, pouring its energy into her lonely heart.

The magic had not left her. She was still an Orchière witch. There were things she meant to do. Plans she had laid through this long day of labor. She could hardly wait to begin.

She remembered the instructions for how to prepare an altar as if she had read them yesterday. Agnes watched, her dark eyes wide, as Ursule lifted the stone and settled it on the table. Ursule took stems from the bunches of rosemary and tarragon and lavender drying beneath the window, and used bits of twine to make bundles to arrange around the crystal. She mixed salt into a cup of water, stirred it with her fingers, and flicked the drops from her fingertips to make a circle of protection.

The air in the cottage seemed to change as she worked, as if the power of the crystal could cleanse it, clarify its atmosphere, fill the little space to the brim with anticipation.

There was study ahead, and work of a different kind than she had been doing, but she was ready. Her life had been returned to her. Drom's satisfied croon outside her door confirmed that it was true.

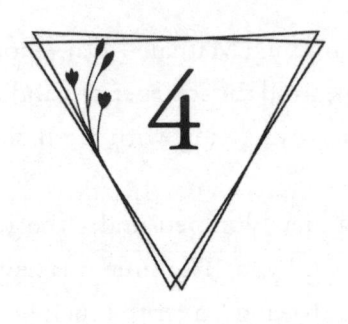

T he next day Ursule waited for a time when her mother was in the garden, clipping back a patch of lavender, to begin to search for the grimoire.

The search didn't take long. The book was in its old place, pushed far under her mother's bed, hidden behind an unused shopping basket. Ursule knew she would have to reveal her secret eventually, but she was too impatient to think about it now. She pulled out the book and carried it to the table.

She turned the pages with delight, savoring the different hands that had written in it, the bits of wisdom they offered, advice and instructions and recipes. She sensed the voices of her ancestresses rising from the pages in swirls of energy and encouragement. She could do so much! She could try so many things!

In her excitement, she forgot about Agnes until she felt her gaze tingle the back of her neck. She swiveled to see her mother, holding a bunch of sweet-smelling lavender stalks and staring at her, openmouthed.

Ursule's stomach dropped. In a vanishing voice she said, "Oh, Maman, I—"

Agnes interrupted her with the palms-out gesture that meant *No!*

"It will be all right," Ursule said hastily, closing the book, placing a protective hand on it. "No one will see it but us, and—"

Her mother dropped the lavender stalks to the floor in her hurry to stride to the table. She reached for the book with both hands, hissing alarm.

Ursule, though it distressed her, shot to her feet and blocked Agnes from touching the grimoire. "Maman—Daj—don't. Please. I need this book. I need the recipes and the instructions and the spells—"

Agnes fell back, her eyes wide with fresh shock. She lifted both palms. *What?*

"I—" Ursule's shoulders slumped under the weight of the old, old secret. "I was going to tell you. The time was never right."

Her mother lifted a shaking finger to touch her eye, then to point at the book, then to touch her eye again. *Reading?*

"Yes." Ursule strove for a pragmatic tone, as if this was not going to be monumental news. "Yes, I can read. I—"

Agnes hissed again and struck her breastbone with her fist, three times, hard enough that Ursule could hear the blows. *You deceived me!*

"I'm sorry!" Ursule seized her hand to make her stop. "I never meant to surprise you like this. I—that is—I was going to tell you," she stammered, her words spilling over each other. "I was going to do it years ago, but then the witch hunters came—"

She felt the spasm that shook her mother's body at the mention of the witch hunters. Ursule led her to her stool and helped her to sit, then knelt beside her. "I'm sorry," she said again. Agnes gazed at her for a heartbeat, then buried her face in her hands.

Ursule put both arms around her. "I'm so sorry," she murmured. "I know we never speak of it. Now I've shocked you twice."

Agnes began to weep, her shoulders trembling with the remembered horror that had stolen her voice. Ursule rocked her, patted her, once again the daughter become the mother, the protector, the strong one. The thought wearied her, but there was nothing to be done about it. She murmured, over and over, "Don't cry. Please don't cry. It won't happen again."

At length, Agnes's tears ceased, and she drew a shuddering breath. She straightened and pointed at the book. Again, she pressed her fist to her chest, not with the force of shock this time, but her meaning still clear. *You deceived me.*

"I didn't mean to." Ursule pushed herself up from the floor and went to the sink, avoiding her mother's accusatory gaze. "Keeping secrets was our habit. You said yourself that some secrets should be kept. And it was already hard, being so different from the rest of the clan, with no man in our wagon, and Uncle Arnaud always after us about not bringing in enough money. If he knew—if they knew—I could read..." She gazed out the little window into the hazy summer day, the branches of the oak tree drooping under the heat, its yellowing leaves barely stirring in the still air.

She had been the least important of all the Orchières. Plain. Quick to anger, often crosswise with her uncle, with her cousins. Her secret had bestowed on her a sense of worth. Letters and words, written on signs and broadsheets and in the rare book she could get her hands on, spoke to her in a way that seemed magical. She could hear the voices, understand the thoughts, of people she would never meet, never know, who would probably refuse to speak to her in person. At the loneliest times, when she felt as insignificant as a pebble on a beach, she would hug her secret to herself, and try to believe it would one day make a difference.

That day had come at last, and she couldn't help wishing it had not been darkened by her mother's hurt feelings. She made herself smooth her resentful expression before she looked away from the window.

"I was little when I realized I could read." She crossed to the table and pointed to the page she had been memorizing. "Letters like these began to speak to me, on their own. I thought they spoke to everyone until I heard Uncle Arnaud making fun of someone who was holding a book. I didn't want him to laugh at me. Everyone already laughed at me because I didn't talk."

She touched her mother's shoulder. "I was only three when it started. Then, as I grew up, the opportunity to tell you—to explain—it never came."

It was difficult, having this one-sided conversation. "Look at this, Maman." She opened the grimoire again and turned to the page she had been reading. "This page says, *Potion against the wasting disease.* I might be able to save Mimi."

Agnes's tears were still drying on her face, and her mouth trembled, but she managed to curve her lips, just a little. She reached out to touch first Ursule's heart, then her own. *Love.*

Ursule smiled back at her. "Why did the Orchières stop reading?"

Her mother pointed to the book and then to herself, shaking her head with a rueful expression. *I couldn't.*

"Was it harder because the *grands-mères* wrote it in French? And Uncle Omas, Uncle Arnaud—I can guess they couldn't read, either? I can guess that—only the witches—"

Her mother shrugged, rubbed the last tears from her cheeks, and rose. She gathered up the scattered lavender, then moved to the counter to begin slicing bread and cheese and tomatoes for their lunch, ordinary tasks to restore order to her world.

"That was it, wasn't it, Maman? Only the witches could read." Agnes, without turning, shrugged again.

Relieved, Ursule bent over the grimoire once again, but a glimmer from the scrying stone caught her eye. She grinned at it over her shoulder. "Soon. Very soon."

Agnes turned from the counter, palms up. Ursule pointed to the crystal. "The *grands-mères* say they're ready to work."

· · · · · ·𖦹𖦹𖦹 · 𖦹𖦹𖦹· · · · ·

The potion for the wasting disease was all bitter herbs—mustard seeds, bay and sage leaves, barberries, mugwort. While Ursule went about her afternoon chores, Agnes brought in the mustard, bay, and sage, then foraged along the river for the barberries and mugwort that didn't grow in her garden. When Ursule came into the cottage at the end of the day, everything she needed was laid out on the stone counter. She hugged her mother's shoulders. "Thank you, Maman. This is wonderful."

Ursule read the recipe again, hoping to do everything right.

Chop six leaves of bay and sage. Add a palmful of mustard seeds, crushed, with twelve barberries and a stem of mugwort still in bloom. Boil together in cider, with a pinch of ash from the cookfire.

"It's meant for people," Ursule said. "But should it not work for beasts as well?"

For answer, Agnes brought her a bit of gray ash, cupped in her palm, and spilled it into the pot. Ursule read the rest of the instructions.

While the candle burns, speak the name of the one who is ill, and bless it, three times three times, stirring the potion the while. Let it rest where moonlight shines. In the morning, administer to the afflicted while speaking the blessing again, three times three times.

"Do you know, Maman, it's Lammas today?"

Agnes inclined her head in acknowledgment.

"We haven't celebrated a Sabbat in a long time. Let's do that tonight, along with making the potion. I just need a new candle."

Agnes turned to a cupboard for one of the candles she had fetched from the Kerjean cellar, then went to the fire to stir up the embers. Ursule prepared the herbs, careful to follow the proper order. When everything was ready, she settled the pot on the hearth and let it boil while she ate her supper. When her nose began to tingle at the smell of simmering cider laced with the pungence of sage, she judged it had boiled enough and pulled the pot out of the embers.

The potion was still steaming when she set it in the center of her altar. She took up a smoldering twig from the fireplace to light the candle and grazed the top of the crystal with her fingertips. It glimmered in response, and her heart fluttered with excitement.

She was about to begin when her mother put up a hand. *Wait.* She hurried into the bedroom and returned with two narrow scarves of linen draped over her hands. They had been bleached to a near-perfect white and sewn with delicate stitches.

"Maman!" Ursule breathed. "What are these?"

For answer, Agnes unfolded one of the scarves and let it drift over Ursule's disordered hair. The unblemished surface of the linen made her stained skirt and smock look even dingier by comparison.

"It's beautiful," Ursule said, stroking it with work-grimed fingers. "Did Grand-mère wear something like this when she worked?"

Agnes nodded as she put the second scarf over her own head. The crystal winked approval. All was in order.

"I found a rite in the grimoire. We'll begin with that."

Ursule didn't know whose hand had recorded the words, but they seemed oddly familiar, as if she had known them once, in another time, another place. She liked the feeling that gave her, the sense of continuity, the comfort of timelessness. She raised her two hands above the altar as she recited:

On this Sabbat of Lammas, we honor our foremothers: the seer Violca, the prophetess Liliane, the Lady Yvette, Maddalena of Milano, Irina from the east, and all the others whose precious names have been lost. We vow to pass the craft to our daughters so long as our line endures.

She glanced up to see her mother watching intently. In the light of the candle her eyes shone like the black stones beneath the flowing river, and the strands of white in her hair glimmered silver.

"You remember?" Ursule whispered.

Agnes made a gesture, her right hand over her left shoulder. *Long ago.*

"We vow to pass the craft to our daughters . . . Maman, because you saved the grimoire, you are passing the craft to your daughter. To me."

Agnes smiled, her face alight with satisfaction.

"But is this the end?" Ursule said. "I have no daughter, nor any hope of one."

Agnes's smile faded and she made one more gesture, a hand to her temple, then the palm upturned. *Who knows?*

Ursule inclined her head in acknowledgment of this wisdom, then turned back to the altar. Now she had only instinct to guide her. She didn't know how to ask, what to say. She was a little embarrassed about it, wanting so much to work a real rite, to prove she could, not sure how to proceed.

She hesitated, biting her lip. Agnes reached out to her, past the drift of the veil, and touched her breastbone, then made a fluttering gesture with her fingers.

It was a new sign for them, one Ursule wasn't sure of at first, but then she realized. It was like Violca's voice. *Stop trying. Believe.* Agnes was saying the same thing in her wordless way.

Ursule gave her a small, grateful smile, then closed her eyes and waited. Silence stretched around the altar, but it was a comfortable silence, marred only by the hiss of candlewax and the two women's breathing. Ursule tried to listen to those small things, adding the gentle scrape of a tree branch against the wall, the faint clicking of Drom's claws on the roof. She felt her mind relax and expand, rise above her daily concerns, connect with the stream of energy that must flow around her always.

When the words came, she spoke them without thinking. Her voice was soft, clear, quick. She didn't consciously choose what to say but took care not to let her consciousness block the flow. *Believe.* She had to trust that the right words had come to her mind.

Mother Goddess, in your daughter's aid,
Bless this potion newly made.
Strengthen leaf and stem and flower;
Imbue them with your healing power.

The crystal glowed as if it held a tiny, faraway sun. It made Ursule smile beneath her veil of linen as she stirred the potion with a spoon, murmuring, "My sweet Mimi, bless her, my little Mimi, bless her, our own Mimi, bless her." She repeated the whole three times. When she was finished she laid down the spoon, slid the scarf from her head, and stepped back.

The potion had ceased steaming. The light in the scrying stone faded quietly, as if its little sun were setting. Soon only candlelight flickered across the gray quartz. Agnes let her own scarf fall to her shoulders as the candle guttered out, emitting one final puff of the honeyed scent of beeswax.

The cottage lay in darkness except for the slender bar of moonlight falling through the window onto the counter. Ursule shifted the pot, angling it so the light of the Lammas moon glistened on the surface of the potion. "There," she said softly. "It's done." She ran a hand across her middle, where the ache of magic was releasing. "I feel it," she whispered.

Agnes held out her hand for the linen scarf and folded it with her own. When that was done, she surprised Ursule by bringing a small, squat pan from the back of the fireplace. It was still warm, and as she uncovered it, the scents of yeast and sage and rosemary rose from it.

"What is—oh!" Ursule said. She bent over the pan and took a sniff. "Lammas loaf!"

Agnes smiled as she cut two squares of the fresh bread, and set them on saucers with the honey pot between them. Ursule pulled up her stool, reached for the pot, and dripped fragrant honey over the bread.

In the old days, the Orchière clan would have gathered on this day, singing, sharing the Lammas loaf, telling stories. They would have taken crumbs of the loaf to scatter around the perimeter of their camp, to celebrate the harvest and honor the Goddess of Plenty. The children's faces would be sticky with honey. The adults would build up the fire and toss in stems of thyme and oregano, dried and bundled with bits of ribbon, smiling at the children's cheers as the herbs flamed up.

She took a bite, and the taste of it, smoky sweet honey contrasting with tart rosemary and spicy sage, made her close her eyes under a wave of nostalgia for what could never be again. Agnes, too, must be remembering, thinking of her brothers, her nieces and nephews, her sisters-in-law. Here they were in their drab little cottage, day after day, night after night, the colors and smells and excitement of the traveling life lost to them.

Ursule supposed they would never know what had become of the clan. Their ruined wagon was an epitaph for their lives as travelers, as true Romani. Despite Madeleine's insults, they were no longer really *gitanes*.

But they would always be Orchières. And tomorrow, she hoped to prove she was still a witch. She took her certainty to bed with her that night and slept soundly, comforted by what was to come.

U rsule found Mimi much worse the next morning. The goat huddled in a corner of the pen, shivering, though the August morning was still and hot. Ursule could see from the gate that Mimi's udder was flat and empty. She was on her feet, but barely, leaning against the slats of the wooden fence, her head hanging low.

The goats looked much alike, mostly white, with gray beards and patches of black over their shoulders. Ursule loved their graceful curling horns and thready little beards. She adored watching the kids frolic through the pasture, little silvery mites shining against the green of the grass. She hated parting with them. She always hid in the byre when Remy carted them away to be sold, leaving Mimi and Bibi bleating after their babies.

She was sure Mimi had picked up the wasting disease at her last breeding. Remy didn't keep bucks but took the does to a farm near Auray. Bibi had gone to be bred at the same time, which meant she would be next, if the potion didn't work.

Ursule rattled the grain bucket, and Bibi trotted eagerly toward her. Mimi didn't move.

Goats were easy feeders, willing to nibble almost anything, especially from Ursule's hand. This morning, she carried two chunks of bread in a saucer. She had soaked them with the potion that had rested all night in the moonlight. She held one of them out to Bibi, who took it eagerly. Her long, flexible tongue flicked up every cidery morsel, then licked and licked Ursule's palm until it was dry.

"Good girl," Ursule said. She gave Bibi's poll a scratch, then gently pushed her toward the byre. Bibi obediently tripped inside, where her feed of hay waited in the stanchion. Ursule carried the saucer across to where Mimi stood, her eyes dull and her long ears drooping.

"Mimi. See, Mimi. I have something for you." One ear flickered, weakly. Ursule knelt in the dirt to cradle the goat's head with one hand. With the other, she set the saucer on the ground and picked up the bit of bread to offer it. Mimi gave a hoarse sigh, her nostrils rippling, but her lips didn't open.

Ursule sat back on her heels, dismayed. She could hardly poke the bread down the goat's throat. Mimi could choke on it. She could force it into her mouth, but if Mimi wouldn't swallow—

"Mimi," she murmured. "My poor little Mimi. Could you just try?"

"*Zi buna!*"

Drom's greeting startled Ursule so that she almost dropped the bread. The raven was staring down at her from the nearest fence post, his thick beak clacking as he rocked from side to side. His ebony feathers gleamed, showing elusive flashes of purple along the wings. Again he croaked, "*Zi buna!*"

"*Zi buna*, Drom," Ursule said. "This is not for you, though. Mimi's very sick."

The raven cocked his head, regarding the goat. He clacked his beak one more time, then spread his wings and fluttered down to the ground, right in front of Mimi.

The sight of him, inches from her nose, roused her. She jerked backward, and her head came up. Ursule swiftly thrust her palm forward.

For the space of three heartbeats, nothing changed. Mimi stared at the raven while Ursule tickled her lips with the bread. Drom clacked his beak and did his side-to-side prance.

When he began to croon, Ursule's neck prickled. She had never heard this particular sound from him: low, throaty, more cat's purr than bird's call. A spasm rippled between her hip bones as Drom repeated the sound, again and then again, only pausing to breathe.

Mimi's long eyelashes fluttered as she blinked, once, twice, three times. Her mouth opened, just a little, and her tongue stretched to scoop the bit of bread from Ursule's palm. Ursule kept her hand under the goat's chin, lest the remedy fall out. Everything was still except for Drom's odd, low call. Mimi didn't chew. Ursule barely breathed.

When Mimi swallowed at last, Drom's crooning instantly ceased.

"Drom," Ursule said. "What did you do?"

He rustled his wings in a way that could only be described as boastful. *"Zi buna!"*

"Zi buna indeed, you rascal! Thank you."

He clacked once, stretched his wings, and was aloft, lifting out of the pen, soaring away into the trees. Ursule sat back on her heels again, her eyes on Mimi.

She knew well from her decade of husbandry that no remedy worked instantly, but her potion was no ordinary remedy. Even as she watched, the goat's shivering eased. Seconds later her knobbly legs straightened, and her head came up. Ursule's belly relaxed. Mimi's long ears lifted. Even her eyes began to brighten. The little goat who had come so perilously close to death was reviving before Ursule's eyes.

She was still too thin, her hip bones jutting under her skin, but she tottered off toward the byre without being told. Ursule sighed, relieved. There would be no milk from Mimi for a time, but she would eat. She would recover. Her milk would return after her next breeding.

Remy would brag that his livestock were the healthiest in the district. Madeleine would sniff, and doubt whether the goat had been ill at all.

But Ursule would know what had happened. Agnes would know.

It was, Ursule told herself as she followed the goats into the byre, a glorious day, and she hoped it was the first of many. A sensation of such power thrilled through her body that she thought she might lift right off the ground to join Drom among the tree branches.

· · · · · ·✦·✦· · · · · ·

By mid-August, Mimi had recovered her health and most of the weight she had lost. Madeleine wanted to know when they could breed her again. Remy told anyone who would listen that the wasting disease would never take hold on his farm because he had nailed icons of St. Francis to every door of his byre. Madeleine scoffed at this, but Ursule overheard her say once that her dairymaid, despite being a lazy *gitane*, was good with sick animals.

Buoyed by the success of the Lammas rite, Ursule hunched over the grimoire every night, burning two candles at once so she could see the pages. Agnes had come to accept this practice, though she took care to pull the curtain over the window after supper and insisted on hiding the book under her bed when Ursule wasn't using it. She made tea for Ursule as she worked, or sometimes honeyed milk. Occasionally, as she grew easier with the idea, she would tap the grimoire with a finger, then touch her ear. *Read to me.*

Ursule read the titles to her mother as they sat in the unsteady glow of the candles: *Potion for the stomach after spoiled food. Simple to ease sneezing. Simple to help a pregnant woman sleep. Potion to speed conception. Charm to heal a broken heart. Potion to heal a burn. Simple to quiet a crying child. Potion for a balding head.*

And the spells: *Spell to reveal a secret. Spell of protection. Spell of concealment.*

When she could lay her hands on enough candles, Ursule turned the pages long past the time she should have been in bed, sometimes persisting until a candlewick drowned in its own wax with a surrendering hiss. At such times she made herself close the book and go to bed, but she often lay awake, watching the slender shaft of moonlight trace its path across the cottage floor, her mind spinning over what she had learned, planning what to try next.

She experimented as autumn approached, starting with a charm to keep the milk fresh in hot weather, then another to sweeten the butter before market day. She made a potion for a rash Remy developed on his neck, although she didn't tell him it was magicked. She made a simple, which she slipped into Madeleine's buttermilk, to soothe her temper, and for three days afterward, Madeleine was almost kindly. She didn't snap once at Ursule or Remy, nor did she press Agnes to speak when she came to pick up an apron Agnes had mended.

The respite didn't last.

"Hardly worth the trouble," Ursule muttered to her mother, when the effects of the simple wore off and Madeleine returned to her crotchety ways. "Or maybe I didn't do it right."

Agnes raised one needle-worn forefinger in warning. *Take care.*

Ursule nodded in response. "I promise. No one will know. It's our secret."

There were other failures: a potion for her own sore muscles that didn't make much difference; a simple to keep the slugs from Agnes's garden, which seemed to attract them more than it repelled them. For each failure, though, she celebrated three or more successes, gaining in confidence each time.

····· ·᠈᠈᠈᠈᠈᠈• ᠁᠁᠁᠁᠁· ·····

Ursule had one great magic she longed to perform. She waited for the day when Agnes was to deliver some needlework in Keranna, and Madeleine wanted fabric for a new petticoat for the Michaelmas fete. Remy said he would take them in the cart so he could ask about a billy to breed Mimi and Bibi. Madeleine rolled her eyes at that, said something about the tavern and too much ale, and off they went.

When the milking and churning were done, Ursule opened the grimoire to a page she had marked with a bit of ribbon.

A spell of undoing

The ingredients weren't difficult—a pinch of pepper from the cupboard, a leaf of wild foxglove, a stem of lavender from the garden, and tincture of horehound, which she always kept on hand. It was perfect for treating constriction of the throat. Even the strand of hair to identify the spell's object was easy, pulled from Agnes's comb.

Whichever *grand-mère* had written it out had been specific in her instructions.

Grind the herbs very fine in a mortar, and add the tincture of horehound and the strand of hair, clipped into pieces. Set the mortar between an unburned candle and the scrying stone. Protect the altar with salted water, then light the candle. Spin the mortar widdershins, three times three times, to reverse misfortune. Crumble the herbs into the candlefire, and speak your petition into the smoke.

Before she began, Ursule found the veil Agnes had made for her, and although she felt a bit odd doing it when she was alone, it seemed right to follow the tradition. She draped the veil over her hair, folding the ends over her shoulders, then stood for a moment before her altar, her fingers on the crystal, concentrating.

As the stone began to glow, Drom crooned from his perch outside the cottage. Ursule lighted her candle, then spun the mortar, widdershins, three times three times. When she finished, the familiar ache thrilled through her middle.

Surely she would succeed in this. People would wonder at the miracle of it. Though she must keep it to herself, she would take great pride in her achievement. She would no longer need to doubt herself. She only wished her uncles and aunts and cousins could witness her triumph.

She crumbled the herbs into the candle, watching their dust turn into tiny flames, then tendrils of silvery vapor. The smell of burning hair was so faint she could barely detect it. She spoke her spell swiftly into the smoke, to finish before it dispersed.

I call upon the grands-mères' power
To heal my mother of her sorrow.
This is the remedy I seek:
Ease her heart, that she might speak.

She intoned it firmly, three times three times. Midway through her recitation, the glow inside the crystal flared high. The candle flamed up, too, spitting bits of beeswax across the table. When she finished, the candle died, its wick collapsing into the molten wax. Drom crooned again, a joyous sound, and Ursule sighed with satisfaction as the ache between her hip bones faded. She stood a moment, her arms crossed over her heart, savoring the moment.

The spell would work. There was no doubt.

···· ·❧❧❦❦ · ❦❦❧❧· ····

Ursule heard the cart return while she was busy with the evening milking, but she couldn't hear voices over the sounds of her animals. She hurried to carry the milk to the buttery, then rushed through her other chores, mucking out the byre, scattering the chickens' feed, filling the water trough. As she crossed the dark barnyard to the cottage, the chill autumn wind chased her, teasing at the hem of her skirt.

Agnes was at the counter, slicing apples into a pan. She didn't look up at the sound of the door, nor did she react when Ursule greeted her. She started on another apple, and Ursule saw that her hands on the knife were shaking.

"Maman?"

There was no response.

"Maman, stop! I'm afraid you're going to cut yourself."

Agnes's shoulders heaved as she drew a deep breath. Slowly, with great deliberation, she laid the knife on the counter and wiped her hands on her apron before she stepped back, turned in place, and faced her daughter. With unsteady hands, she lifted Ursule's stained mortar from the sink and set it on the table. She had retrieved the grimoire from its hiding place, and it also rested on the table, beside the remains of the candle Ursule had used.

Ursule frowned at this display. "Daj?" she said uncertainly. "What is this?"

Her mother put the fingertips of one hand on the grimoire while she touched her throat with the other. She held Ursule's gaze as she shook her head. *No.*

Ursule gazed at her, not understanding. "Do you mean—you mean, no, it didn't work?"

Agnes blew out a breath and dropped her hand from her throat. She laid her hand on the grimoire's leather cover, and shook her head again.

"Maman—perhaps if you tried—"

Agnes's lips worked, stiffly, as if they had forgotten how, but she spoke. "No. No!"

Ursule stared, openmouthed, her heart fluttering with excitement. She had forgotten how big and deep her mother's voice was, a surprising voice in such a small person. It sounded rusty now, creaky with disuse, like the hinges of a door too long unopened, but it was there. She had done it!

"Maman—Daj—it worked! Your voice..."

The look on her mother's face stole her breath. She remembered that look: the hollow eyes, the sunken cheeks, the pall of terror. It was the look Agnes had worn after hours of huddling in a shack, listening to the preparation of the pyre on which she was meant to die.

The horror of it had silenced her for ten years. The damage of those hours could not be undone.

Agnes's silence was her protection against the memory. Ursule realized, observing her mother's stricken face, that she would not give it up. She could not give it up.

"You knew what I was doing," Ursule said helplessly.

Agnes pointed to the altar and again touched her throat with her fingers.

"You felt it."

A single nod was her mother's only answer.

"You could speak—"

Agnes threw up her hands, palms out. *No.*

"I thought you would—"

The gesture came again, two palms outward, then repeated. *No. No.*

"It was just—I meant..."

Agnes turned her back and retreated to the counter, where she took up the paring knife once again. Ursule watched her, her mind wrestling with choices. Should she argue? Insist? Perhaps she could coax her to try, to speak a few words, to see that it would not harm her...

No. It was not for her to decide. She had not been the one hauled off in her nightdress by a gang of men. She had not been the one crouching on a dirt floor for hours as the instrument of her torment was nailed together. As much as what happened to her mother had terrified her, horrified her, it was not her trauma. Not her memory. Her mother had dealt with it in her own way, and her daughter would have to let her be.

In silence, Ursule gathered up the mortar and the candleholder and put them away. She carried the grimoire back to its hiding place, her heart heavy with shame. She had tried to perform this magic as much for herself as for her mother. She had been wrong. Wrong to think she could decide someone else's future. Wrong to put her ambition before her mother's need.

Some things could not be repaired, even through magic. Some hurts could not be healed.

It was a lesson she would not forget.

1782

The years rolled on, marked by endless cycles of labor, the sameness of the days occasionally relieved by the work of magic. There was a charm to soothe nervous hens in a thunderstorm, a simple for the swelling of Chou Chou's knees in wet weather, an occasional spell to speed the ripening of the hay or increase the cows' milk production. Ursule's confidence grew, and she added two pages to the grimoire in her own hand, writing down simples she created with herbs from Agnes's garden, one for good dreams, when she heard her mother tossing restlessly in the night, and another to ease Mimi's and Bibi's birthings.

She still missed the traveler's life, but the magic comforted her. The only worry she would admit to, and only to herself, was that there would be no one to pass it on to. Who would learn from the grimoire, as she had? Who would understand the rites, the dedication to the ancestresses? Who would inherit the magic? She feared there was no answer, because there was no one to do it.

She had barely noticed passing into her thirtieth year, then her thirty-first and thirty-second, the seasons tumbling by like leaves spinning on the surface of the river. The only times she saw people were at the chapel of St. Anne, when she and the other servants chatted briefly after Mass, or when Remy hired laborers to help with haying or some job too heavy for the two of them to manage. The sameness of her life, day in and day out, made her feel as drab and dutiful as one of her cows, a creature of work and sleep and little else. On the winter day she turned thirty-three, she had spent an hour staring into the scrying stone, wondering if this was all there would be to her life.

The crystal flickered, as if waiting.

She wanted to ask a question, find something to look forward to, but she couldn't think of the words. She left it in the end, no wiser about what was to come.

In Keranna, the harvest celebration was the feast of Michaelmas, marked by a great bonfire in honor of St. Michael the Archangel. Vicomte Alleyn sent a cask of ale and a pig to roast, and the bakery was busy turning out Michaelmas cakes. Everyone attended the gathering, even the lowliest servant on the most distant farm.

Ursule did the milking early the day of the festival. Agnes had sewn them each a new petticoat and a red kerchief, even though Madeleine would raise a critical brow at a servant wearing a color usually reserved to her betters. Ursule replaced her customary smock with a shirtwaist. She tried to tame her cloud of unruly hair but was too impatient to comb out all the tangles. As she tied the kerchief around her shoulders she felt a little foolish, as if she were wearing a costume not her own, but it was nice to see her mother's approving smile.

As Chou Chou pulled the cart along the road to the village, the bonfire glowed a lurid invitation against the twilight sky, red and bronze flames reflecting on shreds of cloud. Agnes, never easy with fires, clutched at Ursule's arm when she saw it. Ursule patted her hand and tucked it under her elbow to reassure her.

Two other farm families joined them to make a small procession. By the time Remy pulled the cart into a spot beside a half-dozen others, and Ursule settled Chou Chou with a feed of hay and a bucket of water, the fire had begun to burn down. The air was rich with the scents of roasting pork and baking apples, blending with the yeasty sweetness of the Michaelmas cakes arranged on the baker's table. The folk of Keranna were not wealthy—except for the *vicomte* and his family—but at festivals, they celebrated as if they were, and even Ursule felt the wave

of good cheer. The festivals were the only times she felt the spirit of th
people, the only times they seemed as vital and alive as the Romani.

Remy was pulled into a group of laughing men, drinking th
vicomte's ale and swapping stories. Madeleine joined a group of othe
farmwives, all of them dressed in their best petticoats and brightly col
ored stomachers, with bonnets kept pristine for the occasion. Agnes anc
Ursule, like other servants, wandered around the edges of the crowd
taking turns at a few bites of roasted pork, a slice of baked apple. A few
women spoke greetings to Agnes and nodded to Ursule as they did a
church. The only one who spoke to her was Arlette, the barmaid at th
tavern. In the hierarchy of the village, she was the closest to an equa
Ursule had.

Ursule was Remy's dairymaid, of course, but she was also his woman
of all work, and that meant other women didn't know what to say tc
her. The men mostly ignored her, embarrassed by a woman who dic
the same work they did, as if her ability to wield a scythe or repair a car
diminished them in some way.

After twenty years, Ursule had no expectation that anything woulc
change. Still, she couldn't help a wistful glance at a little knot of womer
close to her own age, some with babies on their hips. Their heads ben
together with the familiarity of friendship, of common interests. One
of them looked a bit like Bettina, or the way she supposed Bettina
might look now, her body grown thicker with childbearing, her bosom
fuller, her face harder. Older.

But not as old, Ursule was certain, as she herself looked. Her skin
had been weathered by sun and wind, and her hair had begun to gray.
She wriggled her shoulders to shake off the thought. Agnes gave her
a questioning glance and made a gesture, her fingers sliding across her
forehead. *Tired?*

Ursule shook her head. "No, no, Maman, I'm fine. Let's get some
Michaelmas cakes before we have to start for home."

They turned together, arm in arm, to go to the bakery, but as they
drew close to the shop, Agnes abruptly stopped. She tore her arm from

Ursule's, lifted her skirts in both hands, and hurried away, circling the dwindling crowd toward the waiting cart. Ursule glanced toward the bakery to see what had frightened her mother.

His black cassock and flat hat stood out among the bright waistcoats of the other men, the lace and embroidery of the women. He was a slight, unremarkable-looking person. Ursule thought he had rather a kind face. He was the parish priest, one who seemed to have been pressed into his profession rather than being drawn to it. She was used to him. Agnes was not. She would flee from any priest, even as mild a one as Father Favreau.

He had just taken a bite out of a Michaelmas cake when he caught sight of Ursule. He shifted the cake to his left hand and touched his cap with his right. *"Bonjour, mademoiselle."*

He seemed to her less patronizing than the other men, although he must know how low her status was.

"Bonjour, père." She smiled at him, trying not to look at the sugar that clung to his wispy beard. She focused instead on his carved pectoral cross as she dropped a curtsy.

Aside from the statues, Father Favreau was her favorite thing about the chapel of St. Anne. His speaking of the Mass was all but inaudible, leaving her to think her own thoughts undisturbed. His manner was gentle, unlike the rough farmers or loud businessmen of the village. She couldn't imagine him leading a pack of witch hunters, although she supposed he was expected to believe the same things they did. He read from the same book and said the words of the Mass. He must, she guessed, be obedient to the bishop, and that bishop, if the tales were true, liked nothing better than a witch burning.

An older woman stepped in front of Ursule as if she were invisible and began to chatter to Father Favreau. Ursule moved away, relieved at not having to make small talk. She had no gift for it. Now, just as in her girlhood, it irritated her. She was happy to leave it to others.

As she paid a few *livres* for cakes for herself and her mother, she spotted a broadside tacked to the outer wall of the bakery. She tucked the cakes into her basket and walked around the display table to see it.

The voice at her shoulder startled her. "Shall I read it for you, *mademoiselle?*"

It was Father Favreau. She could read it perfectly well for herself, but farmworkers didn't read. She didn't want yet another thing to make her different.

She said, *"Merci, père,"* and moved aside so he could peer at the printed sheet.

He traced the letters with his finger, his lips moving as he sounded them out. "Ah," he said. "An amusement is coming, a troupe of jongleurs and acrobats." Ursule had to wait in polite silence as the priest puzzled out the rest of the words. "Two days from now." He straightened and gave her an avuncular smile. "Perhaps your master will allow you to attend?"

She gave a diffident shrug. "I'm afraid not. I will have the milking. Stock to feed."

"Ah, yes. The work is never done, is it?" The priest touched the brim of his black hat once more before he strolled off toward the dying bonfire.

The evening was gathering in, folding the village in its autumn chill. Men's voices faded as the cask of ale ran dry, and women were gathering their children to go home. It was time to go back to the cart. Ursule paused to take a last look at the broadside first, noting the flourishes of script, the inevitable misspellings, and the clumsy sketch depicting an acrobat upside down in the air in front of a trio of musicians. The date was written by hand, with drops of ink scattering across the paper.

The last time Ursule had heard any music had been in Belz, when the Romani sang around their bonfire, and Sandor had played his flute on the village green. No one in Keranna, as far as she knew, played any instrument, at least not in her hearing. Remembering Sandor and his *nai* flute stirred a vague longing in her. She leaned closer to the sketch, squinting to see it in the fading light.

One of the trio had a drum of some kind tucked under his arm. Another, wearing either a dress or a long frock coat, held a stringed instrument, a lute perhaps.

The third, his head bent to play, held a flute in his hands. A *nai* flute, with its distinctive curved arrangement of tubes.

Ursule's heart suspended its beat while she tried to absorb what she was seeing.

It wasn't a good drawing, and there could be other players of the *nai* flute in France, but—but here? Paris, perhaps, or Orléans—but Keranna?

She felt the warmth of a body behind her and turned, thinking Father Favreau had come back, but it was Agnes, rejoining her now that the priest had left. She leaned close to the broadsheet as the priest had done, peering at it.

"It's for an amusement," Ursule said. "Coming here in two days."

Agnes tapped the crude figure of the flute player with her finger, then tapped her own temple. *I remember him.*

"You mean Sandor? It might not be him," Ursule said. Her mother tapped her temple again. Ursule sighed. "It doesn't matter anyway. I wouldn't be able to get away. It's two days from now, and it's in the late afternoon. I'll be milking. Sweeping the byre. Feeding the chickens."

Agnes showed her teeth in a silent grin and pointed to herself. Ursule pressed her fingers to her lips, considering. She should refuse, of course. It would be selfish even to ask, but...

She wanted so much to come. She wanted to know if this odd little picture could mean Sandor was the flutist, if that meant he would be here, in Keranna. She wanted to know if he would remember her, after all this time.

And she could return his knife.

⋯⋅⋅ ⟡•⟡ ⋅⋅⋯

Remy, in his easygoing way, granted Ursule's request to let Agnes do the evening milking. He even winked at her, saying, "Good for you to have a little fun, Ursule. Little enough out here with no visitors and no young people. I'll keep an eye on your mother, make sure it goes well." She thanked him as warmly as she knew how. He added, "Might have a problem with Madeleine, though."

She nodded acceptance of this warning, but she wasn't worried. She had already taken care of it. She had renewed the simple to sweeten Madeleine's mood, mixing it into a cup of cider and offering it to her as she labored over the bricks of butter.

Ursule scrubbed her hands and face as thoroughly as she could and tied a clean scarf over her hair. The autumn weather had turned frosty, so she had to wear her ancient coat, but beneath it she wore a new petticoat and kerchief, and she touched her throat with a bit of lavender water in hopes she wouldn't smell too much like the byre.

She wrapped the knife in folds of linen and laid it in her basket. Of course, the flutist might be not be Sandor at all, but she had reason to think it would be.

She had dreamed it. Her dream had shown him playing on the little green, with the shops and houses of Keranna behind him, his autumn eyes gleaming in the last of the sun, and his pretty instrument glowing as its wistful music curled across the drying grass. In her dream, she had stood before him, speaking his name, reaching out her hand to touch him.

She had woken with her body throbbing with longing and her hand stretching outside her blanket, searching for his in the cold dawn air. She tucked her empty hand back into the warmth of her bed, embarrassed by her weakness, glad her mother was asleep. She was silently scolding herself, telling herself it was just a dream, when a familiar voice spoke to her.

It was the voice of One-eyed Violca. The same one she had heard when she and Agnes fled from Belz. The same one that had spoken to her when she found the ruined caravan. *Never dismiss a witch's dream.*

Still, she wondered as she walked toward the village on the day of the entertainment. Was it possible? It seemed too good to be true.

She had almost reached the green when she heard the thrum of a lute, the soft pound of a drum, the hollow notes of a *nai* flute. She paused at the edge of the small crowd that had gathered to listen to the music, and to watch two acrobats in garish tights and tunics leap and tumble across the grass. As in her dream, the last of the sun glistened over everything. The villagers clapped and shouted and shifted back and forth for better views. A half-dozen laughing girls danced in front of the musicians, white petticoats swirling.

The trio had taken up a spot of ground near the cold remains of the Michaelmas bonfire. The scent of burned wood still hung in the air, and two small boys were stamping through the mound of ash, making clouds of it swirl around their knees. The drummer, a scrawny man of perhaps fifty, perched on a three-legged stool with his drum between his knees. The lutenist was smaller, a woman, but plump, with graying hair twisted up out of the way of her instrument. She leaned back in a straight chair, the lute nestled into her skirts, the neck of it stretching past her shoulder. She plucked the strings with clumsy fingers, her notes often at odds with the melody.

The flutist stood a little apart, his head bent, his long fingers splayed over the tubes of his instrument. His slender body swayed with the rhythm of the tune, and his flat belly expanded and contracted as he breathed.

Ursule had forgotten how tall he was, how silky his hair, how pale his skin. His shoulders had broadened in the intervening years, and his arms had added muscle. A man now, in the place of the slender, beautiful boy. His music had matured, too, the tone stronger, more carrying, the timbre sweet and piercing at the same time.

She watched him breathe, and nearly forgot to breathe herself. She listened to his music, and the rest of the world faded from her awareness. As he finished the tune and lifted his head, she saw his fine features, his thick fair brows, his clear jawline, and a warmth began in her toes.

The years had treated him more gently than they had herself, and she remembered the afternoon they had spent together, the way he had listened to her, talked to her, made her feel as if she mattered.

And of course, the way he had saved her from the brutal assault of Dukkar Vila, and been forced to flee because of it.

The warmth spread from her toes up through her body, on into her chest and throat. It burned in her cheeks, bringing a flood of emotion she had not prepared for.

It seemed she had missed most of the performance. As the audience applauded, the acrobats spun closer to the musicians, and when they straightened, the entertainers all bowed together. Ursule stood still, watching the girls who giggled as they dropped coins into the basket at Sandor's feet. They chattered at him, making him blush and duck his head. They postured and posed, vying for his attention, obviously unaware he couldn't see them.

Those girls made Ursule feel as old as the *grands-mères* sitting to one side in their black skirts and caps. She hesitated, wondering if she should even try to speak to Sandor. He might not remember her. Or he might remember her, and wish she had not reminded him of that terrible day, surely the worst of his life. It had been such a long time, and he had no reason to think of her as she thought of him.

But she had come all this way, had magicked Madeleine to keep her from interfering, had allowed her mother to work in her place. It would be cowardice not to approach him, and she would never admit to being a coward. She set her teeth and pushed through the group of girls until she stood right in front of him.

He was wrapping his flute, tucking it inside his scarlet shirt, bending to feel for his hat on the ground. Ursule waited until he straightened, breathing slowly to ease the thudding of her heart. His nearness set her body tingling with its own kind of magic, a different kind of magic.

She had not felt this twenty years ago. She had liked him, liked his music, liked talking with him, had even felt an innocent thrill at the touch of his hand. She had been so young, just a girl, and he only a little older. Now she was a woman grown, honed and hardened by experience, and this surge of desire was both intoxicating and perilous. She swallowed, girding herself for disappointment.

He was pulling on his hat, a black one with a drooping brim, when Ursule said, "Sandor."

He froze, one hand still on the hat, the other pressed to his heart.

"Sandor, you may not remember me. I am—"

He exclaimed, "But it's Ursule! Of course I remember. Your voice is deeper, a bit, but—you are Ursule Orchière, are you not?"

Relief made her voice shake. "I am. It's good to see you, Sandor. You look well. Prosperous."

He smiled, and she remembered how rare were his smiles, how charming the dimple that appeared in his left cheek. He was smooth-shaven, and the dimple had survived the years.

"I am well. As to prosperous—" He laughed a little and patted his chest where the flute was secure under his shirt. "At least I have steady work, even a few students here and there."

His eyes, those lovely blind eyes, searched for her. She put out her hand with a shiver of anticipation, just as she had done in her dream, and when his smooth, soft fingers touched her rough ones, when she felt the welcome pressure of them as he took her hand in both of his, her own eyes stung with unexpected tears.

"Ursule Orchière," he said, somber now, the dimple fading. "I never thought to find you here. Keranna is very far from Belz."

"Yes." Her voice cracked, and she cleared her throat.

"And you're well? How do you happen to be here?"

"I'm well, yes. We've been here twenty years."

"We?"

"My mother and I."

"You don't travel anymore?"

"No, we—no. Not now."

He gripped her hand harder. "It wasn't because of me, was it? Because of—" His voice dropped low, and his hand tightened on hers. "Because of what I did?"

"No," she said hastily. "It was nothing to do with that."

He eased the pressure on her hand and released a long, tight breath. "I worried so about that. Wondered if you were all right."

A thrill ran through her at his kindness, his concern for her. "I was. That is, as all right as I could be, after—after everything."

She took his arm, though it might seem she was holding him in place. She was, in a way. She didn't want him to say goodbye, to walk away from her.

She gathered her courage. "Do you have a little time? A cup of cider, perhaps, for old times' sake? Or maybe you would prefer ale."

The dimple flashed. He said, "A cup of ale would be welcome." To Ursule, the ordinary words felt like a caress.

The eyes of the village girls followed as Ursule put her hand under Sandor's elbow to guide him toward the tavern. Her neck burned at the murmurs, the sniffs, the ripples of laughter. They resented her, those girls, resented seeing her walk off with the object of their interest. Another time she might have snapped at them for their rudeness, but not this time. This was a moment for herself, and she didn't want to spoil it.

The tavern was crowded with men in loose coats and flat caps, their masculine voices rattling out into the peaceful twilight. Arlette, the barmaid, caught sight of Ursule and Sandor and came to say they would have to sit outside. "The master don't let women in here, Ursule," she said. She smoothed her stained apron over her ample hips as she nodded toward a rough wooden table set up outside the tavern. It had the simplest of benches to sit on, a plank balanced on two tree stumps, but it was serviceable. "You can sit there."

"We will, thank you," Ursule said. "A cup of ale and one of cider, if you please."

Arlette nodded and disappeared into the crowd as Ursule led Sandor to sit at the table. The village girls passed close by the tavern, chattering together, smirking when they saw Ursule sitting with Sandor. For one unworthy moment, Ursule was glad he couldn't compare her sunburned face with their pale cheeks, her calloused hands with their fine ones, her thicket of hair with their smooth locks.

Arlette came back as the girls walked on and wrinkled her nose at their backs. "There's some empty heads due for trouble," she said. "Such as them could use a job to do, you ask me."

"*Bien sûr,*" Ursule said.

"Idle hands," Arlette said. "Wait till they have four babes to raise, like me." She set their drinks on the table. "Careful. It wobbles." She gave Ursule a grin, and Ursule felt a little lift of encouragement.

She steadied the table with her elbow and pushed Sandor's cup of ale into his hand. He picked it up and took a long draft. The scent of barley and malt swirled from it, and she saw his nostrils flare in appreciation.

He felt for the surface of the table with his free hand before he set his cup down. "Those were the girls from a little while ago," he said.

"You recognize their voices, too."

"Yes. There's usually a bunch like that, whenever we play."

"They love your music."

"Mostly I think they're bored. Looking for excitement."

"They're laughing at me, sitting here with you, because they're girls from good families, and I'm only a farm laborer."

"Are you?" He looked down at her in that uncanny way of his, as if he could actually see her face. "That sounds hard."

"Sometimes. I like working with livestock. Goats, cows. Chickens." She sipped the cider and found it thin and a bit sour. The Kerjean cider was much better. She had used a charm to sweeten the apples.

Sandor said, "Your *maman* no longer tells fortunes?"

"No!" He blinked at the force of her voice, and she said, more quietly, "Sorry. I didn't mean to snap, but—no. We don't speak of that, ever."

His fair eyebrows arched. "Something happened? Is that why you—"

"Sandor, I can't talk about it. Truly." Sandor couldn't know the story of Agnes being branded a witch, and she didn't want to tell him. One misplaced word could bring the witch hunters after them, even after all this time. *Some secrets should be kept.*

"You can trust me." Sandor took another drink of ale, nearly draining the cup. "You know my secret, after all. You're the only one in the world who does."

"Except Maman," she said softly. "I had to tell her, but we never told anyone else. You can trust her absolutely, because—well—" She didn't mean to say it, but as he waited for her to finish, his autumn eyes glowing through the dimness, her resolve faltered. Agnes's muteness was, after all, not a secret. "My mother no longer speaks."

He frowned. "Do you mean—she no longer speaks—at all?"

"Not at all."

"But, Ursule—how strange!"

"It is, I suppose. I'm used to it now."

"I don't understand. What happened?"

"She suffered a terrible shock. It stole her voice. Forever, it seems."

He fell silent, his long fingers toying with his cup, his chin tucked in a manner that seemed protective. "I lost my sight when I was six," he said in a low voice. "Also forever, I suppose. I always hoped it might return."

Ursule's throat tightened as she imagined Sandor, only six years old, facing life in the darkness. She had to swallow before she asked gently, "Did you also suffer a shock?"

"An accident." He lifted one hand to his temple, and pushed back a strand of hair. Beneath it was a thick, angry scar, several shades darker than his skin.

"Oh! What happened?"

"I was working with my father—he was a stonemason—and I fell against the hearth he was building." He blew out a breath. "That's what he always said, that I fell. The truth is, I broke a stone he had just finished cutting, and he slapped me for it. Knocked my head into the hearth." He drank the last of his ale and set it down with force, a gesture that surprised her in such a gentle man. "I was blinded, immediately. I couldn't work the stone after that. I was—" He spread his hands. "I was useless."

Ursule burst out her first thought. "Useless? At six?"

"So my father said. I was fortunate to have been left my grandfather's flute. The only time my mother ever stood up to my father was when she refused to let him sell it. I left home when the Vilas found me, and I've made my living with the flute ever since."

"Hardly useless, then," Ursule said firmly.

"Unless you think music is useless," he muttered.

She didn't need to hear him say that his father thought music was useless. She wanted to touch his hand, but she wasn't sure such a gesture would be welcome. There were tears in his voice, and she felt instinctively he would be ashamed of them.

"I'm so sorry," she murmured. "About all of it."

Arlette appeared beside their crooked table and pointed to their cups. "Another?"

"I can't," Sandor said. "I need to find Lisette and Armel."

Ursule felt the bite of the cooling air and looked up to see that darkness had closed around the village, swiftly, as it often did at this time of year, as if an unseen hand had drawn a curtain. Reluctantly, she pulled on her coat, but there was still so much she wanted to know. "Did the boat take you to Lorient, Sandor? Did you go home?"

Sandor blew a long breath and palmed his chest. She recognized it as a habitual gesture, making certain his precious flute was where it was supposed to be. Ursule thought the flute must be an object of comfort to him, as the scrying stone was to her. He said, "You remember about the boat."

"I remember everything. I remember the afternoon we spent, and I remember—the other thing—in every detail."

His hand groped across the table, and she slipped hers into it. She knew, when he was gone, that she would savor the memory of the touch of his skin, the grip of his smooth hand on her rough one.

He said, "I always swore I wouldn't be a violent man like my father, but—then that happened."

"It doesn't matter now," she said. "It's forgotten by everyone, except you and me."

"I made a terrible mistake, though," he said. "It haunts me."

"A mistake? You saved me, Sandor. I have blessed you a thousand times for that."

"That wasn't the mistake." He shook his head. "The mistake was to leave my knife. My Spanish dagger. It's distinctive. Someone could trace it to me."

"They won't," she said with assurance.

"How can you know that? The sheriff, there in Belz—"

"They won't because I have it."

"You have it?" he whispered.

"Maman retrieved it for me, so no one would find it, so you would be safe."

"But that's—what a brave thing for her to do!"

"She did it because you saved me." Ursule fumbled in her basket for the knife and brought it out, still wrapped in linen. She laid the knife across Sandor's palm. "Now. It's done. You can put it out of your mind."

He folded his fingers around the knife and traced its shape with his other hand. "Ursule—"

An unfamiliar voice spoke from the darkness, interrupting him. "Sandor! We're off. Come along, or you'll never find your way."

He turned his head in the direction of the voice. "It's Lisette and Armel. The lutenist and the drummer. They're off to the inn where we're staying."

Sandor rose as the drummer came closer. Armel was no taller than Ursule, as slight as a child, but with an old man's face. He said, "Sandor, we have to go. We'll miss our dinner."

Sandor rose, tucking the knife into his shirt next to his flute. He said, "Ursule, how will you get home?"

"I'll walk. It only takes an hour."

"I wish I could escort you."

"It's fine." A tightness grew in her chest at the imminence of their farewell, but she made herself take a step away. "It was good to see you."

"Ursule, wait."

Armel called again, "Sandor, *on y va!* Dinner."

Tension stretched between the three of them, Ursule yearning to keep Sandor at her side, Sandor's eyes searching for her, Armel impatient, shifting from foot to foot. Ursule said, "Will you be back? I'll come to see you again."

He was already walking toward Armel but spoke over his shoulder. "We're back at Christmas. Will you be here?"

She answered, her voice torn between a bitter laugh and the tears that were soon to come, "Oh, yes. I'll be here." *I'm always here.*

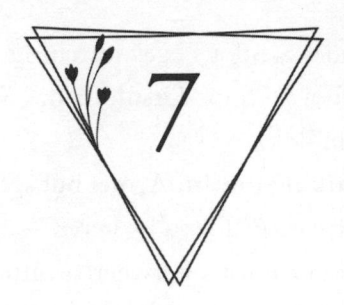

Preparing for winter absorbed everyone at Kerjean Farm. Agnes was busy drying the last of the tomatoes and apples and preserving gooseberries and figs in brandy syrup. Remy had to forgo his daily naps in the hurry to mend the roof of the byre and fill the haymow for the cold months ahead. Ursule chopped wood and stacked it behind the farmhouse and beside the wall of the cottage, while Madeleine salted meat and wrapped it in greased canvas to store in the buttery.

Samhain came and went unnoticed, swallowed up by the Christian All Hallows' celebration at St. Anne and the intensity of the work to be done. The bustle didn't begin to slow until December, when other preparations began. The scents of simmering almonds wafted from Madeleine's kitchen, the first ingredient for her yearly batch of marzipan. She would mold it into tiny figures, miniature pigs and lambs and goats to be given out to the children at Christmas. Agnes had sewing orders to fulfill, new petticoats and shawls, and some of the stiff white bonnets favored by the women of Keranna. Remy cut piles of evergreen boughs to be loaded into the cart and hauled to the chapel. Ursule scoured the countryside for the clouds of mistletoe hanging in poplar trees.

In the Breton tradition, twigs of mistletoe were dispensed as goodluck charms, but Ursule kept a few back. She had a special use for them.

She was glad to be busy. It kept her from counting down the days until Sandor's troupe returned. She often dreamed of him at night, aching, wistful dreams from which she woke yearning for him in both body and soul. Was this love? Or was it simply wanting, because he talked to her, listened to her, as no one else did? She didn't know if there was a difference.

Her mother had coaxed her to describe her meeting with Sandor, but Ursule found it difficult to put into words. She and her mother were practical women. Agnes's family had married her off to an old man, and Agnes had never, to Ursule's knowledge, fallen in love. Ursule herself had been born with a cynical disregard for the notion of romance, and it surprised her to understand that her mother wanted her to have one.

"We just sat outside the tavern, Maman," she said.

Agnes nodded, and wiggled her fingers for more details. *Go on. Tell me.*

"There's not much to tell," Ursule said, avoiding her mother's eyes. "It was good to see him. We talked a bit. I returned his knife, and he was grateful." She felt the intensity of her mother's need to hear something hopeful, something good, and she felt for one brief moment that she was once again the daughter, the little one, to be cared for and encouraged by the mother. "He'll be back the day after Christmas," she finally admitted. "The troupe is going to entertain at the St. Stephen's Day fete."

Agnes touched her empty ring finger. *Married?*

"No. Not married."

Agnes's face lighted with a fox-like grin, and she tapped Ursule's own ringless finger.

Ursule pulled her hand back. "No, Maman, I don't think so. He travels all the time, and I work here so you and I can have a safe place to live. I don't think marriage is possible—and I don't know if he would want it."

Her mother startled her by jumping up from the table where they were sitting, scurrying into the bedroom, and returning with the grimoire. She set it on the table with a thump and tapped it with her fingers.

Ursule gave a disbelieving laugh. "Maman! You don't really think I should magick him?"

Agnes smiled again, shrugged, and spread her hands, palms up. *Why not?*

Ursule chewed on a finger, unable to come up with an answer. She took a surreptitious glance at the crystal in its basket, to see if the *grands-mères* had an opinion on the matter. A faint light flickered uneasily through the linen cover.

It seemed they did.

· · · · · ᵚᵚᵚᵚ · ᵚᵚᵚᵚ · · · · ·

That night, Ursule turned pages in the oldest section of the grimoire, the part that was in Old French. She could make out the words, and they seemed familiar, but only one in three or four spoke to her. She felt as if she were peering at them through an obscuring mist, with only occasional glimpses of their meaning. She turned from page to page, scowling, struggling to understand.

She feared that her gift for language, like the stone itself, had lain dormant too long. The people of Keranna spoke mostly Breton, except for the priest, who spoke in ungrammatical French, and Remy, who peppered his Breton with French expressions. Ursule sat with the grimoire for hours, long past the time she should have been in bed, and when her gift finally awoke from its slumbers, it was like the sun emerging from a bank of cloud. The meaning of the words came clear, all at once, her old talent reasserting itself. She found what she sought a moment later:

A Philter to persuade the reluctant Lover

She read it through, and read it again, then closed the book with a feeling of satisfaction. Though she told herself she wouldn't use it, it was good to know it was there, and that she had understood it.

In the following weeks, she tried not to think of it again, but it was impossible to forget. It haunted her when she couldn't sleep at night, and distracted her as she did the milking, as she churned the butter, as she wielded the ax and stacked the firewood. Her thoughts spun in circles like those the marsh harriers carved in the sky, wheeling and wheeling above the earth. Was Sandor a reluctant lover? Was he a lover at all? Could the philter turn him into one? She had no one to answer her questions. No one to teach her. She was, as always, teaching herself.

Sometimes she convinced herself that if she left things well enough alone, what was between them, if anything, would come right. Then she would fuss about not having time, that he would be off again almost before they started. Their next meeting could be as brief as their last.

Perhaps she should do nothing. Perhaps she should go on just as she was, forever. Or perhaps her mother was right, and she should seize her moment. Use her power.

Her inner struggle angered her sometimes. Men made their own choices, all the time—even blind men. Why should she, a woman, not take what she wanted?

Of course, she didn't know the power of the philter. She had learned enough, self-taught witch though she was, to understand that the effects of magic could be unpredictable. She didn't know if the philter would last, or even if it would work at all.

It was Madeleine who brought her to a decision. Madeleine wanted a wreath for her door. She sent Ursule out into the woods to cut holly, then stood over her, giving instructions, as she twisted and tied the prickly branches into a circle. The thorns pricked tiny scarlet drops from her fingers.

Madeleine, seeing, said, "Just like Our Lord, Ursule!"

"What?"

"There's good luck for you. The holly is the Crown of Thorns, remember?" Ursule didn't, but she nodded. "We leave the berries on to symbolize Our Lord bleeding from the thorns. You're all ready for the Passion!" She laughed as she gave Ursule a clean rag to wipe her hands.

Ursule remembered the Passion, because it was the part of the Catholic practice that most mystified her. The Passion Play acted out the death of their god in a bloody scene with an ugly ending. The

Resurrection followed, which made sense, because Easter coincided with the spring equinox, the time of rebirth, of new beginnings and fresh starts. Nevertheless, the images the Catholics worshipped in their crucifixes and paintings all seemed to be of the dead god, not the risen one.

Madeleine said, with a beneficent air, "There's holly left over, Ursule. Why don't you take it to the cottage? Make a Christmas wreath for yourself and your mother."

Ursule thanked her and accepted the offer. For them it would be a Yule wreath, from a far older tradition than the one Madeleine followed. The Yule wreath symbolized the Wheel of the Year. The holly berries represented fertility and life, not blood and death.

That was the Goddess's practice.

As she finished her own wreath, one of the berries fell into her hand, a cheerful spot of scarlet in her palm. She gazed at it, the bright, tiny promise of new life to come, and felt a twinge in her womb, where no life had grown.

Perhaps it was not too late. Perhaps she could have a daughter to pass the craft to after all.

·····◈≫≫≫·◈≪≪≪◈·····

Take three leaves and two flowers of coltsfoot, along with an inch of the root; add three inches of lovage root, well dried; flowers of lady's mantle; three spikes of mullein; and a twig of mistletoe, crushed. Mix with water that has been boiled and cooled, and let rest on the altar until the morning star rises.

Ursule found coltsfoot growing on the bank of the stream bordering the farm, and lovage root at the back of Agnes's garden. Lady's mantle grew everywhere, as did mullein, and she had already collected mistletoe. She tucked everything into a lidded basket to wait.

On the day of Yule, three days before the Christmas vigil at St.

Anne, Ursule and Agnes planned a quiet celebration. They ate their supper of stew and *pufe*, and Ursule went to fetch the scrying stone from its basket. A knock at the door made them both startle and gaze at each other uneasily. They rarely had visitors, and never at night.

Hastily, Ursule settled the crystal back into its basket and covered it. Agnes, once the stone was hidden, opened the door.

Remy, looking enormous in his heavy winter coat, stood on their doorstep. He carried a small object in his hands, wrapped in one of Madeleine's kitchen napkins. Agnes stared at him, openmouthed. He had never come to the cottage in all the years they had lived here.

Ursule hurried forward. "Remy? Is everything all right?"

"Yes, fine," he said. "Just thought you and Agnes might like a bit of Christmas cake."

"Why, Remy—" Ursule accepted his offering, and stood awkwardly, not knowing what to do or say. "It's—this is a surprise. Uh—uh, *Joyeux Noël.*"

"*Joyeux Noël,*" he said gruffly. He nodded to Agnes, including her in his greeting. "Been here a long time, you two. Don't know what we'd do without you. And it's Christmas."

Agnes came to Ursule's side to take the cake from her hands. She dropped a tiny curtsy to Remy before carrying the gift to the counter.

"*Merci,*" Ursule said, feeling awkward. "Please thank Madeleine for me—for us."

"People are fond of her baked things."

"Yes, I know they are."

Remy seemed to feel as awkward as she did. They didn't usually meet in any social way. He shoved his hands in his pockets and made a gesture with his bearded chin toward the winter sky. "Smells like snow."

"It does."

"*Alors.*" There was something in his face, in his eyes, she hadn't seen before. It made her wonder if she had ever looked at him very closely. Or listened to him. "Madeleine, you know," he said, in a clumsy fashion, as if he wasn't used to talking about his wife. "Madeleine always wanted children. Not having them makes her sad, and that makes her angry."

"Ah," Ursule said. "I understand. A great disappointment for her."

"Worse at Christmastide," he said bluntly. "She gives out those little sweets to the children at St. Anne, then comes home and cries."

This revelation rendered Ursule nearly as wordless as her mother. Finally, she managed, inadequately, "I'm sorry, Remy."

Remy shifted his shoulders. "*Eh bien*. Too late now for us."

It was a strange moment. They had worked together for twenty years without ever speaking of anything that wasn't to do with the farm or the livestock. Ursule wanted to say the right thing, to show sympathy, but she was no better at small talk than Remy. Finally, she blurted, "I imagine that makes you sad, too."

His face colored, and he coughed to cover his embarrassment, and shifted his feet. He said, "*Eh bien. Alors.* Ursule, Agnes. *Bonsoir...*" and was gone, lumbering across the yard to the farmhouse.

Thoughtfully, Ursule closed the door behind him and put her back to it. "How sad, Maman! If he had told me this before—even ten years ago—I could have done something. I might have helped Madeleine conceive."

Her mother nodded again, and wriggled her hand past her shoulder. *Too late now.*

"So I gather." Ursule went to lift the napkin and sniff the sweet, fruit-stuffed cake inside. "But we have a Yule cake. Perhaps it's an omen."

She and Agnes grinned at each other in mutual understanding. They were Romani, after all. They believed in omens.

·····ᐅᐅᐅᐅ·ᐊᐊᐊᐊ·····

For the three days remaining until the Christmas vigil, Ursule tried to be more considerate of Madeleine, but her mistress didn't make it easy. She was impatient with everything: the paucity of goat's milk, the speed of Ursule's churning, the clumps of snow Remy tramped into her kitchen, and as always, Agnes's refusal to speak when she was spoken to.

Because of the demands of the farm, Ursule was spared the long, dark service of the Christmas vigil. She tacked up Chou Chou, helped Remy and Madeleine load the last of the evergreens for St. Anne, and settled them in the cart with a fur robe over their legs against the icy air. They rattled off into the darkness, not to return until at least two in the morning, leaving her free to perform her rite.

With her mother by her side, the altar protected with a circle of salt water and set with four new candles, she uncovered the scrying stone and set a small pottery bowl with her prepared herbs beside it. She had already boiled the water. She and Agnes wore their veils, the bleached linen glowing like moonlight in the dim cottage. Ursule lighted all four candles, then recited the opening rite with a special intensity:

We vow to pass the craft to our daughters so long as our line endures.

Her eyes met her mother's as she spoke the words, and Agnes nodded in understanding. She made a gesture, lifting her hand and spreading the fingers. *If the Goddess wills.*

Ursule poured the water into the pottery bowl and stirred the herbs until they softened and dissolved. She had tied dried stems of white sage into a bundle, and she dipped the tip of it into one of the candle flames and let it burn as an offering to the Goddess. As its sweet smoke swirled above her altar, she hesitated for just a moment, gazing into the scrying stone.

Agnes leaned toward her and touched her elbow. She lifted one palm. *What is it?*

"I'm not sure." Ursule breathed in the scent of the sage and the other herbs, searching in her heart one last time for whether it was fair to command Sandor's love rather than waiting for it to come to her.

But soon she would be like Madeleine, a crone. Soon her chance at motherhood would pass her by. Her chance at ensuring that the Orchière line endured.

Agnes pointed to the crystal. *Look.*

Ursule peered into the stone. It was glowing faintly, as it always did when she performed a rite. Her mother pointed again, with a little shake of her forefinger. *Look closer.*

Ursule bent closer, and looked again. It was rather like standing in the darkness, looking into a lighted window. She saw a brighter spot in the stone, and within the brightness, a face.

A girl's face. A beautiful face, with a halo of fair hair, fine features, autumn eyes.

It was her daughter. Sandor's daughter. A child to inherit the crystal, to carry on the Orchière traditions.

Ursule straightened, and the words she needed sprang to her mind. She stretched her arm out over the altar, aware of her mother's eyes gleaming with satisfaction as she pronounced her rite:

With a witch's power, I command
This potion now beneath my hand
To draw my one true love to me
And bring my precious child to be.

Three times three times she spoke her intention, as the grimoire instructed. The candles flamed up, and the crystal glimmered. Ursule's womb throbbed with energy, radiating into her chest and thighs, her throat, her feet, her forehead. Her outstretched arm grew tired, but she hardly noticed. Her body trembled, not with weakness but with strength, the power of her ancestresses amplified by the crystal, directed by her words.

The cottage itself seemed to thrum with magic, as if a mighty wind had blown in through its window and down its chimney. When the scrying stone exploded with light, Ursule feared for an instant that the crystal itself had shattered.

Her arm relaxed slowly to her side. Agnes covered her face with her hands, the light too bright to bear. The potion in its pottery bowl swirled and eddied as if stirred by an invisible finger. The candles, half-burned, went out with tiny puffs of smoke that evaporated instantly in the cold air. The scrying stone dimmed swiftly, and by the time Agnes dropped her hands from her face, there was only the cool gray crystal, reflecting the faint slant of starlight from beyond the window.

For a time, both women were silent. Ursule found herself breathing hard. Her mother clasped her hands before her, her eyes glinting in the darkness. The air around them began to settle and grow calm, until the night felt like any other, dark and cold and silent.

Ursule was just about to pull off her linen veil when Violca's voice sounded in her ear: *Have a care. The Goddess always exacts her price.*

8

With the philter in a wax-stoppered jar in the pocket of her coat, Ursule set out with Madeleine and Remy for the St. Stephen's Day fete. Her mother had brushed her hair for her, fussed with her clothes, patted her cheek in encouragement. Ursule had hugged her, then hurried out to climb into the back of the cart, one hand in her pocket to steady the precious jar. The December day was brilliant with cold sunshine that glittered on frozen puddles and glinted from frosted treetops.

As the cart jounced toward Keranna on the ice-rutted road, her heart juddered with anxiety. It hardly seemed possible the long-awaited day had finally arrived, and she found a thousand things to worry about.

What if Sandor hadn't come? Anything could have happened to prevent him. What if he didn't want to have a drink with her, or spend any time at all? What if she spilled the potion before she could administer it, or what if she poured it into his ale and then he didn't drink it?

The greatest worry was the one she had still not resolved: what if she was making a mistake? Some part of her conscience struggled to be heard, whimpering from its corner like an abandoned kitten. She both did and didn't want to know what it was trying to tell her.

The plaintive sound of Sandor's music reached her before she saw him, and the weak complaint of her conscience fell silent. She climbed down from the cart, hastily telling Remy not to wait for her, that she would walk home, then hurried toward the source of the music without waiting for a response. She stopped at the edge of the green where the trio was playing and clasped her hands together to stop their excited trembling. Her stomach contracted at the sight of his fair head bent over his flute, his elegant fingers on the instrument. She longed to stroke the line of his jaw. She yearned to circle his lean waist with her arms, and press her cheek to his chest.

Her body ached with need. She wanted him. In every way. At any price.

She stood listening to the trio play while the acrobats tumbled across the green. Several stalls ranged around the space, selling cider and roasted chestnuts and spiced apples. The villagers wore their holiday clothes, bright blue or vivid scarlet waistcoats and stomachers under their winter coats. The shop windows were trimmed with evergreens and featured elaborate crèches in place of their usual wares. Madeleine, with her basket of marzipan figures, smiled for once as children lined up to beg for one.

Ursule waited until the trio took a few moments' respite. Lisette put down her lute and hurried off. Armel wandered toward the stalls at a slower pace, leaving his drum on the stool. Sandor stayed where he was, rubbing moisture from his instrument with a cloth.

Ursule moved closer until she stood directly in front of him. There was no huddle of giggling village girls this time to make her feel old and faded, and she didn't hesitate.

"Sandor, *c'est moi.*"

"Ursule!" He tucked his flute into his shirt before reaching out his hand for her to take. "You're here!"

It was gratifying to hear the pleasure in his voice. "Of course I am," she said, her own voice so bright with happiness she hardly recognized it. "I wouldn't have missed it."

He kept her hand in his, long past the moment of greeting, and his eyes searched her face in his uncanny way. The bustle and color and noise swirled around them, but the feel of his hand and the intensity of that gaze seemed to create a tiny, private space of their own, immune to the winds of activity.

"Shall we have a drink?" he asked.

"S'il te plaît."

It was easier this time, because Arlette remembered them and settled them immediately at the outside table. "Ale?" she asked, in a hurry because of the crowd of men inside. "Cider?"

It was cider this time for Sandor, and Ursule ordered some, too, though she knew it wasn't good. They sat side by side, speaking of little things, Sandor's journey, the conditions on Ursule's farm, the last town where Sandor had played, how Ursule had spent Christmas. Ursule, entranced by the nearness and warmth of him, by his musical voice, by the occasional touch of his hand or elbow, forgot that she was bad at small talk. She had not spoken so freely in years, nor had she said so much, even though none of it mattered in the least, nor was any of it what she really wanted to say or to hear. It was enough just to sit with him, to have all his attention.

Sandor's cider was nearly gone when she remembered the potion in her pocket.

She almost decided not to use it. It seemed a bond already existed between them. The pull of their two bodies toward one another felt like an attraction that needed no magic to strengthen it—but then Armel interrupted their idyll, just as he had before.

"Sandor!" Armel's voice was high and childish, and he sounded as impatient as a child. "Sandor, *allons-y*. Lisette is waiting."

Sandor said resignedly, "I'll have to go. They get tired of having to watch out for me," and put his hands on the table to push himself up.

Ursule felt her chance slipping away, an opportunity as fragile and elusive as a soap bubble floating up from a washbasin. Hastily, she felt in her pocket for the pottery jar. Sandor was already on his feet, buttoning his coat, abandoning the cider he had left.

Swiftly, surreptitiously, Ursule uncorked her jar and emptied it into the mug.

"Sandor!" Armel called again, more cross than ever. "We're waiting!"

"Don't go," Ursule said, in a low, urgent voice. "Tell him I'll take you to the inn."

"Do you know where it is?"

"There's only one. Sit down, Sandor. Finish your cider. I'll make sure you have something to eat."

He hesitated only the briefest of moments before saying to Armel, "You go ahead without me. I'm going to sit a bit longer with my friend."

Sandor could not see it, but the look on Armel's face as he eyed Ursule was anything but courteous. She supposed he didn't know her name, but seeing the black expression on his small features offered no encouragement for her to tell him. He took his time, gazing at her plain clothes, her rough coat, even under the rickety table at her scuffed boots. She stood up and repaid him for his rude look with her most direct stare, the hard gaze she reserved for Madeleine at her worst.

She felt Sandor's faint quiver of anxiety beside her and narrowed her eyes further at the drummer. "I'll guide Sandor to the inn," she said. "No need to trouble yourself."

Armel's eyes flicked from her face to Sandor's, and an insinuating smile curled his lips. "Oh, it's like that, is it?"

Sandor stiffened, and Ursule felt a wave of resentment flow from him. A moment later, when Armel was gone and they had both sat down again, he said, "Armel and Lisette would never get hired without me. They're terrible musicians."

"I noticed that," Ursule said. She watched as he picked up his mug of cider and drained it.

"But they think I'm the burden, because they have to watch out for me."

"That's not fair."

"No." He exhaled a long breath, and his shoulders relaxed. He found her hand with his and gripped it. "It's so good to sit with you, Ursule. So good of you to come and see me! You can't imagine—" He broke off, taking another long, trembling breath.

Her own breath trembled in her throat as she whispered, "What, Sandor? What is it I can't imagine?"

He wriggled himself closer to her, so she felt the heat of his body through his coat, through her own. "It's the loneliness," he said. "Sometimes I can hardly bear it. When you said you might come here, today, all these weeks I've thought of you. I even—" He coughed again, and his voice dropped low. "I've dreamed of you, Ursule. Good dreams. The best dreams." He bent closer to her, so close she could feel his breath on her cheek. The scent of bay rum mixed with the fragrance of the apple cider he had drunk, and she detected a hint of her philter. Her magic. Her power.

He said hoarsely, "I want to make my dreams come true."

Her heart leaped in her breast with such force she couldn't answer him.

······•❈❈❈•❈❈❈•······

Ursule offered to buy Sandor dinner, but he smiled and said he wasn't hungry. She started to guide him toward the inn where he was to spend the night, but as they walked, he pulled her hand through his arm and pressed it with undeniable urgency. They didn't speak again. They had no need.

Ursule knew of places in Keranna, unexpected spots where people could hide themselves. She usually walked wherever she needed to go, so she occasionally stumbled across a pair of lovers in a leafy bower beside the river, or a working man sleeping away an afternoon behind a haymow. She was aware of one or two empty shacks where sometimes vagabonds took a night's shelter. She also knew, because she had helped to clean it after holidays, that the chapel of St. Anne had a storeroom where icons and candles and extra vestments were kept. There was a pile of woolen blankets in that storeroom, saved for nights when the stone flags of the sanctuary floor were too cold to kneel upon.

It was, she was to think later, as if they were surrounded by magic, just as when she performed a rite. Indeed, it was a rite, of a sort. They had no scrying stone, but they had a cold white moon. There was no candle, but a sweet, pure fire burned in her, and an answering fire flamed up in Sandor. There was no grimoire, but their two bodies needed no instruction.

The blankets smelled of damp wool, with a distinct tinge of incense. They were rough, undyed, and scratchy, but Ursule didn't care, and if Sandor noticed, he gave no sign. The icons leaning against the walls or perched on shelves looked down on them, but the faces of the saints were impassive, concerned only with their own tales of love and obsession and sacrifice.

Ursule understood, at last, why the power of magic resided where it did in her body. She let this other magic overtake her, not caring where it led. She didn't let herself think, as she lay in Sandor's embrace, that tomorrow he would be gone. She didn't allow herself to wonder if he would have stayed with her if she hadn't magicked him. She tried not to think that he might never return. She gave herself to the unique rite of lovemaking as eagerly as if it had been she who drank the philter.

They didn't leave St. Anne until the sky began to turn gray and the dawn breeze rattled the tree branches behind the chapel. Ursule had the milking to do in an hour. Sandor had to be ready to depart with Lisette and Armel. Ursule took care to close the door of the storeroom and to lead Sandor out through the chapel quietly, so that Father Favreau, sleeping in the tiny rectory next door, would not hear them.

They walked to the inn, and Ursule said a hasty farewell. "The milking," she murmured. "I can't be late."

He bent his head and kissed her mouth one final time. He said, "I will think of you."

Ursule kept her mouth closed to prevent herself from begging him to return. In silence, she watched him feel his way across the tiny lobby of the inn and up the stairs. She drew her coat collar high around her neck as she hurried away, back toward Kerjean Farm and the endless work that awaited her.

She had gotten what she wanted, and she was glad of it.

It wasn't enough.

Ursule's philter brought Sandor back to her again and again. He found an elderly man, a widower from Auray with bad legs but good eyes, who had a pony cart for hire. Sandor paid the widower to transport him often to Keranna and then on to rejoin the troupe.

Ursule made changes in her life, small things that made Agnes smile. She began to brush her hair one hundred strokes every night before bed, no matter how tired she was and no matter how vicious the tangles. She found a simple in the grimoire for softening the skin, made with oatstraw and a salve of rose hips, and she smoothed it over her face and arms every day. She bathed as often as she could.

She also made the philter two more times, unable to banish the fear that each time she saw Sandor it would be the last.

Whenever the widower brought word from the village that she had a visitor, she tucked the fresh philter into a pocket, then rode back in the widower's pony cart to the inn, where she and Sandor could meet in comfort. She tried to slip up the stairs without being seen, hoping to avoid the whispering of the gossips. She didn't care about that for herself, because she felt no shame and could hardly sink any lower in the eyes of the village. She preferred, though, not having to defend herself to Madeleine.

She understood she was not Sandor's first lover, but she didn't care about that, either. She was his lover now, and she relished every aspect of the role. She discovered sensations in parts of herself she had never thought of, brought to ecstasy by Sandor's long, sensitive fingers, by his seeking mouth, by his lean, hungry body. If she had previously thought of lovemaking as something to satiate the appetite, it seemed utterly different to her now, an exercise in pleasure, to be extended as long as possible.

It was not the lovemaking alone that brought her joy. She loved their midnight conversations, the sort she supposed lovers always had, but so new to her. She thought she and Sandor must be lovers, though neither of them spoke the word. Who but lovers would do the sorts of things they did? Who but lovers would tell each other so many things, intimate things, anecdotes and history and reflections both great and small?

She learned that when Sandor left Belz, he found his father very ill in Lorient, his mother caring for him, unable to take Sandor back into the house. He told her what it was like to be constantly on the road, and lamented having no home he could call his own. She talked about the animals in her care, the endless work of the farm, and the burden of her mother's dependence.

Sandor spoke with affection of the teacher who had taught him to play his flute. Ursule recounted the tale of the little goat whose life she saved, although she didn't mention there was magic involved. He told of meeting Armel and Lisette in a Lorient tavern, where he had been playing for pennies, and his wish that he didn't need them. She described her journey to find the caravan, and how sad it made her to see all their things destroyed, and how much she missed the freedom of being a traveler. He confided his great dream of playing with really good musicians, for a wider audience. He longed, he told her, to be known for his music, not just to play for a few coins dropped into a basket.

She never mentioned Drom. She had no explanation for a raven attaching itself to her, and she didn't want to lie to him. *Some secrets should be kept.*

He repeated, in the depths of the night, his dream of regaining his sight, being free to work wherever he liked. She couldn't tell him her dream of having a daughter to inherit her power—her witch's power—so she asked him to tell her more about the kind of music he wanted to play, the places he wanted to visit.

Ursule's loneliness eased, like laying down a burden she hadn't known she was carrying. Her shoulders relaxed, making her wonder how they had gotten so tight. She slept better, and her nights were rich with memories of their times together, sweet with anticipation of the next ones. Her appetite sharpened, and even the most irksome of her chores failed to irritate her.

She felt startlingly unlike her old self. Desirable. Cherished. When the villagers at St. Anne brushed by her without speaking, she didn't care, because she had Sandor's visits to look forward to. When Arlette and one or two of the other servants gossiped about their romances, she said nothing of hers, but she felt secretly proud of it.

She occasionally looked into the pond behind the barn to see if her appearance had changed, if the simple was working on her skin, if her hair was softer from being brushed so much, then laughed at herself, because of course it didn't matter. Sandor had no idea what she looked like, either when they first met or now. He often explored her face with his fingertips, or tangled his fingers in her hair, but that was not the same.

Each time she returned from being with him, Agnes raised her left hand and squeezed the ring finger with her right.

Ursule knew what she was asking, what she was hoping for. For herself, she didn't care about a wedding, but she knew it was the way her mother saw a woman's life. Despite her own experience, widowed so young with a child to care for, Agnes placed her faith in the security of marriage.

Ursule finally said, after one of Sandor's visits, "I can start wearing a ring, Maman, if you'll feel better, but it won't change anything."

Agnes put her hand to her throat, as if she might try to actually speak her argument, but though the muscles worked, and her brow furrowed, nothing came out. Ursule, seeing, went to embrace her, and murmured into her hair, "Maman, even if Sandor and I were to wed, I would still be a dairymaid. He would be a traveling musician. I wouldn't leave you to travel with him, nor can a blind man do farm work."

Agnes pulled out of her embrace to gaze at her for a long moment, her lips compressed, before she spun around to hurry to the bedroom. She came back with the grimoire and set it on the table.

"Maman?"

For answer, Agnes touched the grimoire with her forefinger, and then touched her eyes. When Ursule stared blankly at her, she did it again. When Ursule still didn't understand, she pointed again to the book, and then to her own throat.

"Oh!" Ursule exclaimed. "You think I should try the spell for Sandor! The *Spell of undoing?*"

Agnes grinned, triumphant, and nodded.

"But, Maman, it didn't work for you. That is, it did, but . . ."

Agnes gestured with her two hands, palms inward, then outward. *Different.*

"That's true. It's different." She had told her mother about the accident that had blinded Sandor. "He longs to see again."

Agnes lifted her palm, then touched her forehead. *Who knows?*

Ursule bent her head, thinking. "Who knows, indeed." She thought about what it would mean for Sandor to see again. He could travel as he wished. They could be a family, have a house big enough for themselves and Agnes. Sandor could have a real home to return to.

She opened the grimoire to review the spell. She would need a lock of Sandor's hair, which shouldn't be hard. The next time he came she would acquire it—and she would also, she hoped, conceive. She had already collected the ingredients to make that potion for herself.

Lulled by these fantasies, she began to drift toward slumber, her breathing easing, her arms and legs relaxing. She was on the very brink of sleep when the voice spoke again. *Have a care.*

Startled, she sat up. "What?" she whispered, not wanting to wake her mother.

Hmmmmm, she heard, a sound at once ominous and impatient, that chilled her heart. She waited for more, for some hint of the meaning, but though she sat there for many minutes, there was nothing.

Ursule lay down again, frustrated and worried. *The Goddess always exacts her price.* She had not forgotten.

She lay awake a long time, anxiety darkening her fantasies of a perfect future. She was tired in the morning, but by the time she rose, she had made up her mind. There was danger in everything, but she was no coward. She would let nothing stop her from pursuing her heart's wishes.

She set about her chores with a sense of urgency. She could hardly wait to get on with the work of magic.

···· ❖❖❖❖ • ❖❖❖❖ ····

The villagers of Keranna no longer lit the balefires of Beltane, but the Orchière clan had always celebrated, dousing the cookfire and replacing it with a vigorous bonfire to mark the peak of spring and the turn of the Wheel of the Year toward summer.

Agnes, following tradition, let the cookfire die early in the morning and swept the ashes out of the hearth. Ursule brought in an armful of firewood. Agnes spent the afternoon spicing ale with honey and cinnamon and nutmeg, a mock mead in honor of the Goddess.

When the darkness came, they lit the fire, and toasted the coming summer with sweet ale. The next day, they would scoop up the cold ashes of their balefire and sprinkle the ashes on the fields to encourage a rich harvest. They always did this before daylight, so as not to have to explain it to Remy, or to Madeleine, who would think it a heathen gypsy practice.

Beltane, Ursule thought, a time to celebrate fertility, was the perfect Sabbat for the two rites she had planned.

After supper, with the table transformed into the altar, and both of them veiled, Ursule began. She started with the easy one:

Potion to speed conception

Take an inch of liver root, peeled and diced small, and another of burdock, both boiled until soft. Blend with a palmful of crushed chasteberries, and mix in a cup of sweet water. Set between the candle and the crystal, and stir until smooth. When the candle is burned, the potion is ready for the infertile woman to drink.

At the bottom of the page, a different hand had added: *It is helpful to call out the name of the expected babe.*

"Léonie," Ursule said firmly, as she raised the cup of potion. "Her name will be Léonie, because a woman in this world needs the heart of a lion."

Agnes, her eyes aglow in the candlelight, crossed her hands over her heart and smiled approval. Ursule tipped up the cup and drank, swallow after bitter swallow. It roiled in her stomach, but the crystal glowed with a steady light, and when the potion threatened to come back up, she pressed her hands to her mouth until the nausea subsided.

"It's done," she said to her mother. She patted her stomach and grinned. "Let us hope the Kerjeans don't expel us from our home because their unmarried dairymaid fell pregnant."

Agnes made a gesture, two fingers of one hand tapping on the opposite palm. *Do the second one.*

"Oh, yes," Ursule said. "I haven't forgotten."

She fetched a fresh fat candle, the mortar with its pepper, foxglove, and lavender already prepared. She added the horehound, then took up her mother's sewing scissors. On Sandor's last visit, a sweet interlude in which he was able to stay for two days, and when he and the widower had come to the farm to have dinner in the cottage, she had begged a lock of his hair. It was for luck, she said, and he had laughed, but bent his head willingly. Now she clipped the strand into tiny bits, and added them to the mortar.

Remembering that moment, she smiled. That visit had been nearly perfect, except for Drom scolding and squawking the entire time their guests were here. When they climbed into the widower's cart to leave, the raven had swooped low above their heads, angrily clacking, until Ursule had shouted at him to stop. He had disappeared then, up into the branches of the oak tree, and had not shown himself for three days.

Ursule blinked, recalling herself to the task at hand. She felt her mother's questioning gaze and gave her head a shake. "It's fine. I was distracted."

When she had sprinkled salted water around the altar and lighted the new candle, she spun the mortar widdershins, three times three times. She pinched up the herb mixture with her fingers and crumbled it into the candle flame. The fragments caught fire, sending starry bits of fragrant ash swirling upward.

May the grands-mères *aid me on this night*
To give my beloved back his sight.
Bless my spell with witches' art,
To heal his hurt and ease his heart.

The crystal flared with light. The candle burned high, as it had before, the wick consuming itself until its flame died in a puddle of wax.

"It worked!" Ursule exclaimed in triumph.

Outside, from the oak tree, Drom crooned his usual approval of magic done, but in her ear, she heard Violca's voice again, that eerie sound of admonition: *Hmmmmm.*

Ursule conceived her daughter on Midsummer Eve. Her mother had made her a Litha amulet of rue and rowan and basil, tied up in a scrap of bleached linen, and Ursule carried it with her when she went to meet Sandor in Keranna. Hours later, when she bid him farewell in the warm dawn of the summer solstice, she knew she carried their child in her womb. When she reached home, she took the amulet from around her neck and hung it beneath the eaves of the cottage near the front door, to beg the Goddess's protection through her pregnancy.

Agnes was waiting for her, tea made, a loaf already sliced on the table. She met Ursule at the door, her eyes wide with hope.

"Sandor has begun to see a little," Ursule announced, tiredly, proudly. "He thinks it's some sort of miracle. He says he sees shadows, flashes of light, things he hasn't seen in thirty years."

Agnes clapped her hands together in congratulations, and Ursule nodded. "It's a powerful spell. I wish I knew who created it. I suppose the *grands-mères* were afraid to sign their names."

Agnes then laid her hand on Ursule's belly, raising her eyebrows in question.

Ursule placed her hand over her mother's, both of them sensing the life that had begun in her womb. She half expected to see a flare of light pierce the web of their fingers. As it was, her hand felt warmed by the glow of creation, the ultimate magic. "The potion worked, too, Maman. Can you feel it? She's coming, my Léonie."

Agnes gave her silent laugh and freed her hand to point to herself.

"Oh, yes, of course!" Ursule laughed. "You're quite right. *Our* Léonie! She will be an Orchière. The line continues."

Agnes put her arms around her to hug her close, and despite her fatigue, Ursule felt as if she could float right off the floor, borne on a cloud of hope and happiness.

·····∗∗∗∗∗∗∗ · ∗∗∗∗∗∗∗·····

Nearly three months passed before Sandor returned. Ursule kept busy with her usual chores, and with simples to ease her morning sickness, but she peered up the road at any sound of a traveler, hoping to see Sandor, or perhaps the widower with his pony, come to collect her. Lammas passed, and then Mabon. The slant of the sun through the turning leaves intensified, seeming to turn all of Brittany to gold, an effect Ursule usually loved. This year, anxiety dimmed the bright autumn days.

She worried because she had not renewed the philter the last time he came, having focused on the *Spell of undoing.* She tried to tell herself it wouldn't matter, that what was between them had strengthened, deepened, that he wanted it as much as she did. She did her best to breathe away her fears, to savor the precious months of her pregnancy.

Her belly had barely begun to swell, but her hair and skin and eyes shone under its influence. Agnes cooked enormous meals for her, cassoulets of hare and capon, great rashers of bacon, quantities of fresh bread and butter. She watched every bite that went into Ursule's mouth, always urging her to eat more, until her daughter laughed, "Maman, if I eat another bite there will be no room left in my belly for the babe!"

Once Agnes pointed to Ursule's stomach and then to the buttery, where Madeleine was working, and drew a scowl on her forehead with her forefinger.

"I know," Ursule said. "I could make another simple for Madeleine before I tell her, but that wouldn't be permanent, would it? If she decides to throw us out, the simple won't change things." She was pulling her boots on for the evening milking. She straightened, and caressed her stomach in a way that had become habitual. "I'm going to tell her straight out. Remy, too. Since you're here to help with the babe, meaning I can do my work, Remy won't care. Madeleine will go on about me being unmarried, I expect, but she'll get over that. Half the girls in Keranna are pregnant before they marry."

Agnes pointed toward the buttery again, then pinched the side of her mouth with the fingers of her right hand, an odd sign Ursule had seen only once before. She had told her mother about the village girls laughing at her when she was sitting with Sandor, and Agnes had made the same gesture. *Jealous.*

"You think Madeleine will be jealous?" Ursule asked, pausing in the act of pulling on her dilapidated coat.

Agnes circled her own abdomen with her hand, then held it out, palm up, empty. *Barren.*

Ursule paused in the doorway, though the cows had begun to low from the pasture. "Do you feel sorry for her?"

Her mother patted her fingertips together. *Of course.*

"It would be easier for me to be sympathetic if she weren't so difficult."

Agnes shrugged, and turned to stir up the fire to prepare their supper. Ursule hurried off to the buttery to fetch the clean milk pails. As she sat beside one of the cows, her forehead against the warm flank, she tried to imagine an easier Madeleine, a Madeleine with babes to scold instead of herself. She couldn't do it.

· · · · ·꧁ · ꧂· · · · ·

Ursule dreamed of her reunion with Sandor, and it was different from her usual dreams, every detail unnaturally sharp-edged, as if carved with a knife. In it, she saw Sandor walking along the road to Kerjean Farm, all on his own, a stick in one hand, his hat pushed back so that his face shone in the sun. In her dream she ran to meet him, calling his name. He stopped at the sound of her voice, but as she came close, he pulled back. She called to him again and again, and kept moving, trying to reach him, but every time she came close, he backed away. She woke with an ache in her throat, as if she had been trying not to cry.

A dream. Only a dream, she told herself, a fantasy made strange by the changes in her body, by her eagerness to tell Sandor about his daughter, by her longing to learn that his vision had returned in full.

Never dismiss a witch's dream.

She didn't need One-eyed Violca's voice to remind her. She went about her work with a sense of dread, and tried to banish it by working harder than ever. She cleaned the byre until there was not a cobweb or a speck of muck anywhere. She gave Chou Chou's harness a thorough soaping before hanging it up for the winter, wondering as she did it if Chou Chou could work through another season. He was getting old, and she should advise Remy to look for another plow horse. She helped her mother dig the last of the potatoes and carrots and onions from the garden, laboring from dawn till dark, so when she fell into her bed she was too tired to dream, too tired even to worry.

On the very day the babe quickened in her womb, Sandor returned. She would think, forever after, that it was no accident.

That morning, she had just begun her breakfast when she felt a movement in her body. It wriggled in her stomach like a tiny fish, making her gasp and drop her spoon. She felt as if she had swallowed a minnow from the shallows of the river.

Agnes was at her side in an instant. Ursule guided her mother's hand to her belly. "She moved," she crowed. "Can you feel it, Maman? She's moving!"

Agnes knelt beside her daughter, their hands side by side, awaiting another sign of the infant coming to life. The porridge grew cold as they followed the movement with their fingers. When it stopped, the babe seeming to rest, Agnes pushed herself up. She took Ursule's bowl of porridge, which had grown cold, and scraped it into the bucket they kept for the goats. She filled it again from the pot at the hearth, and Ursule hurried to eat so she could go out to check the chicken coop.

She had just stepped out of the henhouse with a basket of speckled eggs, still warm from the nests, when she felt a tug in her mind, a premonition. She turned and saw Sandor walking down the road to the farm.

It wasn't precisely like her dream. His hat wasn't pushed back, but pulled down to shade his eyes. He wore a coat she hadn't seen before, with a high collar, and a scarf tucked inside. He did carry a stick, though, and he was alone. Walking by himself.

Walking on his own! Joy surged through Ursule, and the babe, tucked into her *maman*'s body like a kitten in a basket, seemed to feel it, wriggling and stretching. Or perhaps she recognized her papa coming down the road, striding along with confidence, without hesitation, not feeling for the road with his stick, but letting it swing free beside him.

Ursule set the basket of eggs on the nearest fence post and ran to meet him. When she was within a few yards, he stopped walking, staring at her. She stopped, too, to catch her breath and to drink in the sight of him. She wished she had washed her face, changed her clothes, but even so, her smile was so wide it hurt her cheeks.

She was about to speak when he said, "Who are you?"

The wary expression on his face made her heart clutch, and the babe went suddenly still. His eyes were different, the golden brown shaded now to the color of oak bark, more winter than autumn. His mouth, always so soft and vulnerable, looked harder than she remembered. He carried himself differently, too, his chin up, his neck stiff.

"Why, Sandor—" Ursule stammered. "You must know—you must have known, since you've almost reached the farm—"

His brow furrowed, and his eyes searched her face. It wasn't the same gaze it had been, the blind, seeking look. This was clear, narrow-eyed, assessing. "Ursule?"

"*C'est moi.* Surely you expected me."

He took a single step closer. Now he held his walking stick at an angle, blocking his body, so she couldn't embrace him. "I did," he said. "I just—"

A chill gripped her, beginning in her solar plexus, shivering up through her heart and making her throat ache. She didn't move toward him. She folded her arms across her body, protecting herself. Protecting the babe.

"You just what?" she said, and she heard the harshness in her voice. She sounded angry, but she couldn't help it. It was better than admitting to the other feeling, the one threatening to burst out of her, to destroy her composure.

He said, "You're not as I pictured you."

It was the cruelest thing anyone had ever said to her, and it pierced her heart as surely as if he had stabbed her with his Spanish dagger. She gripped her elbows so tightly her fingers went numb. In a strained voice, she said, "Not as you pictured me?"

She was suddenly aware of her shapeless smock, the mud and muck staining the hem of her skirt, the state of her fingernails and, probably, her face. She wanted to turn, to flee from that gaze, that judgment, but she didn't. She stood her ground, fueling her temper as if she were stirring up a fire, goading it to rise, to be stronger than her hurt. Her voice grew harsher. "I'm a farm laborer, Sandor. How did you think I would look?"

"I—I don't know—" He hesitated, and she watched him wrestle with his emotions. She could see, all too clearly, his disappointment doing battle with his wish not to distress her.

It was too late. "You should just tell me," she said in a flat voice.

He blurted, "You're very dark."

"I'm Romani. You knew that. You were in the caravan. Traveled with the clan."

"I never saw them."

The truth of this struck her like a blow. Before she could catch herself, she stumbled backward as if he had slapped her. For a horrible moment, she couldn't catch a breath past the devastating ache in her chest.

His features softened then, and for a moment he looked a bit more like his usual self. He shifted his walking stick to his side. "I'm sorry," he said. "I've had so many surprises in the past weeks. My vision returned—as you can see—and everything startles me. Places I thought I knew. Food that doesn't look like I thought it would. People—people's faces." His gaze dropped to his boots as he spoke the last, as if even he understood what an unworthy thing it was to say. To think.

To feel.

The fantasy of the last months fell away from Ursule as swiftly and completely as if she had shed a garment. His eyes, clear now, functioning again, were as easy to read as the page of a book. The bond between them was broken, all at once, sliced clean through as if she had chopped it with her hatchet. Her great love—her friend, as she had thought—was no better than Madeleine. No better than the witch hunters who pursued gypsies when there was no one else to look down on, to despise.

Why had it never occurred to her that her appearance might matter to Sandor? She had only wanted him to be whole again, to have what he desired, to be free. Sandor, who had been blind for so long, and knew what it was to be different, to be set apart—the realization all but crushed her.

She would have to think about all of it, in time, in solitude, but this was not the moment. This was a moment for holding her head up, for letting her pride protect her, for behaving as if what he thought didn't matter.

"Come along to the cottage," she said. "You must be hungry."

"Not hungry," he said, "but I'm thirsty. It's a bit of a walk from the village."

One I have made a thousand times. "My mother will give you some cider. It's much better than the cider in Keranna."

She almost reached out to put her hand under his elbow, to guide him as she used to do, but she caught herself in time. They turned and walked together, side by side, the rest of the way to the farm. They didn't touch. Neither of them said a word.

As they stepped through into the cottage, Drom settled on the roof above the door, stepping from side to side, his neck bowed, his glittering eye fixed on Sandor. He didn't make a sound, either.

······•᚜᚜᚜•᚛᚛᚛•······

Agnes turned from the sink as Ursule and Sandor came in. A smile started on her seamed face, then immediately faded as she took in Ursule's stiff features and Sandor's awkward greeting. Ursule said, "He can see, Maman. Sandor's vision has returned." She settled Sandor on the stool her mother usually used. "I promised him some cider."

Agnes gazed at the two of them, her face drawn with sudden anxiety. She hurried out to go across to the buttery for a pitcher of cider. Ursule excused herself to go to the bedroom to tie up her hair and change her smock, though it seemed a futile effort. When she came out again, her mother had returned and was pouring a cup of cider. As Ursule sat down opposite Sandor, Agnes poured another cup, then made a swift gesture, pointing to her eyes, lifting her palm in question before she tucked her hands under her apron. She backed away to stand by the sink, as if to escape the tension that thickened the air around her daughter and her lover.

Ursule said, "My mother would like to know when your vision came back. And what that was like."

Sandor had taken a draft of the cider. He set his cup down and nodded to Agnes. "It came slowly at first. Flashes of light, shadows, shapes. I didn't know what was happening, if it would get worse or better. I was lying awake at night, worrying about it, and then, about a month ago, it returned all at once. It was—it made my head ache." He pressed his hand to his shirt, where Ursule knew he carried his flute, though she couldn't see it.

His gaze swept the cottage, and Ursule saw it anew through his eyes: the uneven flagstones, the rough-hewn furniture, the stone sink and wooden counter. Her mother in her long apron and heavy boots. Herself in a clean smock, but her nails grimy and her neck stained with sweat. She felt shame, and resentment, but she also felt pride at having given him this gift, even though it had cost her everything.

Sandor drained his cup of cider, and Agnes stepped forward with the pitcher and refilled it. He nodded his thanks and said, "I hadn't seen a thing since I was six years old. The colors, the textures, the shapes— it's hard to take in. I feel as if I'm a different person. A seeing person. People expect more of me, and I—" He shook his head and left the thought unfinished.

Ursule knew she should probably encourage him, ask more questions, but she couldn't do it. It took all her concentration to behave as if nothing were amiss. Just the same, her mother clearly knew something was wrong. When Sandor and the widower had come to the cottage, it had been a friendly evening. Agnes had smiled, listening to everyone else talk as she served up stew and freshly baked bread, mounds of sweet butter, a pot of fragrant honey. Now, tears glimmered in her eyes, and she raised trembling brows. *What's the matter?*

Ursule gave her mother a tiny shake of the head. *Later.* She ran her hand over her forehead, a hand that ached as if she had burned it. All of her ached, in truth, and the babe in her womb lay still, withdrawing from the unhappiness that gripped her *maman.*

Pain poisoned the air, and Ursule breathed it in as if it were smoke from the hearth, or the fug of the byre. She knew that Sandor felt it, too: the disillusionment, the disappointment, the regret. Perhaps he also felt shame, but she would never know that.

They made shallow conversation. He spoke of his travels, told how he had left Armel and Lisette, described forming a more successful trio of his own. She made herself ask him where he was going next, and he told her.

She didn't ask when he would return. She knew already that he would not.

She didn't tell him about the babe. She would not use her child as a weapon, nor as a lure.

Ursule kept her chin up. She made her voice steady. She couldn't smile, but she held her dignity intact, even as she escorted Sandor out to the road and said a stiff farewell, as one stranger might to another. She watched him stride away up the lane. From the oak tree, Drom glared after him.

Ursule collected the basket of eggs on her way back into the cottage. They had gone cold. She carried them inside, set the basket on the table, and dropped onto a stool.

Agnes signed furiously with her open hands. *What happened?*

Ursule said simply, "He saw me." Her throat ached and her eyes burned, but there were no tears. Not yet.

Agnes stood stock-still, her eyes blazing, her body rigid with fury. Her mouth worked, and a moment later she made a hissing sound, as if she were an angry cat. She made a fist with one hand and struck it into the other palm, so hard Ursule thought it must hurt.

"Yes," Ursule whispered. "It seems only a blind man could love me."

Agnes shook her head, and crossed the room to kneel beside Ursule's stool. She took her daughter's chin with one hand and stroked her face with the other, her eyes brimming. She made no sound, but her lips formed the word. *Beautiful. Beautiful.*

Ursule bent her head to lay her cheek in her mother's hand and let the pain wash over her. Drown her. But only for a short time, only this one day.

She had her daughter to think of. She had the Orchière legacy to care for. She would endure, because she must.

11

The next morning dawned clear and cold. The cows and goats breathed out clouds of mist, and ice glazed the puddles in the barnyard. Ursule felt as if she were frozen, too, her muscles stiff, her mind rigid as she fought not to think about Sandor. She had not felt the babe move since the day before. She had cried with her mother, gone to do her chores, come back and cried herself to sleep. Today she was determined to be done with tears.

As soon as the milking was finished, Ursule returned to the cottage to bring out the scrying stone and the grimoire. Sluggishly, as if every movement caused her pain, she arranged the altar to create the *Charm to heal a broken heart.*

Agnes hovered over her, her own eyes swollen and lips tremulous with shared misery. Ursule hugged her and said firmly, "No more sadness, Maman. I'll make this charm, and that will be an end to it. We have Léonie to think of."

Agnes patted her back and kissed her cheek, then went off into her garden. Ursule suspected she went there to cry some more, since the garden had already been put to bed for the winter, but she appreciated her mother's effort to respect her wishes.

She ground lavender and sage and rose hips in her mortar, reducing them until she could pack them into one half of an emptied walnut shell. She put the other half of the shell on top, and tied the whole together with a bit of thread. She laid the charm between the crystal and a new candle, sprinkled it with salted water, and recited the short spell from the grimoire:

Lavender and sage and rose hips' art
Heal the sting of that cruelest dart,
Restore the bearer's wounded heart.

She would be the bearer. She let the charm lie between the burning candle and the stone, gazing at it dispassionately until the crystal glistened assurance that the infusion of magic was complete. She picked it up and tucked it inside her chemise, saying to no one, "Let that be an end to it."

Violca's voice, soft with sympathy, sounded in her ear. *Hmmmm. We are with you, child.*

Ursule gave no reply. She blew out the candle, restored the crystal to its basket, and covered it. She slid the grimoire under her bed, then washed the mortar and pestle and put them away. As she started out on her way to speak to Madeleine, she touched the charm where it lay against her breast and hoped its power was equal to its opponent, the power of love.

····· ·⟫⟫⟫⟫ · ⟪⟪⟪⟪· ·····

Madeleine opened the door to the farmhouse, and the scent of simmering apples billowed out into the frosty air. She stood in the doorway, drying her hands on her apron. "Yes? You need something, Ursule?" Her face was red, and perspiration brought iron-gray curls slipping out from beneath her scarf. Behind her, a bushel of apples waited on the floor beside the sink. A fire blazed on the hearth, its flames licking the big pot that swung from the chimney crane.

"Yes. I need to tell you something," Ursule said. "You're not going to like it."

"What new misery are you bringing me?" Madeleine leaned against the doorway, scowling down at Ursule on the bottom step. "Please don't tell me you've decided to leave. You're going to marry that man, I suppose! And what am I supposed to do about Agnes when you do?" She shook her apron, and shreds of apple peel fell about her feet.

Ursule tipped up her chin to look directly into her mistress's eyes. "I'm not marrying anyone," she said. "But I'm with child. I thought you should know."

Madeleine's narrow lips parted. She drew a breath, but held it. It seemed she couldn't think what to say.

Ursule said, "I hope you and Remy won't throw me out, but I will understand if you do."

"Ursule, I—*mon Dieu*—how on earth?"

"How? The usual way," Ursule said, but without the customary edge in her voice that Madeleine so often inspired. The memory of lying with Sandor, of being held and kissed and caressed, shivered at the edge of her mind, threatening to break through the barrier she had set up through the sheer force of her will.

Madeleine gave a tiny, derisive snort. "Well, obviously, but—I suppose he has refused to marry you."

"He doesn't know."

"You didn't tell him? He was here yesterday!"

"I did not tell him." Ursule drew a long, slow breath and let it out with a puff. "It's not what he wants, so there was no point."

Madeleine slid her hands down the front of her apron, across her midsection. It was a gesture so similar to the one Agnes had made that Ursule half expected her to lift up her empty palm afterward. *Barren.*

She didn't, though her hands lingered over her stomach before she dropped them. In a voice Ursule had never heard from her, softer, even melancholy, she said, "I love children, though I never had any of my own. I hope you know how fortunate you are, even if he won't stand by you."

"I do." It was the closest thing to a friendly conversation they had ever had, and Ursule didn't know what to make of it. Her mistress was not angry. She appeared—*wistful* was the word that came to Ursule's mind. Her mouth softened. Her eyes, so often snapping with temper, were mild, looking Ursule up and down as if she could see the pregnancy under her clothes.

The next moment, Madeleine tightened the strings of her apron, and her manner turned brisk. "Well, now, Ursule. We must make a list. You'll need things—baby clothes, blankets. Remy can build you a cradle, he's quite good with that sort of thing. And we'll send for the midwife to come and see you."

Ursule had no interest in meeting the midwife, but she kept the thought to herself. She said, with complete sincerity, "*Merci, merci beaucoup*, Madeleine. That's very kind of you."

"*De rien.* A baby changes everything, doesn't it?" With a pensive smile and suspiciously shiny eyes, Madeleine turned back to her apples, closing the door behind her.

Ursule touched the charm again, feeling the ridges of the walnut shell through the fabric of her smock as she walked back to the cottage. Had the pain receded a bit? Perhaps. Or perhaps this feeling of relief was just that Madeleine had taken her news so well.

As she opened her own door to go in to her mother and explain the surprising response of Madeleine Kerjean, the babe stirred again in her womb. Ursule ran her hand over her belly and whispered, "There you are, little one. Good, good. It will be all right, *ma chérie*. We're going to be all right."

The Lady Yvette

*T*hey say the Lady Yvette was a baron's daughter, beautiful and headstrong, who fell in love with a handsome rom. She abandoned her family's stone castle, with its maids and cooks and gardeners and grooms, to travel with him in his caravan. No one remembers the name of the witch of his clan, but she had power enough to recognize magic in the Lady Yvette. She took the noble girl under her wing and taught her the craft.

It was not long before the student surpassed the teacher in skill. She excelled at simples and potions and scrying, but her spells were more powerful than any practitioner who came before her. When her Romani lover betrayed her, she magicked him so that his hair and teeth fell out and his skin wrinkled up like an old man's. After he fled the caravan in shame, the other women began to ask the Lady Yvette to scry on their own husbands. The men of the clan learned that they could keep no secrets from the Lady Yvette, and they took the greatest care not to offend her.

They say the Lady Yvette could make anyone do whatever she wanted them to do. She could make a crying baby laugh, or a boar lie down to wait for the hunter's knife. She could sweeten a mother-in-law's temper, or bring a lazy suitor to pay his bride price. All the clanswomen wanted her with them when they were in labor, and every mother with a sick babe sought her out for her aid.

They say the Lady Yvette ensorcelled a hunter who stumbled upon the clan's midsummer revelry and caused him to give her a daughter to inherit her power. They say he gave her a son as well, but she made him take the boy back to her family to inherit a different kind of power.

The Lady Yvette lived to the great age of eighty, when on a Samhain eve she disappeared. Some say she made a besom and magicked it to carry her up into the sky to join her ancestresses. Others say she magicked herself to become young again, to return to her barony and live once again as a lady among the maids and the cooks.

Whichever is true, no Romani ever saw her again, but they tell tales of a baroness-witch who could make any man, however strong, obey her wishes.

The
BOOK OF
THE WITCH'S
DAUGHTER

1794

M aman, where's Léonie?"

Agnes was on her knees in the garden, pressing potato eyes into shallow trenches and covering them with soil. Ursule hurried to help her up and steadied her until she caught her balance. Agnes pointed toward the farmhouse.

"With Madeleine again? She should be helping you."

Agnes flicked her fingers over the back of her other hand. *It doesn't matter.*

Ursule clicked her tongue as she bent to brush dirt from her mother's skirt. "It does matter, Maman. She's ten now. She knows better." She straightened and tucked Agnes's hand under her arm to walk to the cottage. "Leave the potatoes. And your trowel. I'll finish it for you."

Agnes had developed a nasty limp. Ursule thought it was because her bed was too hard for her aging hips, but when she said so, her mother waved off any suggestion of a fresh mattress. Agnes saw to it that Léonie's was always plump with fresh straw, but she ignored her own. Ursule added to it when she could, when her mother wasn't watching.

Ursule hadn't seen Léonie since early morning. She should have guessed that her daughter would be embroidering with Madeleine and stuffing herself with almond cakes instead of helping her grandmother plant potatoes. She would feel better when she could lay eyes on her and lead her back to the cottage. There she would be protected by the charms Ursule had hung from every beam and eave.

No one else in Keranna believed the Revolution could reach them. They were too far from Paris, everyone said. A village in the provinces, with a tavern and an inn and a tiny chapel. No wealth to speak of. Hardly worth looting.

Ursule suspected they were wrong. The crystal had shown her dark clouds over the farmland, a sky split by bolts of lightning, the green splashed with what looked like blood. When word had come, just before Samhain, that the revolutionaries had put the queen to the guillotine just as they had King Louis, Ursule could guess what was coming. The execution of Marie-Antoinette had put a match to the pyre of what was already being called *La Terreur*. The Terror. France was lost, and not even Brittany was safe from the madness.

When Ursule heard the news, she busied herself at her altar, making every charm of protection she could find in the grimoire and inventing some of her own. She bundled sage leaves with ribbon, sewed pouches to hold poppy seeds and mistletoe, packed walnut shells with herbs. She made a charm for the chapel of St. Anne, too: three river stones in a cloth bag, joined together with melted wax from the candle of a blessing rite. She would hide the bag in the storeroom when she next went to Mass.

As Ursule helped Agnes through the door of the cottage, Léonie came running, calling in her lilting voice, "*Désolée*, Maman! *Désolée*, Grand-mère! I lost track of the time."

She burst through the door behind them, ran to fetch a stool for Agnes, then turned in a swirl of petticoats to pour a glass of cider for her grandmother. As she pressed it into Agnes's hand, Ursule stood watching, bemused.

Not for the first time, she marveled that this mercurial, delicate creature could have come from her own body. It was as if Sandor had fathered Léonie alone. The girl was pale-skinned, with eyes more gold than brown, and a head of silky fair hair. She was long-legged and fine-boned as a new foal, nothing like Ursule. It was true, as Madeleine often pointed out, that she didn't look like a *gitane* at all. Even at ten, when children started to become awkward in their changing bodies, Léonie was as graceful as a swan.

Her resemblance to Sandor had ceased causing Ursule pain. She had put away the walnut charm when she realized the flash of her daughter's dimple no longer made her press her hand to her breast, and the elegance of her slender fingers wielding a needle didn't stir memories of Sandor's fingers on his flute.

She had given up wondering if things might have turned out differently had Sandor not regained his sight. When any flicker of resentment rose in her breast, she suppressed it. He had given her Léonie, after all. Violca had warned her about the employment of great magic, but she had done it just the same. She had made her peace with the choice.

And there was Madeleine. Léonie was the daughter Madeleine would never have, a sweet, sunny girl who lifted her dark moods and always made her smile.

Remy had said as much to Ursule. "Your daughter is the best thing that has happened to my wife in years. I hope you don't mind that Madeleine spends so much time with her."

Ursule had shaken her head. "Léonie loves running over to the farmhouse. Sewing. Cooking. Not one for farm work."

"Madeleine spoils her."

"We all do. It doesn't seem to do her any harm."

She had been right, she reflected, as she watched her daughter fuss over her grandmother, producing some of the almond cakes she and Madeleine had baked that morning, insisting that she try one and compliment it. This last remark was accompanied by her quicksilver laugh, one that never failed to bring a smile to Agnes's face. Léonie was very much her own person, not interested in farm work or gardening, and even less, to Ursule's great disappointment, in learning to read. Still, she was kind and affectionate, obedient in her own fashion, generous in her attentions to Madeleine and Remy and the host of friends she had made at St. Anne.

Léonie chattered now about embroidery and the ingredients for almond cakes, throwing in an anecdote about a boy at chapel getting scolded by old Father Favreau, who never scolded anyone. She had prattled endlessly as a toddler, mixing her languages as she followed her mother through the garden or into the barnyard. Ursule hadn't corrected her, because the tumble of French and Breton, dotted with bits of Romani, always made her laugh. Drom used to follow them on their rambles, croaking and gurgling, sharing the merriment. The years of Léonie's childhood had been happy ones for everyone.

· · · · · ·✦· · · · · ·

After supper, with the table cleared and the dishes cleaned, Ursule laid out the scrying stone and a fresh candle. Léonie said, "Maman, what's that for?"

Ursule clicked her tongue. "Today is Ostara. I told you yesterday. We're going to celebrate and make an offering to the Goddess."

"Oh, Maman!" Léonie came to her and kissed her cheek. "You and your gypsy ways!"

Agnes patted her palms together to get her granddaughter's attention, and when Léonie turned to her, she gave a shake of her head and pressed her forefinger to her lips.

"Sorry, Grand-mère. But don't we make enough offerings at St. Anne?"

Ursule twisted two twigs together to make a spill and carried it to the fire. As she thrust it into the flames, she said, "Those are completely different, *ma fille*. You should know that."

"God, Goddess... What difference does it make? Isn't Holy Mass enough?"

"The Mass isn't part of our practice, Léonie."

"I go to Mass every week, Maman. You go almost that often."

Ursule paused, the spill burning in her hand. "I've always thought it best to blend in with the community, but—" She bent and put the spill to the candlewick. "Our own tradition is important, and you need to understand it."

Agnes, coming out of the bedroom with the veils in her hands, nodded agreement. She had made one for Léonie, too, who wore the veil to please her, dimpling at Agnes's look of pride when she draped it over her head.

Ursule began the opening rite:

On this Sabbat of Ostara, we honor our foremothers: the seer Violca, the prophetess Liliane, the Lady Yvette, Maddalena of Milano, Irina from the east, and all the others whose precious names have been lost. We vow to pass the craft to our daughters so long as our line endures.

"Now you repeat it, Léonie," Ursule murmured. Léonie rolled her eyes, making Ursule scowl. "Don't be disrespectful. I'm passing the craft to my daughter, just as I vow with each rite—and I mean every word!"

"But, Maman, I don't know if I want to learn the craft."

"Léonie! How can you say that? This is who we are!"

Agnes intervened, patting her hands lightly together and shaking her forefinger at her granddaughter. Léonie sighed, but she wouldn't refuse her grandmother. She put the ends of her veil back over shoulders and lifted her hands above the altar. She had grown so tall that she no longer had to stand on a brick to reach above the candles. Agnes nodded at her granddaughter, and Léonie began to recite:

On this Sabbat of Ostara, we honor our foremothers: the seer Violca, the prophetess—um—the prophetess—

"The prophetess Liliane," Ursule prompted, but Léonie had no chance to say it.

The sound of men stamping and yelling in the lane pierced the night, shattering the dim peace of the cottage. Agnes gasped and snatched the veil from her head, then from Léonie's. They heard Remy shouting, and an instant later, Madeleine's scream split the darkness. Ursule hastened to blow out the candles and to move the scrying stone to its basket, her hands shaking with urgency.

Léonie cried, "What is it? What's happening?"

Ursule tore her own veil off and pressed it into her mother's hands. "Maman! Take Léonie into the bedroom and stay there. Don't come out no matter what!"

Léonie shrank back, ready to precede her grandmother into the other room, but Agnes folded her arms and shook her head. Ursule said, "Daj—" as her daughter began to sob in fear.

Agnes shook her head again, even as the noise intensified outside. It was clear she understood that the Terror had reached Kerjean Farm. When torchlight began to glimmer through their little window—fire, her greatest fear—she trembled, but she seized up a knife, the long one she used for jointing chickens, and put her back to the table so she could face the door.

Ursule said in a low voice, "Léonie, go into the bedroom this minute."

"But, Maman, what—"

"It's the revolutionaries, *ma fille*, and they want nothing so much as to spill blood. From what I've heard, they're just as happy with gypsy blood as any other."

"Maman!"

"There's no time to argue. Go now."

With a cry, Léonie seized up the veils and ran into the bedroom, closing the door behind her. An instant later the cottage door flew open with force, banging against the wall, knocking a pot from its hook. In the doorway stood Madeleine, red-faced and white-lipped, just a coat over her nightdress. The racket from the lane swelled in through the open door like a rogue wave.

Madeleine, near hysteria, shrieked, "It's Remy! They'll kill him! The lambs! They'll—"

Ursule caught up her own coat, seized the nearest charm from the beam by the door, and thrust her feet into her boots. "Stay here, Madeleine. With Agnes. With Léonie. I'll get a pitchfork from the byre."

"You can't!" Madeleine gabbled. "They'll kill you, too! They'll see you're a—you're—"

"A *gitane*, I know," Ursule said. "But I can't leave Remy to fight them alone."

She was on the doorstep when Agnes caught up with her to press an amulet into her hand. She offered the kitchen knife as well, but Ursule hissed, "Keep it. And if you need it, use it!" She hurried out, leaving Madeleine cowering behind the table and Agnes in front of it, her knife straight out, ready for battle.

Ursule slung the amulet around her neck and pushed the charm into her bodice as she strode toward the lambing shed. The mob—perhaps a dozen ragged men—were now milling about under the oak tree, their torches burning so high Ursule feared the tree would catch. Two of them ran to bang on the farmhouse door. Two others were already at the lambing shed, where Remy, barefoot and in his nightshirt, had made his stand.

He had braced himself with a hand on either side of the doorframe, and as Ursule crossed the barnyard toward him he roared, "Not a single lamb! We're poor enough here, why would you take what little we have?"

One of the attackers brandished a hatchet, and the other sneered, "Poor? With this farm?"

Ursule palmed the charm under her chemise and shouted, *"Attendez-vous!"* They spun to stare at her. "The *vicomte* owns everything in the district. Surely you know that!"

The man with the hatchet shook it in her direction. "We need food and we mean to have it!" He took a menacing step toward her.

The man with him, smaller, a bit younger, cried, "Hubert, don't! It's a woman!"

"Why do I care?" He took another step, the hatchet ready to strike.

Fury drove all thought from Ursule's mind. This was too much like the mob of witch hunters who had torn her mother and herself from her clan. Then she had been a girl. Now she was a woman, grown strong with hard work, and she had no patience with evil. Without hesitation she thrust her pitchfork at the man called Hubert.

The tines caught in the fabric of his coat and went no farther. Still, he squeaked with panic and fell back, almost into Remy's outspread arms. His eyes wide, he dropped the hatchet to explore his belly beneath his coat with both hands.

Ursule's voice was hard with anger. "I haven't hurt you yet, *monsieur*, but my handle is long, and my weapon sharp. You will have no lamb from this farm. Go your way."

"Madame," the younger man said. "We only—"

She whirled on him. "What are you fighting for, do you know?"

"Freedom," he said, a little weakly. "From those who oppress us."

"Do we oppress you? A farmer, his dairymaid, a poor family?"

Hubert began, "Sacrifices—"

Ursule spun again, her pitchfork poised. "Make your own sacrifices, *crétin!*"

Hubert tried to grab at the pitchfork, but Ursule was quick. This time she punched the tines all the way through his heavy coat. He screamed, and when she wrenched the pitchfork free, the torchlight showed bloodstains on the tines.

Remy exclaimed, and the wounded man sobbed curses, obviously having breath to spare. Ursule suspected she had frightened him more than she had hurt him, but she didn't care either way. She thought of her mother, armed with only a kitchen knife, and her young, defenseless daughter, and she readied the pitchfork to strike again. Her charm grew warm against her breast, and her mother's amulet vibrated in answer.

"Hubert, *on y va*," the younger man begged.

Hubert pressed his hands to his middle and stumbled away after his companion, breathing in noisy, panicked bursts.

The two men who had broken into the farmhouse emerged with a laden basket bobbing between them. The torchbearers gave a ragged cheer, and someone shouted, "Is there more? Good things?"

One of the men with the basket crowed, "We got bread, some sausage, cheese. Two cooking pots, some spoons. There's plenty more!"

The man who had asked the question was an unusually big man, tall and wide, and he seemed to be some sort of leader. He gestured to two more of the mob, and those men started toward the farmhouse, passing the limping Hubert without a glance.

Remy panted, "Give me the pitchfork, Ursule," and she handed it over. He strode toward the looters, his steps as heavy as those of a workhorse.

Ursule ran after him. "*Chut!* Remy, wait."

She slipped the charm from her chemise and pressed it into his free hand. He gave her one swift glance before he started again toward the mob. Ursule followed, whispering a charm of protection as she gripped her mother's amulet:

Blessed Mother of us all,
Let no harm to us befall.
Let the enemy fail this hour,
Banished by your greater power.

Remy moved with surprising speed, more swiftly than Ursule had ever seen him. He reached the mob's leader with the pitchfork in both hands, its bloodstained tines aimed straight at the big man's middle. The big man pulled what looked like a dagger from his belt and brandished it, but the pitchfork was already digging into his waist. He looked down at the pitchfork in surprise, as if he hadn't expected it to actually touch him.

"Call them back," Remy grunted. "Or you'll feel the bite of these tines, and no mistake."

The big man had small, piggish eyes, and they narrowed now until they almost disappeared. He shifted his dagger into his fingertips with a practiced gesture, and Ursule's heart nearly stopped. He was readying his blade to throw, straight at Remy's chest, vulnerable in only his nightshirt.

Remy stiffened. The big man pulled back his arm. Both of them breathed shallowly, urgently. Ursule said again, softly, swiftly:

Let our enemy fail this hour,
Banished by your greater power.

Time seemed to freeze. Ursule could have sworn her breath froze, too, poised in her lungs, unable to move either in or out. She had no air with which to repeat her plea. The noise of the mob faded from her hearing, and she saw only Remy, his pitchfork ready to plunge into the body of his enemy, and the enemy poised to release his dagger, sure to be lethal at such short range.

For an awful moment Ursule felt she had seen this before, had watched it happen once, in another place, another life, another time. Both men would die horrible, bloody deaths. The mob would take what it wanted, get away with it all, go on about its vicious business of laying waste to peaceful farms and villages.

From somewhere above her head, Drom gave a long, curdling call, and the scene broke. The raven, wings spread wide and legs extended, dropped down to claw at the mob leader's hand. The knife spun away and fell to the ground, and Remy pulled his pitchfork away from the big man's belly. A clap of thunder sounded from the clear sky, and Drom, his eerie cry echoing through the night, swooped this way and that, scratching at the heads of the mob. Hats fell off, and one man cried out as the raven's claws dug into his scalp. More thunder sounded from the starry sky, deep and rolling. Ursule's bones vibrated with it, and Drom's cries grew louder, more joyous, as if the raven and the thunder were making their own strange music together.

It was too much for the mob. Shrieking in confusion and fear, the little crowd split apart, scattering this way and that ahead of Drom's talons, then treading on each other as they crowded into the lane to race away from Kerjean Farm. The men with the basket dropped it to the ground in their haste to escape from the raven. Their leader seized up his dagger and ran, no braver than the rest of them.

Remy, panting and wet with perspiration, held the pitchfork high, as triumphant in his nightshirt as a knight in armor with a dragon dead at his feet.

Ursule came to stand beside him as the last of the mob disappeared up the lane. She said, "Are you all right, Remy?"

With shaking arms, he lowered the pitchfork. He dug the tines into the dirt and leaned on the handle as he tried to still his frantic breathing. He gasped, "All right for now. They could be back." He fished her charm out of his pocket. "What is this?"

Ursule didn't answer.

2

The morning after the attack on Kerjean Farm, Remy rode into the village to discover how things were. He returned just as Ursule was pouring out the milk. He stood in the door of the buttery, grim-faced, and Ursule listened in horror to his account of the chaos in Keranna.

"They ransacked the tavern. Destroyed the chapel and broke the cidery's apple press to splinters. Took everything the bakery had on its shelves and bashed the baker over the head, though it looks like he'll recover. Father Favreau disappeared."

"Oh, no," Ursule breathed.

"It's not about the Revolution anymore. It's about greed, and blood-lust. They say the streets of Paris run with blood, even now."

Ursule remembered the smells and sounds of men obsessed with shedding blood. It seemed to her that it must dwell eternally beneath the veneer of civilization. "I fear they won't be satisfied until the whole country lies dying."

"We have to protect Kerjean," Remy said. "Madeleine is terrified they'll come back."

"I'll do all I can, Remy."

"Those charms you make. I don't know what they are—maybe don't want to know—but I'll be grateful if you put up one or two, maybe the byre, the lambing shed—the fence."

Ursule said, feeling wary, "If you wish. Best not to tell Madeleine though."

He grunted acquiescence. "I'll tell her I'm putting up St. Michael medals. She'll like that better." He pointed to her charm. "Don't know why, but this made me feel braver."

She handed it back to him. "Please keep it, Remy. Wear it, if you can. At the least, it can do no harm."

He stuffed it down his shirt and shuffled his feet, averting his eyes. "You're a good girl, Ursule. Lucky day for me when you came to the farm."

Ursule forbore to say it had been years since she was a girl, but his words touched her.

"I'll go to the chapel," she said, "to see if anything can be saved. Tell Madeleine if I find something useful, I'll bring it to her."

"The altar cloth. She made it herself."

"I remember." Ursule finished pouring the milk into the cold buckets, then crossed the yard to the cottage for her coat and her walking boots, and to tell Agnes where she was going. Léonie demanded to come with her, but for once, Ursule was firm. "Stay with your grandmother. In the cottage, mind you. Don't leave her alone."

Agnes had recovered from the frights of the night, though none of them had slept much. Her knife was back in its place. She touched her temple as she shook her head. *Don't worry.*

"I'll leave the charm I meant for the chapel," Ursule said. "Right outside the door."

Agnes nodded approval, and Ursule set off through cool sunshine to see what could be done at St. Anne.

When she reached the chapel a number of village women were already there. Arlette had an empty burlap sack over her shoulder to carry away anything of value that might have survived. The Delac dairymaid had come, still in her milking apron, and two of the cleaners from the *vicomte*'s manor, with brooms and dustpans.

Everyone was quiet in the still morning, speaking softly as if they were at a funeral. It felt that way, in truth. The old chapel had stood for years, and to see it in ruins, its stone walls broken and its windows smashed, was like witnessing a death.

Ursule murmured to Arlette, "Do you know where Father Favreau is?"

Arlette made the sign of the cross. "Hauled him off to the guillotine, no doubt. Nobody safe these days."

"Oh, no. Not Father Favreau, that gentle soul!"

"They got His Lordship, too."

"The *vicomte*? Truly?"

The two from the manor house came closer. One said in a hushed tone, "Dragged him off in the middle of the night. Her Ladyship was in a pure panic. She stuffed the children in the carriage and set out for the coast. They say she's sailing for England, quick as she can."

There were more signs of the cross, and murmured prayers for the safety of the children, before they turned to the chaos around them.

The women stepped cautiously through the rubble of scattered stones and broken timbers. The St. Anne statue was only a mound of ashes in the churchyard, a painted shard here and there revealing what it had been. The statue of the Virgin lay in three big pieces among the debris. One of the village women knelt beside it, weeping.

Ursule went to the storeroom, where she found the stack of blankets intact. She pointed it out to Arlette, who jammed it quickly into her bag. The icons were gone, burned along with the St. Anne statue. The candlesticks and chalices had been carried off to be melted down.

Ursule stood in the center of the mess, her hands on her hips. There didn't appear to be anything else to salvage.

Look again.

Ursule started, surprised as always by Violca's voice in her ear. Arlette said, "*Eh bien*, Ursule, goose walked on your grave?"

"Probably," Ursule said. As Arlette started out of the storeroom, she hung back. The other women were hauling the broken pieces of the Virgin's statue outside, chattering instructions to each other, and the cleaners were sweeping up pieces of wood and plaster. Ursule waited to be certain no one was watching as she took a closer look at the wreckage of the storeroom.

The mob had destroyed anything they couldn't carry away. A cabinet in one corner, which might have been usable, had been smashed into splinters. A shelf had been torn from the wall, and it looked as if someone had stamped on it, rendering it useless. Ursule crouched to sift through the litter of wood and iron fittings.

"Here we are again," she muttered, recalling the search through the broken caravan so many years before. She might have given up, but she knew that when Violca spoke, it behooved her to listen. She had no idea what Violca expected her to find, but it was sure to be something worthwhile.

As she turned over scraps of wood, she touched something she thought was an iron hinge. She almost dropped it, but a quiver in her belly made her look closer.

It was a bit of iron, but it was not a hinge. It was egg-shaped, hollow, with a tiny window of shadowy glass. Ursule held it in her open hand, and as she gazed at it, wondering, she heard the excited clacking of a raven's beak.

Drom. She hadn't realized he had followed her here. And now she knew what it was she had uncovered.

In their hysteria, the looters had missed the most valuable object in the chapel. This little reliquary held a fragment of finger bone from the remains of St. Anne, and Ursule knew, as she folded her fingers around it, that it was an amulet of great power. One-eyed Violca wanted her to have it.

She thrust it into her *posoti*, and with a wave to the other women still laboring over the fragments of the Virgin, she started the walk back to Kerjean Farm, the heavy reliquary bumping her thigh with every step.

····· ᚛᚛᚛᚛ · ᚜᚜᚜᚜· ·····

The looters passed through Keranna twice more. The Delacs lost three lambs, and the manor house was overrun, with paintings and hangings disappearing and the remaining servants fleeing for their lives.

Kerjean Farm was untouched. Ursule had hung her charms where

Madeleine wouldn't see them. She overheard Remy telling a neighbor that he had hung St. Michael and St. Anne medals at the gates, and that had protected Kerjean from the marauders.

The Terror seemed to last forever to the traumatized citizens. Ursule saw to it that Léonie, and Agnes, too, always wore a protective amulet, and for herself, she put the reliquary of St. Anne on a string and wore it around her neck, though it was heavy enough to make her head ache. Then, on a sunny August afternoon when Ursule and Léonie were following Madeleine on her tour of the market stalls, a man jumped up on the tavern's outside table and began to shout that Robespierre and a thousand of his followers had all been fed to the jaws of *Madame la Guillotine*, and the Reign of Terror was at an end.

Madeleine turned to say over her shoulder, "Thanks be to the Virgin! We can stop running to the windows anytime we hear a noise in the night!"

Ursule frowned. She wasn't sure she trusted such news coming from a man she had never seen before. She stole a surreptitious look at a broadside being passed around and saw that, although the number of the executed was closer to a hundred than a thousand, Robespierre had indeed added his own blood to that of the thousands of his victims now staining the cobblestones of the *Place de la Révolution*.

She allowed herself to hope that the time of wars and slaughter had passed, and the quiet of the ensuing weeks and months reassured her. She stopped nagging Léonie to wear her amulet, but she left her charms in their places around the farm, believing they could do no harm.

She was glad to watch Léonie grow up in peace, lively, pretty, happy. She was not so happy to see that, as Léonie grew taller, she seemed to also grow away from her mother and her grandmother. It was natural, Ursule told herself. A young woman should have her own thoughts, her own desires. She wished, just the same, that Léonie would not disdain the wonders of her inheritance. Every time her daughter referred to Ursule's "gypsy ways," Ursule felt her dream of a continuing Orchière line slipping away.

She wondered if she dared do something about it. There was a *Charm of persuasion* in the grimoire, an old, old entry. Perhaps she could bend her daughter's will to hers.

She had the herbs she needed. Sage, for purity of intention. Wild yam for calm. She had a little box of wormwood leaves, too, which she had preserved on an impulse. It was, according to the grimoire, the organizing ingredient.

She thought of her previous failures, but she told herself that the Goddess must understand the need to preserve the craft. Surely she would pay no price for keeping the promise she made at every Sabbat rite.

She made the charm on an afternoon when Remy had taken Agnes into Keranna to deliver some sewing, and Madeleine and Léonie had tagged along to go to the shoemaker's and the chandler's shops. It was simple enough, a bit of grinding and chopping. She spoke the short rite over the finished product, the herbs wrapped in a green oak leaf and tied with scarlet thread. The crystal glinted on her altar. The candle flame was pale in the sunlight.

Mother Goddess, your daughter requests
That you with your power this charm invest
To persuade the daughter of my heart
To give herself over to the witch's art.

She extinguished the candle and passed her hand over the crystal, which had gone dark. A sense of unease came over her, displacing the customary sense of satisfaction at a successful rite. She picked up the tiny bundle of the charm and pressed her other hand over the reliquary beneath her chemise.

She couldn't do it. She had, in the end, to listen to her heart, and her heart spoke clearly. The answer was no.

She would not force her daughter as she had forced her lover, not because she was afraid of the Goddess's price, but because she knew in her soul that anyone who accepted the mantle of the craft should do so willingly. Léonie must walk her own path, however it pained her mother.

Ursule took the little charm, a *Charm of persuasion*, and tucked it inside an empty jar.

Hmmmmmm. One-eyed Violca's voice was gentle, approving of her decision.

Ursule wished Violca would speak to Léonie.

1800

U rsule led the Ostara rite around the altar in the cottage, her sixteen-year-old daughter and her silent mother beside her. Candlelight flickered over their faces and glowed on their veils, and the scene lifted Ursule's heart.

The crystal glittered as if it understood, and her mind expanded in response, stretching beyond Kerjean Farm, beyond Keranna, beyond Brittany. She felt Violca with her, and the other *grands-mères*. She felt St. Anne, also a grandmother, who must have been a witch of immense power to leave such a deep mark on a hard world. Ursule's heart swelled with love for them all until she felt as if she could leave her physical body behind and float with them among the high spring clouds.

It was Léonie's cough that brought her back to the cottage, to the candlelit altar, to her family. "Maman," Léonie whispered. "Aren't we done yet?"

Ursule smiled at her daughter and saw Agnes's silent laugh. "Yes," she said, her dry tone denying the ecstasy she had just experienced. "Yes, *ma fille*, we're done. Put out the candle, and you can go to bed. Blessèd Ostara."

Léonie dimpled at her. "Blessèd Ostara, Maman. Grand-mère." She bent, holding her veil back with one hand, and blew out the candle.

When she had disappeared into the bedroom, Ursule pulled off her veil with a sigh of disappointment. "She still doesn't believe it, Maman. She doesn't understand."

Agnes shrugged and flicked her fingers over Ursule's hand. *It doesn't matter.*

"Doesn't it? If she doesn't inherit my ability, or isn't even interested in it, then...the line dies. Despite everything we've done to preserve it, how hard we've worked, how many chances we've taken—it comes to an end."

Agnes smiled, shook her head, and touched her forehead. *I don't think so.* She pointed to Ursule, then to herself, opening her hands and her eyes wide. *You surprised me!*

That made Ursule chuckle, and from the oak tree outside the cottage, she heard Drom's sleepy cackle in answer. "It's true enough, I suppose. I surprised you—surprised myself! I suppose the Goddess has her own plan."

Agnes made a tiny circle with her forefinger. *Always.*

As she cleared the altar, Ursule said, "Before we know it Léonie will want to marry. Have a husband, children. She has enough of the young men of Keranna dangling after her."

Agnes patted her cheeks. *Beautiful.*

"Yes, she's beautiful. I wish she could also be wise."

Again, the shrug.

Ursule felt a sudden longing for the clan, and the caravan, the life of true Romani. The Romani stayed together, grew old within the circle, rarely had to say goodbye until the final farewell. She didn't speak of it, because she knew it was painful for Agnes, but she couldn't help wondering if, had Léonie been born among the travelers, she might have followed a different path.

Well, no point in thinking about that, Ursule told herself as she put her things away. *It's in the Goddess's hands.* She smiled, thinking of her mother's sign for *always,* and then she sighed again, accepting. *The Goddess always exacts her price.*

But some prices were higher than others.

· · · · · ◦◦◦◦◦◦ • ◦◦◦◦◦◦ · · · ·

In the glow of the Michaelmas bonfire Léonie made her choice known among the young men dangling after her. Ursule, sitting with Agnes among the elderly village women, spotted her daughter slipping into the shadows beyond the green, hand in hand with a slender dark-headed youth. Louis Martin, Ursule thought. From the manor house.

The two were laughing, oblivious to the crowd. Their light steps and the intimate glances they gave each other made Ursule feel every one of her years even as her heart lifted with happiness for her daughter. Léonie would be seventeen next spring. It was time.

She elbowed her mother and pointed, but the young pair had already disappeared. "It appears your granddaughter has made her choice, Maman."

Agnes followed her pointing finger and gave a vague nod.

"Are you tired? I can take you to the cart to rest," Ursule said.

Agnes nodded again, and Ursule helped her to her feet. They put on their coats and picked up Agnes's basket with its little trove of Michaelmas cakes. Agnes held tight to Ursule's arm as they started around the green to where the new horse, Andie, waited with the cart.

Madeleine, out of breath, her cheeks pink from the heat of the bonfire, caught up with them when they were halfway there. "Have you seen Léonie?"

Ursule said, "I believe she's out walking with that young man from Manor Farm. Louis Martin, isn't it? Dark, rather tall?"

"Oh." Madeleine frowned even as she stepped to Agnes's other side to offer her another arm. "Oh, I see. I wanted her to—well, it doesn't matter."

"I can give her a message. I expect he'll walk her home." *I hope she's more careful than her mother was.*

Madeleine lifted her brows. "Really? Well, then. I suppose it doesn't matter now, but the new priest is here. I wanted to introduce her."

"To the priest?" Ursule blinked in surprise. "Why?"

"We're going to present the altar cloth to him. Well, to the chapel, now that they've rebuilt it."

"Is it finished?"

"Almost. There will be a special Mass. The bishop will come from Vannes."

Ursule felt the shudder that ran through her mother's body. Even now, the thought of the bishop who loved to burn witches gave them both the horrors. The bishop was old now, but if the rumors were true, his fervor had survived the passing years, and he was still inspiring young priests with his obsession. Ursule pressed her mother's hand closer beneath her elbow, to tell her she understood.

"Yes," Madeleine went on, "there's going to be a blessing for the altar cloth, and for the statue of the Virgin. They repaired that. There was nothing left of the St. Anne statue to repair, sadly, and the thieves stole the reliquary as well. Sad to think of that precious bit of bone gone to a horde of heathens. They probably sold it."

Ursule pressed her mother's hand again, acknowledging their shared secret.

She was still wearing the reliquary under her chemise, close to her heart. It gave her dreams sometimes, dreams she described to her mother over their morning porridge. St. Anne had been the *grand-mère* of the god the Catholics worshipped. In Ursule's dreams, the saint was old and wrinkled, weary of bearing children, tired by the constant supplications of the faithful. Ursule felt a kinship with her. She understood what it was to be a woman with responsibilities she could never lay down.

Of course no one would build a chapel in Ursule's name, nor would she have wanted one. She wouldn't want a statue, either. Still, it would be a fine thing to be remembered by those who came after. What else could a woman ask of the world?

She felt the reliquary move against her breast, and she sighed. Her daughter cared more for the Catholic practice than she did the Romani one. Ursule had tried to tell Léonie that it made no sense to her that only men were allowed to say the Mass or handle the sacraments, but Léonie dismissed the issue with her usual merry laugh. "I don't want to say the Mass in any case, Maman. And have to learn all that Latin? Why would anyone want to?"

······•❧❧❧•❧❧❧•······

Louis Martin's family had stayed on at Manor Farm after the *vicomte*'s death at the hands of the rebels. They had farmed there for generations. When the *vicomtesse* fled, leaving the manor house empty, the Martins moved into it.

"Maman, you should see it," Léonie enthused. "So many rooms I couldn't count them!"

"I didn't know you had been there," Ursule said.

"Oh, yes, Madeleine and I went to luncheon there after the blessing of the chapel," Léonie said. "You should have gone with us."

"I was working."

"You always are! Anyway, it's huge. Two fireplaces, and everyone in the family has a bedroom all to themselves."

Ursule made no comment. Agnes winked at her from across the table, but Léonie didn't notice. She prattled on, hardly pausing for breath. "Of course the looters took all the good things, paintings and hangings and so on, but they left a lot of furniture. It's really heavy, and I don't expect they could carry it away. There's a lovely long table, with real chairs that have arms on them. The windows look like the ones in the church in Auray, pointed at the top."

Agnes pressed her hands to her forehead in a pretend coronet, and both Ursule and Léonie laughed. "Yes, Grand-mère, it is a bit like royalty."

"I suppose I need to meet Louis's parents," Ursule said. "If he's courting you."

Léonie's cheeks pinked. "He is, Maman."

"And how do you feel about that?"

Léonie's blush deepened. "I like it," she said, her eyes wide with excitement. They were bright gold in the morning light, catlike. "He's everything a girl could want."

"Is he indeed?"

"Don't you think he's handsome, Maman?"

"Handsome is nice. I would care more to know if he's honest. Intelligent. Reliable."

"Of course he is!"

Ursule suppressed her smile and saw that Agnes was doing the same. She said, "You seem very sure."

"I am, absolutely! He wants to marry me and take me to live in the Manor House."

"That sounds a bit grand for a dairymaid's daughter."

Artlessly, with a wave of her hand, Léonie said, "Oh, but the Martins think of me as Madeleine's daughter, really! Because I always go with her to church, and into the village."

Ursule knew her daughter had not meant her remark to hurt, but it did. It struck her directly in the solar plexus, stealing her breath, turning her stomach. She left the table and crossed swiftly to the sink, one hand pressed over the pain. She was pretending to wash a pan that was already clean when she felt Agnes's arm around her and the gentle squeeze of her hand. Through the window, she saw Drom flutter across the yard to perch on the sill and croon at her, his black eyes glittering with sympathy.

Ursule blinked away her betraying tears and leaned into her mother's embrace. "It's all right, Daj," she whispered. She cleared her throat, patted her mother's shoulder, and turned back to her daughter.

"Well, young lady," she said, speaking a bit more firmly than she had intended. "Whatever the Martins may think about your parentage, I still think I should meet them."

It was clear that Léonie didn't notice anything amiss. She said pertly, "Of course you should, Maman, but you never say anything when you meet new people."

"No. I suppose I don't."

"You won't have to worry about that, though. Madame Martin never stops talking! You won't need to say a word."

······⠶⠶⠶·⠶⠶⠶······

What Léonie had said was true. Madeleine and Ursule were invited to luncheon at Manor Farm, and from the moment they climbed down from the cart, Isabelle Martin produced a stream of chatter nothing could divert. She commented on everything from the sultry autumn weather to the dearth of good fabrics since the Revolution, from the terrible prices she was getting for Manor Farm's cheeses to the gossip about a neighbor's wayward son.

Ursule, feeling like a dressed-up child in the new petticoat and scarf Agnes had sewn for the occasion, let the wave of talk flow over her, nodding encouragement now and again, inserting *Oui* or *Non* where it seemed warranted. Madeleine, slightly overdressed and delighted to be dining in the manor house, tried occasionally to say something, but it was like trying to stem a river at flood. She cast a side glance to Ursule, widening her eyes with amusement.

There were, as Léonie had said, a great many rooms in the manor house, and a staircase that led up to still more. They had entered through a wide hall, which at one time must have held a desk and benches where the bailiff or the *vicomte* could meet with tenant farmers. Now it was empty, and their footsteps echoed against the high ceiling and unadorned walls. Madame Martin led them through to a room with a long table and an assortment of chairs ranged around it. Bowls and plates rested on a sideboard. Ursule glimpsed a kitchen beyond. The hearty crackle of the fire suggested the hearth must be enormous.

When a servant in cap and apron carried in a tureen of soup, Ursule realized this entire room was used only for meals, a phenomenon she had never seen before. She eyed the splendor of it all with uneasy wonder and hoped it was Louis himself who had turned her daughter's head, and not the magnificence of this house.

Léonie and her suitor sat side by side, murmuring to each other. Ambrose Martin, dark-haired and lean like his son, had greeted the visitors with shy courtesy, eaten his soup and bread hastily, and fled into the fields. The servant, a middle-aged woman with a receding chin and a nose shaped distressingly like an egg, clattered plates and pans while Madame Martin, oblivious to the racket, rattled on.

The Martins were no grander than the Kerjeans, just tenant farmers like Madeleine and Remy, subject to the *vicomte*'s authority. Their occupation of the manor house had a temporary feel. If the *vicomtesse* decided it was safe to return to Brittany, she might reclaim her house at any time.

A sudden silence made Ursule realize she had stopped listening to her hostess. Evidently there had been a question, something that required a reply, while she had been staring around her. Her cheeks burned with sudden embarrassment. "*Excusez-moi, madame.* I was distracted by your house. It's very grand."

"Isn't it? I've always thought so." Madame Martin puffed up her bosom and ran her hands over her stomacher, which looked as if it had been made for a slimmer woman. She was remarkably plump for one of the working class, with round pink cheeks and a full bosom. Léonie had said Madame Martin had four older children, off now to their own lives, their own farms. Ursule thought she and Louis's mother must be close in age, though she was weathered and wiry as an old fence post, while Madame Martin looked sleek, like a well-fed hen.

Thinking this, she almost flicked the fingers of one hand over the back of the other, one of Agnes's signs. *It doesn't matter.*

She never did learn what her hostess had asked her. Léonie and Louis excused themselves, popped up from the table, and disappeared into the garden.

Madame Martin heaved a dramatic sigh as she watched them go. "My last one," she said. "Now they will all be married."

Ursule had not considered the matter of the marriage settled. She bit her lip, trying to think of a diplomatic way to point out that she had not yet given her approval. Madame Martin burbled on, "Madeleine tells me she has already bought silk for a wedding dress and discussed the date with Father Bernard. She wants to invite the whole village!"

Ursule felt as if someone had dumped a bucket of cold water over her head. Her mouth opened, but no words emerged, and she stared at Isabelle Martin as if the woman had uttered some obscenity. A moment later she threw Madeleine an accusing glance. Madeleine had the grace to flush and spread her hands as if to apologize.

Madame Martin, insensible of these interactions, beamed at Ursule. "You didn't know!" She reached across the table to pat Ursule's brown hand with her smooth white one. "Isn't it a lovely surprise? Madeleine is so good to dear Léonie. It's going to be a beautiful wedding!"

Ursule, fulfilling her daughter's prophecy, could find nothing to say.

···· ·〞〞〟〟· 〟〟〟〝· ·····

Agnes declined to attend the wedding, as she refused anything to do with a priest, and when the November morning dawned with ashen clouds glooming above the frozen lane, Ursule was glad her mother had stayed home. Andie's hooves slipped on rime, even on the well-traveled road, and a sharp wind cut right to the bone. Agnes would have been incapable of walking by the time they reached the chapel. As it was, Ursule and Remy and Madeleine shivered as they tied Andie to a hitching post, and they teetered into the chapel, wary of the icy stones.

Léonie had come in the Martins' carriage, one that had belonged to the *vicomte*. They found her waiting just inside the door, out of the wind. She looked achingly lovely in her new petticoat, a thickly embroidered stomacher, and a pointed cap of Breton lace. Ursule's eyes pricked with tears at the sight of her.

Madeleine fluttered to Léonie to give her hair and her cap unnecessary adjustments. She was openly tearful, a lacy handkerchief pressed again and again to her eyes. Léonie patted her shoulder but looked above her head to smile at her mother. Ursule, quelling her own tears, gave her daughter a tiny wave and a private wink.

The chapel was crowded with villagers and farmers eager to see the Martins as successors to the *vicomte* and *vicomtesse*. They bowed and curtsied so much that Ursule was embarrassed for them. She hung back, taking cover behind the Kerjeans, until Isabelle Martin spotted her, ordering, "Louis! Escort Madame Orchière!"

Ursule didn't have time to be surprised at being called *Madame*-anything. Louis obediently came to her side and offered her his arm.

"A big day, is it not?" he said, flashing his white smile. He looked wonderful in a well-cut coat that Ursule suspected had been lifted from the *vicomte*'s wardrobe. It was hard to remember that he was merely a farmer. He had a tendency to charming gestures, patting her hand where it rested on his arm, nodding graciously to people who called his name.

She let him lead her to a pew at the front, a place she never sat. She wished she didn't have to now. The eyes of her fellow farm laborers and dairymaids burned into her neck, and she fought an impulse to turn around and snap, *I know! I know I don't belong here.*

She sank onto the hard bench of the pew, careful of her own new petticoat. She kept her head down, only peeking up beneath the brim of her hat—a hat lent by Madeleine—to see the neighbors gathering. The chapel was cold and drab, the clothes dark, the atmosphere solemn. At a Romani wedding everyone would have worn their brightest clothes. There would be music and dancing around a roaring fire, the bride adorned with a wreath of ivy and mistletoe and the groom in a scarlet vest.

Ursule sighed and leaned back, letting the thought slip away. It was not to be. She wondered, truly, if she was Romani anymore. Léonie certainly wasn't. She linked her hands in her lap and stared down at her work-swollen knuckles.

When the priest appeared from the back room of the chapel, the low murmur of conversation ceased. A little rustle came from the door, where the wedding couple prepared to make their entrance. Madeleine and Isabelle Martin hurried to sit next to Ursule, scarves fluttering and handkerchiefs at the ready. Everyone turned to watch the bride and groom walk forward.

Everyone, that is, except Ursule. She stared straight ahead, transfixed by the priest.

They hadn't met, but she knew his name. Father Bernard. He was very young and tall, thin to the point of gauntness. A mop of ginger hair framed his bony face and close-set, pale blue eyes. One of his eyes rolled from time to time, and he blinked often, possibly trying to control it.

His features were unprepossessing, but it was not that which made Ursule shiver, as if the November wind had battered its way into St. Anne. A premonition stopped her breath, interrupting her heartbeat.

Her daughter walked past her to kneel beside her bridegroom. The priest began to intone the marriage service in a nasal voice. The wind rattled the windows, and puffs of incense blew from the altar above the heads of the congregants. Ursule took in almost none of it.

This priest radiated evil. Ursule could hardly believe no one else in the congregation felt the dark heat spilling out over the altar, a sensation that made her squirm against the hard back of the pew. She half expected the Bible beneath the priest's hand to burst into flames when he touched it. When he placed the Communion bread on Léonie's tongue, Ursule shuddered. It was like watching a snake slither between her daughter's lips. When Father Bernard pronounced Léonie and Louis a married couple, he smiled, showing small yellow teeth, and Ursule's stomach churned as if he had blown brimstone into her face.

She didn't realize the ceremony was over until Léonie was bending over her to kiss her cheek, Louis beaming beside his bride. Ursule rose, stiffly, and watched as the two made their way out of the chapel, accepting congratulations as they went. In a daze, Ursule followed Madeleine out to the cart, where Remy already waited on the bench. They climbed in, Remy chirruped to Andie, and they followed the Martin carriage out of the churchyard and into the road that led to Manor Farm.

Fortunately for Ursule, the noise of the wind and the rattle of the cart meant it was all but impossible to talk. Her silence went unnoticed. She pressed her palm over the reliquary where it hung against her breast, asking St. Anne's little bone to soothe her anxiety.

The wedding breakfast was a modest affair, attended only by the Kerjeans and Ursule, the Martins, and the newly wedded pair. In the dining room, the adults toasted the young couple with cider and ate an indifferent casserole of eggs and potatoes, followed by a slumping wedding cake that tasted unpleasantly of soda. Ursule privately thought that the Martins' servant could use a charm to improve her cooking.

Madeleine was smiling and weepy by turns throughout everything. Remy blustered, speaking a little too loudly, clearly daunted by the grandness of the house, and making a great show of his gift of cash to the newlyweds. Ursule observed all of it in her customary silence.

Neither Louis nor Léonie paid any attention. They were absorbed in each other, eyes shining, lips soft, hands linked throughout.

When Ursule embraced Léonie in farewell, she clung to her daughter a moment longer than she should have, then walked away as swiftly as she dared, not looking back. She was already in the big empty hall, starting for the door, when she heard Léonie call her name.

"Maman, wait!"

Ursule turned back to see her daughter running toward her, pretty silk skirts swirling around her ankles. "Léonie?"

"Oh, Maman." Léonie threw her arms around her mother and squeezed her so Ursule could barely breathe. "It all happened so fast, didn't it? I barely spoke to you all morning, but I want you to know—that is, Louis and I want you to know—we want to you to come visit as soon as we're back from our wedding journey. Promise me!" She released Ursule but held on to her hands and smiled down at her.

She looked so happy, glowing with excitement and pride and the glory of being in love, that Ursule was almost undone. She managed to say, through a great knot in her throat, "Of course, *ma fille*. Of course I will. And you must come to Kerjean Farm to see your *grand-mère*." *And me. Please, please come to see me.*

For answer, Léonie kissed her forehead, squeezed her hands, then spun about to fly back to her bridegroom. Ursule was grateful her daughter didn't see the shameful tears drip down her cheeks. She palmed them away before Madeleine and Remy emerged from the dining room and led the way out to the waiting cart. By the time she reached the cottage and sat down to tell Agnes all about the wedding, she had regained control once again.

·····•·≫≫≫·•·≫≫≫·•·····

The day after the wedding, Ursule stepped into the buttery with her pails of milk and was startled to see Madeleine hunched on a stool beside the butter churn. Her face was buried in her hands, and her shoulders were shaking. "Madeleine? Are you ill?"

Her mistress lifted a face so full of misery that Ursule clicked her tongue with concern. She set her pails down too hastily, spilling a bit of milk onto the flagstones, and went to offer Madeleine a clean handkerchief. "You're weeping," she said. She had never seen Madeleine cry. She scolded when she was upset. Gently, Ursule asked, "What's the matter, Madeleine? Has something happened?"

Madeleine tried to answer, but only a sob emerged, and then she was crying in earnest, openmouthed, out of control.

Ursule put a hand on her shoulder, something she had never done before. Madeleine's bony shoulder was hot, though the buttery was icy cold, and Ursule suspected she had been weeping for a while. She waited, allowing Madeleine to shed her tears. When they finally subsided, leaving Madeleine sniffling but quiet, she dropped her hand. She bent to wipe up the spilled milk and set about emptying the buckets and washing them, giving her mistress time to recover herself.

"I'm sorry," Madeleine said after a time, her voice thick with tears. "It just struck me, all at once, that she won't be back. I mean, visits, but not back to stay. That it's forever."

"You mean Léonie." Ursule set the buckets upside down on the counter to drain and turned back to watch Madeleine push herself stiffly up from the stool, wiping her eyes one more time. The realization struck Ursule that Madeleine, like Agnes, was entering her old age.

"I've never loved anyone before Léonie," Madeleine said. "No babes of my own. No grandchildren to comfort my old age. Then Léonie..." She made a vague gesture in the direction of the cottage.

Ursule bit back the remark she might have made, folding her arms across her breast to discipline herself. "We all miss her," she said.

"Yes, of course, but I—" Madeleine stopped midsentence.

"I understand," Ursule said, before she could soften the edge in her voice. "The child you never had." *My daughter. Mine.*

Madeleine blurted, "And now I have nothing to look forward to."

"You have Remy."

"Oh, Remy!" At this Madeleine snorted. "It's been years since we've had anything to say to each other. There's nothing left between us but habit."

Ursule felt a spasm of sympathy for big, awkward Remy, drowning his loneliness with brandy in the woods or ale at the tavern. She wanted to be angry with Madeleine for assuming she could miss Léonie more than she herself did, but somehow she didn't feel it. Somehow it felt as if there were enough sadness to go around. "Madeleine, Léonie will have babes. Perhaps you will love them, too."

Madeleine drew a trembling sigh. "Perhaps. Perhaps I will. I just don't know." She was gone a moment later, her back stiff with embarrassment at having broken down before a servant.

Ursule watched her go, shaking her head in wonder that after their long association, Madeleine Kerjean could still surprise her.

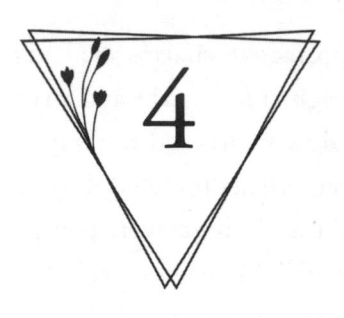

U rsule had not yet finished the churning when she heard the sound of a strange horse's hooves in the yard. She propped the paddle against the side of the churn and started for the door of the buttery, then stopped. The reliquary grew suddenly warm against her breast, warm enough that she plucked at her smock to lift it away from her skin.

She opened the door just enough to peek out, then drew swiftly back and shut it as quietly as possible.

What was he doing here? Even the sight of him, climbing down from his horse, made her skin crawl. His flat black hat, the spikes of red hair sticking out beneath it, all reminded her of that awful moment at the wedding, when she had to watch him putting the Communion wafer between Léonie's lips, and her stomach had turned in horror.

Moving with deliberation, trying to think of an explanation, she returned to the churn. She had just finished and was pouring the buttermilk into the waiting pitchers when the door opened.

Madeleine had put on a clean apron and smoothed the tight bun of her hair. "Ursule!" she said sharply. "Where's Agnes?"

Ursule's skin crawled again. "Why are you looking for her?"

"Father Bernard is concerned that she doesn't come to Mass, and he's come to inquire."

"Madeleine, can't you explain?"

"There's something else."

Ursule felt the stirring of premonition in her solar plexus, and it made her feel as if she were going to be sick. Madeleine held up something in her palm, and Ursule had to hold back a gasp.

It was one of the protective charms she had hung about the farm. It looked innocent enough, a few herbs and a river stone tied up in a bit of silk with a ribbon now weathered and frayed, but it held a great deal of the Goddess's power. It had protected Kerjean Farm when the Delacs and the Armands and the Colberts were being raided, again and again.

"It's Agnes's, isn't it?" Madeleine said. "Father Bernard found it hanging from the fence out by the road. I recognize this silk from a petticoat she made. And the ribbon was for the hat that went with it. What sort of nonsense has she been up to?"

"I don't know what you're talking about."

"She won't go to Mass. She won't talk."

"Can't talk," Ursule snapped, her temper beginning to rise.

Madeleine ignored that, shaking the charm in Ursule's face. "Father Bernard says he recognizes heathen practices when he sees them."

"That's ridiculous!" Ursule's temper flared, but there was danger here.

"Ridiculous? He's a *priest*, Ursule! A man of God."

He's a demon. But she didn't dare say it.

Instead, she palmed the reliquary beneath her chemise and drew a steadying breath. "If Father Bernard wants to ask about that silly little thing, he can ask me. Where is he now?"

"He's in the house, having a cup of tea."

"Good. When he's drunk it, send him to the cottage."

Madeleine shook a finger at Ursule. "You be polite! It's kind of him to come to visit. To ask about Agnes."

"Is it? Perhaps it would be kinder if he were to mind his own business and leave my mother alone."

"Ursule—"

Ursule put up a hand. "Tell him where to find me." She set her jaw and pushed past Madeleine to march across the yard to the cottage. Once inside, she shut the door behind her and leaned against it, her temper cooling quickly in the face of her anxiety. She took a quick glance around the cottage and saw nothing that would give her away. Herbs hung in their usual places, bundled and tied. The only candle was the one they used at night, resting in the middle of their uneven table. The crystal and the grimoire were in their usual hiding places.

Agnes wasn't there. But the *Charm of persuasion* still rested in the empty jar where she had tucked it so long ago. She took it out, and as she held it in her hand, she said softly,

Mother Goddess, your daughter requests
That you with your power this charm invest
To persuade the evil one coming near
That there is no magic or witchcraft here.

She felt a strong urge to add something, to extend the spell, but there was no time. She heard his steps outside her door. He pushed it open without waiting for an invitation.

Ursule thrust the charm into the pocket of her skirt and turned to face him.

He didn't bother to remove his hat when he stepped inside, nor to scrape the dirt from his boots. He had recovered her charm from Madeleine, and he held it out now, shaking it in front of her face. "What witchery is this?"

The word sent a shudder through Ursule. She stiffened her spine to hide it and thrust out her chin. She had to tip up her face to look into his unsteady eyes. She moderated her voice but kept a firm grip on the charm in her pocket. "Why, Father Bernard, whatever do you mean? That's just a child's toy."

"Didn't you make it?"

Ursule's lips parted, ready to tell the lie, but it wouldn't come forth. It was her mother who had been the actress, good at lying to people, at making them believe falsehoods. Ursule's fault was being blunt, blurting uncomfortable truths, and now...

If she said she hadn't made it, who would they think had done it? Someone else would be accused of witchery, come under the eye of this demon priest, and it would be her fault.

She was about to shrug and refuse to answer, but the cottage door burst open, and Agnes dashed in. Her hair was so wild Ursule thought it must be deliberate, and her scarf was loose from her bodice. She snatched the charm from the priest's bony hand and clutched it to her bosom, grinning like a mad thing. She smacked Father Bernard's arm with her hand, as if he had been teasing her and she was amused. Though she made no sound, she twirled and laughed and tore at her hair, all with the charm pressed to her chest.

Acting. She was acting. And Bernard, though he pulled away, was convinced.

"She's mad, isn't she?" he demanded of Ursule.

Ursule, gazing in wonder at her mother, mumbled, "She's not really—not really—"

Agnes waved the charm over her head, smirking, then ran to her sewing box and pulled out a piece of ribbon that matched the faded one on the charm. She shook both of them, laughing as if it were all a great jest.

"This is the woman who doesn't speak?"

At last Ursule was on solid ground. "My mother is unable to speak."

"Well," Bernard sniffed. "I don't want her coming to St. Anne if she behaves like this."

"It's not—" Ursule began, but stopped. She said instead, "Do you know, Father Bernard, I think you're right. It could be disruptive."

"It's disrespectful!" he thundered, brushing at his sleeve where Agnes had touched it. "Someone should have explained to me."

Agnes continued her silent laugh, and Ursule could imagine what Madeleine would have to say about this performance. "I'm sure Madame Kerjean thought you knew. Everyone in Keranna knows Maman doesn't speak." She pressed the charm in her pocket and added, "It's getting very late, isn't it? It will be getting dark soon. You had best be on your way."

For a terrible moment, as the priest's good eye fixed on her while the other rolled away, she thought the charm might have failed to persuade him, but then, with a small, deflating sigh, Bernard backed toward the door. Agnes stood still, watching him, the remnants of her manic grin clinging to her face.

Ursule watched to see that the priest mounted his horse and started up the lane. When she felt certain he would not turn back, she closed the door and leaned her forehead against the cool wood for a moment, relishing a moment of relief.

She lifted her head and turned to see that her mother was as calm as if it had not been more than thirty years since she made her living convincing people of untrue things.

Agnes dusted her palms together. *Good riddance.*

Ursule went to embrace her. Moments later they tossed the offending charm into the fireplace, and as it caught the flames and burned, they watched its magic disappear up the chimney.

"I hope that's an end to it," Ursule said softly. Her solar plexus quivered again, briefly.

Agnes made the sign with her uplifted hands that meant, *Who knows?*

"Only the Goddess, I suppose," Ursule said.

Agnes twirled her forefinger. *Always.*

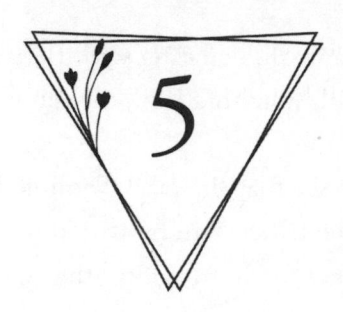

On the eve of Imbolc, when Ursule and Agnes had hung sprigs of rowan outside their cottage to honor the Goddess, and Father Bernard would be planning his Candlemas celebration, Léonie and Louis appeared at Kerjean Farm. It was their first visit since the wedding.

Ursule was in the lambing shed, spreading fresh straw for the birthings to come. She heard the horse's hooves on the still-frozen road and came out in time to see her daughter, in a bright blue cloak, step out of the carriage. Léonie didn't see her mother but gave Louis some command over her shoulder as she dashed across the yard. She burst into the cottage without knocking, which made Ursule smile. Agnes would be startled, but delighted.

Louis stayed back to loop the horse's traces over a branch of the oak tree. Above his head, Drom stepped back and forth on a branch, watching in ominous corvid silence.

Ursule hurried to help her son-in-law. "*Bonjour*, Louis," she said, trying to sound casual, as if carriages drew into the yard of Kerjean Farm all the time. "How good to see you."

He gave her his white smile and inclined his head as if she were a person of importance. He was a lovely young man, with his shining black hair and eyes dark as a gypsy's. She could see why he had won out over his rivals for her daughter, although the manor house and the carriage must have helped.

He said, "*Bonjour, madame.* We've come with great news!"

"I'll be glad to hear it," Ursule answered. "Does your horse need a feed?"

She led the way into the barn and went to a bin to heft out a sack of oats. Louis hastened to take it from her, and this time he called her Belle-mère, mother-in-law. "Let me do this."

"Oh," she said, reluctant to give him the dusty sack. "You'll get your nice shirt dirty."

He took a firm grip on the sack. "You forget, Belle-mère. I'm just a farmer like you." That made her laugh, and she let him take it from her. She pointed to a feed bucket, and he shifted the sack to one arm as he lifted the bucket with the opposite hand. "Go hear Léonie's news. She's bursting with it!"

"Thank you, Louis. I will, then. Help yourself to whatever you need." As she crossed the yard, she grinned up at Drom, perched on the high back of the driver's bench of the Martin carriage. "Zi buna, you rascal."

He fluttered his wings, glossy in the cold sunshine, and made no answer.

In the cottage, Ursule took in Agnes's glowing expression and Léonie's proud stance beside her grandmother. She brushed bits of straw from her hands before she went to embrace her daughter. She took her pretty cloak to hang on a peg, then turned, lifting her eyebrows and spreading her hands in anticipation.

Léonie cried, "I am with child!" as if no new bride had ever conceived so swiftly.

Ursule's lips twitched. "That's wonderful," she said, and urged Léonie to a stool.

"It's just what I've always wanted," Léonie said. "A family of my own. A whole family, maman and papa and children, all together."

Ursule bit her lip, and turned to the sink, trying to quell the sense of reprimand from her daughter. She had never lied to Léonie. Léonie knew she had never married, that the man who had fathered her had disappeared. Ursule understood that, as always, her daughter hadn't meant to hurt her feelings. She cleared her throat to ease its sudden tightness. "I'll make some tea while you tell us all about it."

She busied herself with the pump. By the time she had hung the kettle in the hearth and stirred up the fire, she had regained her equanimity. She brought another stool to the table, listening as Léonie burbled on about the preparations.

"The midwife says in the autumn, Michaelmas, more or less." Ursule thought, *Ah, Mabon,* as Léonie exclaimed, "I can hardly wait to have my own baby to hold."

"It will come soon enough," Ursule said. She couldn't resist touching Léonie's stomach. "How do you feel?"

"I feel fine. Not ill in the least. The midwife says I should eat lots of cheese and butter, and drink cider every day. She says I shouldn't exert myself when it's hot, and I shouldn't kneel in church, and Louis and I shouldn't—well, that's the hardest thing—" She blushed, breaking off the sentence, and a moment later began a new topic. "Madame Martin has ordered a cradle from the woodworker in Keranna, and she says that with her five pregnancies, she always—"

Ursule let the flood of words wash over her, content simply to have her daughter home for the moment. Louis came in, and Léonie told him to fetch the extra stool from the bedroom. Her tone was a bit peremptory, Ursule thought, but he didn't seem to mind. The stool was a rickety thing someone had rescued from the ruined chapel, and he had to sit down with care as it rocked from side to side. The table was so small the four of them could barely fit around it.

Ursule was suddenly aware of the drabness of the cottage, the paucity of its comforts. It smelled of goat because of her boots by the door, something she usually didn't mind. She supposed the manor house never smelled of livestock, and she felt a moment of shame. She watched her mother's painful hobble as she rose and moved to the cupboard to fetch the teacups and wished she could have provided Agnes with a better house, a good bed, a servant to do the heavy work.

Louis had to shift his elbow to avoid getting a splinter from the table, but he smiled indulgently at his bride as she talked. Ursule remembered how easy it was to bear discomforts in the presence of the beloved one.

She had a fleeting image of a pile of rough, incense-scented blankets, a couple too much in love to care, but she banished it. How wonderful it must be to have someone look at you the way Louis looked at Léonie!

Léonie paused for breath, then laughed. "Oh, I'm sorry, Maman, Grand-mère! I've been talking on and on, and neither of you has had a chance to speak. How was your Christmas? I didn't see you at the St. Stephen's Day fete, though Madeleine was there. Did she tell you? Louis and I went with his parents, and..."

On it went. Ursule and Agnes had not celebrated Christmas, of course. Léonie should know they would have observed Yule instead. Ursule had skipped the fete because Agnes was having a bad day with her hip, and she had concentrated on making a potion for her pain.

When she could, she asked Léonie if she had told Madeleine yet that she was expecting.

"Oh, yes, I gave her the news at St. Anne. You weren't at Mass, Maman!"

"Your grandmother hasn't been feeling well," Ursule said. "I don't like to leave her."

She looked down into her teacup, watching an errant leaf swirl at the bottom as she suppressed the spurt of jealousy that shot through her. Madeleine knew about the babe before she did and had not bothered to tell her.

"Oh, Grand-mère, I'm sorry!" Léonie exclaimed. "Are you better now?"

Agnes put up a hand, palm out. *It's nothing.* But the hand trembled, and Ursule experienced a cold feeling in the center of her body, a sense of dread that had come over her all too often in recent weeks, ever since the visit from the demon priest.

Louis said, "We should go. We mustn't tire you, *madame.* Nor you, Léonie."

Léonie said briskly, "I don't feel tired at all, Louis."

He hesitated, obviously not wanting to disagree with her.

Ursule intervened. "I have the milking to do in any case. But it's so good to see you, Léonie. And you, Louis." As she rose from the table, she felt a spasm in her own hip, which she wished away with ferocity. She was going to be a grandmother—the real grandmother, however Madeleine might trespass—and she couldn't let her body fail her now.

She stood in the lane, waving, as Léonie and Louis drove away, back to Manor Farm. Léonie leaned out the carriage window to wave back and to throw her mother a kiss.

Madeleine emerged from the buttery at just that moment, saying, "Was that Léonie?" She shaded her eyes against the glare of sunshine on half-frozen leaves, peering after the carriage. "Why didn't she come to see me?"

Ursule hurried off toward the byre, pretending she hadn't heard, ashamed of the fleeting sense of triumph that brought a flush to her cheeks.

· · · · · ✦✦✦✦✦ · ✦✦✦✦✦ · · · · ·

The dream came early the next morning, before the winter dawn arose to nudge Ursule out of her bed. This time it was not Violca. It was St. Anne. St. Anne as a grandmother, in a black robe, aged and worn and exhausted. She appeared in Ursule's dream with the clarity of a vision.

Ursule saw her standing over a grave, a Christian grave, with a carved stone cross at its head and a handful of colorless flowers at its base. A mist stirred behind her, but through the shifting fog Ursule glimpsed the churchyard of Keranna, with the stone-walled chapel beyond. Anne held up a finger, the way she did in the painting of her Ursule had once seen in Auray. Ursule supposed the bit of bone in her reliquary could have come from that very finger. Anne lowered the finger to point at the grave and then, slowly, lifted her hand and placed it over her heart as she bowed her head.

Ursule tried to ask whose grave it was, but she could make no sound. Anne stayed where she was for a time, her head down, her hand on her breast, then turned and melted into the mist. Ursule struggled to call after her, and the effort woke her.

She lurched up from her bed, her heart thudding. Agnes still slept. Ursule took her smock and skirt from their peg and carried them out of the bedroom just as one of the cows began to low. A goat joined in, bleating her own message into the still morning.

What Ursule wanted was to gaze into the scrying crystal, beg the grandmothers to tell her whose grave she had seen in her dream. As always, she had to wait until after the milking and the churning, the feeding of the stock, the cleaning of the byre. Gritting her teeth against a wave of frustration, she pulled on her clothes and put her feet in her boots.

Never dismiss a witch's dream. Ursule wondered how it must feel to be a normal woman who could say, *Oh, it was just a dream*, and put it out of her mind.

······ ❧ ❧ ······

Two ewes began their labor at midday, and Ursule had to help Remy get them into the lambing shed. She sat with them until the lambs appeared and began to totter around their mothers in search of their first meal. By then, it was time for the evening milking. She wasn't able to carry the scrying stone to the table until all the stock was settled and darkness enfolded the farm. Agnes urged her to eat supper first, but she had been in an agony of wondering all day.

She didn't think the grave could be Agnes's, because she would never bury her mother in a Christian grave. She supposed it could be her own, since she attended Mass, though it would be against her will. That damned priest wouldn't care what she wanted.

Her greatest fear was one she dared not name.

She used the Imbolc celebration as an excuse, so as not to frighten Agnes. They pulled the curtain over the window and began as always with the recitation of the ancestresses:

On this Sabbat of Imbolc, we honor our foremothers: the seer Violca, the prophetess Liliane, the Lady Yvette, Maddalena of Milano, Irina from the east, and all the others whose precious names have been lost. We vow to pass the craft to our daughters so long as our line endures.

Agnes had brought in the Yule greens that had been drying behind the cottage. She placed them in the hearth, and as they burned, Agnes and Ursule let the smoke drift around them, an act of purification for the coming spring. Ursule's impatience had grown almost unbearable but she knew her mother took comfort in these traditions. She forced herself to wait until the last bit of mistletoe and holly had crumbled to ash before she turned to the crystal.

Ursule passed her hands over the chilly top of the stone and peered inside with a whispered prayer:

Reveal, grands-mères, *what is to be*
And show what is required of me.

The stone had been waiting for her. Light flickered through it at once and a mist—not unlike the one in her dream—drifted through the crystal parting almost at once to show Léonie, kneeling in a pool of white silk, like the dress she was married in, her fair hair tumbling down her back. A small, dark woman stood before her, an amulet glowing at her breast, her hands on Léonie's head. In the background, half-hidden by the shifting mist, was the grave with its Christian cross and offering of flowers.

It took a moment for Ursule to realize that the dark woman was herself. "What does it mean?" she whispered.

The familiar voice of One-eyed Violca sounded in her ear. *She will need great magic, beloved child. She will need a great witch.* And then, almost inaudibly, *Prepare.*

······ ∗∗∗∗∗∗ · ∗∗∗∗∗∗ ·····

For three days, Ursule moved through her routine in an anxious cloud. Rising from a troubled night on the fourth day, she decided to do exactly as Violca had said. She would prepare.

Like all women, she knew the risks of pregnancy and childbirth. She had borne her own child without difficulty, aided by her mother, but as a farm laborer, she had assisted in dozens of births—goat kids, calves, lambs—and she knew the multitude of things that could go wrong. A calf could be in breech position. A lamb's legs might be tangled up. Sometimes a goat lost her kid in one bloody rush, and all too often her life as well.

Ursule got out the grimoire and began searching its pages for everything to do with childbearing. Agnes raised her eyebrows and pointed at the old book. *What are you doing?*

Ursule didn't want to frighten her mother. She strove for a casual tone. "I want to get some things ready, to help Léonie when her confinement begins."

She used bits of discarded ribbon from Agnes's sewing box as markers for the pages she found. There was a simple for fatigue, and one to enhance the appetite. One of the ancestresses had written a recipe for a salve to rub on a pregnant woman's belly, and in the same hand was a potion to bring in the mother's milk. Ursule had used a philter to ease the pain of labor for herself, and she would have that ready.

None of these were unusual or dangerous conditions, though. There was something else. *She will need great magic.*

Ursule sat over the grimoire for hours, her head in her hands, and wondered what she should do. Prepare, of course, as Violca had said. But prepare for what?

She took a long, seeking breath and felt the reliquary tremble against her breast. She drew it out and held it in her palm. It seemed to pulsate against her skin, although that could have been the throb of her own blood.

She wrapped her fingers around it and closed her eyes. Would Anne, grandmother of a god, heed the plea of a gypsy witch? She opened her eyes and looked down at the reliquary with its precious memento. It couldn't hurt to try.

Finally, she left the grimoire lying open and went to find Drom. He was perched high in the branches of the oak tree, and he peered down at her as she leaned against the rough-barked trunk, the reliquary in her hand. The old oak had stood strong through times of too much rain or too little, weeks of burning sun, seasons of clouds and darkness. Its limbs spread like those of a many-armed dancer, sometimes clothed, sometimes winter-bare, as they were now. Drom fluttered down to settle on her shoulder, the dig of his claws a sign that it was time to do something.

Ursule had watched people praying for years at St. Anne. It always seemed a foolish thing, to think words without speaking them, and expect the spirits to hear. She preferred the Romani way. She wondered if Anne had a preference.

But the reliquary, made powerful by a fragment of the saint's bone, had come to her by design. Anne was a great witch, and surely she would not have allowed that to happen had she not meant for Ursule to have it. Perhaps she wouldn't mind the mode of petition so much as she would appreciate its sincerity.

With Drom on her shoulder, Ursule walked across the yard and around the byre. The goats poked their heads above the fence of their pen to watch her with their bright dark eyes, their little beards jiggling with curiosity. The cows paid her no attention. Andie, grazing in the pasture, lifted his head at the sound of her footsteps. When he recognized her, he returned to cropping the short winter grass. She glanced back at the buttery, glad to see no sign of Madeleine. She needed to be alone.

Beside the pond was a tiny niche created by the arching branches of a willow tree. Their tips trailed in the water, and the spring leaf was beginning, peppery and fresh. As she pushed through the drape of branches, Drom fluttered off her shoulder and settled onto the carpet of last year's leaves. Ursule knelt beside him, her aging bones grateful for the softness of the leaf fall, her eyes soothed by the green-filtered light.

She said, "I have no plan, Drom. Only a mother's need."

He tilted his head and rustled his feathers in sympathy.

"Anne was a mother," she said. "And a grandmother. Do you think she'll listen?"

Drom emitted one soft *clack*.

"I don't know what else I can do."

The raven moved closer, until his wingtip brushed her folded knees. He dropped his head to his chest in a graceful gesture of patience.

Ursule had no candle, no crystal, no herbs, only the reliquary.

She raised it in her cupped hands to let the dark glass catch the greenish light. The glass gleamed ever so slightly, as the scrying stone might have done, enough that she could glimpse the tiny, white, ancient relic within. Her heart stirred at the thought of the woman who had once flexed this finger. Gooseflesh rose on her neck, and she closed her eyes.

Mother Goddess and Grand-mère Anne,
Heed a mother's plea.
Guide your daughter's mind and hand
To save our Léonie.

It wasn't the Christian custom to make petitions three times three times, but the Catholics revered the number three. Surely three times three would not offend the saint, and it felt proper to follow the Orchière custom. Ursule pronounced her petition the full nine times before she lowered the reliquary to her folded knees. The willow branches caught her voice, blurring it to a whisper, and she felt certain no one outside her little bower would hear.

She knelt there for a long time, breathing the cool damp air. The raven's head drooped lower, and Ursule rested, too, her chin on her chest. She banished all passing thoughts, leaving her mind open and ready for the message when it came.

From the byre, a cow began to low, but Ursule didn't move. One of the goats gave a plaintive bleat, but still Ursule stayed where she was, though her knees began to ache and the chill of the February evening crept through the drape of willow leaves to sting her cheeks.

All the cows were lowing when it finally came to her, as clear in her mind as if someone had painted her a picture.

She saw Léonie lying on a bed, her feet raised on a stack of cushions, her fair hair spread on a pillow. Her eyes were squeezed shut as if in pain. In one hand she held a cluster of bristly teasel stalks, gathered together as if for a nosegay. In the other she held a small corked bottle.

No one would hold teasel stalks that way, because the spines were too stiff and sharp, but Ursule understood that the image was not literal. This was what Léonie would need when the trouble started. The bottle meant that she, Ursule, must concoct a tincture of teasel. She had never experienced such a clear image without the scrying crystal, but she had absolute faith in it. Anne had interceded.

Gratitude eased Ursule's heart. There was trouble ahead, but she had a plan.

She lifted her head, and though her stock was calling her, she took one more moment to offer thanks to the Goddess. To the great witch Anne, who had aided her in her effort, she whispered, "I will keep you with me always, Grand-mère Anne. Thank you."

At last she struggled to her feet, stretching out her aching knees. Clumsily, her feet stinging with pins and needles, she hurried to the byre for her evening chores.

I n the evenings, after the milking was done, Ursule set to work pack-
ing a basket with things Léonie might need. She made the simples
for fatigue and for appetite, and wrapped them in burlap. She made the
salve to ease the stretching of a pregnant belly, and the potion to bring
in the mother's milk, wrapping and stowing them with the simples. She
made the philter against labor pain, too, corking it tightly, nestling it
in a bed of straw. She did all of this in the light of the Orchière crystal,
burning a great many candles in her rites, until she began to worry that
Madeleine would notice how many disappeared from the pantry.

Her mother's brow furrowed when Ursule asked where she might
find a patch of wild teasel. Agnes made fists of both hands and touched
them together, twice. *Dangerous.*

"I know, Maman. I will be careful, but I'm going to make a tincture.
Just in case."

Agnes's frown deepened, and she raised one finger and then both
palms. *In case of what?*

"I don't know. But I want to be ready."

Agnes touched her forehead, then pointed to the basket they used
for collecting herbs. *I know where to find it.* As she picked up the basket
with one hand, she drew a frown across her brow with her forefinger.
I don't like it.

"Maybe we won't need it," Ursule said, and wished she could believe
that was true.

Agnes brought her the teasel, and Ursule made the tincture and
added it to the basket before she completed her final task. She cut a

nice thick branch of willow from the tree by the pond and sliced off the twigs that emerged from it here and there, smoothing the whole into a solid staff. A walking stick, but far more. Using an awl, she dug an opening at the top just the size of the reliquary. She fitted the reliquary into the space and braced it securely. She set the staff, with its precious relic, beside the door, ready to accompany her when the time came.

Agnes pointed to it and raised her eyebrows in question. Ursule said, "I can't wear it around my neck all the time. It's heavy, and the string pinches my neck. But I want it with me, and a walking staff seemed a good place to keep it."

Agnes made no other comment, but it was clear by the anxiety on her wrinkled features that she knew Ursule expected trouble.

The summons came two weeks after Beltane. The farm was busy, on the brink of summer. There had been long hours in the fields as well as the regular labor of milking and churning and feeding, and Ursule hardly had a moment to herself. She had just come in from the coolness of the buttery to the sunwarmed cottage when she heard hoofbeats galloping along the lane. Her solar plexus shivered with premonition, and she stepped swiftly out again, shading her eyes against the midmorning sun to watch Louis rein in a thick-legged horse beneath the oak tree. He leaped down from the saddle and left the reins dangling as he strode across the yard.

He started speaking before he reached her. "Belle-mère, it's Léonie. She's been complaining of pain in her back, and this morning it's in her belly, too. She began to bleed. My mother sent for the midwife, but Léonie wants you. Needs you, she says!"

His voice was steady, but his cheeks bore two flaming red spots, and white lines showed around his mouth. He nodded to Agnes when she appeared in the doorway, but kept his eyes on Ursule. "Will you come?"

"Of course. I'll have to talk to Madeleine—"

He interrupted her. "Léonie said I could do the milking, and anything else Remy wants. I'll stay until you send for me. Until we know she's all right." He looked at Agnes now. "Will you let me sleep in the cottage?"

Agnes nodded, her eyes wide with alarm.

Ursule said, trying to sound calm, "I'll go now, then. My mother can show you around the byre, where the things are. Madeleine and Remy—"

"I'll explain to them. Léonie said they would understand. But go swiftly, will you? I'm afraid—I think it's bad."

Agnes pressed a hand to her mouth, as if even she, eternally silent, might cry out. Ursule said, "I'll get my basket. I have some things ready."

"She said you would. I don't know if you can ride a horse?"

Ursule had never done so, and would have preferred to walk, but that would take too long, and her basket was heavy. She eyed the horse and the hard-cantled, uncomfortable-looking saddle. It looked daunting, but she would let no one call her coward. "I'll figure it out."

She hurried into the cottage to collect her basket, a coat against the nights that could still be chilly, and a nightdress. Agnes followed her to add a hairbrush and comb to the basket, and an amulet for protection. She was about to add a packet of sandwiches, but the basket was full. Ursule waved them off. "No, Maman, see if you can get Louis to eat them. He looks as if he needs some food. Give the basket to him, will you, so he can tie it behind the saddle? I'll change my shoes."

She hurried out moments later, her staff in her hand. Agnes stood by, helplessly twisting her hands as she watched Louis help Ursule onto the horse. The animal was bigger and wider than Andie, with broad hooves and feathered pasterns, a horse bred for the plow. Once in the saddle, Ursule felt small, her position precarious. The ground seemed very far away.

She tried not to think about that as Louis shortened the stirrups as far as they would go. They were still too long, but she said, "Never mind. I'll manage."

The staff was awkward in her hand, and she braced it across the saddle, where it stuck out too far on both sides. It would catch in the bushes, she feared, and she would have enough on her hands trying to keep herself from falling. "Do you need that?" Louis asked.

"I do."

"Give it to me, then. I'll tie it under the stirrup." He slid the staff beneath her knee and secured it with deft knots. The feel of it there reassured her.

"I'm off," she said, lifting the reins. "Try not to worry, Louis."

"Don't you worry, either," Louis said. "I know how to milk cows."

"And goats?"

"I'll learn." Louis stepped back. "Don't worry about Bijou, here. He knows his way back to Manor Farm. Just give him his head and hang on."

"I'll do that." She clucked to the horse and laid the reins against his neck. He executed a slow, plodding turn until he was pointed in the direction of Manor Farm, then set off at a steady walk without any urging from his novice rider. She found it wasn't at all difficult to stay in the saddle as long as she didn't have to guide him.

She had just reached the turning of the lane, where she would be out of sight of the farmhouse, when she heard the *whirr* of Drom's wings and the soft rush of air as he soared down past the trees to land on Bijou's withers. The horse threw up his head, and his ears flicked backward, but he seemed to find the raven an acceptable passenger.

"*Zi buna,*" Drom said, quietly, catching Ursule's mood.

"*Zi buna,* my friend. I'm glad you're with me."

······ ⚬⚬⚬ · ⚬⚬⚬ ······

Ambrose Martin was waiting in the wide drive of the manor house. Bijou clopped to a stop, and Monsieur Martin hurried to help Ursule down from the saddle. She stood on shaking legs as he untied her basket and her staff. "The midwife is coming," he said, "but your daughter asked specially for you. I hope you don't mind."

"No. Grateful," she said. "I'd like to go straight in."

"Bien sûr." He turned, her basket in his hand, and led her toward the wide steps at the front of the house.

She was glad of her staff as she followed. Her feet were numb from trying to stay in the stirrups, and her thighs trembled. She knew she would be terrifically sore the next day.

Monsieur Martin was not a man to make unnecessary conversation. He led her straight through the great shadowy hall, and she hobbled after him, up the wide staircase to a spacious bedroom. He stopped at the door, handed over her basket, then sped back down the stairs, unabashedly fleeing from the doings of women. Ursule rolled her eyes at such behavior from a man with five babes of his own.

Isabelle Martin appeared at Ursule's knock. She looked harried, her apron wrinkled, and her scarf was coming out of her bodice. She began to chatter the moment she saw Ursule, but Ursule didn't hear a word.

Léonie lay on her side in a big bed, her eyes squeezed closed, her face pale and dripping with perspiration. Ursule forgot about her shaking legs and numb feet, crossing the room in three quick strides. She propped her staff against the bedstead, barely registering the massive carved headboard or the matching wardrobe against the opposite wall. She set her basket on the bedside table and sat gingerly on the edge of the mattress. "Léonie, dear heart. I'm here. It's Maman."

Léonie's eyelids lifted, just enough for her to see her mother, and one of her hands groped for Ursule's. "Maman—the baby—"

"Do you feel her? Still moving?"

"Everything hurts so much," Léonie groaned. "My back. My belly." Her eyelids closed again, and she said, almost inaudibly, "I'm bleeding, Maman. I think I'm losing her."

As I might lose you. A mother's nightmare.

Ursule became aware of Isabelle's flow of talk now, something about the midwife coming, about waiting until she arrived, about pork broth, which she apparently believed healed everything. Ursule blew out an irritated breath. She needed silence, and she needed to be alone with her daughter. She wanted to open a window to let the fresh spring air sweep out the miasma of blood and sweat and fear, and then she had to look under Léonie's nightdress, assess what was happening.

There was no time for courtesy. She used Madame Martin's Christian name, and spoke in a peremptory tone. "Isabelle, can you fetch your servant? Then you rest. I'll manage here."

Improbably, her words managed to break through the stream of Isabelle Martin's words. She broke off, diverted by having a task to perform. She murmured assent and disappeared, closing the door behind her.

Ursule rose and went to the window to lift the sash as high as it would go. A welcome gust of air swept through, bringing with it the fresh scents of new hay and young leaves, the faint tinge of the river carrying up to the house. She went back to the bed and gently folded back the coverlet that lay over Léonie. She peeled up the hem of Léonie's nightdress, which was sticky with blood.

"Let's get this off, shall we, *ma chérie*? That will feel better. I'll find you a fresh one in a moment." She pulled the coverlet back up to Léonie's shoulders. The girl was drenched in sweat, and when Ursule touched her skin, her fingerprint lingered. She needed water, and quickly.

She would clean her later. At this moment, there was no time to waste. The servant with the egg-shaped nose appeared in the doorway, and Ursule said, "I need fresh water. Not from a bucket, mind. You have a spring? Good. Get a pitcherful. And close the door when you go out."

She had never in her life given orders as if she were someone of consequence, someone entitled to tell another person what to do and how to do it. She should probably be surprised that the servant didn't question the orders of a *gitane*, but she was doing what she must. She could return to her modest ways when it was over.

She lifted her basket onto a chair beside the window and took out the stoppered bottle of tincture. She went to Léonie, slid one hand beneath her slender neck, and gently lifted her head. With the other she thumbed the stopper out of the bottle, then tilted it above Léonie's mouth. "Open for me, dear heart. Just a little."

It was vital to administer the tincture as soon as possible, but too much would be dangerous. As Léonie's lips parted, Ursule whispered,

Mother Goddess and Grand-mère Anne,
Guide your daughter's mind and hand.

She spilled a drop into Léonie's mouth, then another. She glanced toward her staff and saw a glimmer of light from the reliquary in its top. She let another drop fall between Léonie's lips, and the light swelled to a glow, then went out all at once, as if an unseen hand had pinched the wick of a candle, telling her it was enough.

She let Léonie's head rest once again against the sweat-drenched pillow, and went back to her basket for the philter against pain. This was less difficult, a straightforward remedy, and she administered it without hesitation. Léonie gave a sigh of relief a moment later, and her groans ceased.

The servant came back with a pitcher of water and a glass in her apron pocket. She set both on the bedside table, and Ursule nodded her thanks. "I need cloths and water for washing, too." The woman curtsied and bustled out again.

Ursule made Léonie drink a full glass of water before she began to slip the soiled sheet from beneath her and then, when the servant returned with washwater, to clean her. Without being asked, the servant brought a fresh sheet and a towel. Ursule crossed to the wardrobe and rummaged through it until she found a nightdress, and by the time she got it over Léonie's head and her arms through the sleeves, Léonie was half asleep. A bolster lay at the foot of the bed, and Ursule propped Léonie's feet on it. She and the servant remade the bed around her, and by the time they finished, Léonie had stopped perspiring. Ursule touched her arm and was heartened to see that no print of her finger remained in Léonie's skin.

Ursule looked across the bed at the servant. She remembered her from her visits to the manor house before the wedding, but they had not been introduced. Exhausted now, she said, "I'm Ursule Orchière. I apologize for not knowing your name."

The woman said, "They call me Édi."

"Édi, I thank you for your help. And now, one more favor. I'm thirsty myself."

"Fetch you a glass," Édi said, and disappeared, leaving Ursule to watch her daughter sleep, and to murmur thanks to the Goddess and St. Anne.

·····❖∷∷∭∭∭•∭∭∷∷❖·····

In the days that followed, Ursule slept on a pallet in Léonie's room. She drew it close to the big bedstead so that Léonie's slightest movement would wake her. If the bleeding began again, she dosed her with the teasel tincture. It was frightening, and she didn't rest well, but at the same time, it was a bit like a holiday. Édi brought her meals up from the kitchen. They were simple ones, much like the ones at Kerjean. She kept the big window open for the fresh summer air to fill the room, so she heard the lowing of the cows at milking time, but they were summoning the Manor Farm dairyman, not herself. She worried a bit about her goats and chickens at Kerjean Farm but could only trust that Louis would do all that could be done.

In need of air, she took a few minutes to go outside and roam the grounds. Once there had been manicured hedges and cultivated flower beds. Now, the laurel hedge rambled wherever its roots took it, and its branches stretched across the footpaths to catch at a walker's clothes. The flowers, purple iris and red poppies, yellow tulips and white lilies, had proliferated and reflowered any which way, bigger ones like the lilies and iris choking out the more delicate varieties. Weeds pierced the tangle of colors, rising above the struggling flowers like battlefield warriors standing over the fallen. Last year's blooms decayed in thick layers, their mustiness overpowering the fragrance of this year's blossoms.

Ursule strolled slowly, letting the sun on her shoulders refresh her. She took in the disorder of the garden and wondered idly what Agnes might make of it. Drom appeared and followed her, croaking his impatience at her being indoors so much.

"I can't help it," she told him. "My girl needs me. You have to take care of yourself."

He croaked, mournfully, *"Zi buna."*

"I know. You don't have anyone to talk to."

He cocked his head at her, his black eye seeming to shine as if with tears, then flew up into the trees that edged Manor Farm. "Sorry," she called after him, before she turned and went back to the sickroom.

Léonie didn't speak much for the first two days, but as she began to feel better, she asked after her husband, and when Ursule explained, she gave a tremulous smile. "I told him to go, and he didn't argue at all. He's a good man."

"I'm glad, *ma fille*," Ursule said. "Madeleine drove over in the cart to see you, but you were still recovering. I sent word to Louis so he'll know you're feeling better."

"Will Madeleine come again?"

"I have no doubt," Ursule said. "Now, you rest. And keep your legs up."

"I will."

While Léonie slept, Ursule did, too. She couldn't remember a time she had slept in the daytime or, because Léonie no longer needed the tincture every few hours, right through the night. By the time she judged Léonie was out of danger, she had begun to feel as lazy as the farm cat sunning itself in the drive.

Madeleine returned and, being allowed in at last, fussed over Léonie, offering to brush her hair, asking if she would like to have a new nightgown. She carried with her a jar of cider, although as Ursule had not been at Kerjean to magick it, it was slightly sour. She had made a batch of almond cakes and brought a brick of Kerjean butter.

Ursule supposed that when the baby came, Madeleine would shower the little one with gifts, imagine herself as the infant's grandmother, and behave as if she were.

Ursule was wrong.

Three weeks after Lammas, the baby girl entered the world, squalling and kicking at the indignity and discomfort of being born. The midwife was in the house at the time but enjoying a sip of tea in the kitchen with Édi. It was Ursule who held Léonie's hands as she labored, who gave her carefully measured drafts of the pain potion, who massaged her belly when she began to push, and who encouraged her when the work seemed too hard to do. Ursule received her first grandchild into her own work-hardened hands, wrapped her in the waiting linens, and laid her on her mother's breast.

"Maman, look at her!" Léonie breathed. To Ursule's critical eye, Léonie looked well for having just given birth. Her hair was lank with sweat, and her cheeks red, but her eyes shone with joy. "Isn't she the most beautiful baby you've ever seen?"

"Except for one." Ursule smiled as she used a damp cloth to wipe Léonie's face. Despite the dangers of her pregnancy, and Léonie's weeks of enforced idleness, the childbirth had gone quickly for a first baby. In moments the afterbirth was safely delivered, and bundled in burlap into the waiting basin.

The midwife, a tall, thin, scowling woman, didn't make an appearance until all of this was done. She had spent the first hours of labor either trying to give Ursule orders or recounting stories of perilous confinements she had attended, ghastly tales of bad deliveries in which she was inevitably the heroine. Ursule had finally commanded her to stop frightening Léonie, and the woman had simmered with resentment ever since.

Now she stood in the doorway, her hands on her hips, glaring first at Léonie, sitting up with her babe at her breast, and then at Ursule. "You should have called for me!" she accused.

"Didn't you hear the babe calling?" Ursule crossed the room to hand her the basin. "Take this downstairs," she said. "For Monsieur Martin to bury."

The midwife stared at her, wordless with fury, but when Ursule pressed the basin into her hands, she took it, spun about in a swirl of petticoats and pristine apron, and marched down the stairs.

Ursule's own apron was spotted with blood and fluids, and her smock was wrinkled and stained, signs of a hard job well done. She took a moment to wash her hands and splash water on her overheated face, then returned to the bedside to gaze with pride at her daughter and her brand-new grandchild.

Léonie freed one hand from beneath the swaddled infant to take hers. "Maman, thank you," she murmured, her voice thready with fatigue. "Without you, I don't think she would even be here."

"Do you know her name?"

"Oh, yes!" Léonie said, turning her gaze down to the babe. The little girl had a head full of dark hair, and looked as if she would share her *grand-mère*'s dusky complexion. "Yes, Maman, I planned to name our first child after Louis. She will be Louisette. Isn't that pretty?"

"It's beautiful. The perfect name for a Lammas child."

"Will you send word to Louis? I can't wait for him to see his daughter."

"Of course. I'll go to Kerjean today, and Louis can come home at last. First, though, I'm going to give you a simple to help bring in your milk."

"And you will tell Madeleine about Louisette?"

"*Bien sûr.*" Ursule rose and began to gather her few things together. She fetched her staff, with its reliquary of St. Anne, and brought it close to the bedside. "I want to bless the babe, Léonie. A *grand-mère*'s blessing."

Léonie gave her a tired, happy smile.

Ursule lifted the staff above the two of them, her daughter and precious granddaughter, and said softly,

Mother Goddess and St. Anne,
Bless this babe beneath my hand.
Let her days be full and long.
Keep her well and safe and strong.

Léonie's dimple flashed above the babe's head. "Oh, Maman," she said, half asleep already. "You and your gypsy ways!"

Ursule pushed back a lock of her daughter's hair, then let her fingers trail across the sleeping infant's head. "It's a good blessing," she said.

"A perfect blessing." Léonie moved the baby to her shoulder as if she had done it a thousand times before, then put her head back against her pillows. "I can't keep my eyes open."

"Nor should you. Well done, *ma fille.*"

Léonie's lips curled. "I have never been so happy in my life!"

"I remember that feeling." Ursule bent to kiss her forehead. "Sleep a while. The simple is on the bedside stand. Don't let that fool of a midwife touch it!"

Léonie laughed, sighed, and slept. Louisette, cradled against her shoulder, slept, too.

······ ❖᠁ • ᠁❖ ······

After weeks of living in the manor house, with its spacious rooms and tall windows, the cottage at Kerjean Farm seemed primitive. Ursule thought it must have been a hardship for Louis, living here for the past weeks. She hoped Remy had not taken advantage of her son-in-law's youth and strength.

She found Agnes at the table, a bit of sewing in her lap, and went to embrace her. "A daughter, Daj, just as we hoped. A beautiful little girl. Louisette!"

Agnes hugged her, laughing her silent laugh, a few happy tears slipping down her wrinkled cheeks. She gave the twinkle of her fingers that always meant Léonie.

"Yes, she's well. After all the trouble, the birth went smoothly. Where is Louis?"

Agnes pointed toward the byre, and Ursule hurried out. Her son-in-law had heard Bijou's hoofbeats, though, and met her halfway.

"Léonie was safely delivered of a daughter this morning!" Ursule announced.

"The babe is well? And Léonie?" Louis asked.

"The babe is healthy. Léonie's tired, but she's well. Longing to see you."

Louis hesitated, glancing over his shoulder at the byre, where Ursule supposed he had left some chore half-finished.

She laughed. "Go, Louis. I'll finish whatever it is."

He pushed back his hat, and gave her his white grin. "Thank you, Belle-mère. I don't like to leave you with the work, but..."

"Don't be silly. I've had enough of a holiday! Get your things and go home."

"And is she—is she still calling the babe after me?"

"Yes, of course she is," Ursule said, with an indulgent smile. "She's to be called Louisette, and I think it's lovely. She's an absolute treasure."

Louis barked a joyous laugh, then startled Ursule by bending down to kiss her soundly on both cheeks. "I'm a papa!" he chortled, before dashing across to the cottage. Ursule went to lead Bijou to the water trough, then to let out the stirrups for Louis's long legs.

In moments, Louis was on his way, urging Bijou to a heavy-footed gallop almost before they were out of the lane. Ursule smiled after him, then went in to change into her work clothes. "I'm going out to the byre, Daj," she said. "To see how things are."

Agnes, now at the sink shucking corn, pointed to the farmhouse. *Madeleine.*

"Oh," Ursule said. "You're right. Madeleine will want to know."

Agnes pointed again, then pinched her right eyebrow. *She worried.*

"She had reason," Ursule said. "I was worried, too. I hope she let you know after her visit that Léonie was improving."

A nod, and another point.

"I'm on my way."

She knocked on the farmhouse door, and it opened almost immediately. She found Madeleine dressed to go out, her hat already on her head, a basket on her elbow with several jars in it. Madeleine said, "The baby came, didn't it? I saw Louis's horse in the yard."

"Yes, this morning." Ursule smiled up at her mistress, ready to celebrate with her.

"I'm going there now, right away," Madeleine said. "Remy will drive the cart. And how is Léonie?"

"She's well, and her babe is healthy. Such a pretty little girl, Louisette."

"Oh, it's a girl? That's too bad." Madeleine pulled a shawl over her shoulders. "I'm sure Louis would have liked a son."

Ursule's smile died on her face, and she stared up at Madeleine in disbelief. "Louis didn't say that at all!"

"Well, he wouldn't, would he? But we know how men are." Madeleine stepped out on the doorstep and pulled the door closed behind her. "There's Remy with the cart. You'll see to the churning, won't you? It was one thing Louis wasn't very good at."

As Andie pulled the cart out into the lane, it was Remy who thought to call congratulations to Ursule on becoming a grandmother. She could see, also, as soon as she went into the byre, that Remy had assisted Louis in keeping things in good order. The haymow was full, the stanchions were clean, even the chicken coop had been raked out. There were half-completed repairs on one of the stanchions, and she took up her hammer to finish them. It was milking time when that was done, and she was glad to see her cows and goats again, although she was tired when it was all finished.

She patted the last nanny's bony spine on her way out of the byre, and a moment later Drom fluttered down to perch on her shoulder. She said, "Holiday's over, isn't it, old friend?"

He ruffled his wings, and croaked, *"Zi buna!"*

"*Zi buna* indeed," she said, chuckling. "A very good day."

When she went into the cottage for supper, she tried to explain Madeleine's odd response to the news of Léonie giving birth to a girl. Agnes listened, her brow creasing as she dished up stewed hare with onions.

She was still frowning when she joined Ursule at the table. She took one thoughtful bite, then set her spoon down. Ursule was too hungry to wait, and she almost burned her tongue on the savory stew as she watched her mother trying to work out what it meant.

Finally, Agnes pointed to the farmhouse, her sign for Madeleine, then spread the fingers of both her hands, palms down. *Selfish.* She did it again, pointing to the farmhouse, making the sign. *Madeleine is a selfish woman.*

"Yes," Ursule said. "She's selfish." The edge taken off her sharp appetite, she set her own spoon down. "But she adores Léonie. I thought she would be delighted."

Agnes shrugged and spread her hands. *Who knows?*

"I still think it's odd." She picked up her spoon again. "By the way, Louis left things in good order in the byre. He's a hard worker, I gather."

At that, her mother smiled and fluttered her fingers above her heart. *Lovely.*

"He is lovely, isn't he?" Ursule said with a smile. "It was nice you had company, and I do think our Léonie is a lucky girl to have chosen him. I suspect he'll go on spoiling her the way the rest of us always have."

Agnes nodded and resumed her own meal. Ursule finished her bowl of stew, ate a second, and devoured two thick slices of bread with the good Kerjean butter. Her cows gave much better cream than the ones at Manor Farm. The Martins' byre could have used one or two of her charms, she thought. Their cidery, too.

Louis's churning, however, was perfectly fine.

····· ·≫≫≫≫·≪≪≪≪· ·····

It was odd to be awakened once again in the early morning by the low-ing of cows and the goats' bleating. At Manor Farm, she had learned to sleep through it. She rose, though it was hard to leave her warm bed. She shivered in the autumn chill as she crossed the yard to the byre. She had never really thought about her age, but she was watching Agnes get old, and that meant she was aging, too. Fifty-two didn't seem like so very many years, but the stiffness of her hands as she began the milking made her wonder.

When she carried the milk pails across the yard to the buttery, she found Madeleine scrubbing out butter molds. Ursule remembered, noticing that Madeleine's hair was now completely gray and the lines around her mouth and eyes deeply graven, that Madeleine was older than herself.

She set her pails on the counter. "Do you know, Madeleine," she said, turning to her mistress, "Maman and I have been with you and Remy for almost forty years."

"Have you?" Madeleine went on scouring the mold in her hand. "That seems a very long time."

"It does, doesn't it?" Ursule poured out the milk and turned to washing the buckets. "I believe Isabelle Martin and I are the same age."

"But so different," Madeleine said.

"Well, of course. She lives in the manor house, and I—"

"I meant, she's not Romani, is she? Nor is Louis."

Ursule set her bucket upside down with a clang. She drew a breath to cool the heat of her temper, wiped her hands on a towel, and turned to face Madeleine. "Do you have a point?"

Madeleine ignored the harshness of her tone. "I meant that you look different."

"You mean I look darker."

"Well, of course. Gypsy blood."

Ursule put her hands on her hips and gave in to her temper. "What about it?"

"It's very strong, isn't it?"

"Léonie is fair."

"And that's so interesting. But of course, that man—her father—he was fair. And Louis has light skin, but his hair is dark and his eyes—"

Ursule snapped, "Madeleine, we're not a herd of cows, bred for color!"

Madeleine noticed, at last, that Ursule was angry. She slowly set down the butter mold and brushed water drops from the front of her apron. "The babe," she said, with a hint of her old sourness, "Léonie's babe. She's almost as dark as you are."

"Good!" Ursule bit out. "Then, perhaps, Madame Kerjean"—she emphasized *madame*—"you will remember who is really Léonie's *maman* and Louisette's *grand-mère!*"

Ursule was distantly aware that Madeleine's mouth dropped open, but she didn't stop to hear any retort she might have eventually thought of. She spun about so fast that her apron flapped around her as if she were a giant bird. She stamped out of the buttery and across to the chicken coop. Drom followed, swooping this way and that above her head and making a sound she did not doubt was a laugh.

8

Two weeks before Yule, Léonie and Louis came to Kerjean Farm to show their new daughter to Agnes. Ursule met them in the barnyard, helping Léonie down from the carriage, smiling at the kisses her son-in-law bestowed on her cheeks. Louis went to water Bijou while Ursule and Léonie, with Louisette in a blanket in her arms, started toward the cottage.

"I should warn you," Ursule said. "Your *grand-mère* isn't very well. Her hips bother her, and the winter cold makes it worse."

"You can't do anything for her, Maman?" Léonie lifted the baby to her shoulder and reflexively patted her back.

"I'm doing all I can, *ma fille*. I can help with her pain, but I can't repair her bones. She's just getting old, as we all must do."

Ursule had been observing Agnes's decline daily, but when they went into the cottage and she saw the dismay on Léonie's face, she realized how dramatic it had become. She had begged a comfortable chair from the farmhouse, one Madeleine wasn't using, and these days, Agnes spent most of her time in it. She didn't try to rise when Léonie came in. She stroked the babe's cheek with a trembling finger but made no attempt to hold her.

Léonie made a good job of hiding her consternation. She pulled a stool close and sat with the sleeping babe on her lap. When Louis came in, it was clear he, too, was startled by the change in Agnes.

Ursule made the tea, and as they sat down to drink it, Madeleine fluttered in with a plate of almond cakes. "Léonie!" she exclaimed. "I had a feeling you might be coming, and then I saw the carriage! I know these are your favorites." She set the plate in front of Léonie, nodded briefly to Agnes and Ursule, and said, "Louis, how are you? And your mother?"

Louis had risen from his stool and gestured to it. "Please, sit down, Madame Kerjean." He stood behind Léonie, his hands in his pockets. "My mother is busy planning the christening, as you can imagine. It will be just after St. Stephen's Day. I'm sure you'll want to be there—all of you."

"Bien sûr!" Madeleine said, with an airy wave of her hand.

Agnes didn't bother to sign anything, and Ursule saw Léonie reach out to squeeze her grandmother's hand. Long ago, Léonie had stopped asking why Agnes had never set foot in St. Anne, and Ursule had never tried to explain. *Some secrets should be kept.* In that, at least, they were still Romani.

Ursule sat in silence, struggling with the idea of facing the priest again. Her *Charm of persuasion* had rid her of him once, but she could imagine the accusing glances those cold eyes would cast her way. Her granddaughter's christening trapped her between preference and duty.

Léonie said, "Maman? You will come, won't you?"

Ursule made herself smile, avoiding Agnes's eyes. "Of course, *ma fille*. Of course I will come."

· · · · · ⁘⁘⁘⁘ · ⁘⁘⁘⁘ · · · · ·

In the end, Ursule was not present for Louisette's christening. The night before, Agnes began to have difficulty breathing and could no longer walk. She made no signs, but when Ursule settled her into her bed, she looked up from her pillow with wide, frightened eyes.

Ursule saw that a lamp still burned in the front window of the farmhouse, so she kissed her mother's forehead, then pulled on her coat and boots to hurry across the yard. At her knock, Remy came to the door. His shirt hung loose around him, and he was in his socks, as if he had been getting ready for bed. "Ursule? Something wrong?"

"Remy, yes, I—I think—" To her horror, Ursule felt a sob rising in her throat, choking her voice. Her face crumpled like a child's, and she put up her hands to hide it.

"*Chut, chut,*" Remy said, the way he did when he comforted a ewe in labor. He clumsily patted her shoulder. "Ursule, come inside. Madeleine's gone to bed, but I can give you some tea, or some water...Fetch Madeleine if you need her..."

Ursule followed him inside, the first time she had stepped through the farmhouse doors since Léonie was small. "Don't wake Madeleine," she said, when she had regained control of her voice. "There's nothing she can do. Oh, Remy, it's Maman. I can't leave her to go to the christening, so if you and Madeleine would explain for me...I think my mother is dying."

She swallowed hard. She had known what she had to say, but now that she had spoken the words aloud, the unrelenting truth of it gripped her, tightening her throat again, threatening those painful tears.

Remy clicked his tongue and went to pour her a glass of water. He brought it back and set it in front of her. "Maybe a spot of brandy, Ursule," he said, gruffly, as if being gentle embarrassed him. "Settle your nerves."

"I'm all right," she said, and suddenly, at the kindness of this big, awkward man she had worked with for so long, she was. Her voice steadied. "I won't take the brandy, Remy, but that's good of you. It's natural, isn't it? Maman is seventy-three, and this has been coming." She drank the water and set the glass down. "I think I can help her sleep a little."

As she stood up, he did, too. "Do you want me to come and sit with you?"

"No, thank you," she said. "If she's not better in the morning, though—the milking—"

"I'll do the milking either way," he said, and when she opened her mouth to protest, he added, "No arguments, Ursule."

"*Merci beaucoup,* Remy," she said softly. "I'm grateful."

"I'll check on you after the milking is done."

"I will be glad of it."

······· ·᠊᠊᠊᠊᠊ ·· ·······

Agnes Orchière left the world at the same moment her great-granddaughter was squalling in the hands of the redheaded priest. Ursule had given her mother a simple to ease her way, and she was sleeping peacefully when she drew her last breath.

Ursule was sitting beside Agnes's bed, holding her hand and contemplating her still face, when she heard the noisy rattle of the cart wheels returning from St. Anne, followed by the quieter ones of the Martin carriage. She laid Agnes's hand across her breast and went to the door.

Léonie was just climbing down from the carriage. Louis stepped down after, holding the babe still wrapped in her lacy bearing cloth. Léonie dashed across the yard to Ursule, and Louis followed, leaving the horse standing where it was.

"Maman, is she—am I too late?"

Ursule put her arms around her tall daughter and held her close for a long, poignant moment. When she released her, she saw that Léonie had already begun to cry, informed by the unusual show of affection.

"I'm sorry, *ma chère*," Ursule said gently. "She died about an hour ago. Come in and see her, and say your goodbye."

She led Léonie into the bedroom, where Agnes lay so still and silent. Sobbing, Léonie knelt beside the bed. Ursule stood behind her, a hand on her shoulder. Even in the sadness of the moment, she couldn't help noticing the clothes Léonie wore: a heavily embroidered stomacher, an elaborate skirt hemmed with lace. She supposed the men who had looted the manor house had missed more than one wardrobe full of the *vicomte*'s and *vicomtesse*'s things.

Louis came to stand in the doorway, taking in the sight of his wife crying beside Agnes's body. Ursule reached for her granddaughter, needing the comfort of a babe against her heart.

Louis settled the infant into her arms. "I'm sorry about your mother, Belle-mère."

"Thank you, Louis. I'll take Louisette out by the fire, shall I? It's cold in here."

She left them with Agnes and went to sit in the armchair beside the hearth. She looked down and found the babe's dark eyes open, fixed on her face.

"Hello, little one," Ursule whispered. "Our newest Orchière."

She traced the tiny features with her finger, and the infant's mouth worked as if she were trying to smile. Ursule murmured, "You were baptized a Martin, but you will always be an Orchière to me, clan or no clan." The little one blinked, and Ursule sighed. "Oh, sweeting. Your *grand-mère* wants you to learn the gypsy ways, but I suppose you'll be a good little Catholic, won't you?"

Louisette's eyes suddenly screwed shut, her face reddened, and she began to emit loud wails of impressive fury. Léonie came running, and Ursule handed over the babe, then gave up the armchair so mother and babe could nurse in comfort.

Louis went out to help with the horses. Léonie shifted the babe from one breast to the other. Her eyes and lips were swollen with crying, but she gave her mother a tremulous smile. "You'll want to perform a crossing rite," she said.

Ursule nodded. "It's our way."

"I'll send Louis back to Manor Farm so I can help you."

"Oh, Léonie. If it's not too much trouble—"

"And then," Léonie went on, turning businesslike, "you and I can do what needs to be done for poor Grand-mère. Louis can come back tomorrow with one of the farm laborers to dig the grave. I know she wouldn't want to be buried at St. Anne. I was thinking of that little hill beside the river."

Ursule found she was staring at Léonie, openmouthed. She made a sound that was half a laugh, half a snort of disbelief. "It seems you have everything well in hand."

"Well, Maman. These things have to be done."

"Are you sure Louis won't mind?"

"Quite. He never minds anything I want to do."

Ursule shook her head, amused despite the sadness of the day. "*Ma fille*, does anyone ever say no to you?"

Léonie shook her head. "No," she said with equanimity, as if such a circumstance were the most natural thing in the world. "No, no one ever does."

Ursule breathed out a long sigh and reflected on the enviable power of beauty.

· · · · · ·⟫⟫⟫⟫· ⟪⟪⟪⟪· · · · · ·

Ursule set up her altar with a new candle and the crystal and rested her staff with the St. Anne relic on the wall behind the table. Léonie settled Louisette into the old cradle Remy had made when Léonie was born, then went into the bedroom for their veils.

When she emerged, she said, "It's so strange to see Grand-mère just lying there. She was always so busy, cooking or sewing or digging in the garden."

"I know, sweetheart." Ursule took her veil and draped it over her head, and watched with nostalgia as Léonie did the same. "We will send her on her way, and when we see her again, she'll be as busy as ever."

"I hope so." Léonie stood before the altar, her hands clasped before her. "Father Bernard says the dead have to suffer the fires of purgatory before they can enter heaven. I can't bear to think of my gentle *grand-mère* going through anything like that."

"I don't believe a word of it," Ursule said, without heat. "I see our ancestresses in the crystal, and there are no fires."

"Oh, Maman," Léonie said, with an air of indulgence. "You don't really."

"Don't what?"

"Don't see the *grands-mères*. You just say that."

Ursule reached out to smooth the veil over Léonie's shoulder. "Never mind, *ma fille*. You can think of it as my gypsy ways, if you like, but I want you to know that your *grand-mère* Agnes is not going to be burn-ing in purgatory or anywhere else. Listen in your heart, and you'll find she's still there."

Léonie's eyes filled with tears. "I haven't seen her much lately. I should have tried harder."

"She understood. You have your own home now, a husband and a baby to care for."

Ursule watched the tears spill down Léonie's cheeks and marveled. Her face didn't crumple, nor did her nose run. Her cheeks shone with tears, and her lips glistened as if they had been polished. *It's no wonder no one refuses her anything.*

Ursule said quietly, "Come now, Léonie. Let us send our beloved on her way."

She lit the candle, sprinkled salted water around the altar, then spoke the old rite. She recited the *grands-mères'* names—Violca, Liliane, Yvette, Maddalena, Irina—and added one more, softly. "Agnes Orchière, voice-less in life, set free to sing in spirit."

She took up a palmful of cleansing sage, sprinkled some into the candle flame, and scattered the rest over the altar.

Mother of us all, we pray:
Aid your daughter on her way.
Let every step she takes be blessed
And bring her swiftly to her rest.

Warm light blossomed in the crystal. The reliquary caught it and reflected it back to the altar. Ursule pressed her hand to her heart, warmed and reassured, and glanced at Léonie, whose head was still bowed. "Do you not see it, *ma fille*? The light in the stone?"

Slowly, Léonie raised her head. "No, Maman. There is no light in the stone."

"But did you look?"

"I don't need to look. It's just an old stone."

"Léonie, it's not just a stone, it's—"

Léonie turned sharply away, pulling the veil from her head, going to bend over the cradle where her daughter slept. When she straightened, she turned to face her mother, and her smooth young face looked harder, older. "Maman, the Bible says witchcraft is sinful. If I thought there were lights or faces in the crystal that you could see, I would fear for your soul."

"Léonie!" Ursule pushed back her own veil and gazed at her daughter in horror. "How can you say that to me?"

"Father Bernard," Léonie said, as if she hadn't heard, "says his mother was cursed by a witch. She put a lump in her breast and killed her!"

Ursule unwound her veil and began folding it to still the tremble in her hands. "Léonie," she said, in a low voice. "Please listen to me. Don't put your trust in priests. Especially don't put your trust in this Father Bernard."

"But, Maman—"

"Léonie! Why would some poor woman curse the priest's mother? Why would she want her to die? People just look for someone to blame, someone to take responsibility for tragedy. Sometimes things just happen!"

"But you think you're a witch, don't you, Maman?"

Ursule held out her hand for Léonie's veil. "Give that to me. You won't be wearing it again."

"Maman, I only meant—"

"You've chosen the church over my tradition, your grandmother's tradition. I understand that. But if anyone hears you say I'm a witch, you will put me in the gravest possible danger."

"I wouldn't do that, Maman, I—"

"Do you know what happened to the poor woman your priest accused?"

Léonie drew a sharp breath and put her hands to her lips.

"You do, don't you? No doubt he boasted of it. What was it?"

"She was sentenced to be burned as a witch," Léonie said, through her fingers.

"So some poor old woman suffered a ghastly death because of a superstitious priest!"

"It didn't happen, actually. She died the night before it was to happen."

"That's disgusting, Léonie! Poor pitiful creature, hounded to death by an awful man!"

"He's a priest!"

"He's a monster, as is his witch-hunting bishop, and if you call me witch, I will face the same fate as that poor old woman."

"I won't say it again. I promise you, Maman. On my life, I promise you." She dropped her hand and unwound her veil from her shoulders to pass to Ursule. "I only meant to help you tonight, because I know the rite means so much to you. I didn't mean to upset you."

Ursule took the veil and folded it with painful care. She didn't know if it would ever be used again. "Let us have peace between us, *ma fille*," she said, but her voice was heavy with sorrow.

They didn't speak of their quarrel again that night, nor ever. They prepared Agnes for burial, tenderly washing her, dressing her in her best petticoat and scarf, brushing out the gray mass of her hair and plaiting it.

Louis obediently appeared the next morning, with the farm laborer at his side. Léonie showed them the site she had chosen for the grave, and the two men went to work. Remy went out to join them, carrying his own shovel. At noon, Léonie took the men bread and cheese and ale. At midafternoon, they came to the cottage to announce that the grave was ready.

Remy fetched Madeleine from the farmhouse. She had made it known that she wasn't pleased to have an unchurched grave on her farm, but now that it was clear it was going to be, she kept her thoughts to herself. The six of them formed a procession behind Louis, who carried Agnes's blanket-wrapped body in his strong arms. Léonie carried Louisette, still in her bearing cloth. Ursule brought her staff and leaned heavily on it as they climbed the little hill. Drom soared overhead in slow circles, following their progress.

As the men lowered the body into the grave, Ursule closed her eyes, not wanting to see her mother disappear beneath the earth. Remy and the farm laborer shoveled the dirt back into the grave while Louis kept his arm around Léonie and the babe.

Madeleine muttered, "There should be a priest. This isn't decent."

"Never mind, Madeleine. We said our prayers last night." Ursule felt the slight vibration from the reliquary radiate down through her staff and into her hand, and she silently thanked Anne for her sympathy.

When the dirt was smoothed over the grave, Remy said, "Ursule, would you like a marker?"

"Thank you, Remy. I think I'll bring up river stones and make a cairn."

It was done. Louis and Léonie and the laborer from Manor Farm embraced Ursule, said farewell, and were gone. Madeleine disappeared into the buttery. Remy stood beside the doorstep of the cottage, his hat in his hand.

"Are you all right, Ursule?"

"I am. Thank you for everything, Remy."

"Well. Well." He cleared his throat. "*Eh bien*, you know I'm here if you need something." He lumbered across the yard toward the byre.

Ursule called after him, "Remy, I'll do the milking tonight."

He paused and looked back her. "Are you sure?"

"I want to do it." She wanted to escape the emptiness of the cottage, not ready to feel Agnes's absence. She wanted to forget the quarrel with her daughter. She wanted the company of her cows and her goats, the comforting chatter of her hens.

Drom settled on the roof above the door of the cottage, clearly more subdued than usual. She said, quietly, "*Zi buna*, Drom."

He gave a low chirp, and said, "*Zi buna. Zi buna.*"

It was enough. It would have to be.

Ursule celebrated Imbolc in solitude, with only Drom to watch from the cold February darkness, his eyes glittering faintly through the window. She brought out the little bundle of veils and held it to her breast. The scent of her mother's hair still clung to one of them, and a spasm of longing pierced her. She hastened to set up her altar before her energy failed. She couldn't give up her practice now. She would do this to honor the *grands-mères* and their centuries of tradition.

The ritual comforted her, and when she finished, the glow of the Orchière crystal reminded her she was not truly alone. Her ancestresses were always with her.

She had not bothered to build up the fire, as Agnes might have done, and the cottage was cold. She stirred the embers just enough to warm a cup of milk with a bit of honey in it, and went to bed, wrapping herself with an extra blanket against the chill. For the first time since her mother's death, she slept soundly, and woke rested.

It was Sunday, but she would not be going to St. Anne again, not so long as Father Bernard presided. Madeleine would criticize, but she preferred suffering her mistress's sharp words to breathing in the aura of evil emanating from the priest. She had already made the mistake of thinking she could raise her daughter in the Romani tradition while allowing her to participate in the Catholic one. She saw no point in adding to her misery.

She was still in the byre when she heard the cart clatter away up the lane, Andie's hooves loud on the still-frozen ground. She finished the milking, returned to the cottage for a cup of tea and a slice of bread and butter, then crossed the yard to the buttery to begin the churning.

She was working the plunger when Drom appeared in the doorway, shifting from foot to foot just beyond the lintel. She smiled at him and said, "Drom! *Zi buna.*"

Instead of answering, he crooned at her and flapped his wings.

"What is it?" she asked, and immediately heard the distinctive rumble of wheels that meant the Martin carriage was coming down the lane. She propped the plunger against the side of the barrel and hurried to the door, wiping her hands on her apron as she watched Louis pull up Bijou's reins, then hop down to assist Léonie from the carriage, Louisette bundled in her arms.

Ursule hurried toward them and reached eagerly for her granddaughter. "How nice to see you!" She cuddled the babe's warm small body and pressed her lips to Louisette's downy head, breathing in the faint smell of incense that clung to it. "I hope everything's all right?"

Léonie startled her by circling her with her arms, nearly crushing little Louisette, who woke and began to grizzle. "Maman," Léonie said. "We have news."

"Come inside, then," Ursule said. "I'll make a fresh pot of tea. Did you come straight from the chapel?"

"We did." Léonie kept an arm around Ursule as they turned together to cross the yard. Over her shoulder, Léonie said, "Louis, unhitch Bijou, will you? We'll be here a while. Don't forget the basket."

Louis obligingly began unbuckling the traces.

"You do rather order him about, don't you, *ma fille*?"

Léonie squeezed her shoulders and dimpled. "Don't I just?" she said.

Ursule laughed and led the way into the cottage. "If I'd known you were coming I would have—I don't know—cooked something."

"Don't worry, Maman. I brought luncheon for all of us, and in memory of dear Grand-mère, almond cakes."

"What a treat, Léonie. That was very thoughtful."

Léonie dimpled again and reached for the babe, who was beginning to whimper in earnest. She settled herself into Agnes's armchair to nurse. "I'm going to have to wean Louisette a bit sooner than I thought," she said.

Ursule, filling the kettle at the sink, turned to face her daughter. "Oh, *ma chère*. Already?"

Léonie's smile was joyous, as if the anxiety of the past year had faded utterly from her mind. "Yes, Maman! Another Martin babe on the way, and maybe a boy this time!"

"My goodness. You—you seem to be in a great hurry."

"I want a big family, Maman, and so does Louis. Everything is perfect."

"I'm glad you're happy," Ursule said, as she slid the kettle onto the hob. "But it's awfully soon, isn't it?"

"*Oh la la,*" Léonie said, blithe as a babe herself. "That's what my mother-in-law said, and she with five children in ten years!"

"Perhaps she's worried about you."

"As you are, Maman?" Léonie deftly shifted Louisette from one breast to the other and smiled up at Ursule. The kettle began to simmer just as Louis came in from the cold, stamping his feet and rubbing his hands.

Ursule didn't want to remind her daughter of the dangers of her first labor. There was no point now. She went to take her son-in-law's coat and accept his kisses on her cheeks. Louis handed her a full basket. The mouthwatering aroma of roasted meat rose from it.

"Happy news, is it not, Belle-mère?"

Ursule smiled and agreed despite the quailing of her heart. "Come, Louis, sit by the fire and get warm."

It was the happiest day Ursule had spent since her mother's death, despite her worries. When Louisette finished nursing, Léonie made Ursule sit in the armchair to hold her. She cuddled the sleeping babe as Léonie flitted between the sink and the table, laying out a luncheon of roasted pork, boiled eggs, a wedge of cheese, and freshly baked bread. She directed Louis in the setting of the table, making Ursule pinch back a smile.

When the luncheon was ready and the babe settled in Léonie's old cradle, the three of them sat at the table and ate and talked and laughed.

They were nibbling at almond cakes and sipping tea when they heard the Kerjean cart rattle into the yard.

Madeleine came straight to the cottage, still in her coat and hat. She knocked once and stepped inside without waiting for an answer. "Léonie!" she said, as if there weren't two other people in the room. "Wouldn't you be more comfortable in the house?"

Léonie spoke more coolly than Ursule had ever heard her. "Of course not, Madeleine. Why should you think that?"

Louis rose to offer his stool to Madeleine. It was the crooked one, which Madeleine took in with a glance. Her lip curled, ever so slightly, and she shook her head. "No, thank you, Louis," she said. "I merely wanted to invite you to the house. Since you're here."

Léonie said, "Would you like to see Louisette? She's sleeping in the cradle."

Madeleine said, too quickly, "No, no, I won't disturb her. But come to the house before you leave. I have something for you."

She was gone a moment later. Ursule had not spoken a word, nor Louis. Léonie, serene as if there had been no interruption, said, "Maman, another almond cake?"

To please her, Ursule accepted another, though she had already eaten twice as much as she usually did at a meal. Before she bit into it, she said, "Were you not a bit—*brusque*—with Madeleine, *ma fille?*"

Léonie made a rather prim mouth, and nodded. *"Bien sûr,"* she said, without hesitation. "I'm a mother now. It changes things, doesn't it?"

"What things in particular?"

"Eh bien, it's all well and good that Madeleine is fond of me, but Louisette comes first." As if she had heard, the infant began to grumble from the bedroom, and Léonie jumped up to fetch her.

Louis, leaning forward with his elbows on the table, said in an undertone, "Léonie thinks Madeleine doesn't like babies."

Ursule struggled for an answer that would not offend him. She couldn't tell him Madeleine objected to the babe looking like a gypsy. Indeed, the idea was so offensive she had trouble accepting it herself.

She stammered, "R–really, Louis? I always thought—that is, Madeleine adored Léonie as a baby."

"But not Louisette. Don't you find that strange?"

Ursule was saved from answering by Léonie returning with the babe in her arms. As she sat down, Léonie said, "It's everything, isn't it, Maman? Having a babe to love. Being a mother. I'm sorry that Madeleine never experienced it. I want nothing more in the world than this."

Ursule could not doubt her sincerity. Her daughter was the very picture of maternal contentment. She had gained weight, her cheeks plumping, her autumn-gold eyes sparkling. Her dimple flashed as Ursule admired her.

"You look very well, *ma fille*." She felt her daughter's happiness radiate through her own body, and her spirits rose.

Louis said, "She does look well, doesn't she? We're both grateful to you for that."

Ursule would not demur. What he had said was true. Léonie would have died without her aid, without the intervention of the *grands-mères*, and of St. Anne, guided by her skill. By her power, granted to her by the Goddess, carefully husbanded and honed.

And now, she must prepare. She might need to do it again.

······•≈≈≈•≈≈≈•······

Léonie and Louis fell into the habit of coming to Kerjean every Sunday after Mass. Ursule looked forward to their visits all week, and the anticipation lightened her labors and eased the solitude of her nights. They always brought food with them, prepared in the Manor Farm kitchen. Ursule supplied tea and cider, and simples to support Léonie's growing pregnancy. She dandled Louisette on her knee, marveling at how tall she was growing, how lively she was as she began to crawl. As spring wore on and summer began, she relished the little one's first steps and chuckled over her first word. It was not precisely intelligible. It might have been *button*. Just as easily, it could have been *bird*. Either way, it charmed Ursule and reminded her of how talkative Léonie had been.

Louis didn't mention Madeleine again. Léonie sometimes said, if Ursule asked if she was going over to the farmhouse, "I've already seen Madeleine, at Mass today." Other times, she would cross the yard in response to Madeleine's request, but she always took Louisette with her, and the invitations from Madeleine dwindled.

Finally, as the summer solstice approached and the lovely arch of Léonie's belly grew more prominent, Léonie said, "Do you know, Maman, I can't understand what's wrong with Madeleine. She pretends Louisette doesn't exist."

"Does she indeed?" Ursule kept her gaze averted, teasing Louisette with a doll made of cloth and yarn and buttons for eyes. The babe, seated on a blanket at their feet, seized the doll with a squeal of triumph and immediately put it in her mouth.

Léonie smiled down at her, but when she looked up at Ursule, her mouth pulled tight, making her look older than her eighteen years. "She doesn't look at her. She never asks about her. I suspect she would rather I left her with you when I go to the farmhouse."

"Ah. I see."

"Can you understand it?"

Ursule answered without hesitation. "Louisette is the most precious thing in the world to me, aside from your own self, *ma fille*. I will never understand."

"It makes no sense," Léonie said. The edge of anger in her voice, so unlike her usual sunny nature, made Ursule's neck prickle. "Remy is fond of her. He even carved her a little wooden duck, which she loves. But Madeleine ignores her."

It would have been all too easy to explain, but Ursule bit her lip and kept silent. It would only hurt Léonie. It would change nothing. It would not even assuage her own resentment, which now seemed pointless.

A hint of fire glinted in her daughter's eyes. "I think Madeleine's jealous. Does she think I should place her above my own daughter? And now there will be another child. I can't be soothing Madeleine when I have my babes to think of."

"No," Ursule said. "Of course your babes come first. Madeleine will have to learn, as all mothers do, as you will yourself one day. Our children grow up. They move on. It's the way of the world."

Louisette crowed and waved her now-sodden doll in the air. Mother and grandmother both chuckled, and Léonie bent to pull her daughter into her lap. "I hate to think of that day, Maman. I love having Louisette as my own little girl."

Ursule folded her hands, warmed by a sense of justice. "That's as it should be, *ma chère*."

······ ❖❖❖❖ • ❖❖❖❖ ······

Léonie's pregnancy advanced smoothly this time. Her confinement came much too early, but proceeded without difficulty. The midwife was called, but Ursule ejected her from the bedroom as Léonie began to labor in earnest, and she was once again drinking tea with Édi when Léonie's second daughter arrived.

Anne-Marie looked so much like an Orchière that Ursule nearly clapped her hands at the sight of her. She was considerably smaller than Louisette, a tiny sprite with a sprout of black hair and velvet brown eyes. "Another Lammas babe," Ursule said, as she laid the baby in Léonie's arms.

Léonie whispered, "She should have been a Mabon babe, Daj."

Her daughter's use of the Romani word startled Ursule. She looked closer at Léonie's weary face. Her eyelids were drooping and her lips slack.

Ursule pulled the blanket up around mother and child. "Never mind, *ma fille*," she murmured. "She'll catch up. We'll help her."

Louis had arranged for one of the farm laborers to fill in for Ursule as she came to attend her daughter, so he was in the house for the birth. He dashed up the stairs when it was accomplished, and hurried to kiss his wife and gaze fondly down at his newest offspring.

"Oh, *ma petite*," he said. "So little and fragile. Belle-mère, is she healthy?"

"She's all right. She's just small."

Louis touched his wife's pale cheek. "And you?"

"I'm well, Louis. But tired. I'm sorry it's another girl." Léonie's voice was thin, and her eyes bore dark circles beneath them, but she smiled and snuggled her newborn close to her chest.

"Never mind," Louis said. "Next time."

Ursule waited until both babe and mother slept, then drew Louis out of the room and shut the door softly behind her. He gazed down at her, frowning. "They're truly all right?"

"Yes. But Léonie is going to need more rest than she did with Louisette. And if I may speak plainly to you—" She raised her eyebrows.

He nodded and said, in a voice tight with worry, "Of course. Please."

"She will need more time to recover before she bears another child. Of course you want a boy, but this one—so soon after the first—"

Ursule was glad to see that although Louis flushed an uncomfortable red, he held his ground. She added, "I'm a plainspoken woman, Louis. My work has made me that way."

"I'm a farmer, too. I understand these things."

"Good." She patted his arm, then let herself back into the bedroom to tidy up. As she went about picking up towels and arranging the simples she would leave for Léonie, she reflected on how fortunate her daughter had been in her choice of husband. She might have married him for his charms—or for his big house—but he clearly adored his wife.

That adoration could be a problem. Another pregnancy, too soon after the first two, would be dangerous. She had already had one near-tragedy. Another—

Ursule clicked her tongue, scolding herself. She had a second beautiful granddaughter, another girl of the Orchière line. It was even possible that this was the girl who would carry on the tradition.

She must focus on that. And she would, of course, beg the *grands-mères* for their help.

On the eve of Samhain, when the infant Anne-Marie was three months old, Louis and Léonie resumed their habit of visiting Ursule after Mass. Anne-Marie was still small for her age, but she had begun to smile at everything. Her lips curled up to show her bare gums, and her cheeks scrunched up to turn her dark eyes into glowing half moons.

Léonie handed her to Ursule as soon as they came into the cottage, and Ursule gladly settled into the armchair to cuddle her. Louis carried Louisette in, set her on the floor, then went back outside to see to the carriage.

With a half-toothless grin, Louisette toddled across the uneven floor to Ursule. "Grand-mère?" Her consonants were mushy, but her intention was clear.

Ursule smiled down at her. "*Oui*, Louisette. I'm happy to see you again."

Louisette pointed to Anne-Marie. "*Ma soeur,*" she said, her voice charmingly husky for one so small.

"Yes indeed," Ursule said. "Your sister."

Louisette patted her own chest. "*Grande soeur.*"

"Yes. Big sister."

Louisette gave a businesslike nod, as if she had come just to settle the point. A moment later, she toddled off to examine Ursule's milking boots. Ursule laughed as the little girl plopped onto the floor to try to fit her own feet into them. Léonie sat on a stool, exhaling a long, exhausted sigh. Ursule, lifting the sleeping baby to her shoulder, cast Léonie a searching look. "Are you all right, *ma fille*?"

"I am," Léonie said, but in a wan voice.

"You look pale to me," Ursule said. "And too thin."

"Well, Maman," Léonie said, with a pale little laugh. "I feel as if I've been nursing infants for two straight years."

"So you have," Ursule said. "I've made you a tonic, to strengthen you, and also a simple. It's over there on the counter, the stoppered bottle. I think you should use it, Léonie."

"What is it for?"

"To prevent pregnancy."

Léonie's eyes widened, their gold-brown color deepening to an alarmed nut-brown. "Maman!"

"What?"

"That's—that's a sin!"

"According to the men who run your church, Léonie? Shouldn't the decision to bear a child be your own?"

Léonie's pale cheeks flushed, but she protested, "It's—it's the word of God."

Ursule experienced a nearly overpowering urge to spit on the floor. Instead, she snapped, "It's not the word of the Goddess." From the oak tree outside, Drom gave a warning squawk. The babe in her arms squirmed, and she realized she had tightened her hold on the poor little thing. She loosened her arms, kissed the little girl's head, and took a long, slow inhalation. "Léonie," she said, in a calmer voice. "I wish you would think for yourself, instead of letting that—that *priest*—do it for you. In our tradition, women—"

"Don't, Maman!" Léonie averted her gaze, and the flush on her cheeks receded too quickly.

"Don't what?"

"Don't talk about—about those gypsy things! People will think I'm a *gitane*."

"Ah. So now you're ashamed of being Romani."

Léonie swallowed hard, her slender throat working, and Ursule experienced a pang at seeing her daughter upset. "I'm not," Léonie said, her voice cracking on the words. "Not really. It's just—it's just easier."

"To pretend?"

Léonie swallowed again and lifted a tearful face to her mother. "I don't want you to be ashamed of me."

Ursule clicked her tongue and pressed her cheek to the soft head of her granddaughter. "Never mind, *ma fille*. I would never be ashamed of you."

"You don't want me to have more children?"

"I don't want you to overtax your health."

"I know," Léonie said wearily. "I do know that."

"*Eh bien, ma chère*, your life is your own. I wish your decisions could be, too."

"*Désolée*," Léonie whispered.

"*De rien*, my dearest heart."

A silence fell between them, broken by Louis's return. He carried a basket, which he set on the table and began to unpack. "Léonie made a cake just for you, Belle-mère," he said cheerfully, oblivious to the atmosphere in the room. Louisette scrambled up and ran to her papa to be picked up. Anne-Marie began to whimper, and as Ursule and Léonie changed places so she could nurse, the afternoon settled into a familiar pattern, a family luncheon, babes to mind, conversation that was of no consequence.

Ursule didn't mention the simple again until the visit was over, and Louis was gathering his family to start for home. He started out to the carriage with Louisette in one arm, the basket in his other hand. Léonie, Anne-Marie on her shoulder, started after him, but Ursule held her back, holding out the stoppered jar with its simple.

"Take it, *ma fille*," she said. "In case you change your mind."

Léonie gave her a bleak glance. "It's too late, Maman," she said, her voice dry and resigned. "It's already too late."

······ ❦ ······

Ursule arranged her table for Samhain with a heavy heart. She set a place for Agnes, in memory, and one for Violca. On an impulse, she set one for St. Anne, with a whispered invitation for the Christian grandmother to join the Romani ones. The darkness of the coming winter

:losed around the cottage, as if it couldn't wait to banish the light, to welcome the cold and shadows.

She ate a bowl of soup, though with little appetite. She left the extra places where they were as she brought out the Orchière crystal and a fresh, fat beeswax candle. She sprinkled sprigs of rosemary around the altar and laid one at each place of the missing ancestresses.

When the candle was burning and her veil draped over her hair, she began, though the silence of her house and the blankness of the empty places made her feel stiff and slow. Her voice was low, uncertain, as she spoke the traditional opening and then her prayer.

Mother of us all, I pray,
Lead my daughter in your way.
No priest nor man let her obey,
Nor falsehoods lead her steps astray.

The answering glimmer in the crystal came quickly, a faint star burning in a gray sky, as small and forlorn as Ursule felt. She waited, head bowed, until it faded. She blew out the half-burned candle and gathered up the unused bowls and spoons and put them in the cupboard. When she lifted the dark crystal, she saw her reflection in the surface and stopped, gazing at it with surprise. Her face was distorted by the curve of the stone, but she saw enough to realize that the last vestiges of her youth were gone.

She put the stone in its basket and covered it without taking another look. Her appearance didn't matter. There was no one to look at her. And even if there were, there was nothing to be done about it. She went to her bed, and fell asleep marveling at how swiftly a life could pass.

· · · · · ◦◦◦◦◦ • ◦◦◦◦◦ · · · · ·

Isabelle was born before Anne-Marie was weaned, and she was even smaller than Anne-Marie had been, with dreamy-looking eyes and a cry so faint Ursule could barely hear it.

"Three daughters," Louis murmured, looking down at the tiny doll of an infant.

"Indeed." Ursule heard the note of disappointment in his voice. She feared what that meant.

She was right to worry. Little Isabelle was only a year old when Léonie conceived yet again.

"Louis wants a son," she said wearily, on one of their visits. "I couldn't refuse him."

"Léonie—" Ursule began, but her daughter put up one thin white hand.

"Don't, please, Maman. I know this wasn't—I know you worry."

"It's the lot of a mother, I suppose." Ursule looked away, not wanting Léonie to see that it was not worry revealed on her face, but real fear.

"Please don't blame Louis. It's natural for a man to want a son."

Why? Why should he want a son when he has three perfect daughters? She didn't speak the thought. She knew the answer. Every woman knew the answer to that question, and some even agreed with it.

"I know what you're thinking, Maman." Léonie's voice was that of an old, tired woman, a woman resigned.

"I wonder if you do, *ma fille*," was all Ursule said. All she dared say, lest she burst into tears. The deed was done now, and although she could offer a remedy, she had no doubt her daughter would refuse it. Her prayer had gone unanswered, deflected by Léonie's submission to her husband, to her church—to that awful priest.

She wished with all her heart she could forget the dream that had so frightened her during Léonie's first pregnancy, but it had not faded in the intervening years. When she thought of it, she clutched the reliquary and begged St. Anne to intercede.

· · · · · ⠿⠿⠿ · ⠿⠿⠿ · · · · ·

Léonie's fourth pregnancy was almost as frightening as her first. Ursule made simples and potions and lotions, and she created a protective amulet of sage and mugwort and mistletoe, bound up in a bit of linen and tied many times round with silk thread from Agnes's old stores. She blessed it at her altar, sprinkling it liberally with salted water, and when she went to Manor Farm to see Léonie, who was spending most of her time sleeping, she tied it to one of the slats beneath the mattress.

Léonie was brought to bed of twins, both girls, and for once, Ursule was glad of the midwife's presence. She needed the extra pair of hands as the labor went on through the night, as Léonie began to tire and need more and more help. Ursule seized the moments when the midwife was out of the room to administer drops of the potion against pain, and to ask the *grands-mères* for support.

When both infants were finally born, and the midwife departed with the basin and the afterbirth, Ursule sat beside the bed, watching her exhausted daughter with two tiny, dark babes at her breast.

Léonie said, her voice a mere thread of sound, "How am I going to do this?"

Ursule tried to sound reassuring, but she had her own doubts. "I'll strengthen the simple to bring in your milk, Léonie."

"You will use your magic, Daj?" Léonie's voice broke on the last word, and Ursule felt a scattering of gooseflesh over her neck and arms.

"Of course I will use my magic, *ma fille*. You are not alone. The *grands-mères* are always with you."

When Louis had met his new daughters, Florence and Fleurette, Ursule gathered up her things and followed him out of the bedroom, leaving Léonie sleeping and the babes side by side in a cradle. "I must get back to Kerjean, Louis," she said, feeling almost as weary as Léonie. She let her staff rest against her shoulder as she leaned on the wall behind her. "I've left things on the table beside Léonie's bed. She knows how to use them. I'll come tomorrow with another—"

She broke off, not knowing how to say what she must. He watched her, his brow creasing. "They're all right, aren't they? The babes? Small, I know, but perfect little mites."

"Yes, Louis, your daughters are all right. Small, as you say. It will be hard on Léonie to feed them."

"I'll do everything I can to help her."

"I know you will. But, Louis—this is hard for me to say, but—there must be no more babes for you."

His eyes widened, and the color rose and fell in his cheeks. "No—no more?"

"I know it's hard. You're young, and it's a great sacrifice, but I fear Léonie will not survive another pregnancy. You see how thin she is, how worn down."

"I do," he said, and dropped his head.

"I know you wanted a son."

His shoulders slumped. "I did, but—I should have—we shouldn't—"

Ursule put her hand on his forearm and squeezed the firm muscles. "Hush, Louis. *Mon fils*. It's natural for the two of you, nothing to be ashamed of."

He drew a shuddery breath and lifted his eyes to hers. "If she will recover, I promise I will—that we won't—"

"She can recover. We'll see to it."

"She must. We need her."

So do I. She released his arm and pushed herself away from the wall. "I must go home now, Louis. Thank you for sending your dairymaid to Kerjean."

"I'll order up the carriage."

"Merci beaucoup."

Once she was on her way, with the farmhand driving Bijou, Ursule let her head drop back against the seat, beginning to plan the simples she would make to strengthen Léonie, to help her through the nursing of two babes. She had little faith in the availability of a wet nurse, even for Manor Farm. She wondered if she could convince her daughter not to have another child.

Louis had promised, but she knew how hard it would be. She recalled perfectly how she had hungered for Sandor, so long ago. Would she have been able to make the sacrifice?

She started to doze, having not slept at all during Léonie's labor. Just as her eyelids drooped, she remembered what Léonie had asked her: would she use her magic? And she had once again, in her need and her fatigue, called her *Daj*.

It seemed her daughter was still Romani after all. It was something to cling to.

U rsule had loved everything about Léonie's childhood: the sweet sounds of her breathing as she slept, her sunny little face at the table, the patter of her bare feet running through the yard. As she watched her granddaughters grow, she recalled those moments with an intensity that shook her. She knew how the light steps of little feet turned into pounding, how the eager face at supper closed and withdrew. She watched her granddaughters for all of these things.

Louisette was imperious and bossy. Anne-Marie was sensitive, often weepy. Isabelle was dreamy and quiet, and the twins, even at four, had established distinct personalities. Fleurette was shy, letting Florence do the talking for both of them. Indeed, Fleurette spoke so little that Ursule sometimes wondered if she had a voice at all. The resonance with her memories of Agnes was eerie, a pattern repeating. She coaxed Fleurette to talk to her, to say what she liked or what she wanted, but the little girl inevitably looked to her twin to manage the questions.

Léonie no longer looked like the young, fresh girl who had so happily entered into motherhood. She was too thin, and her shoulders had begun to round. Her face had hollowed, leaving shadows beneath her cheekbones, though she was just twenty-six.

Despite this, Ursule began to breathe easier for her daughter as the time passed without another pregnancy. Léonie faithfully brought the children to spend time with their grandmother every Sunday afternoon. At first, Louis came as he had always done, but little by little he found other things to do, and over time, he stopped coming at all. Denis, the latest farmhand, drove the carriage and disappeared with Remy to his hideaway, always emerging smelling of brandy.

"Why is Louis not with you?" Ursule finally asked her daughter. She wanted to avoid the subject, but Léonie's sad look meant she couldn't put it off any longer.

"He's busy," Léonie said.

"That's not an answer, *ma fille.*"

Léonie shrugged and bent to stop Fleurette from pulling her twin's hair. She called to Louisette to take the twins outside. "Show them Grand-mère's raven," she said. "Anne-Marie and Isabelle, too. See if you can get him to speak to you."

When the children had gone out, Léonie said, "I can't believe that old bird is still with you, Maman."

"Don't change the subject, Léonie." Ursule spoke as gently as she could. "What's wrong between you and your husband? Has he begun saying no to you at last?"

That brought a pale smile to Léonie's face. "Not exactly," she said. She lifted her eyes to her mother's, and Ursule saw that they were not the sunny golden-brown she loved so much, but autumn-dark, the color of fallen leaves in winter. "Louis is having an affair."

"Léonie! Surely not. How do you know?"

Ursule watched in amazement as Léonie put a hand to her solar plexus, the seat of magic, the nexus of intuition. "I just know, Daj. I knew the first time it happened, as if I were standing in the door of her cottage, watching them."

"You have the power," Ursule said, her own voice tremulous with wonder despite the grimness of the news. "You *do* have it."

"Only this little bit. And only when it comes to Louis, I'm afraid."

A memory gripped Ursule. She closed her eyes, but that didn't stop the image of her younger self standing in the lane, suffering the blow of hearing Sandor say, "Who are you?"

She drew a long, noisy breath and opened her eyes to find Léonie watching her. "You know how this feels, don't you, dearest Daj? I haven't forgotten. I'm so sorry."

She reached out to her mother, and they joined hands, the old woman

and the young. They shared the ache of betrayal, of sorrow and abandonment, but beneath the pain, a small part of Ursule exulted. *Her daughter
had the power.*

It didn't matter that it was narrow, and focused. It was there, a seed
from which a mighty vine could grow, because if Léonie had it, one of
her daughters might as well.

But first, Ursule thought, as she squeezed and released Léonie's hand,
they would deal with Louis's failing.

"I think it's because we don't sleep together anymore, Maman,"
Léonie said after a bit. "We—we used to do that a lot, but now—"
Her tiny shrug was one of the saddest gestures Ursule had ever seen her
make.

"I can give you a potion against conception, remember. I offered it once."

"Father Bernard always says—well, you were right, Maman. I should
have taken it, purgatory or not. Now I've lost my husband—at least,
lost his love."

"I don't believe that," Ursule said. "I know Louis almost as well as
you do. I see the love in him for you, for the girls. I think sometimes
men don't understand themselves, and they do foolish things."

She pushed herself up and went to the door to look for her granddaughters. They were chasing each other through the goat pasture,
tall Louisette, petite Anne-Marie, quiet Isabelle, the inseparable twins.
Two black-and-white goat kids gamboled around them in the summer
sunshine. The beauty of them all, the perfection, was stunning, and it
made her furious.

She turned back to Léonie, and now her voice was hard, her heart
harder. "Who is this strumpet?" Anger thrilled through her blood.
"We're going to put an end to this, *ma fille.*"

Léonie sniffled, and she put a hand over her flat, empty womb. "You
can't make Louis love me again, Maman."

"I don't need to," Ursule said. "He never stopped."

······•⫸⫸⫷⫷•⫸⫸⫷⫷•······

The strumpet's name, Ursule learned, was Babette, and she was as different from Léonie as a woman could be, short and soft and red-haired, with blank, pale eyes. Ursule knew this because she saw her in the crystal. She was a squat little dairymaid, nothing like her own elegant, long-limbed daughter. It was not possible that Louis could prefer her.

Léonie had made Ursule promise that neither Babette nor Louis would be harmed. Ursule, still in the clutches of her fury, gave her promise without defining what was meant by harm. Some part of her knew that had Agnes been here, she would have argued for calm, for objectivity, but it was more gratifying to indulge in her anger. She would not forgive these two for hurting Léonie when she was weakened by bearing Louis's children.

"We'll wait for the solstice," she said. "For Litha. Keranna will be having its Midsummer Fete, and everyone will be in the village."

"What should I do?"

"Come here to me, and bring the girls. Say you're not up to a festival, dancing far into the night, managing the children."

"But Madame Martin will say—"

"Tell her you promised to spend Midsummer Night with me. I'll give you a simple to make her amenable."

Léonie flashed her dimple at that, and Ursule took heart. She hadn't seen her daughter's dimple in a long time.

"I will need something of Louis's. A lock of his hair would be perfect."

"I can get that." Léonie fell silent for a moment and said, softly, "I know I teased you about your gypsy ways, Daj. I wish I had not."

For a moment, Ursule couldn't answer. She had longed so for her daughter to recognize what she was—to honor it—that this moment made her press a hand to her breast. "Léonie—*ma fille*—" Emotion made her voice break, and for a moment she forgot her anger in a rush of love and gratitude for her daughter's acknowledgment.

"I'm sorry, Daj. I was wrong."

Ursule swallowed, sighed, and stroked Léonie's cheek with her fingers. "Never mind, *ma chère*. It doesn't matter now. It doesn't matter in the least."

· · · · · ◦◦◦◦◦ • ◦◦◦◦◦ · · · · ·

The spell was very far back in the grimoire, even farther than the *Philter to persuade the reluctant Lover*. Some cramped hand had written at the top, *Spell to quench Lust*. At the bottom, in a different hand, was a warning: *Take care that the Spell is not cast too wide*.

Ursule studied the spell and made note of the ingredients, but she sniffed at the warning. She was confident in her abilities. Surely the past years had proven her adept in the craft. She would need to hurry, though. Litha was only two days hence. She took the ingredients one by one and prepared them according to the recipe.

Cardamom was already in her kitchen, left by her mother some long-ago season. Clove was there, too, and she ground them together with her mortar and pestle. Licorice root would be somewhere in Agnes's neglected garden. She had long ago given up tilling and weeding and pruning, so she was forced to look under overgrown grasses and dig through the remnants of pea vines and wandering squashes to find what she wanted. Sage was in the garden, too, hidden beneath a collapsed tomato plant. She clipped many leaves of it to grind into fine fragments.

Finally, mistletoe. Ursule knew well that mistletoe could be dangerous, but in the case of the *Spell to quench Lust*, no one was going to ingest it, though she would have been happy to feed some to the adulterous Babette.

The thought made her pause.

Her anger had returned, growing more intense as she made her preparations. She had dreamed of dealing with Babette herself, shouting at her, dragging her away from her byre, throttling her. *Never dismiss a witch's dream.*

What was the source of such rage? She wanted to protect Léonie, of course, but her daughter was hardly the first wife to be betrayed. It was always easier to be furious with the other woman than with the errant husband.

She felt a quaking begin in her body and in her mind. Memories spun up into her thoughts, as if they had been buried and were clawing their way out of the deep. Each memory increased the quaking until she vibrated with a fury that had been growing in silence for years. She saw the faces, recalled the scenes as if they had happened yesterday, and with each one her ire grew.

She thought of Dukkar, who had tried to rape her.

She remembered the witch hunters, hauling her mother away like an animal.

She watched Sandor walk away up the lane, abandoning her.

There was Madeleine, calling her *gitane*, then behaving as if Léonie belonged to her.

And there was Louis, shattering the fantasy of her daughter's perfect romance.

It was as if these events had lurked together in a dark corner of her soul, feeding upon each other, hiding inside until her spirit could no longer contain their ugliness. They had burst free, like the embers in a banked fire blazing to life, and Ursule was *angry*.

Dukkar had at least paid with his life for his cruelty. But the witch hunters? They had no doubt lived on to torture other innocent females. And Sandor? Madeleine? Now Louis? They had done their damage, dispensed pain to their victims, and gone on about their lives without a thought for the consequences.

It was maddening, and a little frightening. She had the sense that her anger was dangerous in some way, that it might spin out of control. She was a witch at the height of her powers, and her strength was enhanced by her fury. There would be consequences for what she planned to do. *The Goddess always exacts her price.* What price might she be about to pay?

The crystal, ready in the center of her altar, winked encouragement at her. Beyond the window, Drom chuckled sleepily, approving whatever decision she reached.

She avoided looking at her staff with its tiny relic, waiting on the wall behind her. She suspected St. Anne would not approve. She didn't want to know that.

But Grandmother Anne, though Ursule revered her, had not had a line of descendants to protect. She, Ursule Orchière, did. She straightened her shoulders and decided, in a moment of cold clarity, that to protect Léonie and her slim inheritance of the power, she would do whatever was needed.

She would go forward.

· · · · · ·⟫⟫⟫ • ⟪⟪⟪· · · · ·

When Denis drove the carriage into the Kerjean yard and it disgorged Léonie and her five children, Madeleine came to the door of the farmhouse and stood scowling, her hands on her hips. The carriage rumbled back up the lane as the girls ran to the cottage and Léonie followed with a basket and a valise. Remy came to take both from her hands.

From the doorway, Madeleine called, "What are you doing here, Léonie? Do you want to come with Remy and me to the fete?"

The invitation, of course, was for Léonie alone. Remy shifted his shoulders, embarrassed. Ursule gave him an understanding nod as he carried Léonie's things inside.

Léonie paused between the cottage and the farmhouse to speak with Madeleine. Remy was on his way out as she came in, and she thanked him for his help. The children filled the tiny room with their presence, Louisette giving the younger ones orders they ignored, Anne-Marie digging into the basket to bring out toys and a packet of cakes, the twins running back and forth from the bedroom to the table, where Ursule had cider and bread and butter ready for them. Isabelle stood by the door, waiting for permission to visit the cat who lived in the byre.

Léonie said, "The girls are thrilled because they get to sleep on the floor."

Ursule chuckled. "They may not be so happy when they learn how hard it is." She took the packet of cakes from Anne-Marie's hands. "What did you say to Madeleine?"

"I told her I don't want to leave the children. She didn't seem pleased about that."

"I should have given her a simple, too, I suppose."

Léonie smiled. "Perhaps you should. It certainly worked on Madame Martin."

The girls surrounded the two of them, clamoring to be allowed to go and see the goats. Léonie gave a nod, and the twins dashed out of the cottage, the others following more slowly. Isabelle turned toward the byre in search of the cat. "I've made a mild potion to put in the girls' soup tonight," Ursule said quietly. "We'll want them to sleep soundly."

Léonie sighed. "You should give me one to take home," she said dispiritedly. "Sometimes I think I will go mad for children waking me at all times of the night."

"You must be more strict with them."

"I know, but I try to keep them quiet so as not to disturb Louis."

The little flame of anger flickered up in Ursule's breast, and she pressed a hand to her chest. *Not now. Later.*

Léonie stood in the doorway to watch the Kerjeans depart, and when she turned to Ursule, she was scowling. "I suspect if Madeleine could work a spell to make my children disappear, she would."

"That would be evil, Léonie. I think she's just sad. Lonely."

"When she saw the twins, she said they looked like *gitanes*, as if there was something wrong with them."

"I'm sorry," Ursule said. She could have said a great deal more, about prejudice and selfishness and meanness of spirit, but as was her way, she left the words unsaid. She said only, "Call the girls in for supper, will you? We'll get them to sleep, and then we can begin."

· · · · · ·｡ﾟ⋆⋆ﾟ｡· · · · · ·

The casting of the *Spell to quench Lust* took a long time. The herbs had to be blessed, sprinkled around the crystal, then scraped up again. Ursule named them as she fed them, bit by bit, into the candle flame, speaking their names as she did so. "Cardamom, to clear confusion.

Clove, to calm the body. Licorice root, to cool the fires of lust. Finally, sage, to purify the body of shameful desires."

The sun had set an hour before, and the cottage was dark except for the candlelight. Léonie, her face as pale as her white linen veil, stood back a little from the altar, her eyes enormous in her thin face, her slender figure wreathed in the fragrant smoke from the burning herbs. When Ursule nodded to her that the moment had come, she held out her palm. In it was the lock of Louis's hair she had brought for their rite. It glinted darkly in the uncertain light of the candle, a short, thick, curling strand.

When Ursule took it into her own hand, the flame of her anger began to flicker again. As she spoke the spell, the lock of hair beginning to burn in the flame of the candle, her anger spread to her belly, to her throat, down her arms and legs, burning into her brain. The acrid scent of burning hair seemed to intensify it as she spoke the words of her ancestress:

Mother of All, your daughters pray
An end to infernal lust today.
As fire dies beneath the tempest's flood,
Remove the craving from his blood.

She spoke them into the smoky air three times three times. Léonie's breath quickened as the light in the crystal began to swell. *You see it.* But Ursule wasn't finished. Her anger grew, flaring like the crystal's light. She felt as if she were on fire, and nothing would relieve her but the final stroke.

She had set her staff ready, leaning against the table. She lifted it now and held it high. Her voice rang against the flagstones and echoed against the slanting roof of the cottage. There was no sound from Drom, perched above the window, but she could *feel* him, and the sense of power he gave her was intoxicating.

She proclaimed:

I claim the power of the Orchière line
To protect and defend that which is mine.

As an Orchière witch, I now command
The woman who caused this to be henceforth banned!

She heard Léonie gasp, but she would not be distracted. She spoke her spell again, the personal part of the spell that came from within her, from the deep well of hurt and sorrow and pride. She shook her staff and spoke it again, and again, and again, losing count of the repetitions, not caring, her whole being vibrating with the force of her conviction, her strength, her resolve—her endless, unforgiving rage.

"Daj!" Léonie cried at last. "Daj, stop!"

Ursule whirled to face her daughter, her staff held high, her body thrumming with energy.

Only then did she see the stream of light flashing between the crystal and the reliquary, a slender fork of lightning, as the leaping of a flame from one log to another.

Slowly, reluctantly, she lowered the staff. Léonie pointed to the little window above the sink, and Ursule turned, her body stiff now, and aching, as if she had been in a battle.

The summer night was ablaze with lightning. A fierce wind rattled the window and battered at the door. The oak tree's branches scraped across the roof, and Ursule heard Drom, safe among its leaves, cackling wildly as the sudden storm shook Kerjean Farm, drenching the buildings and the pastures.

Take care that the Spell is not cast too wide.

"Daj—what's happening?" Léonie cried.

In her ear, Ursule heard Violca, and there was laughter in the disembodied voice. *It is a great work of magic. Well done, daughter. Well done indeed!*

Ursule was in the act of sliding her veil from her head when something moved in her peripheral vision. She whirled, just in time to see Louisette slip back into the bedroom.

· · · · · ⠏⠵⠵⠵ · ⠵⠵⠵⠵ · · · · ·

The storm, as Ursule learned when Madeleine and Remy had fled for home through the downpour, had battered the entire district. She heard the cart rattle into the yard and ran out to help unhitch Andie and get him into shelter. She carried a blanket out to dry him and heated a bit of mash to warm him up.

Madeleine disappeared into the farmhouse immediately, her hair dripping and her skirts sodden. Remy, his coat and hat running with rain, bundled the harness into the byre. "I'll give it a soap tomorrow," he said. "Just now I'd better see to Madeleine. She's shaken up."

"What upset her?" Ursule had found another blanket, a dry one, and she strapped it around Andie so he wouldn't take a chill. The wind had died down, but she worried it might come back. The goats were packed together beneath the shelter of the trees in their pasture. The cows had taken cover under the eaves of the byre.

"She was terrified by the wind and the lightning," Remy said. "Trees came down around the green. One broke through the roof of the tavern."

"Was anyone inside?"

"Everyone was out at the bonfire. Screaming, running, as if the Terror had come back."

Ursule's heart quivered. Was it compunction that stirred in her breast? Or was it pride?

"I hope no one was hurt," she ventured.

"I don't know. The fire went out, and we hurried back here, but the road went to mud so fast—I have to see to Madeleine, Ursule. Thanks for coming to help."

He started off across the yard toward the farmhouse, but he paused and looked back. "The little ones are all right? Léonie?"

"Slept right through," Ursule said.

"Lucky. Not much of a fete."

"There will be others."

"*Eh bien*, I suppose." He lumbered off and disappeared into the house.

Ursule, spent, trudged back to the cottage and in through the door. She found Léonie warming milk at the fire. Louisette, wide-eyed and ousle-haired, sat at the table. Through the half-opened door, Ursule aw the other girls still sleeping on their makeshift pallets.

"It would seem, Daj," Léonie said, "that it's time to teach your granddaughter your gypsy ways."

Ursule gazed at her daughter and then her granddaughter, a thrill of hope easing her weariness. "Do you know what you're suggesting, *ma fille?*"

"I do," Léonie said. "You can trust Louisette. She's almost nine years old. She wants to learn to read and I want her to learn the—the other things you have to teach her."

Ursule crossed to the table and sank down on a stool opposite Louisette. The girl looked back at her with an eager expression, her eyes bright with intelligence, her mouth soft with trust.

"Please, Grand-mère," she said quietly.

"What will your papa say?" Ursule asked. She glanced up at Léonie. "Won't you need to ask Louis?"

"No. It doesn't matter, in any case," Léonie said sharply, with a touch of her old spirit. "He won't say no to me. Not now."

"You're sure of that?"

Léonie placed her palm on her solar plexus. "I know it. It's over."

"Excellent." Ursule turned her attention back to her granddaughter. "Louisette, can you keep secrets? The ones you're going to learn are very big secrets, even dangerous secrets."

Louisette's dark eyes glinted with excitement. "I love secrets!"

"I think we all do," Ursule said. "But these must be kept. Above all things, these secrets have to be kept between me and you and your *maman.*"

"What about Anne-Marie? Isabelle?"

Ursule nodded approval of the question. "It's good that you think about that. We have to wait to share these secrets until they're at least as old as you are, and maybe older."

"From my other *grand-mère*, too?"

"Does that worry you, Louisette?" Ursule asked. "Do you feel that's disloyal?"

Louisette tossed her head. "No! She never listens to anything we say, anyway."

"That much is true, Daj," Léonie said. "But, Louisette, this means Father Bernard, also. Even at confession, if he asks you, you mustn't tell him any of our Orchière secrets."

"I never tell him anything," Louisette said offhandedly. "He smells bad."

Noises sounded then from the bedroom, the other children beginning to stir, to throw off their blankets, to call for their mother.

"Ah. The simple wore off," Ursule said, as Léonie rose and started in to the bedroom.

Louisette said, "Simple?"

Ursule put a finger to her lips. "Yes, Louisette, a simple. It's one of the secrets. We can start with that, if you like."

Louisette popped up from the table, a look of fierce pride on her young face. *"Formidable!"* she said, but in a whisper, before she ran back into the bedroom to boast to her sisters that she was to be allowed to stay with Grand-mère, while they had to go home to Manor Farm.

W hy is Louisette staying if Léonie's gone?" Madeleine demanded. She had appeared on the cottage doorstep the moment the Martin carriage, with a chastened-looking Louis driving, had carried Léonie and the rest of the children away. "You're not keeping her, I hope!"

Ursule left the sink, where she and Louisette were washing and drying dishes, and met Madeleine at the door. She took her by the arm and propelled her ungently outside, then closed the door behind them both. "I am keeping her, in fact. I have things to teach my granddaughter."

"Oh, to *read*?"

"Among other things."

"We're not going to become a crèche, Ursule."

"Kerjean Farm will not be a crèche, but the cottage is my home, Madeleine, and Louisette is going to stay with me for a time."

"Well," Madeleine said, jerking her arm free. "As long as it's not for too long."

Ursule's temper flared, but recalling her fury the night before, she drew a long breath and held it until its flame died down. When she spoke, the tone of her voice belied the intensity of her meaning. "Madeleine. Louisette will stay with me as long as she needs to."

"Huh! We'll see what Remy has to say about this."

"Shall we go and ask him now?"

It was a sly question. Remy had a weakness for Léonie's children, and Louisette in particular. He had taught her to whistle, and some Sunday afternoons, when it was time for the Martins to be going home,

Léonie found Louisette near the pond behind the byre, learning tunes from Remy.

Madeleine knew all of that. She didn't answer, but stalked away toward the buttery. Ursule watched her go, trying but failing to feel sympathy. Madeleine could enjoy Léonie's girls as Remy did. Instead, she had offended the one person she most cared about and isolated herself in a shell of resentment and envy.

Drom, however, was delighted that Louisette had stayed behind. She had taught the old raven to whistle a fragment of melody, and though it was hardly perfect, it was charming. Now he danced back and forth on a branch of the oak tree, whistling his bit of tune to entice Louisette outside.

Ursule grinned up at him. "I'll send her, rascal." She went into the cottage, where Louisette was putting the breakfast things away.

"Drom is calling you."

Louisette flashed a happy smile, a girl on the eve of a great adventure. "I'll go see him, Grand-mère, but just for a little while. I want to get started!"

As she ran out into the hot summer morning, Ursule had to lean against the counter for a moment, her hand on her heart. So much had happened, and so fast, that trying to take it all in made her feel shaky. She was pleased to have Louisette to teach, and to have earned Léonie's trust, but the drama of the night before unnerved her. Had she really caused all of that?

Louis had told of lightning flashing from a clear sky, and a huge cloud bank rolling over the horizon, carrying a torrent of rain that drenched the village moments later. A battering wind had knocked down trees and frightened two cart ponies so badly they broke free of their tethers and galloped off into the night. The ancient oak that had shadowed the tavern for years split in two, and one half collapsed onto the tavern's flat roof. The bonfire had been drowned in an instant, leaving the green in darkness, people shouting for their children, calling for each other.

And Babette? Neither Léonie nor Ursule asked after her, but Ursule felt certain the strumpet was gone. Scared off, or dismissed for immoral

behavior, it didn't matter. Nor would Louis miss her. The spell had
been effective.

Ursule had pressed the simple on Léonie to prevent conception, and
Léonie accepted it, but with no joy in her face. "I don't know if I'll
need this, Daj."

"Can you not forgive Louis his moment of weakness?"

"Yes. I can do that. But I don't know if he will love me again—or if
I will love him. Something broke in all of this."

"What is broken can heal, *ma fille*."

Louisette burst back into the cottage, her cheeks pink with running,
her eyes bright and eager. Ursule went to fetch the crystal. The rightness
of this moment filled her with gratitude, no matter the roughness of the
path that had led to it, and she would let no doubts spoil her appreciation.

We vow to pass the craft to our daughters so long as our line endures.

Praise the Goddess, the line continued. She set the crystal, still covered
in its folds of linen, on the uneven table. "Close the door, Louisette.
What we're going to do, no one must know but you and me. Do you
understand?"

"Yes, Grand-mère." Louisette's voice had begun to deepen, her chin
to grow firm and prominent. Witch or not, the girl would be a woman
to reckon with.

"Knowing these things, *ma chère*, will make you different. Set you
apart from other girls. Are you sure you can live with that?"

Louisette tossed her head. "I can't wait!"

"Very well. Let us begin." Ursule gently slid the folds of linen away
from the scrying stone. A shaft of summer light fell through the little
window directly onto the cool, glistening quartz, and she ran her palm
over it with a reverent gesture.

"This," she said, "belonged to the *grand-mère* of the *grand-mère* of
your *grand-mère*. It will one day come to you, and you need to know all
about it."

L ouisette soaked up everything Ursule taught her: herbalism, read-ing, the making of simples and potions, the history of the Orchière line. In time, Anne-Marie joined them, and then Isabelle, so that for several days each week Ursule had a houseful of girls to teach and to feed. The years passed swiftly this way, the happiest and most satisfying ones of Ursule's life.

Her granddaughters intrigued her, each of them with their own innate gifts. Anne-Marie was the most like her mother, interested in cooking and sewing. Ursule had never had more than basic cooking skills, and though she wished Madeleine would take to Anne-Marie, perhaps teach her as she had taught Léonie, her wish was in vain. Mad-eleine was increasingly withdrawn, only emerging from the farmhouse to shape the Kerjean butter. She barely spoke to Ursule, and never to the girls. Fortunately, Anne-Marie took to reading with enthusiasm, and Ursule managed to acquire a cookbook so she could experiment.

Isabelle took over the management of the chickens, feeding them, mucking out their coop, filling their water trough. Each day she col-lected their eggs as proudly as if she had laid them herself. She named every hen, as Ursule had always done with her cows and goats. When the sisters quarreled, Isabelle usually fled to the henhouse for comfort, or to the byre to cuddle the cat.

Louis, when he brought the girls to Kerjean, no longer flashed his white smile, although he always kissed Ursule's cheeks when he arrived. Lines had appeared around his eyes and his mouth, and she worried.

Léonie seemed even more unhappy than Louis. Ursule recognized the misery in her daughter's eyes. Time had worn away the pain of Sandor's rejection, but she had not forgotten how it felt. It didn't seem possible that Léonie, still beautiful despite everything, and so sweet-natured, should suffer the same hurt as her mother.

She waited for a moment alone with her daughter and asked her bluntly, "Are things no better between you and Louis?"

"They're all right," Léonie said, with an air of resignation. "I suppose I couldn't expect things to go back to the way they were before."

"At least she's gone."

"Babette? Oh, yes. That same night. No one has seen her since."

"Do you think Louis cares?"

"I don't think Louis cares about very much lately. He does what needs to be done—the farm work, taking care of the girls, helping his mother—but his heart isn't in it."

"He feels guilty."

"I expect so."

Ursule glanced toward the reliquary, still set into her staff, propped beside the door. It gave her no answer, but then, this was not a matter St. Anne would care to be part of. It was a matter for a witch willing to take a risk. *The Goddess always exacts her price.* It was a hard thing, to choose between her daughter's unhappiness and the danger of working yet more magic. It seemed a small thing to revive a love that had gone astray, but she knew all too well that the cost of magic did not always match its reward.

She bowed her head and considered, searching her heart for an answer. After a time she looked up into her beloved daughter's melancholy face, and she understood. It was better to take a chance on a happy life than to merely endure a sad one.

She said softly, "Perhaps I can help, *ma fille.*"

"Would you, Daj?" Léonie took Ursule's hand, twining her long, slender fingers with Ursule's work-worn ones. "I'm so weary of being sad."

· · · · ·꙳꙳꙳ • ꙳꙳꙳· · · · ·

A third time, Ursule performed the *Spell of undoing.*

She waited until a day when all the girls had gone back to Manor Farm. Louisette, who had seen Ursule gathering her materials, asked if she could stay. "I know you're planning something, Grand-mère. I can help you."

Ursule had hugged the girl to her. "Not this time, *ma chère,*" she murmured, her cheek against Louisette's hair. "Best not."

"But why?"

"I can't explain to you, dear heart. You'll have to trust me."

Some secrets are better kept.

She waved them all off, noting Léonie's drawn expression as she settled the girls in the carriage. It was a great pity, and it had gone on long enough.

····· ·≫≫≫• ≪≪≪· ·····

May the grands-mères *aid my hand and heart*
In the practice of the witch's art,
That Louis and Léonie will both forgive
And find a loving way to live.

The crystal glowed with a steady golden light. The candle burned steadily, its flame swelling until all the herbs were consumed. It was not the triumphant conclusion of the spell to restore Agnes's voice, nor the fiery one to restore Sandor's vision. The completion of this spell felt mature to Ursule, a quiet, contemplative finish. There was no perfect ending, no dramatic restoration of the love Louis and Léonie had once had for one another, but there was hope for peace between them, and a return of the affection they had once felt.

The hour had grown late. Ursule was exhausted. She cleared the altar, took off her veil and folded it, stowed the crystal in its basket, and moved the candle to the center of the table where it could burn itself out while she undressed for bed. She lay down on her pillow with a sigh that came from the deepest part of her soul.

I'm so tired, Grands-mères.

It was not Violca's, but a different voice that answered her, a high, fragile voice that creaked with age. *Your road is a long one, my child. Rest will come when it comes.*

Ursule's eyes blinked open. *St. Anne?*

Grand-mère Anne. I am with you.

Grateful tears filled Ursule's eyes. She turned on her side, and wept them into her pillow.

· · · · ·⋙ · ⋘· · · · ·

Despite the subdued atmosphere that surrounded her *Spell of undoing*, Ursule knew immediately there had been a change for her daughter and son-in-law. They came with the five girls after Mass with an enormous basket of food.

The twins came into the cottage with their dolls while the older girls scattered: Isabelle scampering to check on the hens, Anne-Marie running to stroke the goat kids who crowded to the fence to greet her, and Louisette off in search of Remy and a whistling lesson. Léonie touched Louis's arm as he lifted the laden basket to the table. "The books first," she said. "Maman will be so pleased."

The look Louis gave Léonie made gooseflesh rise on Ursule's arms. He said only, *"Bien sûr,"* but his face was relaxed, and he smiled, first at Léonie and then at Ursule. He pulled out two books that had been tucked between the sandwiches and cakes Édi had packed for their luncheon.

"I know you're a reader, Belle-mère," he said, as he handed them to Ursule. "I only read a little, figures and things to keep the farm accounts, but Louisette has been clamoring for things to read. I found these in a little shop near the harbor in Auray."

As she took the books from Louis's hand, Ursule returned his smile, a glow of pleasure easing the fatigue that had become her constant companion. "Has Louisette seen them yet?"

Louis laughed. "No, because I wasn't sure what they were about. This one especially."

The books were old, and their covers showed lots of use, probably from the saddlebags of the peddlers who bought and sold them. The one Louis pointed to had a picture of a man and a woman embracing. "It's a romance," Ursule said. "Louisette will have questions, but she's old enough to understand."

The other book was a treasure, a collection of herbal remedies. She told Louis that, and as she held it in her hand, she thought of how she had longed for more to read when she was a girl, when she had nothing but the grimoire and a few posters and street signs.

"You can give them to the girls whenever you're ready," Louis said.

"I think you should do it," Ursule said. "So they know their papa bought them specially."

This made both Louis and Léonie smile, and when the girls returned, all of them, parents, children, grandmother, ate their excellent luncheon in congenial fashion, talking of nothing, laughing at everything. The afternoon was perfect, a little, shining jewel of a day, and Ursule was to remember it for years after, when her daughter looked happy again, her grandchildren were carefree, and her son-in-law beamed on his family, at peace with his lot.

Léonie embraced her when she said goodbye and whispered, "Thank you, Daj."

Ursule was to think later that she should have warned Léonie then, should have asked if she needed more of the simple against conception, should have sworn she would bring it herself, even if she had to carry it to Manor Farm on foot. But it had been such a lovely day, and Léonie looked as content as the barn cat lying in a ray of sunshine.

Ursule savored the moment, returned the embrace, and waved goodbye.

The Goddess always exacts her price.

L éonie conceived her sixth child a few weeks later. It was a sign that her marriage had healed, but it was too much for her fragile body to withstand. Her last pregnancy was like her first, with pain and bleeding and fear. Ursule did all she could, just as before, but Léonie wasn't strong enough. She lived only long enough to deliver her babe, and to hold her for an hour before she looked up at Louis and said, her voice breaking with grief, *"Désolée, mon cher. Je ne peux pas."*

Louis cast Ursule a pleading glance, but though she had begged the *grands-mères* for their help, there was nothing more to be done.

Léonie's eyelids sank down, as if holding them open was impossible. Her eyelashes lay long and damp against her white cheeks, and her pale lips trembled.

"This is the one, Daj." She tried to kiss the babe's head but had not the strength. Her head fell back on her pillow, and her hands lost their grip. Ursule hastened to take up the infant just as Léonie spoke her last words. They were so faint that Ursule, with the babe in her arms, had to bend close to hear Léonie breathe, "The one you've been waiting for."

······ ❧ ······

In the midst of the ensuing sorrow over Léonie's death, the weeping children, the stunned widower, even Madame Martin wordless with shock, there was the new babe to think of. Ursule, riven by grief herself, did not allow herself to give in to tears. There was no time. Tears could come later.

"Louis, what is her name?"

Louis, white to the lips, said through a dry throat, "Nanette. Her name is Nanette."

"Very well," Ursule said, with a dignity and control she didn't feel. "Nanette will need goat's milk, Louis. I don't think you have goats in your byre."

He shook his head, and she saw his throat work.

"I'll take her to Kerjean," Ursule said. "My goats will feed her. As it's spring, we have new kids and several milkers. I will need Louisette to help with the chores, and Anne-Marie to cook for us."

"I—I'll get the carriage—" Louis's voice broke.

"Yes." It seemed best for Louis to be busy, as they would all be for some time. "Yes, your mother and Édi can do what needs to be done. You can come back and sit with Léonie later. I'm going to ask Louisette and Anne-Marie to get their things."

"They're crying," he said, his eyes and voice bleak.

"Of course. Let them cry as much as they need." *I will cry forever.*

In the end, Isabelle also insisted she go to Kerjean with her older sisters, and when Fleurette and Florence realized their grandmother was leaving, they clung to her, noisily weeping, until Louis agreed to take them all. They crowded into the carriage with two swiftly packed valises. Madame Martin didn't come down to see them off, but she gave them a stiff wave from the window where she and Édi were washing Léonie's body.

The new baby, swaddled in Ursule's arms, was the only one of all the family, except for Ursule, who didn't weep. Ursule gazed down at the tiny triangle of her face, the wide dark eyes, the bud of a mouth that pursed, seeking the breast that would never come.

"I'll do my best," Ursule whispered. "Precious little Nanette. Are you the one, *ma petite*? Did your *maman* know?"

She felt eyes on her and glanced up to see that Louisette's tears had ceased. The girl said, in a voice far too hard for one so young, "Everything has changed, hasn't it, Grand-mère? Nothing will ever be the same."

"You're right, *ma chère*," Ursule said. There was no point in false assurances. It was better to face the truth. "Nothing will be the same."

····· ·⟫⟫⟫⟫⟫·⟪⟪⟪⟪⟪· ·····

They had only been back in the cottage for an hour when Remy came to stand in the doorway, gazing at Ursule with the motherless babe in her arms. She tried to speak through the tightness of her throat, but he held up one of his huge hands to indicate there was no need. "I came to tell you I'll be doing the milking. Madeleine will do the churning. You're to stay here and take care of the babe."

Ursule's brittle self-control nearly shattered before his kindness. She had to bite her lip to keep from sobbing aloud. He stayed just long enough to say, "I'll build a room on the cottage for your little ones. Can't have them sleeping on the floor like peasants."

Ursule could only nod agreement. He nodded in return, as if they had held a real conversation, and walked back across the yard.

Days passed. Ursule gave the children a simple to help them sleep, but nothing to stop their tears. It was right that they should mourn.

The older girls sorted out the housework between them. Remy did all the milking. Ursule still crossed to the buttery once a day to churn, since Madeleine flatly refused to do it. She didn't come to see the babe, nor to offer her condolences. She attended the funeral at St. Anne, but when it was over, she retreated once again into the farmhouse, evidently for good. Anne-Marie took over the shaping and stamping of the butter, guessing at the technique and trying different ways of doing it until she had it right. In no time she was doing the churning as well, and seeing her strong young arms working the paddle assured Ursule that the butter would be fine. She hung a charm above the churn to make sure.

She didn't go to Léonie's funeral. It was not just that she had sworn never to see the redheaded priest again, but that she couldn't bear to see her dream become reality, to see her daughter laid in the earth beneath a Christian cross, with pale, scentless flowers dropped onto the raw dirt. She couldn't stand the eyes of the parishioners on her, or Madeleine's weepy gaze. She stayed at home, caring for Nanette, watching over the twins, while the three older girls went with their father to bury their mother.

When they returned, Louisette, eyes flashing, came to stand before her grandmother. "Father Bernard said you should have come."

Ursule felt the uneasy quiver of premonition in her solar plexus. "I imagined you explained to him about little Nanette?"

Louisette's voice was even deeper than usual. "I did, of course. He gave me this look—well, one of his eyes gave me a look—" She grimaced. "He said he hopes my *grand-mère* isn't teaching me heathen ways."

"Ah, Louisette..."

The girl's smile was fierce. "I said I had heard his bad eye was the mark of the devil, and then I walked away, left him standing there."

"Louisette, my darling girl, you are a force of nature."

"I'm not going to Mass anymore."

"I understand how you feel, *ma chère*, but what will your papa say?"

"He says God has abandoned him. He's not going, either."

Ursule blew out a slow breath. "The demon priest will blame me for all of it."

"*Oh la la,*" Louisette said blithely. "No one cares what he thinks. He can't hurt us."

Hmmmmm.

. . . . · ﹏﹏ · ﹏﹏ · . . . .

Louis came to Kerjean every day for the first months, though the travel time cut into his work at Manor Farm. As the year wore on into full summer and then the busy harvest, his visits grew more infrequent. When Ursule made a brief visit to the village, Arlette, who always knew everyone's business, told her Louis was keeping company with the sheriff's daughter, and that she had already been out to Manor Farm.

Madame Martin sent word that she was not well enough for the carriage ride to Kerjean to visit her grandchildren. Monsieur Martin came to deliver her message, but awkwardly, embarrassed by the position he found himself in. He didn't embrace his granddaughters, although he brought them sweets. He didn't come again.

As time went on, it became clear to Ursule that the girls were her charges now. She was glad to have them, but worried. She began to make simples to strengthen herself. If she fell ill, what would become of the girls? And how long could they go on living at Kerjean?

One day, when the first raw edges of her grief had dulled, she approached Remy as he left the byre. He stopped and snatched off his hat as if she were someone of importance, which brought a tremulous smile to her face. Only in Remy's presence had she been able to shed her tears. His gruffly kind presence was a shield, a cover under which she dared release her emotions. She didn't understand why that should be, but there were so many things demanding her attention that she couldn't find time to think about it.

Now she said, "Remy, I should speak with you."

"*Eh bien*, Ursule, any time. What's on your mind?"

She glanced past him at the byre and bit her lip. It wasn't as clean as it should be, and one of the stanchions had a broken post. "Oh, Remy. The work—it's too much for you."

"Getting old," he said. "No one to take over the farm."

"I know," Ursule answered. The morning was a frosty one, not yet spring, and she wrapped her arms around herself to keep warm. "I can't do the work anymore, either, Remy. It was already getting hard for me, and now, with six children to care for . . ." She shrugged a little. "You've been so kind, adding to the cottage, helping with the girls, but we can't go on this way."

He stared at his feet, shuffling them in the dirt of the yard. "I hoped Madeleine would be glad of children around the place, since she always wanted them. The trouble is—in this case—"

"I understand. She might have wanted children, but not *these* children." Ursule could imagine Madeleine snapping, *Six gypsy girls? Not at Kerjean Farm!*

Remy had no doubt heard his wife say just that.

"I suppose her moment for children has passed, Ursule. I hope you won't think too harshly of her."

"I won't. I understand." Madeleine had never been a woman to change easily in the best of times, and in old age her tendency to inflexibility had hardened into a permanent state.

"I'm sorry to say, Ursule, after all this time we've worked together—I think I'm going to have to..."

When he couldn't seem to speak the words, she finished his thought for him. "You're going to sell the farm."

He nodded, and for a bad moment, she thought he might be the one to weep. His voice was rough with sorrow. "Not yet, though, Ursule. Not yet, especially while *la petite bébé* needs goat's milk. I thought—after the harvest, but before Christmas—I will ask about for a buyer. And then I thought—maybe Manor Farm could take you in? That house has so many rooms, and it's the children's home, isn't it."

It was a statement, not a question. He was right, but Ursule distrusted the Martins. Even Louis had seemed shockingly content to have her take all six of his children into her tiny dim cottage. She tried not to be angry with him, reminding herself that he was still a young man, with his life ahead of him, and a farm to work.

She said, "I don't know, Remy. It should be, but—it seems everything has changed."

"But these are their grandchildren!"

"They have a dozen other grandchildren. And other sons who would like to step into Louis's place, and take over Manor Farm." At Remy's guilt-ridden look, she said hastily, "But we'll see of course. I'll talk to Louis."

She was about to say something else, but Violca murmured in her ear. *Hmmmmm*, and Ursule knew it would be no use.

Dispirited, Ursule left Remy to his work in the byre and trudged back toward the cottage. The new addition looked oddly clean next to the older walls of the original: the wood new-cut, the mortar between the boards still fresh. It was simple, just three walls and a roof, but it had been a great help.

As she approached she heard little Nanette cry, and she hurried her steps, though the movement made her hips hurt. The crying stopped before she reached the door, and when she opened it, she saw Louisette in the armchair, the babe in her lap, the pottery bottle they used already full of milk. Nanette was peacefully suckling at the bit of sponge in the mouth of the bottle.

"Louisette, thank you for taking care of our little one."

"I know how to care for a babe. I'm old enough to have my own, after all."

"Goddess forbid!" Ursule exclaimed, before she could catch herself. Louisette twinkled up at her. "Don't worry. A joke."

"Of course." Ursule smiled at her, but she knew it was true. Louisette would be fifteen at Lammas. A woman. If she were to choose a husband and leave, how were they all to manage?

There were so many questions. Once again, she turned to the crystal.

······◆······

Mabon was approaching. Anne-Marie was fourteen, Isabelle thirteen, and they had been introduced to the Sabbat rituals. Ursule asked Anne-Marie, with her clever fingers, to sew another linen veil while she made the other preparations. Apples were abundant. Madeleine no longer shared her cider, but the Orchières could make their own. Ursule collected twigs of sage, for cleansing sorrow and illness, and branches of rosemary, in memory of Léonie. Finally, she brought out a tiny jar of oil of frankincense, *franc encens* in Old French, the mystical incense said to part the veil between this world and the next.

On the eve of Mabon, she and the older girls waited until the twins and little Nanette were asleep on their cots in the extra room. They laid out the altar, and Anne-Marie produced a perfect beeswax candle she had poured herself. It had faint swirls of color in it that caught the starlight coming through the high window.

"Anne-Marie, you have a gift," Ursule said. "I will teach you to create some charms."

Anne-Marie's cheeks colored with pleasure. Louisette, carrying the crystal to the altar, said, "Don't get above yourself. It's hard work."

"I know that," Anne-Marie said. "Can you do them?"

Louisette tossed her head. "I do other things."

Isabelle shushed them both. "This is serious. No time for squabbling."

Ursule said, "Isabelle is right. This is a time to celebrate, and to ask for guidance."

She had made little bundles of the herbs, and she placed one at each corner of the altar, then sprinkled them with drops of the oil of frankincense. The scent of incense rose in the small room, and Ursule felt as if it rarefied the atmosphere, setting the stage for the work to be done.

When all of them were gathered, with their hands folded before them and their veils draped over their heads, she said, "I remind you again, *mes filles*. You must never speak of this to anyone. Not ever. It is a matter of life and death."

Isabelle's eyes filled with easy tears. "Did Maman know?"

"She did."

"She never told us," said Anne-Marie. "Not anything."

"She was protecting you," Louisette said, before Ursule could explain. "Because that nasty priest would say Grand-mère is a witch, and want to burn her."

Anne-Marie and Isabelle gasped, and Ursule held up her hand. "It's not going to happen, because we're going to keep this secret to ourselves. We are Orchières, and we stand together."

Isabelle said, in a small, pale voice, "Are we not Martins, like Papa?"

"You can be both, *ma petite*. Louisette already understands, because she began her studies first. Now you will also understand, and the younger ones when it's their time. For now—" She nodded to Anne-Marie. "Light your beautiful candle, and we can begin."

It was lovely to have the sweet young voices join in the opening recitation. Anne-Marie and Isabelle were still learning, stumbling over the names, but Louisette's voice, deep and resonant, spoke them without hesitation. Despite the grief of the past months, Ursule's heart swelled with tentative hope. She had lost her precious daughter, the child of her heart, but she had not been left alone.

On this Sabbat of Mabon, we honor our foremothers: the seer Violca, the prophetess Liliane, the Lady Yvette, Maddalena of Milano, Irina from the east, and all the others whose precious names have been lost. We vow to pass the craft to our daughters so long as our line endures.

Ursule glanced up at her granddaughters' faces. Louisette was focused on the candle flame. Anne-Marie's eyes were half-closed, dreamy. Isabelle's filled with tears, and so, Ursule realized, did her own. The room glimmered through the sheen of them.

She went on to welcome Mabon, the celebration of abundance, of farewell to the labors of the year past, of looking ahead to the coming days of darkness, the time of rest. The candle glowed steadily, and the crystal, though still dark, reflected its generous flame.

Finally, Ursule passed her hands over the Orchière stone and made her petition.

Grands-mères, your daughters gather here
To beg you to make our future clear.
Tell us where our home will be;
Show it so that we might see.

She glanced up at the girls' rapt faces, and said very softly, "Three times three times, *mes chères*. Remember to speak your petitions three times three times."

Louisette nodded, and Anne-Marie and Isabelle both murmured assent. Ursule passed her hands over the old stone and repeated her petition. Her voice cracked, but it was clear enough. Steady enough. When she finished the last repetition, the familiar, reassuring glow began. Anne-Marie and Isabelle both gasped, and Louisette's lips curved in a smug expression. Ursule bent forward to look into the old crystal to see what her ancestresses had to say.

A great shame," Remy said, his mouth dragging with disapproval. "A father letting his children go this way."

"He has a new wife now," Ursule said. "She's made it clear she doesn't want to be stepmother to six half-gypsy girls."

"Should have stood up for his children."

"Louis is easily led, I'm afraid. He was with Léonie, and I expect he will be the same with this one."

"He'll regret it," Remy growled.

"I have no doubt." Ursule stepped back from Andie's head, dusting her hands together to rid them of horsehair.

The new spring sun gleamed on Andie's tack, recently cleaned by Remy. He was hitched to the caravan, which, though hardly new, was also clean, its hardware polished and oiled. Its cheerful blue paint was sun-faded and cracked, its yellow trim flaking in places, but the walls and the wheels were in good repair.

Remy had bargained for the caravan, using some of the proceeds of his sale of the farm. When Madeleine objected, he told her in no uncertain terms that it was found money, and he would do with it what he liked.

"Wouldn't have a *sou* if the *vicomte* were still here," he pointed out. "We would have been out and gone without a *livre*."

Madeleine had more to say, of course, a great deal of which Ursule heard through the open window of the farmhouse, but Remy had been unmoved. "Where would we have been, all these years, but for Ursule? And now these young ones, Léonie's girls, what would you have them do?"

That, it seemed, had put an end to Madeleine's complaints, but she had not come to say goodbye, either to Ursule or to the girls.

"You're sure the clan is there," Remy said, shifting his feet as he struggled for words to say his own farewell.

"I'm sure, Remy. The clan is always at Carnac for the spring equinox." It was the explanation she had settled on for how she knew.

"*Eh bien.* I suppose you have everything packed. Can't I do something more to help?"

She smiled up at him, moved by the concern of this big, clumsy, gentle soul. "Louisette saw to it. She's a great one for getting things done."

Remy stopped shuffling his feet and looked directly into Ursule's face. "She must get that from you. Hardest worker I've ever known."

Ursule's eyes began to sting, and she had to look away. "Remy," she began, but then couldn't find words, either.

Isabelle saved the moment by leaning out of the caravan door. "We're ready, Grand-mère. Everything's tied down, and Anne-Marie has Nanette. Louisette will ride up with you so I can keep an eye on the twins."

"I'll be right there." Ursule turned back to Remy. "Is Madeleine in the house? I'm going to say goodbye to her."

He turned his hat in his hand, his cheeks flushing with shame. "I'm—I'm not sure—"

"I know she doesn't want to see me, but I want to see her. I'll try not to upset her."

He bit his lip, jammed his hat on his head, and said, "You come back if they're not there, Ursule. You and the whole lot. We'll figure something out." Before she could respond, he had turned away to lumber across the barnyard. Ursule felt the tingle of tears again as she watched his lonely figure disappear inside the byre.

She had visited Agnes's grave and asked for her blessing on their journey. She had also slipped away to the chapel graveyard when no one was about and knelt beside Léonie's headstone for a long time, saying her farewell, promising she would do her best by Léonie's daughters. There were no cows left. The goats were gone, too, sold along with the farm. Andie was the last of the livestock, and Remy had made a gift of him to Ursule and the girls, saying Andie was getting old in any case, and wouldn't be of service much longer. Soon, a carriage was coming to take Remy and Madeleine to the little house they had bought in Vannes.

Ursule crossed to the farmhouse and knocked sharply on the door. When there was no reply, she knocked again and heard Madeleine's reluctant footsteps approaching.

"What is it?" Madeleine's voice was thin and unhappy.

"Madeleine, it's Ursule."

The door still didn't open. "I thought you had left."

"Come now, Madeleine, you can see for yourself the wagon is still in the yard. Open the door." When nothing happened for a moment, Ursule said, "I won't be seeing you again, Madeleine. This is the last time, after all these years, that you and I will speak."

Slowly, as if the door had grown too heavy to move, Madeleine pulled it open. Ursule, standing below the step, had to suppress a gasp.

It had been weeks since she had seen Madeleine up close, and the change in her was a shock. She had always been lean, but now she had no flesh to spare at all. Her cheekbones jutted, and the tendons in her neck were exposed, as if the skin had been removed. Her eyes were the worst, red-rimmed and hollow.

"Madeleine, you don't look well."

"It's all over," Madeleine said. "The farm is gone. The cart is gone. The house... Léonie is gone."

"You loved her, and she was fond of you, too."

Madeleine's reddened eyes gleamed, but no tears fell. It looked to Ursule as if she couldn't spare the moisture, so dried-up and spent she seemed.

"Don't you want to see Léonie's children one more time before we go?" Ursule said. "This is really goodbye."

Madeleine dropped her gaze and stared down at her feet. "I should have done more."

"For the children, you mean?"

There was a long pause before Madeleine said, in a little rush, "I thought her children would look like her!"

"And instead they look like me." Ursule sighed. "*Eh bien*, I suppose things haven't changed." She put out her hand. "I hope you'll take care of yourself. And Remy."

Madeleine lifted her gaze and, to Ursule's surprise, put her thin, trembling hand into Ursule's. "Goodbye, Ursule. You—you were very good at the churning."

"Thank you," Ursule said. "Your butter was always the best, Madeleine. *Au revoir.*"

Madeleine nodded, released her hand, and stepped back, closing the door in one swift movement. She might have murmured, *"Adieu,"* but Ursule wasn't sure.

Ursule walked to the caravan, where Louisette was holding Andie's reins and shading her eyes against the glare of the rising sun. "You're sure they're there, Puri-daj?" she asked, just as Remy had.

Ursule smiled up at her, approving her granddaughter's use of the Romani word. "I'm sure," she said. "I saw them."

"I couldn't, though. I saw the light, and shadows here and there."

"I'm sorry about that. Perhaps, as you get older—"

"I don't think so, but that's all right, since you always see what we need." Louisette put a hand down for Ursule's staff. Ursule climbed up, steadying herself against the slats of the seat. When she was settled, Louisette lifted the reins. "Shall we start? We have a long way to go."

"Just one more thing." Ursule twisted in the seat to look around the barnyard, the now-empty byre, the abandoned pens, the deserted pasture where the deer had already begun to graze in the early mornings. In the glaze of sunshine, she almost thought she could see the ghosts of her cows, of Bibi and Mimi, the little goats gone so long ago. It seemed if her ears were only sharp enough, she could hear echoes of the chickens chortling as they scratched in their pen.

The animals she had loved were all gone. All except one.

She called, softly, "Drom! Drom, where are you?"

Louisette made a small noise in her throat that might have been a laugh. "Really, Puri-daj? That old raven?"

Ursule said simply, "I need him, Louisette."

Louisette caught her lower lip between her teeth, gazing at her grandmother, then handed her the reins. "I'll go look for him."

But as she started to climb down from the driving seat, Ursule heard the flap and swoosh of wings. A moment later, Drom settled onto Andie's withers, his wings lifting and settling, glistening like ebony in the sunshine.

Louisette chuckled and took the reins back. "You love that bird, don't you, Puri-daj?"

"I don't know if *love* is the right word, but—I'm not complete without him."

"He's terribly old, isn't he?"

"Yes. Uncommonly old, I believe."

"What will you do if—" Louisette broke off. From inside the caravan, behind them, the voices of the other girls rose, chattering with anticipation over the adventure ahead. Nanette squealed, picking up her sisters' excitement, and Ursule heard Isabelle laughing with her.

"I don't think about it, *ma chérie*. Things happen when they happen." *When Drom goes, my own end will be near.*

She didn't tell her granddaughter that. There was no need to frighten her. She didn't know how she knew, in fact, but she felt it in her bones. All she said aloud was, "There's no shame in being old, Louisette."

Louisette, confident in the power of her youth, grinned as she pulled down the brim of her hat and lifted Andie's reins. "Are you ready now?"

"I'm ready. Let us go find our clan."

Irina from the East

*T*hey say Irina was the first of the gypsy witches to come from the east, bringing with her the knowledge and wisdom and magic of the Punjabi. She was a great beauty, exotic and delicate, admired by every man who met her. Wives used to scold their husbands for staring at her. They claimed she used witchery to make her hair lustrous, her eyes wide, her lips full. She had traveled from her country alone, a woman in men's clothing, fierce and dangerous, and more than one man perished for trying to capture her.

They say she used her witchery to multiply the members of her adopted clan, and for this the wives forgave her for her beauty. She enticed hunters and carvers and farriers and metalworkers, who brought along their wives and children, so the procession grew to dozens of caravans. They say she kept them safe though wars of every kind raged through the countryside. On their journeys into the south, they often passed villages that had been razed to the ground, the citizens slaughtered; Irina's spells distracted the warriors. Once, they say, she made an entire band of armed men who meant to raid the caravan turn instead upon each other, and they did not stop fighting until every man of them was slain.

Irina had no interest in the men of her clan or of any country she traveled through. When it was her time to cross over, they say she was still as beautiful as a young girl, with smooth skin and clear eyes and hair as black as a crow's wing, with only a single strand of silver falling across her face.

She had no daughter, but she chose a girl from the clan, a tall, awkward, intelligent young woman named Maddalena. They say she allowed no one to watch the rite through which she transferred her powers to Maddalena of Milano, but there was no doubt that it happened. Maddalena became as powerful a witch as her benefactress.

Irina, though she had come from the east, turned her face to the west at the end. She walked away from the clan to lie down on a rocky promontory overlooking the ocean, where she gave up her spirit. The clan found her beautiful body empty of life and buried her there, in sight of the sea. Her protégée knelt beside her grave for three days and three nights, until the women of the clan lifted her up and carried her back to the caravan.

The
BOOK OF THE
CARAVAN OF
WIDOWS

1

1817

Decades had passed since she last visited Carnac, but Ursule was awash in the sensation of homecoming as her secondhand caravan rolled between the fields of menhirs. She breathed the sea air and sniffed the fleeting scents of sea holly and spurge. The birds circling overhead were sea birds now, herring gulls and sanderlings and plovers. Soon the rush and hiss of waves underlay the rattle of the inland breeze, creating a familiar harmony. Louisette, driving beside her, tipped her face up into the salty wind.

It had been a long day, and the children's excitement at the beginning had dissipated with the lowering of the sun. Louisette turned sun-reddened eyes to her grandmother. "Will we be there soon? I think Andie is tired."

"I'm sure he is. We all are." Ursule's hips ached fiercely from the hours on the wooden bench, and she imagined even Louisette, with her youthful bones, was ready to climb down from it. "We should reach the camp before dark. Not more than an hour, I think."

"We're going to seem so strange to them," Louisette said.

"And they to you," Ursule said. "They live a different life."

They had talked about this at length. Ursule had told the girls as plainly as she could what was happening, but she doubted they understood what a great change it would be. They were young, and it sounded like a great lark to them, a fete that never ended, living in a caravan, traveling here and there, not bothering with shoes or manners.

Leaving their father didn't seem to worry the younger ones. Ursule suspected Louisette was wounded by Louis's abandonment, but the child never said so.

In any case, Ursule had no choice. A Romani grandmother did not leave her grandchildren to be raised by unsympathetic strangers.

The sun had just slipped below the distant glimmer of the sea when Andie clopped down the dirt lane leading from Carnac-Ville to Carnac-Plage. The clan was there, camped in the field of menhirs, exactly as the crystal had foretold. Ursule's heart fluttered at the sight of three colorful wagons and a cookfire flickering yellow through the blue gloom.

"Louisette, pull up here. We need to tell them who we are."

Louisette reined Andie in, and he plodded to a stop, his head drooping wearily. Anne-Marie put her head out the window of the caravan to call, "Are we there?"

"Almost," Ursule said. "You can see the camp just ahead. You girls can get out, but don't go far. I'll go talk to them." She rose from the bench and drew a little breath of pain as she tried to straighten.

Louisette was beside her in an instant. "Let me help you, Puri-daj. Here, I'll get down first." She clambered lightly down, her long legs bending as easily as stems of sea grass, then lifted her hands to Ursule.

Gratefully, Ursule leaned into her support as she made her way to the ground, then stood for a moment, gingerly stretching her legs and her back before limping toward the encampment, supported by her staff. She couldn't resist trailing her free hand across the menhirs as she walked. The stones spoke the welcome of old friends in their cool, unchanging roughness beneath her fingers.

The dusk was thickening as she approached. Someone stood waiting for her, a dark silhouette against the glow of the cooking fire. Ursule didn't realize until she came close that it was a woman, a woman wearing a man's jacket over a long red skirt. She didn't recognize her, but it had been fifty years since she had met another Romani. She hadn't expected to recognize anyone.

She stopped a few feet away. *"Zi buna, mora."*

The other woman, who appeared to be about Ursule's age, wore a *churi*, strapped awkwardly outside her jacket. She dropped her hand to the hilt but didn't pull it from its scabbard. *"Zi buna.* Why do you call me friend?"

Ursule took a step closer. "I'm Ursule Orchière, daughter of Agnes."

The woman put a hand to her throat. "Ursule? It can't be!"

"It is." Ursule took another step.

"But—Ursule—we thought you were dead."

"Not yet."

That won a fleeting smile from the other woman. She looked like she should be plump, round of cheek and arm and hip, but her skin hung empty on her bones. Her face was lined, her straggling hair as gray as the stone of the menhirs. "Ursule—I'm Bettina."

"Bettina!" An image flashed through Ursule's mind, poignantly clear, her friend at fourteen, laughing and boasting, dressed in a bright blue skirt and a white smock over her pregnant belly. Ursule stepped closer to peer into her old friend's face, searching for the remnants of the girl she had once known. She didn't find it, but she supposed her own face held nothing familiar, either.

She held out her hands. "Bettina. It's good to see you!"

Bettina took Ursule's proffered hands. "I can't believe it," she said. "What are you doing here? Is that your caravan?" She pointed to the wagon, where Louisette waited at Andie's head. Drom still clung to the horse's withers, nothing but a shadow in the gloom.

"We've come to join you," Ursule said. She released Bettina's hands. "There's my eldest granddaughter, and inside there are—" She hesitated as she watched Bettina's face close, her lips setting in a hard line, her brow furrowing. "What's the matter?"

"Join us?" Bettina said, a quaver in her voice. "Ursule, we—I don't know if—"

Ursule's spine stiffened, and she looked past Bettina at the three wagons gathered by the cookfire. "Is this not the Orchière clan? I was sure..."

"It is," Bettina said, her voice flattening.

"I'm an Orchière," Ursule said. "As are my granddaughters. Will we not be welcome?"

Bettina blew out a long breath. "I will welcome you, of course. We'll have to see about the others. You'll find out soon enough what the problem is, but as you say, you're an Orchière. I won't let them turn you away."

"Are you the head of the clan now?"

Bettina nodded. "I am."

"How is that possible?"

"There's no one else to do it. Go now, bring your wagon up to the campsite. I'll get the fire stirred up, but I have to warn you. There's not much to eat."

"I have some food with me."

"We'll be grateful if you're willing to share it. Our children are hungry."

····· ❖❖❖ • ❖❖❖ ·····

It took a few minutes to maneuver the caravan into position alongside the others, then to unhitch Andie. Drom fluttered up into the darkness, disappearing as Ursule led Andie to the nearby stream to drink, then settled him with a feed of mash she had pounded smooth for his old teeth. Louisette gathered the younger girls and guided them toward the cookfire.

By the time Ursule joined them, a half-dozen others had emerged from their caravans to squat or sit around the fire pit. Bettina had added an armful of wood, and the flames blazed nicely, a comforting light in the darkness.

Ursule saw, however, that there was little comfort in this gathering. She introduced herself, and the girls, and listened in amazement as the other Orchières gave their names. One was her aunt, Céline, now greatly aged. Bettina introduced her two daughters, Kezia and Rosella, well into their middle years.

There were three children as well, bone-thin and badly dressed. Louisette brought out two loaves of bread from Kerjean, with a bowl of yesterday's butter and a jar of honey, and the children fell upon the food as if they hadn't seen bread in days.

Ursule found a stone to lean against, preferring not to sit until the stiffness had worn out of her hips and back. The sad little gathering gave her a chill despite the heat from the fire.

When the children had devoured the bread and butter, their mothers sent them to bed. Ursule sent Fleurette and Florence, also, with Isabelle to mind them. She held sleepy Nanette, sticky with honey, on her lap, and she signaled to Louisette to stay close.

"Bettina," she said. "Where is Mikel? Where are my uncles?"

"Mikel was killed in the Terror. Omas and Arnaud were dead before that."

"Your daughters aren't married?"

"Not anymore."

"You mean—there are no men here?"

Céline spoke up, her voice as shrill as the scrape of an iron nail across a stone. "Not a one."

Bettina said wearily, "Widows, Ursule. We are all widows."

One of Bettina's daughters, Kezia, gave Ursule a narrow-eyed look in the uncertain light from the fire. "We have no one to protect us," she said. It didn't sound like a complaint so much as a warning.

Bettina said, "Hush, Kezia. We'll explain all of that tomorrow. You can see Ursule is tired, and I am, too. You take the first watch."

Kezia didn't say anything, but she buckled on a *churi* and moved around the fire pit to one of the menhirs that had fallen on its side, pulling up the collar of her coat as she went.

Louisette stood up, impressive in her height. "I can take a watch, too."

Ursule nodded approval.

With the watches organized, the clan retired to their wagons. Old Céline had been helped up into her caravan by Bettina's other daughter, Rosella. Bettina disappeared into the next one, and Rosella into the third. Ursule, with Nanette asleep now on her shoulder, returned to her own wagon, where Isabelle and the twins were sound asleep. Ursule pulled out Nanette's little truckle bed and laid the child in it before she slid beneath her own blankets.

Tired though she was, sleep was slow in coming. She turned uneasily on her pillow, worried by the state of Bettina's caravan. How could they have fallen so low? And how could it be possible she and her grandchildren would not be accepted back into the clan?

She didn't dare wonder what would become of her family if they were turned away.

······ ⟊⟊⟊⟊•⟊⟊⟊⟊ ······

Ursule woke early, when Louisette came in from her watch. As Louisette took off her jacket and lay down, she rose and dressed. Nanette stirred, but the other children slept on, exhausted from the travel and the curious attention of the clan children the night before.

Louisette sat up as Nanette woke and began to whimper. "Do you want me to feed her?" she whispered.

"No, no, you need to rest, *ma chère*. I'll do it." Ursule took the goat's milk she had brought, sniffed it to be certain it was still fresh, then crumbled the last of the bread into it. She carried the little girl outside to sit in the sweet ocean breeze, and fed her with her fingers while she listened to the gulls squabbling over something on the shore. The menhirs stood still and solemn and peaceful, reminding Ursule that while some things changed in essential ways, others didn't change at all. It was what she loved most about the standing stones. They neither moved nor reacted nor noticed the world rushing around them.

"One day," she said softly, "I will take my rest among you, my old friends."

Nanette hummed happily as she chewed a piece of milky bread. Ursule smiled down at her round little face, and a rush of love swept over her. "Don't worry, *ma petite*," she murmured. "I will be with you a while yet."

"Good morning, Ursule. You're up early."

Ursule glanced up to see her aunt approaching, leaning heavily on a stick. "*Zi buna*, Céline," she said. "Yes, it's my habit. I worked as a dairymaid for—goodness, fifty years, I suppose."

"Hard work. And you had to stay in one place."

"I did. My mother wasn't strong."

Céline settled onto a nearby stone, grunting a little. She must be, Ursule thought, well past eighty, a great age for one of the Romani. She peered through the rising light, her papery eyelids drooping so badly Ursule didn't know how she could see past them. She said, in her creaking voice, "How old is the child?"

"Not yet two years."

"Ah. Her mother's dead?"

The words fell heavily on Ursule's heart. She had to take a deep breath before she said, "My daughter Léonie. All these girls are hers. This one was one too many."

"Six daughters. That's supposed to be a good omen."

At a terrible price. But Ursule said only, "Her husband wanted a son."

"So did mine. They blame us, don't they? As if we have any choice in the matter."

A little silence fell. The sun peeked above the marshes to the east, and the camp was enveloped in that curiously clear light Ursule remembered from long ago, the air delicate and luminous, as if everything were gilded. A child's voice sounded from a caravan on the far side of the fire pit, and someone answered. Rosella stepped down from a different wagon and came to stir up the banked fire. She caught sight of Ursule and turned her back with a scowl.

Céline spat a thin stream into the dirt at her feet. "Rosella is a fool," she muttered.

"Why?"

Her aunt squinted at her again, her black eyes like tiny, shining pebbles beneath their wrinkled lids. "You know why they don't want you here?"

Ursule could only shake her head.

"It's the tale they tell around the fire, one of the stories they always tell. It's about you spiriting your mother away from the witch burners on your broom!"

"What?" Ursule exclaimed, and began to laugh. "A broom? I would have loved to have a broom! The two of us had nothing but our feet, and we nearly wore them out getting away."

Céline gave a stiff little shrug. "You disappeared, both of you. How could you have escaped without witchcraft? They think you're a witch."

Ursule's laughter died.

"That's why they don't want you. They call Violca One-eyed, and they call you the Great Witch. They think you'll bring the witch hunters."

"But, Céline—do these women no longer honor the craft?"

"They have no power, and they're afraid. They cower whenever strangers come around."

Ursule looked into Céline's ancient, remote eyes. "Will they turn us away?"

Again, the tiny shrug, as if Céline didn't care much either way. "We'll have to see."

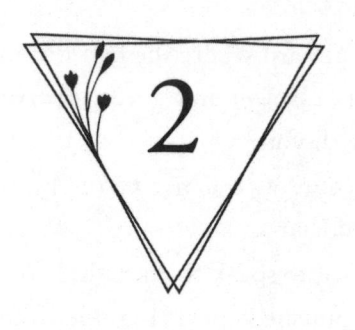

To Ursule, who had labored like a man all her life, the condition of the clan was shameful. The children were not only thin and ragged but none too clean. The women rose late, and heated a thin, meatless soup. When Louisette rose and came to crouch beside Ursule and Nanette, her mouth pinched with distaste at the sight of the bedraggled clan.

Ursule murmured, "They can't help it, Louisette. They were used to having men around. They don't know how to hunt. Probably don't know how to fish. And the Romani never stay in one place long enough to grow any food. I expect they've been begging for whatever food they can find."

"Maybe we'd be better on our own, Puri-daj."

"Six children and their grandmother? That doesn't seem like a good idea. In any case, this is our family, and we can help them."

"How?"

"First, they need food."

She climbed up into the caravan. Anne-Marie and Isabelle were peering out the window at the other Orchières around the cookfire. Fleurette and Florence huddled together on their cots, and Ursule clicked her tongue at them.

"Come on, all of you! Out now. Get to know your cousins."

Anne-Marie and Isabelle pulled back from the window, and Anne-Marie said, "Grand-mère, they smell!"

"I know. Perhaps you can get them to bathe in the stream. But first, take them some food. We have the things we brought from home, a bit of cheese, some apples saved over the winter."

She opened the cupboard where she had stored what food she could. She put the things in a basket and gave it to Anne-Marie. "Go now, and take the twins with you."

Florence slid off the cot, but her twin shrank back. "She doesn't want to," Florence said.

"Florence, let Fleurette speak for herself," commanded Louisette. It never did any good, but she kept trying. Fleurette shrugged, and Florence grinned.

Isabelle said, "Come on, everyone. We can't hide in here forever."

When they had all piled out, Ursule told Louisette, "They're afraid of me, these women."

"I heard what the old woman said. The story about the broom."

"Yes. I can't imagine who made that up—there was no broom. We have to remind them that it's good to have a witch in the clan. They've forgotten, I suppose, despite the stories they tell."

"What are you going to do?"

"When you're dealing with hungry people, food is a great persuader."

······ ◦┅┅◦┅┅◦ ······

It was an uncomfortable day, with the strange children wary of her little flock, and Rosella and Kezia drawing back whenever Ursule came near, as if her very presence were dangerous. Ursule and Agnes had lived with that fear for decades, so she understood it, but she had never expected to be the source of it.

Remy had supplied her little larder with carrots and turnips from the Kerjean cold cellar. Ursule offered them to the widows for their communal pot. Rosella had made *pufe*. She grumbled that it had taken the last of her buckwheat, but when Ursule produced a brick of Kerjean butter, her complaints died away.

Ursule withdrew to her caravan as soon as the evening began to draw in, and the girls went with her. Isabelle settled the twins into their cots, and sat patting their backs and soothing them until they slept. Nanette drowsed in her truckle bed, a rag doll tucked under her chin.

Ursule had the herbs she needed, saved from the remnants of Agnes's garden. There was sage and wild yam, and a small store of wormwood leaves, necessary for the *Charm of persuasion.*

Louisette prepared the altar with a candle and the scrying stone, and Isabelle found the veils in a cupboard. Anne-Marie had already ground the herbs together, and Ursule had salted and blessed a bowl of water. They were ready. Ursule took one glance through the little window to be certain the other caravans were dark and quiet. She pulled the curtain tightly across the window before they began.

The girls chanted the opening rite in low voices as Ursule sprinkled the salted water. Anne-Marie crumbled a bit of the herb mixture into the candle flame, and the sweet, soothing perfume of sage filled the wagon. The rest she poured into a tiny pottery jar, stopping it with a twist of linen. She set it between the stone and the candle and stepped back, fixing her grandmother with a luminous and expectant gaze.

Ursule's heart swelled with pride to see her own family, her own true coven, gathered around the altar to practice the art of their ancestresses. It made her think of a deep, strong river. Louisette was a rock, an anchor in the swirling current. Isabelle's nature was the deep, slow layer beneath the faster surface, a place of rest and comfort. Anne-Marie was like the little silver fish darting through dark water, a flicker of brightness connecting them all. Surely this community was a special kind of magic.

Ursule lifted the little jar in her hands and spoke the rite, changing the words just enough to fit the need.

Mother Goddess, your daughters request
That you with your power this charm invest
To persuade the beasts and fowl and fish
To give themselves over to our wish.

Three times three times, as always. The candle flared and dimmed, and the crystal glowed its confirmation. From the roof of the caravan, Drom clacked his beak.

Ursule raised her eyebrows at Louisette. "You do see the light?"

Louisette said, "Yes, Puri-daj. I just can't bring it up myself."

Anne-Marie and Isabelle nodded, and Isabelle said, "It's beautiful, isn't it? Misty. I wish I could do that, Grand-mère."

"Perhaps one day you will. In any case, it's done now, and tomorrow there will be game in our cooking pot. Go to bed now, *mes chères*. Sleep well."

····•·⁙⁙⁙·⁙⁙⁙·•····

In the dim chill of early morning, Ursule woke Louisette with a touch on her shoulder. They pulled on their boots and wore coats over their nightdresses. Ursule took up the pottery jar with its charm and handed Louisette a sharp kitchen knife. Once they were outside, she said softly, "You must be quick when the moment comes. Merciful." When Louisette wrinkled her nose, she said, "Don't shrink from it, *ma chère*. Needs must. We are long on hungry children and short on hunters."

With the charm in one hand and her staff in the other, Ursule led the way past the circle of wagons and into the menhir-studded field. A ground mist lapped at her ankles and curled at the feet of the stones. Ursule found the place she wanted, two minutes' walk from the camp, and chose a fallen menhir to sit on, though the cold from the stone seeped instantly through her nightdress and her coat. Her hips would remind her of this later.

Louisette stood at her side, her knife at the ready. Ursule cupped the charm in her palm and crooned,

Hares, come here at our behest.
Come to us and take your rest.

She didn't need to repeat it. She held the charm down into the swirls of mist, and the hares came, long-legged little brown creatures with long, straight ears and round black eyes. At first two or three appeared, inching through the fog, then half a dozen, their awkward hops lazy, unhurried, as if they moved in a dream. Their ears drooped, and their eyes were sleepy and soft.

Ursule said, "We won't be greedy. Take a brace."

Louisette acted without hesitation, swiftly, one stroke for each that she chose. Throats cut, they fell quietly, without complaint or struggle. The coppery scent of warm blood rose into the cold air. The remaining hares didn't move, still resting trancelike in the shifting fog.

Ursule nodded approval to Louisette. "Good," she said quietly. Then,

Back to your warrens now, dark and deep.
Day is coming and you will sleep.

The remaining hares woke from their trance. Their ears stiffened and rose, their eyes opened wide. In seconds, they scattered into the misty field, strong hind legs propelling them through the stones.

Louisette, looking down at their catch, said, "It's too easy."

"Best that way, *ma chère*. For them and for us. Give thanks for their sacrifice." She settled the charm into the pocket of her coat and pushed herself up. "Now. Has anyone taught you how to skin a hare?"

········ ❖⟩⟩⟩⟩⟩ • ⟨⟨⟨⟨⟨❖ ········

By the time the rest of the clan were up and out of their caravans, Ursule and Louisette had dressed the hares and built up the fire. Anne-Marie went to the stream with a pot for water, and they dropped the jointed hares in it to stew through the day. The children of the camp, drawn by the scent of simmering meat, crept close to Ursule and her grandchildren, forgetting their wariness in their eagerness to know the source of the smell.

Rosella and Kezia came, too. They peeked into the simmering pot, and Kezia said, "We haven't had meat in so long. How did you manage?"

Louisette answered in a pert tone. "My *puri-daj* is an adept at the craft. You should be grateful instead of afraid."

Bettina, coming up behind her daughters, chuckled. "Ursule, your granddaughter has a quick tongue."

"She's an Orchière. Most of us do."

Later, when the clan had made do with soup to break their fast, the children, awkwardness forgotten in their enthusiasm for the feast to come, went off with Anne-Marie to look for wild onions and fennel, and anything else that might be added to the stew. Kezia and Rosella carried baskets of laundry to the stream while Bettina and old Céline drowsed in the thin spring sunshine.

Louisette stirred the pot, picking out the bones when she spotted them, saving them in a bowl to make broth. "I have a question, Puri-daj."

Ursule was resting on a stone near the fire, tossing in twigs when the flames began to die down. "Yes?"

"The charm of this morning, and the other things...How do you know what to say?"

Ursule slowly shook her head, gazing into the glow of the fire. "I can't explain it. The words come to me, the right words to express my intention. Part of the gift, I suppose."

"I wish I had the gift."

"You have other gifts, *ma chère*. Leadership. Strength. Spirit."

"But not magic."

"Magic is not always a blessing," Ursule said. *The Goddess always exacts her price.* "I think you must trust that the Goddess knows what's right for you."

· · · · · ·⟩⟩⟩⟩⟩⟩ • ⟨⟨⟨⟨⟨⟨· · · · ·

The clan feasted that night on stew rich with meat, onions, and fennel, and spiced with the hardy rosemary that grew between the menhirs. The spring night was comfortably cool, and the women and children, bellies full at last, sat around the dying fire until stars sprinkled the black sky and nightjars began to trill. The fire had dwindled to scarlet and black embers when Old Céline began the storytelling. She recounted the tale of One-eyed Violca, then went back further in time to the fable of the prophetess Liliane, who had foretold the coming of a great flood.

When she stopped, Kezia said, "Maman. Tell the story of Ursule, the great witch of Brittany."

Ursule started at this, her spine stiffening. She turned to fix Kezia with an angry glance, but Bettina touched her arm.

"You should hear it," Bettina said. "Then you'll know why the clan is fearful."

"But it's not true."

"Do you think the other tales are true?"

"The other tales could be true. This one isn't."

Rosella, with one child on her lap and another at her feet, said, "Ursule, why don't you hear the story, and then you can tell us what really happened?"

It was a reasonable thing to say, and Ursule pressed her lips together and argued no more. She was aware, before Bettina began speaking, of Drom, perched on one of the standing stones just beyond the fading glow of the fire, shifting from side to side as he did when he was waiting for something.

"Long ago," Bettina began, "when the Orchière clan traveled with the Vilas, there was a young girl, only thirteen. She had been born in the dark of the moon, and no one knew who her father was. They say she had a birthmark on her shoulder in the shape of a broom. She was neither pretty nor rich, but she was clever, and she had a secret. Her mother—" Bettina paused, and Ursule understood this was the way she always told the story, with the same rhythm, the same emphasis in the same places. Bettina had probably created it.

"Her mother," Bettina went on, allowing her voice to drop low, just loud enough to carry around the circle. "Her mother was a seer. A teller of fortunes. And the girl, little Ursule, was a—*witch*!" At this, all the listeners gasped, although Ursule had no doubt they had heard the story a hundred times. "Everyone thought the days of the witches were past, until Ursule.

"Ursule's mother did well telling fortunes, and brought in many *livres* for the clan. Ursule, the clever little witch, helped her in her work, because she saw things her mother couldn't see. Saw too many things, indeed."

Bettina paused again, and everyone around the circle waited, rapt, for her to go on. From the darkness, Ursule heard Drom groan, as if he felt the tension, too, and she gripped her hands together in her lap.

"The word began to spread about the little witch and her mother, the fortune-teller. The women came from nearby villages, wanting to know their futures, wanting to know their husbands' secrets. The word spread, all the way to Vannes, and when it reached the bishop's ear, he sent his witch hunters to Belz.

"The witch hunters came one dark night and carried Ursule's mother away to be burned. That very night, Ursule magicked a dog to lead her to her mother, and she carried a magicked broom with her. She struck the lock on the prison door with the handle of the broom, and the chain fell into a hundred pieces, setting her mother free. Ursule put her on the broom, climbed up behind her, and flew her away from that place. When the jailer came to the prison, he found the door open and the witch gone.

"The witch hunters searched for days. The bishop was furious and had the poor magicked dog killed and the jailer thrown into his own jail, but all for nothing. The Romani are the only ones who know that the little witch, so small but so powerful, was Ursule." Here Bettina slid a sideways glance at Ursule. "The Romani say the great witch Ursule carried her mother away on her broom to a secret place, where no one could find them. No one ever saw them again, but—" Another practiced pause. "In the dark of the moon, if you look up into the stars, you may see the silhouette of the great witch Ursule on her magicked broom, come back to Brittany to see how we do."

Bettina blew out a long breath and stopped speaking. In the darkness, Drom gave one admonishing croak. No one said a word until Old Céline cackled, "And here you are! Do you still have the broom?"

U rsule had hidden her gifts for so long that sometimes, living once
again with the Romani, she felt oddly exposed, as if she had forgotten to put on her clothes before stepping out of her wagon.

Everyone knew who she was and what she could do, and it made them
greedy. Persuaded by the brace of hares that first day, the clan fell into the
habit of asking her to do it again—or rather, they asked Louisette to ask
her. The children began to fatten, and the worried looks on the women's
faces eased, little by little. They had hare and winter teal and trout for
their cookfire. Once, Ursule lured a big goose that had been browsing
near the stream, and it fed them all for three days. Still, neither Kezia nor
Rosella was brave enough to speak to her directly. She hadn't yet decided
how she felt about that, whether she should be offended or amused.

She worked hard for them, just the same. In addition to the *Spell of
persuasion* she made charms, some to sweeten the soap and candles they
made, others to smooth and tighten the weaving of their baskets. All
these things sold well at the market, better, Bettina assured her, than
ever before. When Kezia and Rosella carried their wares into Carnac-
Ville on market days, they always returned triumphant, bringing back
beans and bread and buckwheat, with the luxury of a few coins left over.

Bettina didn't repeat her wild tale of Ursule and Agnes disappearing
on a broom, but no one had forgotten it.

On an afternoon spitting with rain, the three Orchière children,
with Fleurette and Florence in tow, crowded up into Ursule's wagon
to get dry. Ursule and her family had been enjoying a quiet afternoon,
secluded by the pattering rain. Louisette had been reading a book, and

Ursule and Anne-Marie were working on a salve for the horses' feet as they prepared to move on to another camp.

It was the first time the Orchières had been inside. They fingered the cushions, looked inside the pots and bowls, and climbed onto the cots to try the mattresses, until Anne-Marie snapped at them that they were muddying the blankets. There were far too many people in the cramped space. Isabelle, rocking a drowsy Nanette on her lap, told them to keep their voices down. It did little good.

They needed a bit of discipline, Ursule thought, as much as they needed a good wash.

Having snooped into every corner of the wagon, a dirty-faced girl of perhaps eight or nine came to stand in front of Ursule, her hands on her skinny hips. "Grand-mère Ursule? Can we see your broom?"

Ursule said, "There is no broom, I'm afraid."

"Did you lose it?" The other children clustered around her now, eyes bright with curiosity.

"There never was a broom, *mes enfants*," Ursule said. "It's just a story."

"But you're a witch!"

It was the same girl, with a shrill, insistent voice. One of Kezia's.

Louisette stepped in. "Renée! Has your mother taught you nothing?"

Ursule had to suppress a smile. Louisette had always had an imperious nature, but now, with a passel of unruly children needing a firm hand, she had come into her own.

Louisette drew herself up and glared. She was as tall as her father now, and she had the voice of a man as well. "You listen to me, Renée, and the rest of you, too. We do not say that word about Grand-mère, not among ourselves, and especially not where anyone else can hear. You don't know who might be lurking among the stones, or crossing to the stream to fish, or—or anything! Do you want to bring the witch burners down on us?"

One of the younger children began to sniffle, and the third, one Ursule thought was a boy, though it was hard to tell, turned pale. "The w-witch burners?" he breathed.

"Yes!" Louisette thundered.

Ursule chuckled. "Don't frighten them too much, *ma chère*. They'll all be in tears, and have nightmares."

"I don't care," Louisette said, but in a more moderate tone. "You've done so much for them in such a short time, Puri-daj. They should learn some gratitude."

The little boy said again, in a small voice, "Are the w-witch burners coming?"

Ursule put aside the notes for her potion and patted her knee. "Come here, *mon petit*. Tell me your name."

"I'm Jean."

"Jean. Good. Now, I know Louisette can be very scary." Beyond the little boy's head, Louisette grinned. "But she's right, and all of you need to remember. A bit of power does wonderful things, like bring us better food and even a bit of money, but other people are afraid of it. Just as you're afraid of the witch burners, they're afraid of witches." She said the word softly, almost whispering. "Now, don't cry. I think we might have a few almond cakes tucked away. Would you like one?"

This suggestion banished all thoughts of the witch hunters, at least for the moment. Anne-Marie brought out the almond cakes. She had to divide them in half to make them go around, but none of the children seemed to mind.

When the rain stopped and the children ran out into the fields to search for frogs, Ursule and Louisette and Anne-Marie seized the moment's peace to talk. Isabelle laid Nanette down for her nap, and Ursule noticed the child was getting too big for her little truckle bed. She would have to share someone's cot soon.

Louisette began. "I still think we might be better on our own. Safer."

Anne-Marie said, "But these people need us. The children were starving."

Isabelle came to sit beside Ursule on her cot. "Anne-Marie is right. How can we leave now, knowing the children will go hungry?"

"We're not going," Ursule said. "But I'll speak to Bettina about everyone being careful."

"But, Puri-daj," Louisette began.

Ursule stopped her with a shake of her head. "I don't want us to be alone. I'm getting old, Louisette. You're going to need other people around."

"You're not old," Isabelle said. "You'll always be here."

Ursule smiled at her, but she heard Drom's claws scratch on the roof of the wagon, sending a ripple of premonition through her.

· · · · · ·˙˙˙˙˙˙˙ • ˙˙˙˙˙˙˙· · · · ·

"You were all afraid I would attract the witch hunters," Ursule said to Bettina that night, as the younger women cleaned up after their meal. "Now you're glad enough to have me—"

"We are, Ursule," Bettina interrupted. "You're Goddess-sent."

"But, Bettina, the children put us at risk. They have to be taught."

"I know. Kezia told me what Renée said, and she swears she scolded her."

"So did Louisette, and in a most convincing way."

"I can imagine. Louisette is—well, you can't ignore her."

"I hope that will be enough, but we have to remind them—remind everyone, in fact, Kezia and Rosella, too."

"I'll see to it."

"I also think that if we go east, to La Trinité-sur-Mer, perhaps on to Locmariaquer, that would be safer. We're too close to Belz."

"*D'accord.* They still remember, though it was so long ago. They have not forgotten the witch who escaped."

Ursule shivered. Despite the years, the old horror remained, lurking in a corner of her mind like one of the cave spiders hiding in a crevice of stone.

"And," Bettina went on, unaware of her old friend's discomfort, "Louisette and Anne-Marie should have a chance to meet other people, at their age."

"I suppose you're right," Ursule said. "I don't like thinking of it."

"I remember how that felt, but you get used to it. Kezia was only thirteen when she met Philippe, and Rosella was fifteen when she and

Felix married. I had to remind myself I was just that age, and already pregnant with Kezia at fourteen."

"I thought you were too young."

"Oh, I was!" Bettina laughed. "Such romantic notions, as if I were a princess, and not a Romani traveler in hand-me-down clothes!"

"Your husband..."

Bettina's smile faded. "Yes. Poor Mikel. He wasn't a very good husband, but he didn't deserve to die that way."

"What happened to him?"

"We thought, when the revolutionaries turned against the lords, and the king, and the priests—we thought we would have our place at last. Mikel went to join the fighting, but they saw who he was. What he was. It seems being Romani is as bad as being an aristocrat."

"Not the guillotine?"

"No, they just—they were slaughtering everybody in their path, and he was there."

"They came to the village where I was living, too. Smashed everything, hauled away the local priest and the *vicomte*—it was terrible."

"I think it's over now."

"Yes, but people always need someone to hate. Someone to blame. If they knew about me, I would be precisely that person."

Bettina reached for Ursule's hand and gripped it. Ursule looked down at their entwined fingers, remembering how they had looked, so long ago—fresh and strong and smooth. Now their hands were crooked, the knuckles swollen, the backs spotted.

Bettina followed her glance and gave a sour laugh. "It creeps up on you, doesn't it?"

"It does exactly that. While you're living your life, it creeps up on you."

Bettina gave her hand a squeeze and released it. "We'll keep you safe."

It was a brave statement, and it made Ursule smile. "I know you'll do your best."

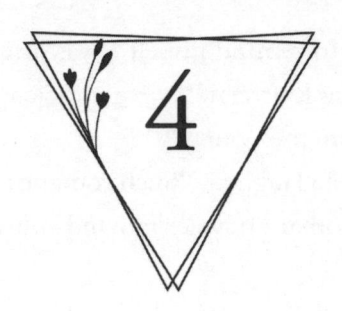

4

The clan traveled single file, pausing when they needed to, keeping a careful watch during the lonely nights on the road. Farmers occasionally came to stand by their gates, eyeing them with suspicion. They avoided villages, trundling along the lanes closest to the sea, sometimes bumping through empty fields. They found a spot on a bluff above the soft sand beaches of La Trinité, with a bit of sparse grass for the horses to crop, and a jumble of black boulders to shield the wagons from the wind. The site gave a view of Men-Dû, the little island rising from the blue water to the south. They were an hour's walk from the town and its lively market. A nearby stream gurgled its invitation of clear fresh water and small silver fish that could be netted up with ease.

On the eve of Samhain, Ursule sent the children out to collect oak leaves, acorns, and pine cones. Anne-Marie poured a wide, shallow candle and studded it with a half-dozen wicks, so each child could light one. Rosella and Kezia, though they grumbled over the extra work, stacked wood and kindling in the circle of stones they had used to create a fire pit. Louisette had already been to the market in La Trinité, returning with a harvest feast of sweet corn and turnips, a wheel of cheese, and apples to bake. Isabelle managed the table, using two planks from the roof of Kezia's wagon, and visiting each caravan to collect bowls for everyone living, and one for each of the dead to be remembered.

Ursule spent the day of Samhain making charms of rosemary and thistle and mugwort, tied together with twine.

By the time the darkness fell, the younger children were beside themselves with excitement, dashing around the encampment, leaping around the unlit bonfire, shrieking with unspent energy and making their mothers beg for peace. Even Florence ran and shouted. Fleurette hung back, silent and shy, but once the torch was put to the bonfire and the feast of vegetables and roasted apples and cheese was laid out, she crowded around the table with everyone else.

After the feast, Ursule sent Louisette to the caravan for the crystal. They used the end of the table as their altar. Ursule sprinkled it with what was left of the herbs and added the acorns and other things the children had gathered. Anne-Marie set her candle next to the stone, and each of the younger children, helped by an adult, held a flaming twig to a wick. When all the wicks were burning, Ursule put one hand on the cool, rounded top of the crystal, the other on her staff with its reliquary, and waited.

One by one, the members of the clan fell silent. The breeze whispered around the black boulders, and off to the west, the tide whispered up and down the sand. The air smelled like Samhain, Ursule thought, salty and fresh, pungent with the scents of roasted apples and simmered vegetables. Even little Nanette, on Isabelle's lap next to Ursule, was quiet, her eyes turned up to the stars. Ursule wondered if the child, like herself, heard the whisper of ancestral voices on the wind.

She breathed a long sigh, and addressed her clan. Her family. "This," she said, "is the Orchière crystal, our scrying stone. It was dug out of a riverbank by the *grand-mère* of the *grand-mère* of my *grand-mère*. One-eyed Violca saw things in it, as did the prophetess Liliane when she predicted the flood, and Maddalena of Milano, who saw the Romani spreading across France. Its power is our secret, our Romani secret, a secret to be kept. Always."

Louisette put her hands on her hips and flashed her fiercest look around the table. The subsiding flames of the bonfire shimmered over the clan's cheeks and hair, and the littlest ones' mouths hung open in wonder. "It's a dangerous secret," Louisette said. "Remember that."

From the darkness, Drom crooned approval of this, and little Nanette crowed back at him, *"Buna! Buna!"* It was her favorite word, and she had been practicing it endlessly. Old Céline cackled in appreciation.

Ursule said, "We will begin with the traditional rite, but first, I want to say to you—to all of you, my grandchildren and Bettina's, Rosella and Kezia, even Céline. We have all had different names at different times, but we are always—we will always be—Orchières. There is power in our line, and in our name. *D'accord?"*

Everyone nodded. Even Renée was quiet, rapt, and Bettina flashed Ursule a grin.

"Good." Ursule raised her hands above the altar and recited the old litany. She felt as if the names had more power this night, generated by so many Orchières gathered together.

On this Sabbat of Samhain, we honor our foremothers: the seer Violca, the prophetess Liliane, the Lady Yvette, Maddalena of Milano, Irina from the east, and all the others whose precious names have been lost. We vow to pass the craft to our daughters so long as our line endures.

Rosella's little boy piped, "Only daughters?"

His mother shushed him, but Ursule held out a hand. "Come here to me, Jean," she said. "You can look into the scrying stone just as the girls do, and if you can scry, then you have the power, too."

The little boy stood on his tiptoes and peered at the crystal. "I don't see anything."

"Not yet." Ursule smiled at him. "But don't give up."

Renée put her nose as close to the stone as she could. "I don't see anything, either."

"We haven't begun yet," Ursule said.

"What are you going to do?"

"We're going to ask the *grands-mères* to tell us something, and we'll see if they answer. Samhain is a good time, because this night the veil between the living and the dead is thin."

Renée fell back a step. "The dead?"

"Yes."

"You mean—dead people will talk to us?"

"Are you afraid of your ancestresses?"

"Well, yes! They're dead!"

"But, Renée, they are always with us. It's why we set extra places at our Samhain table."

"But, Grand-mère—"

"Hush, now." Louisette drew the girl away, and the little boy followed. Isabelle shifted her seat, adjusting Nanette's position. Nanette turned up her face, and when Ursule saw the sparkle of reflected stars in those wide eyes, her heart contracted with longing for Léonie.

She breathed into the ache, and when it eased, she sprinkled a few crumbs of *franc encens* into the candle flames, then propped her staff against her shoulder so she could stretch her arm above the stone. Her voice rose to mingle with the sounds of the sea and the wind, to echo off the unmoving menhirs, to resound from the black boulders that encircled them.

This night of nights, this sacred eve,
Come to us who do believe.
Maiden and widow, child and crone,
We ask your protection in our new home.

The scrying stone shimmered with light just as a huge white moon slid up the sky in the east to cast long silver shadows over the campsite. The watching clan gasped as one, and Jean, clinging to his mother's skirts, whispered, "Grand-mère? Did you see the dead people?"

But it was Nanette who caught Ursule's attention. No one else seemed to notice her staff, the little reliquary with its tiny bone glowing like a miniature moon, but Nanette's eyes, dark and wide, were fixed on it. Her rosebud mouth pursed, and she murmured, in her sweet high child's voice, *"Buna. Buna."*

From the darkness, Drom crooned his agreement.

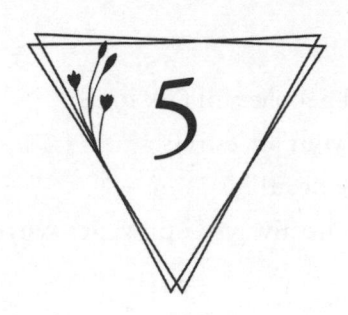

The caravan of widows stayed in La Trinité through the winter, fishing in the stream, hunting in the fields, weaving and making soap and, under Anne-Marie's guidance, producing tallow candles of several shapes and sizes. With the aid of her little talent, they were clearer and brighter than the ones available in the shops, and they always sold out in the market.

Louisette took the children in hand, not only Florence and Fleurette, but Jean and Renée and Rosella's daughter Fara, who was sweet, but rather slow. Louisette bought clothes for all of them in the ragman's stall in La Trinité, and as the weather grew colder, she managed to find shoes as well, though most of them didn't fit very well, and the children avoided wearing them if they could. Louisette insisted they wash weekly, and if they didn't do it on their own, she did it for them, ignoring their cries of protest and attempts to wriggle free of her big hands.

Ursule knew that Florence and Fleurette still wept for their mother, though they tried to do it so no one would see. Ursule pretended she didn't notice, because there was nothing she could do to lessen their grief. *I will cry forever.* At least the twins had each other. And they had Isabelle. Isabelle was the favorite of all the children, including Rosella's and Kezia's. Nanette toddled after her wherever she went, and it wasn't unusual to see Isabelle heading to the copse with three or four barefoot children trailing after her. She loaded their arms with sticks and branches, then built up the fire and sat telling them stories.

As Ostara drew near, Bettina decided it was time to move on. They had exhausted the supply of firewood in the copse between them and the beach, and the horses had decimated the grass in the field beyond the boulders. They needed supplies before they could replenish their wares for the market, and La Trinité seemed to have run out. Or perhaps the village had fewer people willing to sell to the Romani.

"I'm getting restless, too," Bettina said. "We've been in one place long enough."

Ursule had spent fifty years in one place. She no longer remembered what restlessness felt like, but she let it pass. It was a Romani trait.

Bettina went on, "We should travel to Locmariaquer. There are usually other caravans there at this time of year. They go for the oysters."

"Shall we celebrate Ostara first?"

"Yes. It will take us a few days to gather everything up in any case."

It was true. The table had to be dismantled and restored to the top of Kezia's wagon. Various toys and dolls and half-finished projects lay scattered about the encampment, and the black boulders were draped with drying laundry. The cooking pots resting in the cold ashes of the fire needed to be scrubbed with sand and rinsed in the stream before being stored away. All their possessions had to be secured, and the horses' tack cleaned and soaped.

Louisette took charge of all these preparations. For three days, the sound of her snapping orders and calling commands echoed around the encampment, and the day after Ostara, they were ready. By the time they put the horses in their traces, every wagon was in good order and the campsite was scoured clean.

Louisette decreed that Ursule, on this journey, should travel inside the caravan. "Anne-Marie can sit with me on the driving seat," she said. "Puri-daj, it's too hard on you. Anne-Marie, put on a hat. It's going to be sunny and breezy."

No one asked how she knew this, but everyone—including Ursule—did just as she said.

It was cozy for Ursule, sitting on her cot as the wagon lurched onto the path leading to the south. The twins had their heads together over a doll they were constructing out of a discarded scarf, black pebbles from the streambed, and a hank of yarn donated by Old Céline. Nanette, who now shared Isabelle's cot, lay with her head on her big sister's knee, lulled into drowsiness by the movement of the caravan.

Isabelle, idly turning Nanette's dark curls between her fingers, looked up at Ursule. "Puri-daj," she said softly. "I have to tell you something."

"*Bien sûr, ma petite,*" Ursule said. "You can tell me anything."

Isabelle's cheeks colored, reminding Ursule of the dark pink dog-roses that grew along the brook bordering Kerjean Farm. "I had a dream," Isabelle said.

"Is that unusual?"

"No, but this was different. It was true." Isabelle's little chin lifted, and she met Ursule's gaze steadily. "It was like seeing things in the crystal."

Ursule lifted her eyebrows. "Was it indeed, Isabelle? Why is that?"

"Everything was clean and clear, the way the light in the crystal is sometimes. And it was important. I could tell because I remember every detail, every little thing, as if I had seen it in a painting or—or I don't know, when I wasn't asleep."

"And what did you see?"

"There were people dancing all around Louisette and a man. A tall man, strong-looking, but I don't know him. Louisette had a wreath of flowers on her head, yellow trefoil and orange pimpernel, I think, twisted up with lavender. The man wore a scarlet vest. The other people all wore bright clothes, not like ours, all washed out. These were red and purple and green. And everyone was laughing. Even Louisette! She doesn't laugh very often."

"That's a wonderful dream to have."

"It's not just a dream. It's a true dream, Puri-daj. And you were in it, too."

"Was I?"

"Yes, and you had a new red skirt." Isabelle's dark eyes—the Orchière eyes, the Romani eyes—sparkled with wonder at the intensity of her experience. The magic of it.

Ursule smiled at the idea. "I haven't had a new skirt in a long time, Isabelle."

"But you will have one. I saw it."

Ursule didn't argue. *Never dismiss a witch's dream.* She didn't care much about the new red skirt, but she cared very much about Louisette's future. And about an Orchière's true dreams.

······ ·≫≫≫· ·≪≪≪·· ·····

Bettina had traveled to Locmariaquer when she and Mikel were still with the Vilas. Their caravan, in the days when Edouard Vila was still alive, had joined two other clans in a spot on a low cliff overlooking the bay. She remembered a long beach that appeared when the tide retreated, where the men could wade into the water and fish with nets or poles.

With Bettina in the lead, their little caravan set out. The horses were well-fed and rested, and even Andie seemed to have regained a bit of his youthful energy. The larders in the wagons were well supplied. The giddying scent of spring charged the air. Spirits were high, and everyone from little Nanette to Old Céline savored the change of scenery.

It made Ursule smile to see her girls waving at sheep in the farms they passed, or exclaiming over a spring foal bucking in a green pasture. They were definitely Romani, she thought, born to travel, to see fresh sights in every season. Madeleine had been right in this one thing. The Romani blood was strong.

They arrived late in the afternoon, squinting against the angle of the lowering sun on the water as they turned out of the road and worked their way toward the place Bettina remembered.

The village of Locmariaquer nestled on a stretch of marshy land pierced by bodies of water on all sides. The ground was spongy, and the wagon wheels dragged, but they soon found another lane where the soil had been pressed flat. Bettina called back, "Almost there," as they approached a high dune thick with spiky tufts of beach grass.

As they rounded the dune, the children leaned out of the windows, thrilling to the sight of six vivid wagons, blue and purple and yellow, parked in a semicircle around a generous fire pit. Beyond the campsite, several horses grazed in a narrow field that ended at the edge of a low cliff. A handful of children, playing among the wagons, came running to stare at the newcomers.

A tall young man, with a *churi* at his waist, came forward as the Orchières climbed down from their wagons. Ursule started forward to stand with Bettina as they introduced themselves, but Isabelle caught her back. "Puri-daj, that's him! That's the man!"

Distractedly, Ursule said, "What man, Isabelle? I need to—"

"My dream!" She spoke with quiet pride. "I told you it was true."

·····•❧❧❧❧•❧❧❧❧❧•·····

The young man's name, they soon learned, was Claude Roche. He had narrow black eyes, an arching nose, and a manner every bit as imperious as Louisette's. They were, Ursule had to admit, a perfect match.

Observing Louisette fall in love was like watching an unbroken horse struggle against accepting its rider. Louisette was by turns misty-eyed and short-tempered, dreamy and sharp-voiced. Ursule could guess that Claude, too, was riding the same uneasy tide of feelings, the rise of passion often breaking into shreds of foam on the jagged rocks of reality. If it had not been for Isabelle's dream, she would never have believed the pair of them would make it as far as a wedding.

She knew for certain it was going to happen the day Louisette and Anne-Marie came back from Locmariaquer's market with a surprise for her, wrapped in a bit of burlap. When she folded back the burlap and shook out a bright red skirt, she and Isabelle both burst out laughing.

"Why are you laughing, Puri-daj?" Louisette said. "It's for the wedding!"

"Oh, I know, *ma chère*, I do know! And I thank you! I haven't had a new skirt in—well, not since my mother sewed me one for *your* mother's wedding. Goodness. I'm walking around in rags."

"But you still haven't said—" Anne-Marie began.

Isabelle interrupted, her small features glowing with pride. "I told her she would wear a red skirt for the wedding. I dreamed it, and it was true! You, Louisette, will wear a wreath of pimpernel and trefoil and lavender, and Claude will have a vest of scarlet, and we will all dance!"

Florence said, "Dance? I love to dance!" Fleurette, smiling, nodded agreement.

Anne-Marie said, "I had better ask around for where I can find some lavender."

Nanette, wide-eyed at the excitement in their voices, cried, *"Buna!"*

Louisette caught her up in a hug, burying her face in the little one's hair. "You will have a new dress, too, *ma petite*. I will see to it!"

····· ⫸⫸⫸·⫷⫷⫷ ·····

It wasn't long after Louisette moved into Claude's caravan that Anne-Marie wed one of Claude's cousins, a mild-mannered young man named Paul. Ursule appreciated the extra room in the Orchière caravan, but she missed Louisette's decisive ways and Anne-Marie's soothing voice. She supposed it wouldn't be long before Isabelle would choose a husband as well, leaving only herself, the twins, and Nanette. The great blessing was that these marriages took her dear ones no farther than the other side of the encampment. She could see them every day.

Locmariaquer was an easy place to live, and sharing with the Roche clan was, for the most part, peaceful. The work of hunting and cooking and washing was shared by many hands, making Ursule feel as lazy as Drom on a warm day. She and Bettina sometimes sat on a great log that had been washed up by the sea and lugged up from the beach. It was a silvery, smooth piece of driftwood that grew warm in the sun and soothed their aging bones with its heat as they talked of old times and watched the children play. Nanette sometimes climbed into Ursule's lap to drowse, and the sweet weight of a child in her arms felt like an embrace from the Goddess.

The day before Lammas, when preparations had begun for a grand celebration, Louisette found them sitting there. "Puri-daj," she said.

"My sister-in-law's little boy is crying with a stomachache. Do you have something?"

"*Bien sûr.*" Ursule pushed herself up from the stone, appreciating the way the warmth of the sun had eased her stiffness. "I always keep a simple ready for stomachache."

Together they went to the caravan, and Ursule rummaged through a dozen or so corked bottles until she found what she wanted. "This should help," she said. "Ginger and peppermint in a tincture of chamomile."

Louisette grinned down at her grandmother. "With a dash of magic, I expect."

Ursule handed the little jar to her. "More than a dash, I hope, *ma chère*. Give the little boy ten drops, and if he doesn't feel better in half an hour or so, try five more."

Louisette bent to kiss Ursule's cheek. "Thank you. And my sister-in-law will thank you."

"More likely, dear heart, she will tell you to thank me. None of the Roches seem to want to talk to me."

"That's Céline's fault. She couldn't wait to tell the story of the witch Ursule stealing someone away on her broom."

"They believe that? Surely not your husband—or Anne-Marie's!"

"They know your simples have special power, and your potions. The *Charm of persuasion* has brought many a bit of meat or fish into our cooking pots, so yes, they believe the story. They're afraid of you, just as the Orchières were at first."

"But they're Romani! They grew up on stories of witchcraft!"

"I can't explain it," Louisette said with a shrug. "It seems to me if they're that afraid of the power, they're no better than the witch hunters."

"You should tell them that," Ursule said. She opened the door of the caravan. "Go now, take care of the little one. I would go with you, but I expect they would rather not have me in their wagon."

As she took down a bundle of herbs to make a fresh stomach potion,

Ursule indulged in a private laugh. In a strange way, the Roches' fear made her feel powerful. They would do probably anything she asked of them. Or told them.

As she lifted her mortar and pestle to the counter, she imagined how they would feel when she scried something that was to come. She had not yet brought out the Orchière crystal, but when they saw it come to life, her reputation would solidify.

She went on chuckling as she worked, thinking what a wonderful addition to their Lammas celebration the scrying stone would be.

Louisette's babe, Ursule's first great-grandchild, was born just after Imbolc, on a day of cold sunshine and brisk, salt-sharpened wind. He was a loud and lusty boy they named George, and he made his appearance without difficulty. Anne-Marie had never been as strong as her older sister, but she, too, gave birth to her Pierre easily, with the aid of Ursule's potion for pain and then the simple to bring her milk in.

The Roche clan was in awe of Ursule's abilities. They had watched the crystal glow under her hands as if with the light of a full moon, and then they had observed the ease with which her granddaughters gave birth. The next time one of the Roche women had a confinement, she sent Louisette to ask for Ursule's help, and it became the custom throughout the camp.

The Roches remained hesitant to speak to Ursule themselves, so Louisette and Anne-Marie and Isabelle became her couriers, and Bettina her defender. The Roches treated every one of her caravan of widows with deference, as if Ursule's power extended to them as well. Kezia and Rosella walked around with their noses in the air, flattered by the respect even the men showed them.

Ursule and the twins and Nanette lived comfortably in the caravan, each with their own cot, their own bowl, their own cup. Nanette was a talker, as her mother had been, and she spoke in such a polyglot of languages—French, Breton, Romani—that Ursule feared she would never sort out which was which. She was already puzzling out letters from her older sisters' tiny book collection, and Ursule began to teach her in earnest, drawing one letter at a time with a precious graphite pencil, adding the letters together to form words. Nanette was quicker at learning to read than any of her sisters had been. When the Roches became aware that all of Ursule's grandchildren could read, the uneasy distance between them grew.

Ursule would never admit to having a favorite, but Nanette was in many ways the child of her heart, as Léonie had been. The other girls could hardly help but see this, but they didn't seem to mind. They cast indulgent glances their way when the two of them, the old woman and the bright little girl, bent their heads over a scrap of paper or a book. Their tolerance felt to their grandmother as an extra layer of love, of a wish for both Nanette and herself to be at peace.

Ursule wished Louisette and her husband could find the same peace.

The whole clan could hear the shouted arguments from inside Claude and Louisette's wagon. Ursule often paused whatever she was doing to listen, shaking her head. Louisette came to her after one of these noisy arguments, when Claude and Paul and two of the other Roche men had gone to the oyster beds to collect enough shellfish for a stew.

Ursule had been resting outside the wagon, letting the rich May sun bathe her face. She would darken, of course, but that no longer mattered to anyone, least of all to her.

The twins and the Roche children had been sent out to unhobble the horses and let them roam a bit but had stayed to play in the meadow. Nanette, on a blanket at Ursule's feet, was taking her favorite doll apart to see how it was made, then trying to put it back together. Louisette, with her babe in her arms, bent to kiss her youngest sister before she crouched beside Ursule's stool. She smiled, but her eyes were stony.

Ursule patted her cheek. "Are you all right, *ma chère?*"

"I'm all right, but Claude may not be when I get done with him."

Ursule raised her eyebrows. "I wouldn't want to be in his shoes, if you're that angry."

Louisette drew a long breath and gently laid her infant on the blanket beside Nanette's plump little legs. She settled onto her knees and rubbed the sleeping babe's back. "He's not nearly as smart as he thinks he is, my husband."

"Husbands can be a challenge," Ursule said in a mild tone.

Louisette spat into the dirt. "Men!"

That made Ursule chuckle. "I expect they have their own thoughts about women."

"Without doubt!" Louisette snapped. "They think women should do as they're told, and ask no questions!" She lifted her chin and glared across the campsite in the direction of her caravan. At that moment, she looked so much like the statue of an Eastern goddess Ursule had once seen, tall and dark and strong, that she half expected her to extend two extra pairs of arms.

"*Eh bien*, my sweet, and what did our Claude tell you to do?"

"He told me to ask you for the *Charm of persuasion*. I said he could ask you himself, but he won't do it."

"*Oh la la*. Surely he's not afraid of me, too, a strapping big man like that!"

Louisette shifted on her knees to hand Nanette a bit of the doll's body she had dropped. "He doesn't like asking a woman for help."

"So he asks you to do it for him?"

"Apparently he fails to see the irony in that."

"You should tell him he married into the wrong family if he feels that way."

Louisette's lips curved. "Do you know, Puri-daj, I said that very thing."

"Good for you." Ursule put her hands on her knees and pushed herself up, wincing at the pain in her hips. "Of course I will make the charm, though."

"I knew you would. The least he could do is show some gratitude."

"Sometimes, *ma chère*, it takes a long time for them to come to it. Will you watch Nanette? I'll see if I have what I need."

She climbed up into the wagon, bracing herself on the flimsy doorjamb, and went to her herb cupboard. It was cool inside, although later, as the caravan baked in the sun, she would keep the door and the window open to the sea breeze. She began to sift through the herbs she had, making mental notes of what she needed, but as her hands worked, she suddenly thought of Remy Kerjean.

It was Louisette's comment about gratitude. Ursule hadn't known, for such a long time, that Remy was grateful to her. That he noticed what she did, or cared very much, not until Agnes died and Madeleine retreated so far into herself she might as well have been dead. Not until the very end of their long relationship did Ursule understand Remy's regard for her. She supposed Claude might suffer the same kind of constraint, and perhaps for the same reasons.

She piled the herbs for the charm onto the narrow wooden counter and went back to tell Louisette it would be ready the next day. She found her seated on the stool now, her bodice open, her little George eagerly suckling. As Ursule had earlier, Louisette had closed her eyes and tipped her face up to the let the high spring sun shine on her cheeks. Nanette, at her feet, had curled up with her doll and fallen asleep.

Ursule smiled at the scene and withdrew into the caravan, leaving the door open so the warm air could swirl in, bringing with it the assurance that all was just as it should be.

······ ·꞉꞉꞉꞉꞉·꞉꞉꞉꞉꞉꞉·····

The sense of peace and rightness stretched through all of the lovely summer. Everyone ate well, fish and oysters, an occasional fallow deer, vegetables bought from the Locmariaquer farmers. Once, there was a wild boar entranced into docility by the *Charm of persuasion*, and the hunters who brought it down boasted about their feat for weeks. The children fattened and grew, waded in the sea, and played on the beach. Isabelle's pregnancy proceeded without incident. Old Céline died just after the summer solstice, but it was as easy a passing as any Ursule could imagine. They buried her on one of the great dunes, where her spirit could fly free over the sea, to travel to wherever it chose. There was a very Romani funeral, one Ursule wished she could have had for her mother and her daughter, with music and food and piles of fragrant wildflowers on the grave.

The only darkness in all that bright season was Ursule's worry for Drom. She had no way of knowing how old he had been when he joined her so long ago, but he was certainly greatly aged now. She didn't wonder at it, because there were many tales of familiars who lived long lives as witches' companions.

Now, though, he moved slower, and clacked less. He no longer tried to whistle for Louisette, although she coaxed him. Ursule saw her gazing at him once, concern on her face, but when she asked her if she was worried about him, Louisette pretended she wasn't. As autumn approached, Ursule caught sight of a few silver feathers among his ebony cloak, and they chilled her heart. Ravens never turned gray, nor did any other bird she knew. It wasn't natural.

Drom was no ordinary raven, but even a life awash in magic, as his had been, must one day come to an end. Ursule found herself surprisingly shaken by the thought. She couldn't picture her life without his presence, without him descending to ride on her shoulder, or adding his voice to her spells, or simply greeting her in the mornings.

On the morning she found him on the ground outside the caravan, unable to flap his wings with enough strength to rise into the air, she knew the end was near. She lifted him in her arms and carried him inside the wagon, a place he had never been. She made a nest for him on her cot with a bit of old blanket, and brought him a bit of meat and a dish of water. He didn't touch either one.

Nanette had been finishing her breakfast, but she left it and came to put out one chubby finger to Drom's wing. The wing lifted in response, but limply, and fell back to the raven's side as if there were no strength left in it.

Nanette's face was as grave as a child's can be. "Grand-mère, no *Zi buna?*"

Ursule settled with care onto the cot next to Drom. "No, *ma petite.* Drom is very sick."

"Fix him?"

Ursule shook her head, swallowing away a betraying tightness in her throat. "I can't, dear heart. Drom has just gotten old."

Nanette turned her gaze up to Ursule and put a small hand up to her cheek. "Crying?"

Ursule put a hand to her face and realized that, indeed, she was shedding tears for her old friend. She hadn't wept since Léonie. She hadn't thought she would ever weep for anyone else.

Nanette climbed up onto the cot next to her and stretched her short arms around Ursule's waist as far as they would go, doing her best to pat her as Ursule and Isabelle and the others all patted Nanette when she cried. "*Désolée*, Puri-daj," she said, in her way of mixing languages. "*Désolée.*"

Louisette found them that way a little later. Ursule's tears had dried. Nanette had fallen asleep, her head on her grandmother's lap. Drom was also asleep, but it was the sleep from which no creature wakes.

"Oh, Puri-daj. Oh, no. I'm so very sorry." Louisette crouched beside Ursule. "Shall I take him away, while Nanette is still sleeping?"

"That would be best," Ursule said. "Wait for me outside."

Louisette wrapped Drom's body in the bit of blanket and lifted it with gentle hands. Ursule slid out from beneath Nanette's warm head and made certain she slept on before she climbed stiffly down from the wagon.

Louisette was waiting for her. "I'll get Claude to dig a grave."

"Yes, please," Ursule said. "If he won't make fun of me."

"He won't." Louisette's expression and voice were both firm. "He knows better." She handed the blanket-wrapped bundle to Ursule. It had grown cold with shocking speed, and the chill spread into Ursule's body, a warning. A premonition. "I'll be back in a few moments," Louisette said, and strode away across the campsite.

As Claude returned with her, a shovel in his hand, someone spoke to him, asking what he was about, if he needed help. Ursule heard him say, "Never mind. Grand-mère needs something done, and she wants it private."

When he reached her, Ursule murmured her thanks. *"De rien,"* he said, and ducked his head to her. "The dune, Louisette said?"

Ursule nodded, and the three of them set off away from the camp, toward the dune with Old Céline's unmarked grave. Claude set to with a will, digging a nice deep hole, where the scavengers wouldn't find Drom's body. Louisette helped Ursule lower the blanket-wrapped form into the grave, and Claude covered it. He dug up and replanted a clump of the spiky sea grass on the top, and as he tamped down the sandy soil, he said, "It will be safe now."

Louisette said, "Shall we stay with you, Puri-daj?"

"No, thank you, dear heart. Thank you, Claude, for your labor."

Claude nodded. "Witch's familiar," he said gruffly. "Deserves a good resting place."

Ursule, leaning on her staff, said, "I'll just stay a while and say my goodbye."

Louisette bent to kiss her, and she and Claude turned back toward the camp. Louisette took her husband's arm, hugging it to her. Theirs was a complicated union, and it was good to see a moment of accord between them, though Ursule had no doubt Claude would be cross again by the evening.

She watched the pair of them, their tall figures looking young and strong in the morning sun, and she felt her encroaching age as if it were a visitor coming to meet her. It was still a little way off, perhaps just around the corner, but it was on its way.

Stiffly, she knelt down and laid her staff across her knees. She pressed a hand to her chest as she spoke her rite of crossing:

For the gift of you, my friend,
My soul brims full with gladness.
For the loss of you, my friend,
My heart is rent with sadness.

She paused and lifted her staff to stretch it out above Drom's little grave. The reliquary glimmered, its light all but lost in the brightness of the sunshine. Ursule's voice creaked with sorrow.

Don't go far, my faithful one.
I'll join you when my time is done.

The light in the reliquary faded. A breeze blew up from the beach to dry Ursule's tears. She braced herself on her staff as she came to her feet, and stood a moment, looking out to sea.

She must speak to Louisette. She would need to be ready.

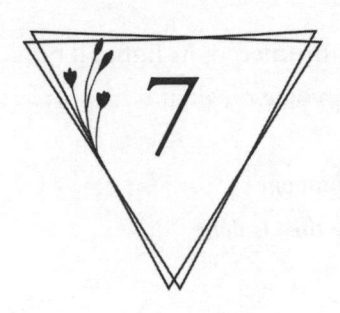

A t Mabon, Claude decreed it was time for the caravan to move away from the coast. The mild breezes of the summer had given way to the raw winds of winter, and they needed a more protected spot. Ursule, during the Mabon celebration, had looked into the scrying stone and had seen the Orchière wagons drawn together in a familiar field of menhirs, just outside Carnac. Most of the Roche families wanted to go east, away from the sea, moving inland to Vannes, but Claude and Paul would do whatever Grand-mère thought best. They both, and Isabelle's husband, too, were afraid of going against her wishes.

Ursule scowled when her granddaughters came to tell her this. "It seems a hard way to earn respect, to make everyone afraid of me."

Louisette said, "They're not so much afraid of you as of what you see in the crystal."

"Do they think I will predict someone's death?"

Isabelle nodded. "Or some other tragedy."

"Do they not think that the crystal might help us to prevent such things?"

Anne-Marie said, "The trouble is, they have to let you do it, let you look into the stone and interpret what you see, and that makes them uneasy. They think they're supposed to be the strong ones, the brave ones."

"Well, their fear is silly, but it could be useful. You can tell them that what the witch wants, besides going up to Carnac, is for us all to be Orchières. One family, with one traditional name. Half the Roches are going in another direction, and it would be good if all of us, Bettina's grandchildren, you and your husbands, my great-grandchildren, were united as one clan."

"Grand-mère," Anne-Marie said. "Bettina is taking her family with the Roches."

Ursule blinked. "Is she? Has she said why?"

"She says she's tired. She doesn't want to lead the clan anymore."

And I am tired unto death. But Ursule didn't say it, nor did she breathe the weary sigh that caught in her throat. "Very well. We will be few, but we can all be Orchières."

"Claude will agree. I'll see to it," Louisette said.

"If Claude agrees, Paul will," said Anne-Marie.

"Roger will, too," Isabelle said, and dimpled, very like her mother used to do. "Or he can just go off with the Roches without his wife."

That made them all laugh, so they parted with smiles, climbing down from the wagon and starting off to their various tasks. Ursule called Louisette back just as she stood on the step. "I need to talk to you," she said. "I thought it best if we spoke alone."

Louisette's smile faded instantly. She knew, Ursule thought. She already knew what her grandmother was going to say.

"Now, don't look distressed. I simply want to prepare you."

"Because Drom died," Louisette said. Her voice was flat, unin-flected, but Ursule saw the pain in the darkening of her eyes, in the deepening of her habitual frown.

"Yes, *ma chère*. Not now, or perhaps even soon, but the day is coming."

"Surely not for years, Puri-daj. You're not so old, not like Céline."

"No, but I had a head start." She smiled at her granddaughter. "My mother used to say I was born old."

"But this is your time to rest, isn't it? You've worked so long and so hard, and held us all together. Now we will go to Carnac and you will rest."

"That sounds nice."

"So we don't have to talk about this again."

"Perhaps not this, Louisette, but I do need you to know that—should it come—you must take charge of the scrying stone, and the grimoire, too. You're the eldest, and it falls to you."

"But none of us can use the stone!"

"Not yet."

"It won't be me, we already know that," Louisette said. "Nor Anne-Marie or Isabelle, and probably not either of the twins. That leaves only Nanette, and she's just a child."

"We leave that in the Goddess's hands. But the stone, and the book— those will be in yours."

"It's a heavy responsibility," Louisette said soberly.

"It is indeed," Ursule answered. "But I have no doubt you will manage it."

Louisette bent to kiss Ursule's cheek. "I don't want you to leave us," she said, her voice catching in her throat.

"That, too, dearest heart, is in the Goddess's hands."

······ ·⊰⊱· ·⊰⊱· ······

So it was that Ursule bid farewell to her caravan of widows, and to the peaceful interlude that had been her time at Locmariaquer. It was hard for her to leave Drom's grave, as it had been hard to leave behind Agnes's, and most painfully, Léonie's, but she knew her loved ones did not actually lie beneath the earth. They lived on in the cool sea breezes, in the slant of autumn sunshine, and with increasing frequency, in her dreams.

She had dreamed of Léonie, laughing, cradling one of her babies, although Ursule wasn't sure which. She had dreamed of Agnes, not silent, but talking easily as she pretended to read someone's future in the crystal. And she felt Drom's presence in her dreams, his gentle claws on her shoulder, his faint croon above the rush of the sea, the rustle of his wings above her head.

Never dismiss a witch's dream. She had not forgotten.

It was clear, as they set out on their journey, that this would be Andie's last. He, like Drom, had lived well past his normal span. It was hard asking him to pull the wagon one more time, but it was an easy road, and not too long a way. Ursule gave him a simple to strengthen him for one more effort, and whispered in his ear that when they reached Carnac, she would set him free.

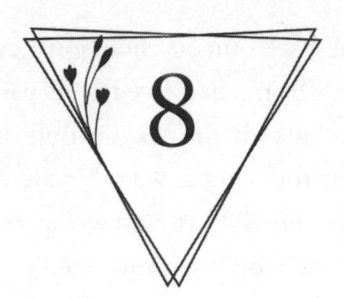

Carnac, 1820

When they pulled up their four wagons among the dozens of menhirs that watched over Carnac-Plage, Ursule felt as if she had come home at last. She left the young people to do the work of digging the fire pit and lining it with stones, and set out with Andie into the field where the other horses were hobbled. She stroked the old horse's neck, ruffled his forelock, then stripped every bit of tack from his head and back. He stood, head down, awaiting his hobbles, but she murmured, "No, my old friend. No more hobbles. You've served long enough, and it's time for you to rest. If you want to stay close, I'll bring you a feed of mash every day, but if you want to wander, you can."

The old horse lifted his head and blew gently against her chest before he plodded gingerly into the field, weary and sore-footed. She watched him go, leaning on her staff, and marveled at the labors of animals in service of people.

She was content to be back in her beloved Carnac. It was a good place, surrounded by the friendly old stones, with water both salt and fresh close at hand. She laid her hand on a waist-high menhir and thought how many people the old stones had watched pass by through the centuries. She stood still, listening to the horses cropping grass, hearing the push and pull of the tide on the beach. Above her head the clouds were clearing before the evening breeze, and the stars began to prick out into the darkening sky, one, three, five, a hundred.

This was a fine place to rest, and not just for Andie. It was a fine place for her. She would rest, watch her great-grandchildren grow, teach them the craft, let others do the heavy work.

As she stood there, a nightingale trilled from the dusk to welcome her home.

She watched Andie until he found a patch of grass to nibble, then turned toward the encampment. Claude had built up the old fire pit, refreshing the stones that surrounded it. Already a lively fire licked up into the darkness. Isabelle, with Nanette at her heels and her babe in a shawl on her chest, bent over a cookpot, stirring something. Nanette's face was tipped up, talking to her. *What language this time?* Ursule wondered, and smiled.

Their little clan settled quickly into the spot. Toys appeared, and baskets for kindling. The twins, getting tall now, ran back and forth at Isabelle's orders, bringing bowls and spoons and laying them on two fallen menhirs that made a creditable table. Anne-Marie was sweeping out her wagon, her babe in a cradle outside the door.

It was a scene of such peace that it brought tears to Ursule's eyes, easy, soothing tears. Her beloved clan was around her, and they were safe and well. She turned back toward her caravan, supporting herself with her staff. Her hips ached fiercely, and her knees were beginning to hurt as well, but she could ignore them.

Then, even as she made her way through the menhirs toward the welcoming light of the fire, she heard the old, vague warning.

Hmmmmm . . .

·····•⸙⸙⸙•⸙⸙⸙•·····

In their Carnac encampment they lived quietly, frugally, peacefully for months. They celebrated Samhain, but modestly. The children were delighted by Yule, with little gifts from all the adults. Louisette and Claude even bought little marzipan shapes to hand out to them, like the ones Madeleine used to make for St. Stephen's Day. Sometimes women came from Carnac-Ville in search of Anne-Marie's potions or Isabelle's pretty candles. Sometimes they paid with *livres*, and at other times traded with trinkets or bits of fabric or sacks of turnips or apples. They eyed the black-eyed men with uneasy interest, and gazed with curiosity at the colorful wagons, at the pot always simmering in the fire pit, and at the old woman who walked with a staff.

Ursule rested and taught the children to speak French and to read. She cuddled the babes whenever she could, delighting in the pliancy of their little bodies so close to her own stiffening one. Everyone called her Grand-mère, including the men. Little by little, their fear of her eased. Once in a while Claude would jest with her. Paul, in his quiet way, would bring her little treats—a scarf he had found at the market, or a handful of beads for her to make into a bracelet. It was a good life, and she woke every morning determined to savor each day.

She had not forgotten Violca's warning. She peered into the scrying stone again and again, looking for an answer.

It was at Imbolc that she saw it. Not a reason for Violca's warning, but a clear vision of a place, a house on a cliff, in a land that was not Brittany. She bent over the stone, gazing at the long, low building, the collapsing fence around it, the byre in need of repair. A hill rose beyond the house, topped by great gray boulders, almost like the dolmens they had passed on their way to Locmariaquer.

"Why are you showing me this?" she whispered.

She received no answer, but Louisette, standing near her, murmured, "What is it, Puri-daj? What do you see?"

Ursule shook her head and took her hands away from the stone. "I don't know, ma chère. I'm not sure yet."

She waited three days before she sent the twins and Nanette off to stay with Isabelle for a night. Alone in her wagon, she brought out the scrying stone, lit a candle, sprinkled salted water, scattered a handful of rosemary across the altar. She brought her staff with its precious reliquary and held it in one hand as she stretched out the other above the stone, and whispered,

Mother Goddess, did I see
A future home beyond the sea?

For answer, the crystal began to glow and showed her again, clearer this time, the long, low house with its roof falling in, its doors crooked on their hinges. It perched on a cliff overlooking the water, and the hill rose behind it with perilous steepness. Most definitely not Brittany. Nor was it France.

She said,

Tell me what it is I see,
This place you choose to show to me.

The light in the stone dimmed and shifted, and the scene changed. There was an island, with a great building rising up from it, a castle, or a cathedral, like the one at Mont St. Michel. Ursule had never been there, but one of the Vilas had and described it in detail. This wasn't Mont St. Michel, though. She had no reason to know that, but she did. She knew it without doubt, and the moment that insight flashed through her mind, the island vanished.

"It's not enough," she mourned, as the stone went dark. "Am I to guess?" She was going to have to find out where there was another island, with another castle, or a cathedral. A landmark.

But why did she need to know that?

Frustrated, she blew out the candle and restored the scrying stone to its basket. There was nothing more she could do about the problem this night, but she had to accept, as she went to her bed, that something was about to disturb the peace of their little camp among the menhirs.

····· ·❦·❧· ·····

The weeks passed undisturbed, past Ostara, approaching Beltane, when they could celebrate the fullness of spring. The thrashing of the winter sea beyond the lane gave way to quieter tides, gentler waves. The horses, even old Andie, were fattening on spring grass, and the Orchière children grew and thrived like the spring lambs of Kerjean Farm.

On a cool, crisp afternoon, Ursule was sitting beside the fire pit, tossing twigs into it to keep the flames high enough to simmer the pottage. Florence came running toward her, Fleurette in her wake, the two of them long-legged and lean as yearling colts.

"Grand-mère! Grand-mère! There's a man asking for you."

"A man?" Ursule reached for her staff and pushed herself up. "What man? Where is he?"

Fleurette turned and pointed. Ursule followed the direction of her finger and caught a breath in surprise. "Remy!"

He lifted his hand in greeting. Behind him, a horse Ursule had never seen cropped the grass. Remy's hair was almost completely white beneath his floppy-brimmed hat. His thick shoulders curved forward, as if he were bearing a weight on his back, and his belly sagged. He started toward her, taking furtive glances at the painted wagons hung with plants and blankets and clothes. He smiled at the little flock of children that clustered behind Ursule, staring at the stranger with unabashed curiosity.

Ursule said, "Remy, how did you find me? Why are you here? Please, come and sit. Florence, Fleurette, run to the caravan and fetch me—I don't know, the teakettle. And put some tea leaves into two cups."

The twins, gazing at her visitor, backed reluctantly away. Ursule patted her stone seat. "Sit, sit, Remy. I can hardly believe it's you!"

"It's me, all right," he said, gingerly letting himself down onto the stone, then nodding when he realized it was warm. "That is, what's left of me."

"You look well," Ursule said, although she thought he looked tired. Very likely he thought the same of her.

"Well enough," he said. He pulled off his hat and turned it in his hands. "I remembered you said you were coming to Carnac, and I guessed you wouldn't be in the town."

The twins came back and pushed the teakettle into the coals. They laid out cups and *pufe*, then stood back, avidly watching their *grand-mère*'s visitor.

"Your grandchildren," Remy said. "I wouldn't have known them."

"Florence and Fleurette. They're fifteen now."

"And Louisette, the tall one? Is she with you?"

"They're all with me, I'm glad to say." The kettle began to whine, and Fleurette whisked it out of the fire to pour out two cups. "Run off now," Ursule said. "I'm going to chat with my friend."

She picked up a cup and passed it to Remy. She watched his big blunt fingers wrap around it and breathed a little nostalgic sigh. She had seen those fingers milking a cow, nailing a board, driving the pony cart. They were crooked now, the joints swollen, and the hair on the back of his hands was as white as the hair on his head.

As if he was aware of her thoughts, he said, awkwardly, "Getting old now, Ursule."

"As am I, Remy. Now tell me about Madeleine."

"Madeleine died the year we left the farm."

"Oh, Remy! *Désolée.* Was she ill?"

He was taking a sip from his teacup, but he put it down on the stone beside him and pulled his hat into his lap so he could turn it. "I don't think so," he said. "It seemed like she just—stopped living."

There seemed to be nothing to say to that. Ursule sipped her own tea, watching Remy from above the rim of her cup, waiting for him to say why he had come so far to seek her out. Instead, he looked past her to the field where the horses roamed. "Is that old Andie?"

"It is. I've retired him, though."

"He must be thirty-five years old!"

"Is he? I wasn't sure."

"You've taken good care of him. But then—with your gypsy ways— I expected that."

"My—my gypsy ways?" Ursule felt a prickle run over her neck and down her arms.

His eyes came up to hers, and then, as his cheeks reddened, he looked down again at his rather forlorn hat. "You were so good with the animals' illnesses, and I knew you had your little charms and things hanging all over the farm. I finally figured you were—well—doing something special to keep Kerjean safe. Healthy beasts, good butter, the sweetest cider. Never made so much money before you came to us."

"Remy, I—" Ursule began, but he put up his hand.

"Don't need to speak of it. It's not safe for you."

"True."

"Why I came, actually." Now he put his hat aside again, and braced his hands on his knees as he looked into her face. "Came to warn you. Someone has betrayed you."

The prickle on Ursule's arms grew into a rash of gooseflesh, and she felt the chill all the way to her toes. "Who—Remy, who could have—"

"We moved to Vannes. I still live there. Do odd jobs. There was a caravan of gypsies came through, and they told this story. A lot of stories, of course, for money, but this one—the bishop heard it, and I fear they will come looking for you."

"The witch who spirited her mother away on a broom. I've heard that story."

"I don't believe it for a moment, never mind your little charms and such."

"I did save my mother from the witch hunters. She wasn't a witch at all, of course."

His mouth worked as if he wanted to ask the question—*are you?*—but he didn't. Instead, he said, "That bishop. The one who thinks he'll be a cardinal if he burns enough witches? This woman—Kezia, I think—kept saying your name until it reached his ears."

"You came to warn me."

"There was another burning," Remy said in a gravelly undertone. "In Vannes."

"Not a Romani, I hope."

"Don't know. Old. No one to speak for her. Awful thing."

"At least I am not alone." Her shoulders slumped under the sudden weight of grief for the unknown victim, and a soul-deep fatigue over the endless cruelty of the world.

"You all right?"

She had to take a deep breath, to draw energy from the sweet sea air and the familiar menhirs, the guardians of her childhood. "I will be," she said.

"Good." He released her hand and pushed himself up from the stone. "*Eh bien*, Ursule. Just wanted you to know."

She made herself rise, though her knees felt weak and her head felt light. Was it fear? Or was it recognition? "Thank you, *mora*."

He bit his lip and shrugged in confusion.

She smiled up at him, the big, clumsy, kind man who had proved to have a great heart. "It means *friend*."

"I thank you." His eyes reddened, and he averted his face in shame over his threatening tears. "This is goodbye, then," he said in a choked voice. "Once again."

"The last time, I fear."

"*Oui. Adieu.*" He hesitated, coughed, then pulled his hat down on his forehead with a gesture of finality. He lumbered away into the waning afternoon without looking back, and she watched him go. There was no doubt in her mind she would never see him again, but then, she had never expected to see him this time.

Even as he mounted his horse to ride away, Claude and Paul appeared, hurrying along the lane from Carnac-Ville with bags of beans and lentils over their shoulders. Their tight-lipped faces and narrowed eyes showed that they, too, had heard the story of the burning. The witch hunters were close.

Ursule turned toward her caravan to fetch the scrying stone. It was time.

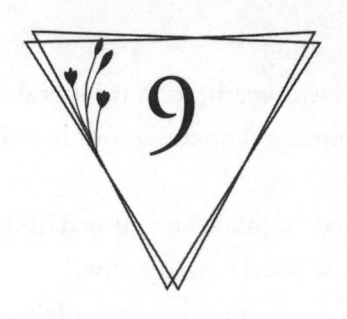

U rsule stayed in her caravan while the clan ate their dinner of two fat hares that had been roasting for hours on a spit over the fire. The smell of sizzling meat carried to her inside her wagon, but she had no appetite, except for the scrying stone.

The *grands-mères* showed her the scene without delay, a dilapidated house facing the sea, a moor rising beyond, an island castle in the distance. There was no mistake. It was the same place, a home for the clan across the water. She yearned toward it, seeing the possibilities of the place, of the house, of the future.

But it was not her future.

She didn't step out of her wagon until Louisette came for her. "Are you coming to eat something, Puri-daj? Claude and Paul have bad news."

"I don't need to eat, and I know their news, *ma chère*. We have work to do."

"They say it's the redheaded priest with the bad eye. Bernard. The one from St. Anne."

"I thought it must be." Ursule handed Louisette the stone pitcher of salted water and the crystal, and she stepped out carefully, leaning on her staff. She could almost hear her bones creak beneath her skin, like the axle of a caravan too long without grease.

"Paul thinks we should go south tonight, but Claude says it's too dark."

"Claude is right. It's not only too dark, it's too late. I know what we need to do, but first, a *Spell of protection*."

"Tell me, Puri-daj."

"Gather everyone around the fire. I know they're frightened, but they have to wait while I cast this spell. It will take some time."

Ursule hobbled behind Louisette to the fire pit, where the stones still dripped with fat from the hares that had roasted there. She waited while Claude and Paul, Anne-Marie and Isabelle and all the little ones sat or squatted near the fire. When they were in place, Ursule took the stone pitcher from Louisette and sprinkled water around the fire pit, including every one of the clan in her wide circle. When that was done, she exchanged the pitcher for the scrying stone. Its smooth surface reflected the flames, glimmering red and gold and orange as she lifted it to shoulder height. She murmured,

Mother Goddess, bless this ground
And all the ones here gathered round.
Embrace them with your loving arm.
Ensure they do not come to harm.

Three times three times she spoke the spell, softly, since the ones who needed to hear it were not with her in the flesh. She was unsteady, swaying from one foot to the other, but she fought to stay upright. The clan watched, tense and wary, the light from the fire reflecting in their dark eyes. The crystal flared between her hands, coruscating waves of light in shades of silver and white, pierced by shimmers of bronze and gold. It was the most impressive display she had ever seen in the stone, and she sensed the awe of the watchers and heard the occasional indrawn breath when the light flashed across their faces.

By the time she finished, her arms were trembling with the effort of holding the stone. Carefully, she lowered it to the ground. She took up her staff and leaned on it as she looked around at her clan. Her family. Her everything.

She drew as deep a breath as she was able, but it was barely enough to support her voice. The fragility of it startled her. "There is a house," she said, then had to stop to draw another breath.

Isabelle cried out, "A house?" but Anne-Marie shushed her.

Louisette said, in her deep voice, "Where, Grand-mère?"

They waited while Ursule drew on the dregs of her strength. "Beyond the sea," she said. "Above a cliff. Long and low, with a thatched roof and broken shutters." She broke off for another breath. "A fence that needs mending. A hill behind it, and a rising moor." Her eyelids fluttered, and she struggled against the faintness that made her head light and her vision blur. She blinked, and focused on their faces. "You must go there. All of you."

Florence asked uncertainly, "But, Grand-mère, how will we find it?"

"You must go in a boat." Ursule didn't know where they would find a boat, but she must leave that problem to them.

She barely heard the resigned sigh of her family. Despite the support of her staff, her legs folded beneath her, and she found herself on the ground, sitting on her heels. She didn't know how long she knelt there, listening to the moan of the ocean from beyond the lane, the whisper of the breeze among the standing stones, the intermittent stamping of the horses. She felt as if she were in a trance of waiting, a suspension of awareness of herself or anyone else. She didn't notice the stiffness growing in her knees or the chill of the wind on her cheeks. Her hair came loose and blew over her forehead, catching in her eyelashes, but she didn't notice that, either.

She remained that way until, sometime far into the night, the thick clouds above Carnac-Plage parted, allowing a narrow beam of moonlight to splash over the encampment. Ursule startled, sitting bolt upright. "Put out the fire!"

A child's querulous voice rose into the quiet sky. "Why?"

Ursule commanded, "Be still. Everyone."

Claude doused the fire with seawater, and the flames hissed out, sending billows of steam ghosting into the moonlight. Ursule worked herself to her feet, though pain shot through her knees and her feet had gone numb. She lifted her staff in both hands and pointed it at the gap in the clouds.

There was no time to wait for the perfect words. There was no time to turn to the stone, or to light a candle, or to do anything but issue the demand, and hope the Goddess listened.

"Hide us!" she hissed.

Slowly, leisurely, the clouds began to knit up the rent in their dense fabric, the edges of the tear folding together, forming a solid layer once again to block the betraying moonlight. The ashes in the fire pit emitted a slender trail of smoke that was nearly invisible in the darkness. Every voice was still, every body tense. Mothers held their children tight. Men clutched their *churis* in readiness. Even the sea seemed to hold itself back, contain its restless movement, and in the ensuing silence, they heard it.

The sound of feet in the lane. Many feet, boots and shoes and clogs, tramping toward the field of menhirs.

"Grand-mère," Anne-Marie whispered. "Shouldn't we—"

"Quiet!"

Ursule lifted her staff once again, and saw that the precious reliquary glinted faintly, though there was so little light. It gave her courage to whisper one more spell. One last feat of magic, to protect her clan:

Mother Goddess, hear my plea:
Hide us so that none can see.
Let my belovèd people be.

A shadow, blacker, deeper, thicker than any natural darkness, fell over the encampment. No one moved. No one spoke. Even the horses were silent, their hooves still, their tails hanging limp and quiet.

The witch-hunting mob drew close, talking among themselves, sometimes laughing, often cursing when they stumbled. Some prayed, monotonously, repetitively. Ursule didn't know how many of them there were, but she sensed the redheaded priest's presence, an ugliness, a sickness among the ordinary folk of the mob. She gripped her staff and bent her head, willing them all to go past.

The clan was invisible to them. No one made a sound, and the mob, so eager to find a victim, to slake the blood-thirst that drove them out into the night, had no idea that they walked right past their goal. The deep, impenetrable darkness shrouded the encampment until the footsteps of the witch hunters had faded into the night.

In silence, the Orchières signaled to one another. The men set watches, out among the menhirs. The women took the children to their caravans, to rest while they could. Ursule, swaying with fatigue, stayed where she was, watching the sky, guarding against the return of the light. She stood there until a cold dawn broke over Carnac-Plage. The sea resumed its hiss and spit, the gulls began to wake, the horses stamped and flicked their tails.

The watchman among the stones was gazing at the lane when Ursule, with a long, exhausted sigh, crumpled to the ground. Her granddaughters were in their wagons, as were their children. There was no one to hold her hand, or to arrange her body when her spirit left it. She died alone, as she had lived, but without regret. Her people were safe. Her labors were finished.

Her spirit rose above the ground, free of pain, liberated from the failings of her body, eager to discover what came next. She looked back just once at the small, wizened form curled among the standing stones, the staff still clutched in its hand. She looked ahead then, up into the brightening sky, and saw the dark, glossy form of Drom riding the thermals, awaiting her.

With a laugh only he could hear, she floated up to meet him.

The Great Witch of Brittany

*T*hey say the great witch Ursule was born in the dark of the moon, and with the mark of a broom on her shoulder, which made her both clever and fierce, though she was small and plain. She was adept at every part of the craft: potions, simples, spells, and especially scrying. She saw things in the Orchière scrying stone and whispered them to her mother, the fortune-teller, whose reputation as a true seer grew so that the two of them became rich.

It was dangerous for a gypsy to be so rich, and when the bishop who loved to burn witches got word of the fortune-teller's success, he sent his witch hunters to seize Ursule's mother and consign her to the pyre, though the real seer was her daughter.

The little witch Ursule magicked a dog to lead her to her mother's prison. She made a magical broom that matched her birthmark, and she put her mother on the broom and flew away with her. The witch hunters who tried to pursue her died screaming in pain, as if they were the ones tied to the pyre that had been meant for Ursule's mother. Those who came after found nothing left of those pursuers but ashes, and they say the ashes never cooled, but would burn the hand of anyone who touched them.

No one knows where Ursule hid her mother, but the tales of Ursule's magic spread through Brittany, whispered from house to house, muttered in secrecy in the churches. They say she could make the blind see, return speech to the voiceless, and persuade anyone—priest or nobleman, baker or chandler—to believe whatever she wanted them to believe. She had a raven familiar who spoke Romani and sang Romani songs. The raven pecked out the eyes of anyone who threatened his mistress. It lived an unnaturally long life, and its feathers were pure silver by the time it died.

They say Ursule magicked a lover into giving her a child, then made her daughter produce six daughters of her own to preserve the Orchière line. Ursule repulsed marauders during the Terror, strewing the lanes and hedgerows with their bloodied and broken bodies. Word spread among the revolutionaries that there was no weapon sharp enough, no man strong enough, to resist the great witch of Brittany.

They also say that Ursule, in a rage at her daughter's husband for causing her daughter's death, destroyed his grand house by calling up a terrible storm. The stone walls fell before the winds and the tiled roof collapsed beneath the thunder, crushing servant and master alike within. Only Ursule's granddaughters survived.

Ursule found a caravan traveling the roads of Brittany, and she claimed it for herself *and her granddaughters. As they roamed, she taught the girls her magical arts, and made them vow to always teach their own daughters. Near the end of her life, she looked into her scrying stone and foretold that there would always be Orchière witches in Brittany, and in Cornwall, Wales, and the crowded streets of London, even in the royal palace.*

They say that when Ursule died, there was no body for the clan to bury. They say she seized a broom and flew up into the sky where her raven was waiting for her. Sometimes, in the dark of the moon, turn your gaze up into the stars. You may see the silhouette of the great witch Ursule on her magicked broom, come back to Brittany to see how we do.

AUTHOR'S NOTES

Ravens in the wild live only ten to fifteen years, but they can live much longer in captivity. Anecdotally, it seems some ravens kept as pets can live into their sixties. They are considered the world's largest songbird, and they *do* learn to speak certain words.

If you're fascinated by ravens, you'll enjoy investigating the ravens of the Tower of London, said to be installed there by Charles II in the seventeenth century. Legend has it that if the ravens should ever abandon the tower, the monarchy will come to an end. Those ravens each have their own name, and they have been known to live as long as forty years.

In researching the Romani, I discovered two wonderful books. The first, a nonfiction, beautifully researched work, is *Bury Me Standing*, by the sociologist Isabel Fonseca. She met with many Romani in Eastern Europe and dug deep into their traditions and challenges.

The second book is fiction, a young adult novel by the great writer Rumer Godden. It's titled *The Diddakoi* and is a delightful read on every level. It explores the urge of the Romani to be always on the move, which is why some cultures call them Travellers.

It's believed that the Romani, centuries ago, spread out from India into various parts of Europe. There are many variations in dialect, both in word choice and in pronunciation. The bits of Romani used in *The Great Witch of Brittany* are taken from glossaries found online and are occasionally combinations of versions of the language.

If you're curious about the *nai* flute, you can find a number of performances online. You will hear its unique sound and watch experts play. I was fortunate to discover examples of this rare instrument in the Musical Instruments Museum in Phoenix, Arizona. The museum is magnificent, with examples of musical instruments from every country in the world. It's well worth a trip.

ACKNOWLEDGMENTS

I am indebted first to the dedicatees of this book, the readers of *A Secret History of Witches* who asked for Ursule's story and inspired me to explore it. It has been a joy to work on it, and I'm very sorry to say goodbye to Ursule Orchière.

This novel is a much better book because of the efforts of Nivia Evans, my sharp-eyed and creative editor. The contributions of Nancy Crosgrove; RN; and Dean Crosgrove, wizard researcher, were also invaluable. My critique group is both savvy and supportive, consisting of the amazing writers Erica Bauermeister and Anna Quinn. Read their books! You'll be glad you did.

The team at Redhook, my imprint at Orbit, is a marvel of ingenuity, energy, and hard work. Any book can disappear into the void without sufficient publisher support. Redhook has been lavish in their efforts on behalf of my novels, and I'm beyond grateful. Working with them has been one of the most satisfying experiences of my writing career.